Christmas
at the
Little Village
Bakery

ALSO BY TILLY TENNANT

Honeybourne series:
The Little Village Bakery

Mishaps in Millrise series:
Little Acts of Love
Just Like Rebecca
The Parent Trap
And Baby Makes Four

Once Upon a Winter series:
The Accidental Guest
I'm Not in Love
Ways to Say Goodbye
One Starry Night

Hopelessly Devoted to Holden Finn
The Man Who Can't Be Moved
Mishaps and Mistletoe

Christmas
at the
Little Village
Bakery

TILLY TENNANT

bookouture

Published by Bookouture

An imprint of StoryFire Ltd.
23 Sussex Road, Ickenham, UB10 8PN
United Kingdom

www.bookouture.com

ISBN: 978-1-78681-067-0
eBook ISBN: 978-1-78681-066-3

*For my Nana Sylvia, whose kindness, courage
and fortitude is inspirational. As is her chicken soup.*

Chapter One

It felt like the world had been muffled. Their breath rose in plumes into the air against a landscape that was white as far as the eye could see. Gentle feathers of snow fell silently, frosting their coats and hair.

Tori gripped Spencer's hand tighter and he looked down at her with a broad grin as they trudged along the path that led to the Old Bakery, his unruly black hair peeking out from beneath a woolly hat and his startling blue eyes alive with humour. Her tiny frame was bundled up in a huge padded coat, and he could barely see her flame-red hair beneath the hat and scarf wrapped around it, but the perfect nose that turned up a little at the end, and the blue eyes set in a face that looked a good deal younger than her twenty-eight years, peeked out at him from the layers, and he couldn't think of a time when she had looked lovelier.

As he drew in a lungful of frosty air, he was filled with joy to see the paths and fields of Honeybourne that meant they were home – at least, his home; though, in time, he hoped that it might become hers too. He had enjoyed his time in Colorado teaching on the exchange programme at a school in Boulder – aside from being the place where he had found Tori it was a beautiful part of the world – but he had been away for over a year, apart from the one brief visit in the spring for the opening of the Old Bakery, and a year was a long time to be parted from the place he felt rooted to.

'I bet you didn't expect to go from snow in Boulder to more snow here,' he said.

'You get snow in England too.'

'Yeah, but usually at Easter, not Christmas,' Spencer laughed. 'One of the supreme ironies of all those songs about white Christmases is that in real life you don't get a flake of the stuff until at least March.'

'I can deal with snow. It'll shake the jet lag off a bit.'

'Maybe we should have had another snooze at home before venturing out to meet everyone,' Spencer said thoughtfully. 'I'm sure they would have understood if we'd put off the reunions until we were feeling right.'

'Best way to deal with jet lag is to battle through it,' Tori announced stoically. 'When you're exhausted, your body won't care whether it thinks it's bedtime or not.'

'If you say so. And is the jet lag being shook off?'

'Not really,' Tori grinned. 'I never said it was a foolproof plan.'

'Maybe it's the wrong sort of snow… How's our English snow holding up against your American stuff?'

'It's a bit wet.'

'Don't you dare add anything to that about it being like the English people…'

'I would never say that,' Tori smiled. 'I love the English people. One in particular I love more than anyone in the world…'

Spencer's grin widened, and he gave her hand a squeeze. He'd waited so long to hear those words. 'I love you too,' he said.

She turned to him with an impish gleam in her eye. 'Oh, did you think I meant you? I was talking about your friend, Millie, obviously.

After all, anyone who can make chocolate cake like she does has to be worthy of my love.'

Spencer bent to kiss her lightly on the lips. They were cold, but yielded and warmed beneath his own. 'That's exactly why I love you, chocolate cake or no. And you're really getting the hang of the British sarcasm thing.'

'I'm not sure that's a compliment.'

'Of course it is.'

Tori raised her eyebrows. The action was just about visible below the rim of her red and blue reindeer-motif bobble-hat. 'Is that the British sarcasm thing?'

'I'm afraid so.'

'Then you'd better watch it, buster. We may not have sarcasm in Boulder but we do have fists.'

Spencer threw back his head and laughed. The sound echoed down the frozen lane. Then he scooped Tori into his arms and planted another kiss on her lips, this one more passionate than the last. 'I really do love you, Tori Annabelle Dempsey.'

'Hey…' She smiled as she pulled away, catching her breath. 'If you do that again we might not make it to the bakery.'

'I'm sure they won't mind if we're late.'

'That's rude. Didn't your parents teach you anything?'

'You can ask them in a couple of days when they arrive back from Spain.'

Tori's smile faded. 'You think they'll like me?'

'Of course they'll like you. Quite frankly, I don't care anyway. I love you, and that's the only thing that matters.'

'You didn't say that when you were stressing about meeting my parents.'

'That's different.'

'How?'

'It just is. Your parents are… Well, let's just say they take a lot more impressing than mine will. And fathers are always more protective of daughters, aren't they?'

'Are they?'

Spencer nodded as he set her on the path again.

'I don't buy it,' Tori said. 'Your parents will be just as tough to crack as mine were.'

'Ah, so you do admit that your parents are tough!'

'Maybe a little.'

Spencer grinned. But then it disappeared. It was bad enough that his parents were going to meet Tori and her parents for the first time, but his anxieties weren't helped by the fact that Tori's parents had met Spencer once before and made it quite clear they hated him. But he tried not to dwell on that. Tori had told him not to worry, and briefly explained that it was all to do with some guy named Hunter that they had earmarked as a potential husband for her. It wasn't Spencer's fault that he wasn't Hunter, she'd told him, but in time they would get over that. Maybe he could salvage things over Christmas, when people were feeling a little more charitable and disposed to love their fellow men?

'Maybe we should have done all this before we set a date for the wedding,' he said. 'What if our parents don't like each other?'

'Well, at least they won't have to see much of each other as yours live in Spain and mine live in Colorado.'

'That will certainly put paid to a life of weekend bridge tournaments.'

'Never mind that, what if they hate each other and it ruins Christmas for everyone?' Tori asked, anxiety creeping into her tone for the first time. 'We can always "forget" to ask them to the wedding, but they're already on their way for Christmas so there's no saving that.'

'My mum would never speak to me again if we didn't ask them to the wedding and Dad always takes her side over everything.'

'Neither would my mom but I'm still prepared to risk it if you are.'

Spencer tried to smile but he couldn't. He wanted to believe it was just because his face was so cold. 'I'm sure it will be fine.'

'No, you're not. You're chewing your lip.'

He clamped his mouth shut and pulled her close. 'This is our first Christmas together – at least officially – and I won't let anyone spoil that, parents or otherwise.'

'I know, I feel the same way. Maybe that's why we're both blowing this thing way out of proportion. I'm sure the folks will get along just fine…' She reached up to kiss him.

'You're right,' he smiled, glancing up at the sky. 'We'd better get moving – I'm sure this snow is getting worse. And there is absolutely nobody else daft enough to be out in it, so we could freeze to death on this lane and nobody would find us until morning.'

'Our passion would keep us warm.'

Spencer raised his eyebrows. 'Is that an attempt at sarcasm again? Because if it's not that's the cheesiest thing I've ever heard!'

'Of course,' she grinned. 'But I'd still be willing to test the theory.'

'It would certainly make for an interesting find when someone stumbles across our frozen corpses.'

'So you don't want to stay out and make snow angels?'

'I'm British. We do tax returns, bad customer service, good tea and late trains. We do *not* do snow angels.'

Tori bent to scoop up a handful of snow. 'Yeah?' she giggled, 'How about snowball fighting? Do you do that, Johnny English?'

'Oh, we do that alright. Are you issuing a challenge, Uncle Sam?'

'That's Aunt Sam, if you don't mind. And yes, I am!'

'You do know I'm a specialist in what's known in these parts as the White Death, don't you?'

She narrowed her eyes. 'What does that mean?'

'It means this!' Spencer scooped her up again and swung her into a snow bank before leaping on top of her and kissing her all over her face. She squealed and tried to push him off, laughing uncontrollably as she did.

'Is this really the White Death?'

'Well, I did moderate it a bit for you. I didn't usually snog the boys at our school in the snow bank, but that's because none of them were quite as hot as you.'

'Spencer!' Tori shrieked as he nuzzled his face into her neck and began to nibble her ears. 'We'll be late!'

'It's your fault – you issued the challenge!'

'But you said you didn't want to freeze to death!' she giggled.

'Ah, but we wouldn't freeze *that* quickly...'

'Ok! You win! I give up!'

They were still kissing when an amused voice interrupted. Spencer shot up to find his best friend, Dylan, wrapped in an enormous, down-filled coat, grinning at them.

'Mr Johns! And Miss Dempsey! Just imagine if the children of Riversmeet Elementary School could see you now...'

'Very funny, Dylan,' Spencer said, hauling a blushing Tori to her feet and dusting the snow from her.

'Not when you get pneumonia it won't be. And I thought I'd had sex in some weird places.'

'We weren't having sex!' Spencer replied indignantly.

'It looked like you were about to,' Dylan replied carelessly. 'Not my business, of course, but it's lucky I came along to spare your blushes.'

'What does that mean?'

'It means that Ruth Evans is about ten minutes behind me – I passed her on the way out to find you. She'd have had the time of her life spreading the news of that little peep show around the village. She's so old now that any hint of sexual activity has to be had vicariously, and boy must she miss it – she's obsessed with how much everyone else is getting.'

Spencer shot an alarmed glance at Tori, but she simply bit back a grin.

'Remind me – who's Ruth Evans?' she asked.

'You mean you don't remember her from earlier in the year when we came to the bakery opening?' said Spencer. 'She grilled you mercilessly as soon as she found out we were dating. She's the biggest busybody on the planet!'

'Certainly the biggest gossip in Honeybourne,' added Dylan.

Tori scrunched her nose up. 'Oh!' she said suddenly. 'Not that little old lady who drank everyone under the table and then asked me the most personal list of questions ever.'

'That sounds about right. Once met never forgotten.'

'Well, if you want to avoid a repeat of that little conversation you'd better get moving right now,' Dylan said, gesturing to the road behind him.

'Right you are,' Spencer said, glancing at Tori with some alarm. But then he relaxed into a grin, and turned to Dylan again, who was now grinning too. 'It's bloody good to see you!' he cried, hugging his friend.

Dylan slapped him on the back, laughing. 'Of course it is! How was the flight?'

'Good,' Spencer said. 'We couldn't sleep a wink last night, though, and it was so weird to be back in my old house after being away for so long. All the noises are wrong and the shadows are in the wrong places.'

'Are you sure you've gone back to the right house?' Dylan laughed as he hugged Tori and kissed her lightly on the cheek.

'How come you're out here anyway?' Spencer asked. 'I thought we agreed to come and meet you at the bakery.'

'We did, but Millie got worried because you hadn't arrived yet and sent me out to look for you. She thought you'd got stuck in the snow or something; you know how she frets about everyone. Turns out she was half right.'

'We'd better hurry,' Tori said, her expression suitably repentant now. 'I'd hate to be the one to stress her out – you both have enough to worry about with baby Oscar.'

'Tell me about it,' Dylan replied as they began to walk.

'Still keeping you up at night?' Spencer asked.

'And some. Night, day… you name it, that boy is awake. The health visitor says to sleep when he sleeps. Easy enough if you're a cat, but a human needs a bit more than ten minutes at a time – especially this human. Millie is like death warmed up. I don't know what we'd have done with the bakery if Darcie hadn't arrived to help. She really is a gift from the heavens.'

'I can't wait to meet her,' Tori put in, 'I've heard so much about this little dynamo of a girl.'

'I'm not sure we can call her girl anymore,' Dylan laughed. 'She is actually twenty-two, she just looks about twelve. She works hard in the kitchens, though, the customers have all taken to her and she's sensible – you can trust her with anything and know that she won't cock it up. She came just to help with the baking at first, but she's fast becoming indispensable in just about every other area, including helping with Oscar. She's just brilliant and Millie loves her to bits.'

'So it hasn't been too much of a problem having her stay at your place?' Spencer asked.

'Not at all,' Dylan replied. 'It's a shame we don't have my old cottage across the way anymore but we've built a little annexe-type arrangement at the back of the bakery and she seems happy enough there. It's got its own door, a wet room and it's rent-free to boot – and you don't get rent-free very often these days so I should think she would be.'

'Is she coping ok with being so far from home?' Spencer asked.

'She seems to be. It's probably not my place to say, but I think she was a bit relieved to get away. She doesn't talk much about it but I don't think she always sees eye to eye with her parents. Dad's a bit of a loser – more interested in his pigeons than other people, and her mother's a nervy type…' Dylan rubbed his chin. 'Come to think of it, Darcie can be a bit nervy too. I suppose that's where she gets it from. I don't think either of them have been parents of the year. Still, Millie being Millie took a real shine to Darcie growing up and took her under her wing – shopping trips and sleepovers and such – got her out of the house, you know? They were pretty close by all accounts and I think Darcie missed her a lot when she moved here.'

'Is it her mum or dad who's related to Millie?' Spencer asked.

'Jane, Darcie's mum. She's Millie's mum's sister.'

'But the sisters are not alike?'

Dylan shrugged. 'No idea. Sounds like Millie's mum was a bit of a loose cannon too, but I only have stories to go by – she hasn't been in touch with Millie for years. I don't know what went on but she upped and left Millie's dad when Millie was twenty-two and nobody knows where she is now, apart from a vague idea that she might be living somewhere around the Snowdonia area. Millie tried to find her at first but kept coming to dead ends, so maybe she just didn't want to be found.'

'The same age as Darcie is now,' Spencer said thoughtfully. 'You know, she's never mentioned to me that her mother had taken off.'

'Keeps it to herself – doesn't want everyone thinking she's bleating about it.'

'It must be hard, knowing that she can't let her know she has a grandson, too,' Tori said.

'I asked Millie if she wanted to try again, after Oscar was born,' Dylan said. 'I offered to help trace her. But she wants to leave things be.'

'If that's the way she copes then maybe it's best we don't say anything about it,' Spencer replied.

'It's good that you're looking out for her,' Tori said. 'And for Darcie too.'

'Well, we try our best. You know Millie, she loves looking after people – would give Mother Teresa a run for her money – so she's loving having Darcie around, though I'm not quite sure who needs who the most sometimes. Which reminds me… Millie says it's a bit late in the afternoon for lunch, but she'll put nibbles on and make a proper dinner later on this evening. That's assuming you can both stay awake that long.'

'Cheeky bastard!' Spencer laughed. 'We're not that old and infirm yet!'

'He meant we might be tired from the flight,' Tori said.

'No, I didn't,' Dylan fired back impishly. 'You may not be old and boring yet, Tori, but this git certainly is! He's pretending to be exciting to impress you, but you'll soon find out.' He dodged Spencer's flailing arm as he tried to land a playful punch, laughing, and they continued on their way.

They were all in good spirits as they fought their way through ever increasing flurries and drifts that had built up along the buried hedgerows, bordering white fields and frozen waterways. Despite the fact that Tori and Spencer were quite wet, they were all laughing uncontrollably at one of Dylan's racier jokes by the time they arrived at the Old Bakery. Or home, as Dylan called it. As he had warned, they briefly encountered Ruth Evans, Honeybourne's own Olympic-standard gossip, who had been delighted to see Spencer home for the holidays, and with Tori in tow, but had then quickly tried her best to draw them into some speculative conversation about whether Colleen, the landlady of the Dog and Hare, had treated herself to a facelift or not. Dylan had tactfully excused them by explaining that Millie was waiting for them so they could start dinner.

'Oh!' Ruth had exclaimed, 'I could have helped her with dinner! I bet she's rushed off her feet as it is!'

Nobody was fooled for a second, even Tori who had met Ruth only once before. Not only would Ruth have helped to cook dinner, but she would have wanted to stay and eat it too. There were some gatherings that were sacred, and this was one of them. Millie, Dylan and Spencer had faced a world of troubles in the past and come through it all together, and friends didn't get much closer than that.

As Dylan opened the front door, Millie looked up, her face bright with expectation, and broke into a huge smile as the blast of arctic air from outside brought with it Spencer, the friend who had been perhaps her biggest and most solid rock on her arrival in Honey-bourne; a time when the fabric of her life had been in tatters. She couldn't have looked more different from the woman he had met eighteen months before. Her dark hair was still sleek, but she wore it longer than the bob she used to have; she'd put on a few pounds with pregnancy, but it suited her. She still had an astonishing feline beauty, but now it was warmer and softer. Another girl stood next to her, a slightly shorter, less obviously beautiful copy, but pretty in her own way. Spencer had to assume that this was Millie's cousin, Darcie – the family resemblance was so obvious. She held a baby in her arms and watched quietly as Millie let out a squeal of delight and threw herself at the newcomers.

'Spencer!' she cried, wrapping her arms around him and hugging him tight. He picked her up and swung her around, laughing. When he put her down, she went to Tori next and offered her a hug. It was a slightly more restrained version for someone she knew less well, but there was no mistaking the warmth in it just the same.

'It's so good to see you,' she said, stepping back, her face split into a huge smile. 'I can't wait to hear all about how life is treating you in Colorado.'

'I think you've seen almost everything on Facebook,' said Spencer, smiling.

'Well, you can tell me again over tea. I've made mince pies too.'

'You've baked?' Tori asked. 'Wow, how have you had the time?' She nodded her head to where the other girl was holding the baby. 'Is this Oscar?'

'Oh!' Millie laughed, skipping over to take the child into her own arms. 'Yes... Spencer, Tori – meet Oscar Hopkin-Smith!' She kissed his head tenderly and smiled up at them with obvious pride.

'He's gorgeous!' Tori crooned, stepping closer and peering down at him.

'He must take after his mother then,' Spencer said.

'Oi!' Dylan laughed. 'He must take after both of us.'

'Um... No, just Millie.' Spencer grinned. 'So, how old is he now?'

'Two months. He's still a bit tiny because he was a few weeks premature but he can't half pack away the milk,' Dylan said, with more than a little pride in his voice.

The baby gnawed on a fist as he stared up at the new faces. 'He's going to want feeding again soon,' Millie commented to no one in particular. 'I never knew that babies could eat so much.'

'Well, he is Dylan's after all,' Spencer said. 'I'm surprised he hasn't asked you for a can of Heineken yet.'

'I'm saving a special one for his first birthday,' Dylan said.

'I bet that's not even a joke,' Spencer replied.

It was then that everyone seemed to remember the sixth person in the room.

'Oh, I'm so sorry, Darcie!' Millie said, turning to her. 'I'm so used to everyone knowing who you are in Honeybourne now that I totally forgot you three haven't met before. Spencer and Tori, this is my cousin, Darcie.'

Darcie put up her hand in a tiny wave, a nervous smile twitching around her mouth. 'Hello...'

'The famous Darcie!' Spencer smiled. 'We've heard so much about you, it's good to finally meet you in the flesh.'

Darcie turned to Millie with a questioning glance.

'All good,' Tori reassured her.

'In fact, all quite saintly,' said Spencer.

Dylan strode over and slung an arm around the girl's shoulder. 'She's our angel, aren't you, Darcie?'

In that instant, Spencer saw it. He'd spent enough years wearing that look of longing that he would have recognised it anywhere. Darcie looked up at Dylan, and it was obvious that she was hopelessly in love with him. Spencer's own smile faded, but as Millie watched the friendly affection the father of her child offered her younger cousin, she seemed unconcerned. Spencer wished he could feel the same, but he had been friends with Dylan Smith for too long to be able to ignore his past. Dylan looked like a loving partner and doting father, happy with a steady life in a rural bakery, but he was still Dylan. Millie and he were perfect, so good for each other… but Spencer wondered whether Dylan was aware of Darcie's obvious adoration and if he'd ever be tempted to take advantage of it. He believed that Dylan had changed since Millie had come into his life, but tiny doubts were inevitable when you knew Dylan like Spencer did. What if all it took was an argument, a day when Oscar was being particularly difficult, when perhaps Millie wasn't feeling quite as amorous as he was… What then?

He tried to shake the thought. He was being unfair to his oldest friend, who looked as happy and contented as he had ever seen him. Love changed people, and nobody knew that better than Spencer.

As Millie busied herself making coffee, Tori took a seat alongside Spencer and took a moment to appraise the bakery. She had seen it before, of course, but only briefly when they had come along to the grand opening – the first and only other time she had visited Spencer's village. After that they had gone immediately on a very exciting whistle-stop tour of UK landmarks – a time she remembered fondly as involving lots of castle ruins, quaint towns with unpronounceable names, rain, teashops, and sex. She had been taken by surprise with his marriage proposal on the day of the bakery opening, despite saying yes, but during the whirlwind of a vacation that followed, she knew she had made the right choice. Spencer was special, not like the jocks and arrogant go-getters her parents had always done their best to push her in the paths of, and he couldn't be more different from their particular favourite – Hunter Ford. Ugh! How could they even think that she would be attracted to a man like Hunter for one second? And yet they had been unerringly obsessed by the idea of her marrying him for the last five or so years and it was clearly the reason they were determined to hate Spencer, no matter how they might deny it. Hunter Ford might have been on his way to becoming District Attorney, and he might have been handsome in a very obvious way, but he was pompous, boring and self-absorbed. In contrast, Spencer was thoughtful, intelligent, cultured and humble, with the kindest heart of anyone she had ever met. And as much as she loved her parents, and had always strived to please them in all other things, in this case she had defied them. It didn't matter that she and Spencer would never live in a five-storey house or send their kids to private school, only that she would have a life she loved with him.

The décor of the bakery had worn into itself a little since her first visit – contrived shabby chic had become real shabby chic; the pastel-painted tables and chairs bore the signs of wear with the odd chip and scuff, and the tablecloths were soft with repeated washing, but the place looked more homely for it. The wooden counter gleamed, a sign that it was polished rigorously on a daily basis, the glass cases displaying the baked goods were spotless and there was a warm, welcoming sweetness to the air. A part of Tori longed for a home like this herself and she could see that Millie and Dylan loved running their little rural business. Perhaps she could find tranquillity and cosiness like this in the wilds of Colorado, even if it did come with bears and towering firs rather than fields of wheat and sheep, but would Spencer be happy there? It was a question they hadn't really discussed properly, and Tori suspected that was part of the reason she still didn't feel quite settled about their future. She suspected that Spencer felt the same, and to discuss it would mean they had to reach a conclusion that one of them might later come to resent.

Dylan ran a hand through his thick, sandy hair, hazel eyes bright with humour as he plonked himself at their table, Oscar over one shoulder in a way that Tori found disconcertingly casual, but that didn't seem to be causing Oscar a bit of trouble as he leaned against his dad looking quite content.

'So,' he began, grinning at Tori. 'He's managed to persuade you to fly all this way for Christmas. It must be love. And to think…' He glanced at Spencer with a look of mischief, 'she still hasn't found out what a total nerd you are.'

'I like nerds,' Tori laughed, grabbing Spencer's hand across the table for a squeeze. 'Geeks and dorks too.'

'That's lucky, because Spencer is all of those.'

'Thanks…' Spencer shot Dylan a wry smile. 'It's good to know you've got my back.'

'It's what I'm here for.'

Darcie and Millie came to the table, each carrying a tray loaded with cups, sugar bowls, milk and spoons. After laying it all out, they took their own seats. Tori reached for a cup and inhaled deeply.

'Smells amazing. Almost as good as the coffee at home.'

'You can't be talking about the coffee they make in the staffroom at Riversmeet School,' Spencer said. 'That tastes like they fetched the grounds from the recycling and gave it another go.'

'No, not that coffee,' Tori laughed. 'It's true; I don't know how they make it so bad.'

'Must be a school thing,' Millie said. 'We all know what school dinners are like.'

'But if it was good coffee, then maybe we never would've struck up a conversation about it that day,' Tori said, smiling at Spencer.

'Is that how you met?' Darcie asked in a hesitant voice that instantly told Tori she was a shy girl, not usually the one to instigate conversations. Their story had obviously intrigued her enough to make her do it now.

'It is,' Tori replied. 'There I was, doing my best to avoid drinking the coffee and this very cute guy sat next to me with a cup of it. I tried to warn him not to drink it but too late and, boy, did he need some counselling afterwards! As soon as he opened his mouth and that accent came out, I knew he was on the exchange programme and had come in place of one of my colleagues. Lucky for me Andy Bartowski's exchange buddy turned out to be a charmer. A week later we were dating.'

'So you fell in love right away?' Darcie asked.

'I wouldn't say right away,' Tori smiled. 'But I guess I knew quickly that I had someone special.'

'It's funny you don't say it like that to me,' Spencer said with a mischievous grin.

'I can't let the adulation go to your head, can I? That would lead to all sorts of trouble.'

'I'll do my best to stay calm in the face of your hero worship.'

Tori shot him a withering look as she spooned sugar into her coffee, but it was only pretend and he let out a laugh that told her he could see right through it. 'So, Darcie,' she said, turning to her again, 'we hear you've settled into your new life pretty well.'

She nodded. 'I like it here,' she replied, shooting the swiftest glance at Dylan, though it didn't go unnoticed by Tori.

'We're so lucky to have her,' Millie said warmly. 'When Darcie phoned and said she wanted to come down to help, I was thrilled. I needed to employ someone, with Oscar being almost due and the business still getting off the ground, but you can never be sure of people you don't know, so who better than my cousin? There's none of that awkwardness with family, is there? I didn't hesitate to say yes.'

'You felt like a change of scenery, huh?' Tori asked Darcie.

'Um… I suppose so,' Darcie replied.

Tori detected some reluctance to pursue the current line of conversation. There was obviously something bothering her, something in her past she didn't want to talk about. It probably had something to do with what Dylan had told them earlier, though it was obviously something she was not going to hear from Darcie herself, and not in company either. Tori couldn't help but be intrigued though, and resolved to ask Spencer what he knew when they were alone.

Millie stepped in. 'Have you and Spencer set a date for the wedding yet? And please don't say no, because I can't believe how long it's taken you. If only I could get Dylan tied down on the question of marriage, I'd have a date inked in the diary quick as you like before he changed his mind.'

'I would never change my mind,' Dylan cut in. 'Although, we're ok as we are, aren't we?'

'Oh, I'm happy enough. I was just saying, if it happens in the future. I mean...' She turned to Spencer and Tori again. 'You announced the engagement back in April and last I heard you still hadn't set the date.'

'I'm sorry to disappoint you but we're no closer to it,' Spencer said.

'Maybe a little,' Tori added. 'At least we have a ballpark of next summer. But we've been so busy with work and it's kind of hard to do when you can't even figure out *where* you're going to get married, never mind when.'

'Sounds like a terrible excuse to me,' Millie said, giving Spencer a glare of pretend chastisement. 'Set a date, for pity's sake, and then you can figure out the venue.'

'Oh, now I'm terrified...' Spencer said, grabbing Tori's hand playfully and shaking theatrically. 'First Saturday in July! Is that ok, Miss?'

Tori smiled at him. 'First Saturday in July it is.'

Spencer's mouth dropped open. 'Really? I mean...'

'I know it was a joke, but Millie's right. How about it? First Saturday of July, you and me? If our diaries are clear, let's get hitched!'

Millie clapped her hands together with a little squeal. 'Yay! Now we have to get wedding magazines and everything! Please let me make the cake! I don't mind sending it to Boulder... or even bringing it over myself!'

'Steady on!' Dylan spluttered, sending coffee spraying across the pristine tablecloth. 'We haven't got the money to go to Colorado to deliver cake!'

'And that's what we're up against,' Spencer said, his smile fading. 'Now do you see why we've put off making concrete plans? Wherever we get married, one or the other of us will have to make sacrifices and lose guests we'd like to have there but who can't make it. And that's only the start of the troubles.'

Tori aimed a warning frown at him to stop the current thread of conversation. She could guess what subject it would turn to – where they were going to live once they were married. And while she was happy to have a high-spirited debate about setting dates and choosing dresses, the rest was something they needed to figure out when they were alone. If only one of them would be brave enough to state truthfully what they wanted and the other brave enough to listen and perhaps be prepared to compromise.

She looked at the faces sitting across from her: handsome Dylan with his arsenal of perpetual banter; Millie who seemed to be everyone's friend; and sweet, inoffensive Darcie. They were lovely people – kind, caring, welcoming. And Honeybourne was full of other lovely people, as she had discovered during her last visit, and it was just like the picture-postcard vision of rural England that she had always imagined. But could she live here? For good? She liked it well enough, but Boulder was home and she loved it dearly. She loved her job at Riversmeet, and the kids in her class, the softball team she coached, camping trips out in the woods of Colorado in the summer with toasted marshmallows and singing by the fire… Could she give all that up to come here? Could she give it all up for Spencer?

She glanced up at him, his face crinkled into a smile that showed the dimples in his cheeks as Dylan made some new quip, but before she'd had time to think about anything else, the door of the bakery flew open and old Ruth Evans burst in, followed by a flurry of snowflakes.

Millie turned to her, mouth open. 'Ruth—' she began, her tone indignant, but she never got to finish the sentence.

'Dylan!' Ruth cried. 'You have to come quick... Doug's fallen off the roof of the Dog and Hare!'

Chapter Two

'Shit!' Dylan stared at Ruth. 'Are you sure?'

'Of course I'm sure!' she squeaked. 'I saw it with my own eyes!'

'Who's with him?' Millie asked.

'Just Colleen,' Ruth said. 'I called on Frank Stephenson on the way here to see if he could help but he wasn't answering his door.'

Spencer would have smiled at this in less shocking circumstances. The trouble with Ruth Evans was that a lot of people didn't answer their doors to her, because it would be hours before they could get rid of her again. Though she meant well, she was a busybody however you looked at it and some people just had too much to do. He glanced at Tori and she turned to him with a questioning look. 'Doug's the landlord of the local pub and Colleen is his wife. You met them at the bakery opening, remember?' he offered as a brief explanation.

'And Frank? Does he work at the pub too?'

'No – he's a farmer...' Spencer turned back to Ruth. 'Is Doug alright?'

Ruth shook her head. 'I don't know. He's talking, but he's not right.'

'That's something,' Dylan said briskly. 'Come on, we're wasting time here. Millie, call an ambulance, would you? I'll jog down there now, see what I can do.'

'Colleen has already called the ambulance,' Ruth said, rubbing her bony hands together.

'Good,' Dylan said. 'Let's go then.'

'I'll come...' Spencer began, then he turned to Tori. 'You'll be alright here if I go?'

'I can come too,' Tori said firmly. 'I know some first aid.'

'So do I,' Millie put in. 'I can help.'

'Oscar needs you here,' Dylan said, planting a brief kiss on her forehead. 'You always want to help, I know, but you said yourself he's going to need feeding soon and nobody else can do that but you right now.'

Millie gave a brief nod. It was obvious to anyone that she wasn't happy, but she understood it was the most sensible plan.

'Could I come?' Darcie asked.

Spencer was about to offer his opinion that maybe it wasn't such a good idea, and that too many cooks spoiled the broth – or at least made rescuing pub landlords in the snow a lot more difficult – when Dylan cut in.

'At this point I'm not bothered who comes.' He disappeared into a back room for a moment, and then re-emerged, flinging a pink coat at Darcie. 'We just need to stop messing about and get over there.'

One by one they filed out, leaving Millie standing in the empty bakery alone with her baby. Even as they closed the door behind them, Spencer heard Oscar begin to cry.

The snowfall had stuttered into powdery stop-start flurries, and the clouds alternated with a low, brilliant sun that peeked out every so often and turned the landscape into a glistening white blanket. It took a few minutes longer to reach the old pub at the heart of Honeybourne than usual, but they were a determined little group. Even Ruth Evans, easily the oldest woman in the village (though nobody knew quite how old), was keeping up with Dylan's long strides and not showing any sign of fatigue. Talk was on a strictly need-to-know basis, with Dylan and Spencer ascertaining the most pertinent details of the accident from Ruth and not inviting speculation of any kind on any other subject – usually the old woman's default setting no matter what the severity of any situation – until they saw the higgledy-piggledy roofs of the old pub ahead. Covered in thick snow, the lower level was scarred by a track leading from the chimney to the roof's edge; there were two figures – one lying down and the other sitting next to him – in the garden below. A set of long ladders was propped against the side of the building and various tools were scattered across the ground beneath.

'At least it wasn't the big roof,' Dylan said as they made their way over. 'We'd have been organising his funeral.'

Spencer gritted his teeth and said nothing. It was a cold observation but he had to agree.

'The snow probably cushioned his fall too,' Tori offered.

The seated figure looked in their direction and began to wave frantically. 'He's here!' she yelled.

Dylan picked up the pace and the others followed, apart from Ruth, who seemed to show signs of slowing up for the first time that morning.

'What happened?' Dylan's tone was terse as he crouched down to get a good look. Doug stared balefully up at him but offered no reply. He seemed alert, though almost as white as the snow beneath him, and he was obviously in a lot of pain. Colleen clung to his hand and faced Dylan, her mascara streaked down her face as she continued to weep.

'I told him… I told him not to go up there…' she sobbed.

'It's ok,' Spencer said gently, joining Dylan at her level. He put an arm around her.

She looked around, and for a moment she seemed confused. 'Spencer Johns?'

'The same,' he smiled.

'I thought you were in America…'

'I told you he was coming home,' Ruth said in an overloud voice. She turned to Tori and added in an equally loud whisper, 'Poor thing. Must be the shock sent her loopy.'

Tori gave her a small smile but then turned her attention back to the distraught woman sitting next to her injured husband.

'I'm home for Christmas,' Spencer said to Colleen patiently. 'And you've got Tori's parents booked in to stay at the pub, remember?' She stared back at him, and Spencer realised that she was probably in shock, just as Ruth had asserted; there was no point in having this conversation while her husband lay on the snow. 'It doesn't matter now. We need to think about Doug, don't we?'

Colleen gave a tiny nod, and then she began to cry again.

'How long did the emergency services say it would be before they got here?' Dylan asked, looking up at a sky that now seemed to be filling with snow again.

'I… I can't remember,' Colleen sniffed. 'But I wish they'd hurry up.'

'He's shivering,' Tori said. 'Colleen, do you have any blankets you could bring from inside to cover him? And a big umbrella would be good too.'

Colleen looked towards the front door of the pub, and then back at Tori with an expression that suggested to everyone that she wasn't quite keeping it together. Clearly, she hadn't really taken in what Tori had asked her.

'I could help you look,' Darcie said in a small voice. She'd been so silent they'd almost forgotten she was there at all.

'I couldn't leave Doug,' Colleen said, gripping his hand so tightly that her knuckles were white.

Doug grunted something along the lines of his being perfectly alright. It was clear that he was a lot of things, but alright wasn't one of them.

'Sure you are,' Dylan said. 'Just humour us anyway.' He turned to Ruth. 'Could you help Darcie find what we need in the pub?'

Ruth looked rather more excited than was appropriate about the opportunity to sniff around unsupervised in one of her neighbours' homes. 'Of course I can!'

She grabbed Darcie by the hand and yanked her with surprising force towards the open doors of the pub, while Spencer called Dylan and Tori closer and lowered his voice.

'One of us should call the ambulance service again. There's no telling what Colleen has done in her state – for all we know she could have phoned Domino's Pizza.'

'Good thinking,' Dylan said. 'It beats standing around here feeling useless.' He turned to Tori. 'You said you knew a bit of first aid… Do you think we ought to move him? He'll go into shock, won't he, in this cold?'

'Well, yes… That's why I asked for the blankets.'

'Then we should get him out of the snow,' Spencer began, but Tori stopped him.

'We can't move him because we don't know what his injuries are and we might do more damage than if we left him in the snow. We'll keep him as warm and dry as we can for now and wait for the paramedics to do their thing.'

Spencer nodded agreement, then he and Tori went back to Colleen to see if they could keep her from the nervous breakdown she seemed about to have, while Dylan looked on with a grim expression, arms folded across his chest. Just as he was about to stride over to the pub to see if the blankets were coming, Ruth and Darcie hurried out, Darcie carrying a duvet they'd clearly stolen from one of the beds and Ruth armed with a parasol from the beer garden.

'This was the best we could do,' Ruth said. 'I couldn't find an umbrella anywhere… If I'd had another twenty minutes to go through the cupboards, maybe, but Darcie wouldn't let me look through all of them.'

'I thought something brought back quickly was better than leaving him out in the snow,' Darcie said in a slightly defensive tone.

Dylan nodded. 'I think that was a good call. He took the umbrella from Ruth and spiked it into the ground as best he could, while Tori proceeded to wrap Doug in the quilt. What little colour he still had was fading from his face even as they worked. Dylan exchanged anxious glances with the rest of them, while Colleen never let go of his hand, the river of mascara now spilling from her cheeks onto her clothes.

'The ambulance is almost here,' Spencer said, shoving his mobile phone back in his pocket.

'Not before time,' Dylan muttered, pulling his own collar up as high as it would go to fight off the cold.

Spencer shot a half-apologetic glance at Tori. Honeybourne was a tiny village, but it seemed to be big on drama. He should have realised he would get no ordinary welcome home.

* * *

Three hours later, Dylan, Spencer, Tori, and Darcie trudged back through the door of the Old Bakery. Ruth had stayed with Colleen at the hospital while Doug was checked over. The immediate impression from the doctors was that he'd broken both his legs, but they were by no means sure that was the full extent of his injuries and there was a whole list of unpronounceable scans and tests they wanted to do before they could say with any certainty. Dylan had instructed Ruth or Colleen to call them the moment they needed any assistance, or when they were ready to come back to Honeybourne, and he would go out, snow or not, to get them.

Millie was pacing up and down, Oscar slung over her shoulder as she patted his back to encourage a burp. She turned to the door as it opened, and the look of relief on her face didn't need words.

'He's at the hospital now,' Dylan said in answer to her silent question.

'What happened?' Millie asked. 'Why on earth was he on the roof?'

'We still haven't got the answer to that,' Spencer said. 'But I bet he could do with one of your herbal healing remedies right now.'

'I haven't made any of those in a while,' Millie said doubtfully. 'And it's no time to go foraging in the hedgerows for all the plants I'd need. Do you think I should?'

'Let the hospital deal with it,' Dylan said. 'There's no need for you to worry yourself. Perhaps you can brew him a tonic once he's home if you really feel the need to pull out all that old equipment and make something.'

'However long that takes to happen,' Spencer said.

'Is it that bad?' Millie asked, rubbing Oscar's back. 'Did they say he'd be in hospital for a long time?'

'Bad enough, I think. The doctors are still figuring out exactly what he's managed to do to himself.'

'Poor Colleen…' Millie murmured. Oscar let out a belch, while Dylan, now coatless and standing in his socks by the fire, took him from her for a cuddle. 'She's so devoted to Doug… I don't know what she'd do if anything happened to him.'

'Well,' Spencer said, taking a seat at one of the deserted tables, 'lucky for him his guardian angel was on duty, because it could have been a lot worse.'

'You've been ok while we were out?' Dylan asked.

Millie nodded. 'No customers, if that's what you mean, so at least I didn't have that to worry about. It was just me and Oscar. The snow is so bad, nobody wants to come out for tea and scones today.'

'I bloody do!' Spencer grinned. 'I believe we were promised tea and mince pies what feels like a very long time ago now.'

'I can do that,' Millie smiled. 'I bet you're freezing.' She turned to Darcie. 'Would you be a love and fetch the stuff we baked this morning through to the counter? We should probably look like a bakery, even if nobody's going to come in to buy anything today. I'll make the hot drinks.'

Darcie gave a quick nod and scurried through a doorway to where the ovens were housed, while Millie took herself behind the counter and switched on various gadgets. Soon, the whoosh of steam and the clanking of china filled the room, and as everyone began to thaw out, conversation turned to speculation about how Colleen and Doug were going to cope. Christmas was only a week away, and while they might be able to get away with closing the pub for a day or so, a week as busy as this was a lot of trade to lose if they stayed shut any longer.

'Won't the brewery send someone?' Millie asked the room at large as she set a mug of hot chocolate in front of Tori.

'The Dog and Hare is a free house,' Dylan said. 'I don't know if it works like that for them as they're not tied to one particular brewery and they own the pub outright.'

'Oh,' Millie replied thoughtfully. 'What will they do?'

'I suppose that's something they're going to have to work out, but for now I imagine they'll be concerned with more pressing matters, like Doug's injuries.'

'It won't help him to get well if he's got the added worry of his business going down the drain though,' said Spencer as Millie handed him a mug.

'Definitely not.'

'Well, there aren't many folks in a position to help – at least not long term,' Dylan said. 'We work long enough hours here but Doug and Colleen's are even longer.'

'Don't forget that we'll be losing money too without their pie orders,' Millie reminded him. 'If there is any way we can keep them open it would benefit us as much as anyone else. Things are tough enough in the winter without tourists passing through, we can't afford to lose our regular customers as well.'

'You might have a point there,' Dylan said, looking around at the café, empty apart from their own small group. His gaze settled on Darcie, who was bringing a tray of bread pudding through from the back kitchens. 'Perhaps we could spare someone to go over and help Colleen for a few hours a day until Doug is back on his feet.'

Darcie looked up from the counter. She glanced at Millie, and then back at Dylan.

'Darcie?' Millie replied doubtfully. 'What will we do without her here?'

'You said yourself that we'll be in trouble without the Dog and Hare's orders.'

'But I can't manage without Darcie.'

'We'll have to if it comes to it. Better that we struggle for a bit than lose that income.'

'It might be a lot more than a bit,' Millie replied. 'You know I want to help, but it could be months before Doug is up and about if he's seriously injured and we could go under either way because I don't see how we can cope with Oscar and this place without any help, whether we get the orders in from the Dog and Hare or not.' Millie's voice rose, and it seemed as if she was convincing herself of the impending doom whatever happened.

'You've just said that we need the orders…' Dylan shushed Oscar as he began to whimper.

'I know I did! There's no need to lose your temper!' Millie snapped.

'I'm not losing my temper—'

'It bloody sounds like it!' Millie gave a loud sniff and turned her back on everyone.

'I didn't mean to upset you…' Dylan said, going to her.

'No…' She flapped a hand at him. 'Ignore me… Hormones and stress don't go well together.'

'I can see what you're saying, Millie,' said Spencer, 'and – as much as I hate admitting it – Dylan might have a point too. The way I see it, we need to call a meeting as soon as we have an update on Doug's condition. Surely Honeybourne hasn't changed that much while I've been away? We're a community who help each other, and I don't see why things should be any different this time. Nobody will want to see the pub closed over Christmas and if we call for assistance I think we'll get it. I mean,' he glanced at Tori, 'we'd go and help for a start – right?'

'Of course!' Tori beamed.

Dylan gave a solemn nod as Millie stepped away from him, now composed again.

'I could go,' Darcie said in the ensuing moment's silence. 'I don't know much about pubs but I don't mind, if it would help. We close at five, sometimes before when it's quiet, so I could go afterwards.'

'You get up at the crack of dawn,' Millie said gently. 'I don't know if you realise what a long day that would be, going on to a pub afterwards where you'd be working way past the time we usually head off to bed.'

'What about Jasmine?' Spencer said suddenly.

Dylan's face split into a grin. 'God, I'm an idiot, I should have thought of that! If anyone knows about that pub it's my sister! She worked in it for a couple of years before she started the craft business.'

'But would she want to be there every night for months?' Millie asked doubtfully. 'Not to mention her three kids and a business.'

'Which brings me back to my original idea,' Spencer said. 'We call a meeting and we recruit volunteers to help out on a rota basis.' He looked at Tori, and she nodded, immediately understanding his train of thought. 'Tori and I will do some shifts – it'll be fun and we haven't got a lot else on.'

'Um… you might be forgetting the small matter of your parents flying in from Spain to spend some time with you?' said Millie.

'Oh, yeah!' Spencer grinned. 'I'm sure we can fit them in somewhere. After all, Tori's parents were planning to stay at the pub anyway so we'll need to make sure it stays open for that reason if no other.

My parents have the spare room at my house and we couldn't possibly fit everyone in. They'll be cool about it too, because they'll be spending more than a few hours in the bar of the Dog and Hare themselves if I'm not mistaken. They'll probably want to help out too.'

'And that little celebration called Christmas,' Dylan added.

'Easy,' Spencer smiled. 'We're practically ready for that. So we've got three volunteers straight away – that's a good start, right? And I'm sure Jasmine will say yes so that's four.'

'We could ask Ruth,' Millie said.

Dylan raised his eyebrows. 'We want to keep their customers, not drive them away. Besides, the way old Ruth Evans packs away the whisky there'll be no profits to show for her doing a turn behind the bar.' He glanced at Millie uncertainly. 'I suppose I could do an hour here and there if you could cope with Oscar on your own.'

'Or I could do an hour at the bar and you can stay home and hold the baby,' Millie replied, planting her hands on her hips. 'This is the twenty-first century, after all.'

'Ok,' Dylan raised his hands defensively, 'I wasn't being chauvinist – I just didn't think you'd want to spend your evenings listening to Frank Stephenson complain about the weather and how things just aren't the same as they were in the fifties.'

'It might be a nice break for an hour, though?' Spencer said, understanding instinctively that perhaps, sometimes, an intelligent, creative woman like Millie might find domesticity a little stifling.

Millie nodded. 'The way I see it, we should hang on until we know what timescale we're looking at, see what Colleen is happy with, and then go from there.'

There was murmured agreement around the room.

'Now that's settled,' Millie said, 'who wants those mince pies?'

Dylan grinned. 'I thought you'd never ask.'

Darcie busied herself tidying the tables. Everyone had left – Spencer and Tori back to Spencer's empty house, Millie and Dylan back to their parenthood, while Ruth Evans was still at the hospital with Colleen. Oscar was crying again, so Dylan had taken him upstairs while Millie sat out in the tiny yard at the back of the bakery, wrapped up against the cold but so desperate for a break that the ice and snow was a small price to pay.

The only noises in the building were the quiet hum of the refrigerators and Oscar's screams, punctuated by Dylan doing his best to soothe him. At first Darcie had found the sound of Oscar crying for hours on end distressing, but now she was learning to filter it out. It wasn't her baby, after all, and she knew that even when she helped out with him, when it all got too much, she could simply hand him back to his parents and go out. Not that there were many places to go in this village.

When she'd lost her job back in her hometown of Millrise, she'd grabbed the chance to leave the Midlands and come and help Millie in Honeybourne with both hands. Not only had she found herself unemployed there, but in Millrise were reminders of a broken relationship that held only bitter memories and parents who didn't seem to care whether she was there or not. She had been miserable, and although she had been desperate for something to lift her from the doldrums of her life, she had been too scared to do anything about it. But then Millie had made the call, and it had sounded like a wonderful adventure – to leave home and start somewhere completely new without the baggage of her old life and in the company of people she knew would keep her safe. Millie had turned her own life around by leaving Millrise – perhaps she could too. Dylan and Millie hadn't been able to promise her much of a wage – pocket money, really – but they had promised a free roof over her head and all the food she could eat in return for a few hours' help in the mornings. She had settled into life with them quickly, and she had enjoyed it at first. But that was before she realised she was falling for Dylan.

She hadn't even noticed the feelings creeping up on her. He made her laugh, he was handsome, and he was kind. He always asked how she was, whether she needed anything, included her in decisions concerning the bakery and listened to her opinions like they really mattered. Nobody had ever shown that much interest in her before, not even her own parents. Not only that, but he was so patient and loving towards Millie and Oscar that it was obvious his heart was good. And then one day, the unexpected jolt in her own as he innocently pulled her into a friendly hug issued the warning. It started as a vague, unexplained longing, and no matter how much Darcie tried to ignore it, the longing kept growing until it was an ache that threatened to break her heart in two. Now, every time she looked at him all she could think of was how his lips might taste if only they were to meet hers. And then she'd look at Millie, her own flesh and blood, more like a sister than a cousin, and the guilt would overwhelm her.

She'd mentioned leaving – her first reaction was to get away from the situation before it got out of hand – but they'd both seemed so genuinely devastated by the idea that she couldn't go through with it. So here she was, stuck in a village where she could never be far enough away from Dylan Smith to forget about him, and forced to watch him love someone else, someone she cared about too.

Her thoughts were interrupted by the slam of the back door, and Millie swept in, bringing the cold with her.

'The sky is so clear this evening, it looks gorgeous, but I think the snow is going to ice over so it'll be a nightmare tomorrow. You weren't planning to go far, were you?'

'I was thinking of going into Salisbury,' Darcie replied, sweeping a cloth across a table. 'I need to get a few last-minute presents.' The truth was that she didn't really need any last-minute presents, but she did need a reason to go out.

'Oh…' Millie said. 'I'm not sure how reliable the buses will be if the roads are too treacherous. Unless Dylan can run you there. He's quite good at driving in snow.'

'I'll probably put it off for a day or so,' Darcie said, rubbing at a particularly stubborn mark on the table. She was giving it far more concentration than it needed, but she couldn't trust herself to look Millie in the eye right now, not when thoughts of her and Dylan alone in the car were filling her head. 'It's a nuisance that I can't drive. I hate relying on you two and public transport all the time…' She took a deep breath, and forced herself to look up. 'About the pub…'

'Yes?' Millie asked, grabbing a sweeping brush from the cupboard. She took advantage of Darcie's hesitation to continue and cocked her head. 'Sounds like Oscar has finally gone down. Poor Dylan must be frazzled, but at least we have an hour now with a bit of luck. I don't know what I'd do without you both – I'd be a crackpot, I'm sure.'

Darcie chewed her lip. She had been about to tell Millie that she'd given it some thought and she wanted to go and help at the pub while Doug was out of action. If at all possible, she'd quite like to live at the pub for a while. Perhaps some distance from Dylan and Millie might be enough to cure her inappropriate feelings for him, but she didn't really want to go back to Millrise if she could help it. It seemed like a good solution and, in such a small place, about as far away as she was going to get without leaving altogether. But Millie had gone and done it again without even realising the pain she was causing. How could Darcie tell Millie now that she needed to get away? How could she leave them to cope when she knew just how much they relied on her?

Millie began to sweep the floor. 'Sorry, what did you want to say about the pub?'

'It was just something about the meeting… When did we decide to hold it? And are we doing it here or at the Dog and Hare?'

Millie stopped and rested her chin on the handle of the brush. 'I suppose we should have it as soon as we know about Doug's condition and what Colleen wants to do. I said I would let Spencer know and Dylan will have a word with his sister to see what she thinks. She was amazing when we were getting the bakery up and running and she has a real flair for organising things like this.'

'Jasmine?' Darcie asked doubtfully.

'Yes…' Millie frowned. 'What's the matter?'

'It's just that she has so much to do already with triplets and her own business.'

'I know, but she always seems to have time to pitch in. She's an absolute wonder woman. I don't know how she does it but whatever it is, she should bottle it and sell it. She'd make a tidy fortune and I'd be first in the queue.'

Darcie said nothing and went back to cleaning the tables.

'It's quiet up there,' said Millie, resuming her sweeping. 'I bet Dylan's fallen asleep with Oscar.' When Darcie didn't look up, she added, 'Is everything alright?'

'Sorry?' Darcie asked.

'With you? I can't help noticing that you don't seem yourself lately. I know life can be a bit quiet and boring sometimes in Honeybourne, and you're younger than me and used to more excitement than this...'

Darcie wished she could say that the craving of more excitement was the only problem she had in life, but she felt there was more than enough of that right now, and not at all the right kind. 'I'm fine. I'm just ready for a break at Christmas, that's all.'

'Do you feel as if you ought to be home at Christmas? I know that it's not always easy to be around your parents, but they are your parents and I'd completely understand if you wanted to be with them for the festive season.'

'You'd miss me – how would you run things on your own?' Darcie asked with a slight smile.

'I know. But I also know your mum and dad will miss you on Christmas Day too, despite what you think.'

'We talked about it and they're fine. They understand that it's probably just this year. It'll give them an excuse to have a quiet one together, perhaps do something a bit different.'

What she didn't add, because they both knew it, was that they would barely notice her absence anyway. It wasn't something that Darcie enjoyed thinking about. She had often wondered whether she would have been less lonely with a brother or sister to grow up with, but she quickly realised that there was no point, because she didn't have either and no amount of wondering would change that. It was a mixed blessing of sorts anyway, as her growing up alone had meant that Millie had always taken a keen interest in her wellbeing, sensing early on that she had very little emotional support from home, and it had drawn them closer than two cousins with such an age gap would normally be.

Millie was silent again for a moment. 'Well, you know we'd hate to lose you, but if you wanted to go home to Millrise, then of course we'd understand... I mean, for Christmas, or if you wanted to go back permanently. You've been brilliant this past few months but it's a long time to be away from your home.'

Darcie paused. Millie always seemed to work out what was going on in her head, and it was unnerving to say the least. Although what Millie had guessed wasn't the whole story, and Darcie was happy for her to stay in the dark about some of the details... Details that could destroy their relationship if they came out. 'I needed a breather, to get away from home for a bit. I'm fine as I am for now.'

'Right, I was just saying... It's not us, is it?'

'What do you mean?'

'We're not getting on your nerves? Me and Dylan? I'm a worrier and I know that's hard work. And Dylan can be a bit full on sometimes, but he's a good man.'

'No,' Darcie replied, wishing now that Millie would just drop the interrogation.

'Is it living with Oscar? He cries a lot and that drives us mad so it must be hard for you.'

'No,' Darcie repeated. 'I'm fine.'

Without another word, she marched out to the kitchens to change the water in her bucket, fighting back the tears that would give her away. Damn Millie's kindness. If only Darcie could hate her for something, however small, she could stop hating herself quite so much for being in love with her boyfriend.

* * *

It was standing room only; it had been a while since the tiny café room of Millie's bakery had been so full. For Spencer it brought back fond memories of the grand opening, when he had first brought Tori to Honeybourne and had proposed to her.

Darcie and Millie were busy plying everyone with hot drinks as they settled in for the meeting, and Spencer smiled with pride as he watched Tori, who had volunteered her services and now stood behind the counter doing her best to figure out how to operate the monstrous coffee machine. Dylan had Oscar strapped to him and was dishing out cakes at the counter. And of course, though the Old Bakery was filled with more noise than ever before, Oscar was sleeping peacefully through it all. Spencer could only imagine how galling that was when he would likely be keeping them awake later that night, but at least it meant people would be able to hear themselves speak when the meeting began.

He turned to Colleen, who sat next to him, drawn and pale, fingers twisted around each other as her edgy glance darted here and there. People waved or mouthed greetings to her as they filed in; some came over to ask briefly how Doug was doing, but Spencer could tell by her distracted replies that she was finding it difficult to hold things together. 'Are you alright?' he asked. 'Do you need me to get anything for you?'

Colleen shook her head.

Ruth, who was sitting on the other side of her, patted her hand. 'We'll have you sorted in no time,' she said. 'Won't we, Spencer?'

He was about to reply when the door opened with a gust and Dylan's sister, Jasmine, walked in. She was with her husband, Rich, and triplets Rachel, Rebecca and Reuben, who all seemed to have grown at least a foot since he had last seen them. But their astonishing growth spurt wasn't the thing that cut short his reply. It was the unexpected reaction at seeing Jasmine after months of being away. She looked as lovely as ever, her candy-pink curls spilling out from beneath a Scandinavian-style woolly hat, flowery wellies and a long plum coat; the cold of the day had brought out the blush of her cheeks and her hazel eyes danced with excitement. She had her own unique style and take on the world, and she didn't look like other women, but he had loved her for this.

Today, she was all that he remembered and all that he had fallen for in the first place. He tried to shake the thoughts away as she searched the room and her gaze fell on him.

'Spencer!' she squealed, before rushing over to his table.

He stood to hug her, and as he pulled her close the scent of her brought back feelings that had his mind in a whirl. Where had this come from? It was sudden and fierce; he had never expected to react this way and he didn't want to. His life was with Tori now, so how could he feel like this?

'I'm so sorry we didn't get to see you before, but Rich has been locked away with a deadline looming and Reuben had flu, which meant that the other two decided to get pseudo flu, and you know how it is…'

'I know,' Spencer smiled. 'It's ok.'

Rich and the triplets joined them, and Spencer wondered how much his face was giving away as they greeted him. This was not good at all.

'Good to see you!' Rich said.

Spencer's mind went back to that thunderous evening the previous year, when he had told Rich that he loved his wife… Was Rich thinking about that now? Or had he moved on? Spencer certainly thought he himself had, but it seemed that some people, like Jasmine Green, were just too beguiling to shake. Spencer and Jasmine had seen each other since the day it all came out, of course, at the bakery's grand opening that spring, but somehow that visit had been so fleeting and so busy, and filled with the excitement of his proposal to Tori, that he had managed to put any thoughts of Jasmine to the back of his mind. It was hard to know what had changed this time, but something had. Perhaps twenty years of being in love with someone was too much to erase in a few short months, no matter what else happened to come along.

He turned to Reuben and offered him a formal handshake. 'How's it going?'

'Are you coming back to school soon?' Reuben asked.

Jasmine and Rich burst out laughing. 'Straight out with it, son!' Rich chuckled. He turned to Spencer. 'They don't care much for the exchange teacher in your place.'

Spencer looked around the room, as if he had suddenly remembered something very important.

'I had thought I might see him around,' he said. 'Does he come to the village stuff?'

'He doesn't even live in the village,' Rich said. 'Drives in every day from Salisbury.'

Spencer nodded. 'Village life too quiet, eh?'

'It might be, although I'm not sure I'd call Salisbury a thriving metropolis.'

'No,' Spencer laughed, 'but at least there are some decent shops and more than one pub.' He looked down at the triplets. 'I probably shouldn't ask, but what's wrong with Mr Bartowski?'

'He's alright, he's just...' Rebecca paused, looking for the right word.

'Weird,' Rachel finished for her. Spencer raised his eyebrows.

'He's not like you,' Reuben offered. 'You're funny.'

'And he's not?' Spencer asked. 'I think that makes him better than me, because I'm not sure teachers are supposed to be funny.'

'You know what we mean,' Rebecca said, blushing.

'You're just nicer,' Rachel added.

'Are you planning to come back soon?' Jasmine asked.

'I'm supposed to, and I already extended my stint in Colorado, as you know, so I don't know how much longer I'll be allowed to stay, but we're not sure where we're going to end up living when we get married. I might apply for citizenship and stay in the US, but Tori is already an EU citizen, on account of her grandparents being Irish, so we could stay here and it would be a lot easier. That's not to say it's the right decision, though, or one she'd be happy with.'

'It's a tough one,' Rich agreed. 'Good luck with thrashing it out – it's been nice knowing you, because if she's anything like Jasmine she will win the debate and you'll end up living in Colorado before you've had time to realise it.'

'That wouldn't be so bad,' Spencer smiled. 'But I would miss Honeybourne a lot.'

'Honeybourne would miss you too,' Jasmine replied. 'A lot.'

He shrugged. 'I expect you're used to me being gone now. I've already stayed on past the year I was supposed to.'

'That's love for you,' Rich said, glancing up to see that Tori was now making her way over, drying her hands on a tea cloth. 'Talk of the devil and she will appear...'

Jasmine elbowed him and he simply grinned.

'Hey, Tori!' Jasmine pulled her into a warm hug. 'Is my best friend looking after you?'

'He is,' Tori's smile was stiff as she pulled away. 'He's making me very happy.'

Spencer shot her a sideways glance. The two women had only met once before, at the grand opening of the bakery, but Tori's reaction to Jasmine's greeting was cool, even when you considered they barely knew each other. Had Tori picked up on something between him and Jasmine that easily and that quickly? He'd done his best to keep it locked away, but maybe his attempts just hadn't been so good. If his feelings were that transparent it could spell trouble.

'Good,' Jasmine replied in a voice full of approval.

'Hi, kids,' Tori added, smiling with more warmth at all three of them, who simply offered shy smiles in return.

Rich hugged Tori too, but was called away immediately by Frank Stephenson shouting to him from across the room. 'Sorry…' He offered Tori an apologetic shrug, and she laughed.

'It must be tough being famous.'

'What can I say?' Rich grinned as he went off to find out what Frank wanted.

'It'll be something to do with scrumpy, no doubt,' Jasmine said, watching Rich go with a shake of her head. 'Anyone would think we lived in twenties America the way they sneak around with that stuff.'

'You want to come and get cakes?' Rachel asked Tori, Reuben and Rebecca nodding eager agreement. Tori offered a quick glance at Spencer, who nodded encouragement, and she was led away to where Dylan was beckoning with a tray of baked goodies.

'She's lovely,' Jasmine said to Spencer as they watched Tori go.

'Yes, she is.'

'You're happy?'

Spencer looked sharply at her. 'Of course. Why do you ask?'

'I just wanted to know. I'm still allowed to care about you... You look well.'

'So do you.'

'Oh, I look like a working mother of three, so you can stop lying,' she laughed. 'But you look great. Life in America suits you.'

'I like it, but I don't know that I want to stay there forever.'

'That could be a problem.'

'I know.'

'Have you talked about it?'

'Sort of. I don't think either of us dares to say what we really want.'

'Which is?'

'I want to come home. But this isn't Tori's home and I don't think there would be enough in Honeybourne for her.' Spencer hesitated. Should he be telling Jasmine this? But something wouldn't let him stop. There was something about Jasmine that invited confidence, whether it was right or not. 'She'd be alright at first, but it wouldn't last.'

'You love each other?'

'Yes, of course we do.'

'Then you'll make it work.'

Spencer gave her a thin smile. 'I wish I could feel that confident about it.'

'You're not sure you love her enough?' Jasmine asked.

'Of course I do!'

'Then what?' Jasmine pressed, seemingly unconcerned by the sudden irritation in his tone.

Spencer let out a long sigh. He knew Jasmine didn't mean to pry, and she wasn't the sort of woman who passed judgement on the choices of others. If she was asking, it was out of genuine concern and there was no need to take his feelings of confusion out on her. He softened his tone. 'It's just a tough call, isn't it?'

'But if you loved her enough nothing else would matter.'

He gave her a small smile. 'You always could see right through me.'

'You're like a brother to me. Of course I do.'

Like a brother. How Spencer had once hated to hear those words from her and yet it was all he'd ever heard… apart from that day she had visited him, after the thunderstorm in which he had almost lost his life, vulnerable and confused about her feelings and not in a place where it was right to tell her how he felt, how he would always feel about her. He could have kissed her then and she would have let him. She might even have fooled herself into thinking she loved him, and he might even have been happy for a while, but it would have been a lie. He had seen enough to know that Jasmine loved Rich and that would never change, no matter who else challenged it. And so he had turned her away, had made the decision to leave Honeybourne and to try to forget about Jasmine Green. It had been the right choice, but there had been times when he wondered about what might have been.

He noticed Ruth sitting at a table close by, eagerly following their conversation. Shit! Why did that woman have to be so damn good at unearthing secrets? And why was she always there at the worst possible moments? Spencer wondered just how long she had been listening and how much she had worked out from what she had heard. Most importantly of all, would she repeat any of it to Tori?

He had just made the decision to take her to one side and try to hint, as subtly as he could, that she needed to keep anything she'd heard to herself, when Frank Stephenson called for order and the whole café fell silent. The meeting was about to start, and it looked as though everything else would have to wait.

Chapter Three

When Darcie had hoped to be given shifts at the pub, this wasn't what she'd had in mind at all. She glanced across to where Dylan sported a white apron tied over his jeans, chatting to the owners of the newsagent as he pulled a pint. God, he made looking good seem so easy, and the sound of his relaxed laughter sent a pulse of longing through her that made her face burn with shame. How had this happened? She had volunteered to take a couple of shifts a week, after Millie had reassured her that they could manage at the bakery without her, and before she knew what was happening, Dylan had ended up doing the same ones after his sister had told him she would be happy to stay with Millie on the evenings he was missing. Darcie had aired some reservations about her ability to work behind a bar, of course, but she had done so believing that Colleen, or perhaps Jasmine, who had done it before, would help her out. The last person she wanted (and also, perversely, the only person she wanted) there was Dylan. But the whole point had been to get away from him. Now she was stuck in purgatory.

She spun around as Colleen tapped her on the shoulder.

'Everything alright?'

'Oh… yes…' Darcie stammered. She handed over the food order that she now realised she had been holding for five minutes while she stared at Dylan and cursed her luck. At least the pub wasn't too busy tonight, because she was sure she would have been no help at all if it had been. 'A couple of pies and gravy for that table over there…' She pointed to two old men playing cards, half pints of bitter in front of them.

'Jim and Saul,' Colleen observed with a faint smile. 'They love Millie's pies. I suspect it's because they love Millie but it's all the same to me as long as the money goes in our till.'

'Why don't they just buy them from Millie and eat them at home?' Darcie asked, instantly realising it was the wrong thing to say.

Colleen simply raised her eyebrows. 'Why do any of the regulars not stay at home? I don't know and I don't want to, as long as they keep us open.'

Darcie frowned as Colleen took the food order slip and went off to the kitchens. She didn't know Colleen all that well, but she had never found her quite so cynical and easy to dislike. She supposed that it was stressful, your husband being in hospital with two broken legs over Christmas, a whole troupe of strangers coming into your pub night after night trying to run it for you while you had to keep smiling for the customers. Colleen didn't look her usual immaculate self either, and that only made Darcie certain that it wasn't Colleen's usual attitude.

Her thoughts were distracted by Dylan's laughter again. This time he was chatting to a slim blonde, probably around his age. She could hear him calling her Amy. *Amy…* Darcie seemed to recall the name from somewhere. She'd heard it mentioned before but she couldn't quite place where and why. Judging by the way Amy was flicking her hair and thrusting her chest out, she was quite partial to Dylan herself, and although he was obviously enjoying the attention, Darcie could tell that he wasn't interested. His loyalty to Millie only made him more attractive. At least if he was a cheating git, like the boyfriend she had left back in Millrise, who had taken it upon himself to seduce practically the only friend she had, Darcie might have been able to hate him instead of longing to be at the receiving end of that loyalty.

He turned to the CD player behind the bar and flicked it on. Instantly, Wham's 'Last Christmas' blasted out and Amy clapped her hands with glee.

'Ooh, I love this one!' she squeaked, and proceeded to croon it to Dylan in a way that made it hard for Darcie to decide whether she wanted to punch her in the face or throw up. She was just thankful that Millie wasn't there, although she suspected the only reason Amy was brave enough to flirt so outrageously was for just that reason.

'Well, it's not long, so I thought it was about time we got the Christmas cheer back in this place,' said Dylan, grinning.

'Five sleeps and counting!' Amy said in a stupid baby voice that was obviously meant to be sexy but just made her sound like she'd been hypnotised by the Teletubbies. 'What's going to be in your stocking?'

'No idea,' he said. 'I don't think I've been good enough for presents. What's going to be in yours?'

'My legs!' she squealed and collapsed into fits of giggles.

Dylan glanced across at Darcie with a knowing smile. He sidled across.

'Pissed as a fart,' he said in a low voice, angling his head at Amy who was still snorting at her own joke. 'Never could hold her booze.'

'Do you know her well?'

Dylan coloured at this question. Darcie had never seen him look embarrassed in that way before. 'She's lived here for a few years.'

'Is she married? I never see her with a man.'

'Her husband works away a lot. I think he's in Düsseldorf or somewhere right now… Some boring finance job or other – I forget.' He lowered his voice. 'She goes a bit stir crazy when he's away. I think she needs a lot of… Anyway, he's not home right now, but I expect he will be any day.'

'Oh.'

'Have you had a go at pulling a pint yet?' he asked. It was obvious he wanted to change the subject. Perhaps it was best to let him.

'Not yet.'

'Want me to show you how to do it properly?'

'Don't you just pull the tap?'

'If you want more head than beer you do, but nobody will want to pay you for it. There's a little knack to getting just the right head. Here…' He scooped up a pint glass from the shelf behind him and handed it to her. 'Tip it this way,' he said, placing his hands over hers as she held the glass beneath the beer tap.

She froze at the contact, barely able to breathe. This was her wildest dream and yet her worst nightmare all rolled into one. His hands were hot as they covered hers, and he moved closer to get a good grip. It was as if he was charged with sexual magnetism, and she could feel it moving through her. The fact that he didn't seem to notice the effect he was having on her made him even sexier.

'Pull on the tap,' he said, 'gently. Make sure the beer runs down the inside of the glass as you keep it at an angle… See?'

She watched the glass fill up, but she could think of nothing but his smell and the feel of his hands over hers.

Then he moved away as the beer reached the rim of the glass. 'You can stop the tap now.' He looked up at her with a grin. 'There you go – you've just pulled your first perfect pint.'

'What shall I do with it?' Darcie asked, feeling a little dazed by the whole experience now that it was over.

He took the pint from her and put it to his lips. 'No point in wasting it,' he said, and winked as he knocked half of it back.

She watched him plant the glass on the bar as one of the men – Jim or Saul, Darcie had no idea which was which – came to order another drink. Thank God there had been plenty of volunteers at the meeting so she wouldn't have to work at the pub too often. Perhaps she could sort out another buddy to come with her next time, but right now, she needed this shift to be over, and quick.

Spencer pushed open the doors of the Dog and Hare, Tori's hand clasped in his, with Rich bringing up the rear. Jasmine had stayed at the bakery with Millie and Oscar, the triplets were all at a slumber party with a school friend, and Rich had been given special leave to come and take the piss out of Dylan as he attempted to be a decent barman. At least, that was how Jasmine had put it. Spencer would really rather have had a quiet night in with Tori, particularly as it was their last night before the parents arrived, but when he'd taken the phone call from Rich, he had found himself persuaded. Rich seemed really far too keen for their company and Spencer didn't dare say no for fear of offending him. The truce between the two men looked solid from the outside, but Spencer wondered just how much of his revelations on the night of the thunderstorm Rich still recalled. Even so, he seemed to be offering the olive branch and, in view of the fact that Spencer had made it clear he wanted to steal his wife that night, any token of forgiveness wasn't something to be sniffed at. And at least Jasmine wasn't with them, because Spencer hadn't been able to get her face from his mind after they had left the bakery, and he knew that he had to. He wasn't sure whether seeing her a lot might make things easier or worse in the long run.

The three of them stamped the snow from their boots at the door and then made their way to the bar, where Dylan greeted them with a broad grin. He looked odd and out of place at that side of the bar, and it was even stranger to see Darcie a few feet away serving a customer, as though Spencer had fallen into some parallel universe. But the thread-bare tinsel and paper chains that festooned the bar and the cracked baubles hanging on the tree – some of which, Spencer was sure, were older than he was, as he could not recall a single Christmas when he hadn't seen the same decorations hanging there – reminded him that he was very definitely in his own universe, though it might possibly have gone a bit mad. This was the place his dad had brought him for his first pint when he turned eighteen, as his dad had done a genera-tion and a different landlord before. It was the place where Spencer had announced his intention to take off to university to his parents, Lewis and Jenny, and where they had bid farewell to the village in a party to end all parties before travelling to Barcelona for a new phase of their lives and careers. The Dog and Hare had been a part of Hon-eybourne almost since its founding and had seen wars and scandals aplenty. A quiz machine bleeping in the corner was the only conces-sion to a modern drinking establishment; otherwise, the place was as unassuming and traditional as Spencer had always known it to be.

'Bloody hell,' Rich said, 'Dylan is working here and yet the build-ing is still standing. It's a Christmas miracle.'

'Oi!' Dylan laughed. 'I have permission to kick out troublemakers tonight so you'd better be nice to me because no other pub will have you.'

'There is no other pub in Honeybourne,' Spencer said. 'You'd better do as he says, Rich, or it'll be special brew in the newsagent's car park.'

'I think I've been barred from there too,' Rich grinned.

'What can I get you?' Dylan asked, looking very deliberately at Tori. 'I'm asking you because I've a feeling I won't get any sense out of these two for at least half an hour after they've stopped making fun of me.'

'Oh, I don't know,' Tori smiled. 'What do you drink in these parts?'

'Despite appearances, we do have bottled beers that probably won't be a million miles from what you drink at home. Stronger, if anything, but not bad.'

'I feel I should have something English,' Tori said.

'How about a snakebite?' suggested Rich.

'Snakebite and black,' Dylan said.

'What the hell is that?' Tori asked.

'Cider, lager and blackcurrant cordial,' Spencer replied. 'Guaranteed to have you vomiting before you've emptied your first glass, so you might want to stick with the beer.'

'Oh!' Tori said. 'A challenge! In that case, hit me with the snakebite, boys!'

'I knew there was a reason I liked you!' Rich said. 'Jasmine would be proud of you for not letting the side down.'

Spencer's gaze wandered as Dylan prepared Tori's drink and Rich poked fun at him. Darcie had been watching them, but she quickly looked away as his eyes met hers. He got the feeling that she needed a friend, and if he was right about her feelings towards Dylan, then perhaps there was no better qualified friend than him. After all, who knew more about unrequited love than he did?

While Dylan and Rich shared their banter, he moved down the bar towards her. 'How are you finding it?'

Darcie looked up from the pad she was doodling on. 'Sorry…' She blushed. 'Did you want to order some food?'

'No, thanks. I just wondered how you were finding your first shift as a barmaid.'

'Oh… It's ok.'

'But you wouldn't want to make a career out of it?'

'It's getting used to all the different drinks people ask for.'

'You'll pick it up in no time.'

'Have you ever done it?'

'When I was a student I did a couple of weeks in a bar in Bournemouth.'

'You'll find it easy when it's your turn, then.'

'I'll have to remember it all first – it was a long time ago,' Spencer smiled. 'How are you finding life in Honeybourne? I expect it's a world away from home, isn't it?'

'It's very different. In Millrise, you knew your neighbours and the people you worked with, but that was it. Here, everyone in the village knows who you are.'

'It can be a bit daunting at first, can't it? I even felt that a bit when I came back from university. I went from being able to mind my own business to being everyone's business, whether I liked it or not. But they're good people and there are a lot worse places to live.'

'Oh, I can see that. I mean, look at the way everyone is helping to run the pub. And Millie told me how everyone helped to get the bakery up and running. I can't think of anywhere else that would happen.'

Spencer nodded vaguely. He couldn't help but wonder what else Millie might have told Darcie about her time in Honeybourne when she first arrived. Now she was as much a part of the village as anyone else, but it hadn't always been so. Perhaps it was better to avoid the subject, just in case he put his foot in it.

Rich wandered over and placed a glass in front of Spencer. 'I got your usual, as you were missing.'

'Hi, Darcie,' Tori said, joining them with a nasty-looking drink clutched in her hand. She took a sip and grimaced. 'Wow!'

'Pretty disgusting, eh?' Spencer said. 'Serves you right for not being warned.'

'I think I could get used to it,' Tori replied stubbornly.

'So what were you two whispering about?' Rich asked.

'I was just telling Darcie that we have a good bunch of people in the village,' Spencer replied. 'Apart from you, of course. I told her to stay away from you.'

'I'm trouble alright,' Rich laughed, 'but the right kind.'

'Is there a right kind?' Tori asked.

'You're looking at it.' Rich puffed his chest out and Tori giggled.

'Whatever he's telling you, don't believe a word of it,' Dylan called down the bar, as he pulled a pint for one of the Jim/Saul combo. Darcie looked across the bar, but she didn't smile or laugh like everyone else. Spencer thought she looked terrified.

'So,' Rich asked, turning his attention back to Tori and Spencer, 'are you looking forward to the parents arriving?'

'I'm not sure looking forward is how I'd describe it,' Spencer said. 'More like battening down the hatches.'

'I'm looking forward to seeing Lewis and Jenny,' Rich said. 'It must be, what, six years since they went to Spain?'

'Seven.'

'Bloody hell, time flies.'

'It does. I've got so used to it now, though, it will be weird having them around.'

'But you've seen them since?' Tori asked, looking confused.

'I have, but usually in short bursts and with some relief once it's over,' Spencer laughed. 'They can be a bit… eccentric.'

'I'll say,' Rich laughed.

'You're not supposed to say,' Dylan cut in as he made his way over to where they were chatting.

Darcie scurried out to the back room at his approach. Spencer watched her go but said nothing, though nobody else seemed to notice.

'I, for one, am seriously looking forward to seeing them again. The place has been far too normal without them.'

Spencer smiled and wished he could be as excited as everyone else for the return of his parents to Honeybourne after seven years away. He was even less excited about the prospect of them meeting Tori's parents, who had decided, for some unfathomable reason, that the Christmas season was a good time to travel to a tiny village they'd never heard of to meet his parents for the first time. She had explained to them that it had been a difficult decision to make but in the absence of another opportunity, it would have to be Christmas if she was going to get acquainted with Spencer's parents, and that they had a lifetime of Christmases ahead for her to make it up to them. But, of course, they didn't want to be parted from her during the festive season. Even more unsettling for Spencer was the notion that they probably wanted to stuff everything up rather than be with their daughter – who had, for all intents and purposes, snubbed them in favour of spending Christmas with her boyfriend and his parents (a boyfriend they had no love for) and probably pissed them off so much that they'd be even more determined to wreck things than they had been before.

Even though he had been living in Boulder for the past year or more, Spencer had only met her parents once. They had been so cold and dismissive towards him that the ordeal had prompted his and Tori's first real argument. After that, they had agreed that it was probably best to keep interaction to a minimum until her parents got used to the idea that the man marrying Tori wasn't going to be some jock named Hunter Ford, as they had wanted, but an Englishman they didn't like very much. Spencer wondered if she had even broken the news of their engagement to her parents at all, because he was quite sure that they would have been on his doorstep with a shotgun if she had. Perhaps he should have asked their permission before proposing to Tori, despite being terrified by the prospect, because by not doing so he may have just compounded their dislike of him to titanic proportions. He had asked Tori about their reaction to the announcement of the engagement and she simply told him things were fine. The whole thing had become such a headache he didn't dare ask anymore, satisfied with Tori's vague responses on the subject. So when he had mentioned that his parents were flying over from Spain to spend Christmas in Honeybourne and that he wanted to go home to see them, he expected her to tell him that she would spend Christmas with her own parents. Instead, the plan had somehow developed into Tori telling him that she wanted to spend Christmas in England with him and his parents, quickly followed by the revelation that her parents had been so outraged by this idea that they had decided to come to Honeybourne for Christmas as well, determined to be with her one way or another. Every time Spencer thought about it, the idea filled him with dread, but he cheerfully tried to ignore it in the hope it was all a bad dream that would go away. Now, with the imminent arrival of both sets of parents, it was impossible to deny that it was very definitely going to happen. God only knew what they would all think of each other or, indeed, what Mr and Mrs Dempsey would think of Honeybourne itself.

He took a gulp of his beer and fondly remembered the days when he had been young and single and life had been no more complicated than the problem of how to get his hands on a new set of Top Trumps. Of course, he had been very young indeed then, but that was pretty much the last time he could remember life being uncomplicated.

'My parents are staying here, at the pub,' Tori said, shaking Spencer from his musings. 'I checked with Colleen and she was still ok with that, as she has the extra help now. And Spencer's parents will stay at his place with us.'

'That makes sense, as it used to be theirs,' Rich said.

'It did?' Tori looked at Spencer, who nodded.

'I bought it from them when they moved away.'

'I didn't know you owned it,' Tori replied. 'That will make Daddy happy.'

'Not outright,' Spencer added, 'there's only a tiny mortgage but it's still a mortgage.'

'Oh. Well, we don't need to tell him about that part,' she replied cheerfully, taking another sip of her drink and this time managing it without pulling a face.

Spencer shot a helpless glance at Dylan, who just grinned. He'd never been the sort for impetuous gestures, but eloping seemed like a very attractive prospect right now.

One snakebite had quickly led to another – and another. Tori wasn't sure at all that she liked the drink, despite the fact that every new glass placed before her was downed, but she did like the jovial atmosphere of the Dog and Hare. Everyone who came in was welcomed warmly, and everyone seemed to know everyone else.

Dylan passed a third (or possibly fourth) drink to Tori from the other side of the bar as Spencer was grabbed by Ruth Evans for an interrogation about something or other. 'On the house,' he said with a smile.

'Why, that's very kind,' Tori said, laughing. 'What have I done to earn that?'

'You've put up with Spencer for a start,' Dylan said. 'That's got to be worth a drink or two.'

'You'll have me worried that I've made a mistake,' Tori replied, taking a sip. 'Is there something about my fiancé I should know? Does he have some dark and terrible secret?'

'Far from it,' Dylan said. He smiled in Spencer's direction. 'He's a good lad, you know, one of the best. And I don't say that about many.'

'He says you were close.'

'We were. Still are, sort of. But I suppose distance changes that. I was sorry to see him go when he left for America, but everyone understood it was something he needed to do.'

Tori was thoughtful as she took another sip of her drink. *Something he needed to do…* It made it sound as though Spencer had left Honeybourne for more than just a change of scenery, but he'd never told her anything different than that. Was he hiding something? She glanced across to see him give Ruth an indulgent smile, his cheeks crinkling into the dimples she had grown to love. She couldn't believe that he would hide anything from her.

'He grew up with you? And with your sister? You were all close, or so people tell me.'

'Yes…' Dylan replied, and Tori suddenly detected a shift in his tone. Was Dylan now hiding something from her, or was the drink causing her imagination to run wild?

'But he was happy, living here?' Tori asked. 'Before he left for the US?'

'Oh, yeah…' Dylan rubbed at a spillage with a bar cloth. 'I think he got a bit fed up of being on his own sometimes, and he had his share of problems, like everyone does, but he was happy. It's a great place to live… Maybe you'll find out, eh?'

'Maybe,' Tori smiled.

'So what do you think of it so far, now that you've had time to get used to village life a bit?' Dylan asked, his tone back to normal, as if the strange moment between them had never happened.

'It's lovely. Quaint. Just how you imagine an English village to be.'

'Ah, you say that now, but wait until all the scandals come out…'

'I bet you know them all.'

'A few, yeah. Ruth, though – half an hour with Ruth and you'll know it all. If you can stand the extra information about her bladder problems, that is.'

'I thought she had irritable bowel syndrome,' Tori laughed, 'at least that's what Spencer says.'

'I think she's got it all. At least she likes to tell everyone she has. Absolutely no memory for what you've told her ten minutes ago or what she's told you a million times about her ailments, but ask her about Frank Stephenson's affair in 1987 and she's sharp as a tack.'

Tori giggled. 'Frank had an affair? He looks so innocent!'

'Don't be fooled by anyone around here. We might seem like a bunch of country bumpkins but there are plenty of dark secrets.' He glanced up to see Ruth sidling along the bar. 'Speak of the devil…' he breathed, and Tori erupted into a new fit of giggles.

'Ooh Dylan,' she crooned, handing him an empty shot glass. 'It's lucky you don't work in here every night, or I'd be an alcoholic.'

'She is...' Dylan mouthed to Tori from behind his hand, and alongside the vague alarm that Ruth might have seen the exchange, she also felt the urge to laugh out loud again. She could see why everyone in this village seemed to love Dylan so much as she felt the full-beam effect of his charm.

'Going to the little boys' room,' Spencer announced, shuffling over and giving Tori a peck on the cheek.

'Me too,' Rich called, following him.

'Together?' Dylan asked.

'When you gotta go, you gotta go,' Rich replied carelessly as he followed Spencer to the toilets.

'Probably selling him fags,' Dylan said with a grin.

'Fags?' Tori asked.

'Cigarettes.'

She frowned.

'Don't worry,' Dylan chuckled. 'It was a terrible joke and I probably should have stopped telling it when I left school.' He looked up to see Terri, the newsagent, at the bar. 'What can I get you?' he asked, making his way over.

'It's good to see them getting along after all that happened,' Ruth said, staring in the direction Spencer and Rich had just taken.

'Who?' Tori asked.

'Spencer and Rich Green.'

'They didn't get along? What happened?'

'Oh, and that Dylan Smith...' Ruth continued, practically drooling as she turned her attention to watch him pull a pint of Guinness. 'What I wouldn't do for a kiss and a cuddle in a dark corner with that one.'

'What happened between Spencer and Rich?' Tori asked again.

'He's changed, since he met Millie,' Ruth continued. 'There was a time when he was a very naughty boy.'

'Dylan was?' Tori asked.

'Oh yes, but that all changed when Millie arrived. I had wondered whether your Spencer was a bit sweet on Millie.'

'Spencer liked Millie?' The conversation was beginning to make Tori dizzy.

'Sorry?' Ruth said, turning to Tori as though she had quite forgotten she was there. 'Oh, no, Spencer was all sweet on someone else… I forget who it was now…'

'Could you remember if you had a minute to think about it?' Tori asked. She suspected she already had the answer, even though she couldn't really say what it was she had seen between Spencer and Jasmine at the emergency pub meeting that had first set the alarm bells ringing. It was more of a vague intuition, something in the way he reacted when she was near. She desperately wanted to be wrong, though, and maybe Ruth would give her that answer.

'He's a lovely boy. You're very lucky.'

'I know,' Tori said, feeling more frustrated by the minute with the way the conversation seemed to be going. She was finding herself with more questions than answers. Dylan hadn't been kidding when he said Ruth's memory was shot. 'Did he have many girlfriends growing up?'

'I don't recall… No, I don't recall any.'

'But he must have had one? You said he was sweet on someone.'

'Why don't you ask him yourself,' Ruth said, nodding in the direction of the gents, where Spencer and Rich had just emerged, laughing. 'It *is* good to see them getting along,' she added. But it didn't look as if Tori was going to get more out of her than that.

* * *

It was gone midnight by the time Dylan and Darcie walked through the front door of the Old Bakery. Millie was fast asleep in one of the armchairs in the back room, where the living quarters were, while Jasmine sat crooning to Oscar, who seemed to be more contented in her arms than Darcie had ever seen him with anyone. Dylan had been a lively companion on the walk home, a bit tipsy from all the free drinks he'd had from customers, and gently teasing Darcie about everything from her serious demeanour to asking when she was going to get a man and have kids of her own. It really wasn't what she needed, and she was only too relieved to walk into the bakery, where she could lock herself away and try to pretend that Dylan Smith and his charming, handsome, stupid face didn't exist.

'Hey,' Jasmine said as they went through. 'How's it been? Enjoyed playing at landlord and landlady?' She wafted a hand in front of her face as her brother leaned over her to get a closer look at Oscar. 'Oh, I can tell by your breath that you've enjoyed it, Dylan. Some things change, like becoming a dad, but other things, like you being unable to say no to a beer, never do.'

'It would have been rude not to when everyone was telling me to get one for myself,' he grinned.

Millie stirred in the chair and he staggered over to kiss her.

'Ugh!' she exclaimed, pushing him off and rubbing her eyes. 'You smell as though you drank more than you served!'

'Is that any way to speak to the love of your life?'

'You just woke me up with a beery kiss! I'm bound to be a bit grumpy.'

'Come upstairs now and I can do better than a beery kiss…'

'Oh God!' Jasmine squeaked. 'Sister! In room!'

Dylan threw his head back and laughed. 'Off you go then, sis! Back to Rich and you won't be in the room then.'

Jasmine frowned and glanced back at the door. 'Where is Rich?'

'Um…' Dylan looked at Darcie. 'Where is Rich? We left with him, didn't we?'

Just then there was a knock at the door. Darcie ran to answer it and Rich stumbled over the threshold. 'Are you there, darling?' he called through as he followed Darcie to the living room.

Jasmine rolled her eyes. 'Thanks, Dylan, he's drunker than you, isn't he? I thought the barman was supposed to keep the punters from getting too drunk.'

'He's not too drunk,' Dylan said defensively, 'he's just the right amount drunk.'

'That is very true, my little hippy chick,' Rich said, practically falling into a vacant armchair.

'So it looks like me walking you home, rather than the other way around,' Jasmine said with a frown.

'You could stay here,' Dylan said.

'Where would they sleep?' Millie asked.

'Oh…' Dylan shrugged.

'I'll go and make some coffee before you go,' said Millie, pushing herself up from the armchair and heading for the kitchens.

'I'll help!' Dylan called after her and followed clumsily. The clang of a metal pot followed as it bounced across the tiles of the kitchen, followed by Millie hissing a curse and Dylan laughing. Jasmine glanced down at Oscar, but the racket hadn't bothered him one bit.

Darcie sat down next to Jasmine. 'Has Oscar been good?' she asked.

'An angel,' Jasmine said, looking down fondly at the little boy who was now dropping off to sleep.

'You always did have a way with babies,' Rich said. 'The baby whisperer, that's what you are.'

'I'm a bit out of practise now,' she said with a smile. 'It's been nice to have a proper cuddle. I know it's hard to trust other people with your baby at first – I was just the same when ours were born – but I think Millie is coming around to the idea of accepting help with him now. She's been asleep nearly all evening, so she must have needed it.'

'I bet she feels amazing now,' Darcie agreed. 'She's been exhausted every day since I got here, even before he was born.'

'The last couple of months are hellish when you're expecting,' Jasmine agreed. 'And then when Oscar was premature there would have been the added stress of worrying about him.'

'Do you think that's why he cries so much?' Darcie asked.

'Maybe some of his mother's stress affected him,' Jasmine said. 'Babies pick up on that sort of thing instinctively.'

'He probably cries because he's realised he's got Dylan as a dad,' Rich slurred from his armchair, his eyes closed.

'If that rule applies then ours should have been suicidal,' Jasmine shot back. Rich didn't open his eyes or reply, but simply grinned to himself. She looked up at Darcie. 'Perhaps I should suggest that I take Oscar home with me tonight? It would give all three of you a rest from the four o'clock alarm call.'

'We have to get up anyway to get the ovens on,' Darcie said.

'Yes, but at least you won't have a baby to worry about as well. That's got to be worth something. Besides, I'd love to have him and my brood are staying with friends so the house is empty tonight.'

'Do you think it's a bit late to take him out?'

'If I wrap him up he should be fine.'

The idea of waking up, just one morning, and not having a screaming baby drowning out the radio in the kitchen as she worked was an appealing one. Darcie didn't think for a moment that Millie would say yes to Jasmine, but she hoped she would. 'Shall I go and ask her?'

There was a loud giggle from the kitchens, followed by a second crash, another giggle and then silence. Jasmine raised her eyebrows at Darcie. 'Maybe not just yet, eh?'

Darcie knotted her hands together and wished she could stop listening. It was obvious that Millie's recent sleep and Dylan's inebriated state had stirred up urges that hadn't been at the forefront of either of their minds for quite a while. They might have been doing many things in the kitchen, but she didn't think that making coffee was one of them.

A few minutes later, Millie appeared with a couple of mugs, Dylan following with the rest. They were both grinning broadly, Millie looking flushed while Dylan just looked supremely pleased with himself.

'We were wondering if you wanted me to take Oscar tonight,' Jasmine said as Millie placed a mug of coffee on the small table next to her. 'I thought it might do you good to have a night off and I have an empty house so it would be no bother.'

'Oh, that's lovely of you,' Millie began, 'but I don't know…'

'I think that's a great idea,' Dylan said. Millie glared at him, but he just gave her a soppy smile.

'Come on, Mill. We haven't had a full night's sleep for ages and you must be as knackered as I am. I bet Darcie would like a night of lovely peaceful sleep too, wouldn't you, Darcie?'

'Um…' Darcie glanced from Dylan to Millie and back again. She knew what she wanted, but she had no idea whether she was really being asked for her opinion or not.

'I've raised three of my own,' Jasmine said gently, 'so I'm sure I can manage little Oscar for one night. You need a rest, even if you say you don't. You were practically asleep as soon as I walked in and took him from you this evening, so I know it's a lie if you tell me you're fine.'

'I've had a sleep now so I'll probably be awake half the night anyway.'

'Are you mental?' Dylan said, taking Millie by the shoulders. 'Let her take him! For the love of God, please let her take him for one night! I'm knackered and I would do anything for one night that doesn't involve being puked on by a very angry tiny person.'

'He's our baby!'

'Yes, and I love him more than life itself, but I need some sleep! You need some sleep... Darcie needs some sleep... Jasmine, not so much.'

Jasmine chuckled. 'I think you're outvoted, Millie. You need to accept that you can't do it all alone and I want to help. I am his aunty, after all.'

Millie glanced at Rich, who was now snoring softly in the chair. 'What about him?'

'We could leave him in that chair and he wouldn't wake up until Christmas Eve,' Jasmine said wryly. 'But he'll sober up a bit once we get some coffee inside him and I'll take him out of your way.'

Millie bit her nails and gazed at Oscar, who was now peacefully sleeping in Jasmine's arms. 'Ok,' she sighed. 'I'm going to be a nervous wreck, but let's try it for one night.'

Darcie cleared her throat.

'What is it?' Millie asked.

Darcie hesitated. 'I wondered if it would help Jasmine if I went to her house with her to look after Oscar. I mean, I know a bit about what he likes and doesn't – not more than you, obviously, Millie – but I've seen what helps to calm him down and I might be more useful there than here. And you can have the place to yourselves.'

'The reason I am going to say no is that you're as knackered as us,' Dylan said. 'And I think you should take advantage of a few undisturbed hours of sleep too. We'll be getting up early enough as it is to start work, and if you really want to help then your assistance here in the morning would probably be more useful. Jasmine has this, don't you, Jas?'

His sister nodded. 'Absolutely. It's really kind of you but I can cope. In fact, I'll enjoy it.'

Darcie gave a small smile. 'If you're sure,' she said.

'Perfectly,' Jasmine replied. 'So if someone could pack a bag for this little fella, I'll get out of your hair and let you all get some sleep.'

The alarm clock still went off too early, despite the unbroken sleep. Darcie opened one eye. It was dark and silent outside, and it felt like the middle of the night. It *was* the middle of the night for most people. The bedroom was cold too. She hit the snooze button and nuzzled into her pillow. As she dozed, she could hear the sounds of Millie and Dylan getting up – the tap being run in the bathroom, whispering and light footsteps along the hallway. It still didn't persuade her to open her eyes. *Just ten more minutes…*

Darcie turned over and looked at the clock.

'Shit!' she cried, bolting up in bed. How had this happened? A snooze of ten minutes had turned into an hour. Millie and Dylan would be rushed off their feet, already behind schedule because she hadn't been up to help them. She dreaded to think what sort of stress was going on down in the kitchens.

Swinging herself out of bed, she pushed her slippers on and ran for the bathroom. In a matter of minutes, she had brushed her teeth, thrown some jeans on and dragged a comb through her hair, and was heading out to the kitchens.

The radio was on. The radio was on *really* loud. Darcie frowned as she heard giggling. She stopped at the doorway. Dylan was twirling Millie around to some old sixties song while the worktops lay covered in flour, blobs of butter and mixed fruit. The kitchens were often messy as they worked, but this was carnage. Millie had flour all over her backside, in her hair, white handprints all over her breasts, while Dylan had smudges of jam on his face. Darcie could tell that they'd put something in to bake by the smell coming from the ovens, but they certainly weren't baking anything right now and they didn't look stressed about her absence either. By the looks of things, Dylan had been busy putting another bun in Millie's oven rather than anything less metaphorical and more useful. They hadn't been missing her help at all because they were barely working themselves.

'This looks sanitary,' Darcie said coldly. But then her face burned as she realised how it sounded and she instantly regretted the comment.

They spun around to face her.

'Good morning!' Millie beamed, appearing not to have noticed Darcie's sarcasm. 'Did you sleep well?'

'Yes,' Darcie said briskly. 'I'm sorry I got up late – I'll start now.'

'Don't worry,' Dylan said. 'In fact, sit down. We've got everything under control, so we thought we'd let you sleep in today. In fact, I'm going to make pancakes for you.'

'Pancakes? But—'

'No arguing. Bottom on chair, right now!'

Darcie began a reply, but then sighed and did as she was asked, pulling a high stool from beneath a worktop to sit. Damn it, why did he have to be so nice? This was torture, and every time she found a reason not to be attracted to him, he went and undid it. And then she was forced to watch him love Millie, who was lovely too and who didn't deserve the traitorous thoughts harboured by her cousin. Darcie imagined that if the moment ever came and Dylan ever lapsed back into his old ways – which Ruth Evans had been only too happy to inform her of one quiet Wednesday afternoon in the café shortly after Oscar was born – she would find the resolve to refuse him, if only because she cared for Millie so dearly. But she couldn't be certain of that, and it was something that tore her up inside, because she wasn't that sort of person and she never wanted to be. Morals for her had always been as simple as right and wrong, and there was no question of the line ever being crossed. But things had become so complicated these days she no longer knew who she was or what she believed. If this was love, she didn't want it.

Dylan pulled Millie close and planted a kiss on her lips, and then he patted her bottom as she pirouetted away from him to check the ovens. 'Right then,' he said, clapping his hands together. 'Pancakes à la Smith…' Whistling loudly along to the radio, he pulled out an old stoneware basin from beneath the units and began to measure in some flour, then adding the egg, milk and water before whisking vigorously. As he worked, he kept looking up at Darcie and smiling. He looked like a little boy doing his first grown-up chore and begging for his mummy's approval, and the whole effect was so ridiculously adorable that Darcie didn't know whether to throw herself into his arms or run away crying. This was too painful and she didn't know how much more she could take.

'I need some air,' she said, leaping down from the stool. Dylan looked up from the bowl, and then glanced out at the dark sky beyond the kitchen windows.

'You're going outside?' he asked, looking confused.

'Just for a minute.'

'But it'll be freezing out there!'

'I'll wrap up,' Darcie called as she ran for the doorway.

Not a light was on in a single window of Honeybourne, and not a sound could be heard out on the streets; it felt as if the whole world had fallen under the same curse as Sleeping Beauty. Darcie blew into her hands as she walked down the lane, not really sure where she was going or why, but only certain that she had to get away and clear her head. The orange glow of the streetlamps was haloed in the frosty air as the stars, more than she had ever seen in the light-polluted skies of Millrise, winked down at her, vast swathes of glittering dust. At least nobody was up and about yet to witness her distress, because she was quite sure that it showed as much as she felt it. People always told her she wore her heart on her sleeve, but she'd never seen that quality as a liability… At least, not until now.

She'd barely gone two streets when she heard her name being called, and the pad of soft-soled footsteps on the pavement behind her. She let out a sound that was half strangled cry, half angry growl. Of course Dylan would come out after her. Wasn't it just like him to be worried? And even if it hadn't been his doing Millie would have sent him out anyway.

'I know there's not much in the way of real tough crime around here,' he said as he caught up, 'but sometimes I think some of the garden gnomes look a bit sinister, so I'd avoid being out alone in the dark if I were you.'

'I'm sure it's fine,' Darcie said, hoping her terse response would be enough of a hint to leave her alone.

'What's the matter?'

'Nothing. I just wanted some air.'

He was silent for a moment, keeping pace, his trainers slapping on the icy channel of tarmac where the previous snows had been cleared from the pavement. 'Millie's worried you might be homesick and you daren't tell us that you want to go back to Millrise.'

'She mentioned that to me. I told her I'm ok.'

'You don't seem it… If you don't mind me saying so.'

'I don't mind, but you're wrong. I'm just… tired, that's all.'

'So you don't want to leave?'

God, she didn't want to leave. And yet she needed to leave, for the sake of her sanity and before she did something unforgivable, something she would never be able to fix, something that might tear his world apart and hers into the bargain. There was no answer she could give to his question, so she didn't say anything at all.

'It's almost Christmas,' he said.

'I know.'

'So… do you want to go home for Christmas? The weather forecast says more snow but if you wanted me to drive you there I'm sure Millie could manage—'

'Please, it's ok. I don't want you to drive me and Millie couldn't manage.'

'Ok,' he said slowly. 'Maybe you want to see how it goes for the next few days? We'll close the bakery for a couple of days over Christmas, and you might feel better and more positive after the rest. If you still feel this way when we reopen, then I'll take you home. How does that sound? And you needn't worry about letting Millie and me down, we're just grateful that you've been here for us so far. Nobody would blame you one bit.'

'Thank you,' Darcie said.

'So, are you coming back inside?'

She halted on the path and turned to him. 'Do you mind if I don't just yet?'

His look was one of exasperation. 'It's five-thirty in the morning! I know I just said we don't have much crime around here but I'd be happier if you didn't walk the streets in the dark like this.'

'Five minutes. I promise I'll be back in and ready for work. I just want to have five minutes alone.'

'You can be alone in the bakery.'

'No, I can't,' she snapped. 'I'm sorry,' she added. 'That was uncalled for.'

He waved away the apology. 'Don't worry about it. We all have our moments when we're not quite ourselves, I know that.'

'Please...'

He let out a sigh, glancing up and down the deserted road, clearly torn. Finally, he relented. 'If you're not back in half an hour, I will send out a search party, and it will be the scarier half of the bakery's management.'

Darcie gave him a small smile. 'Half an hour.'

He nodded and then turned to walk back the way they had come. Darcie watched him retreat until he was swallowed by the darkness. She took a lungful of frosty air and made a decision. She'd see Christmas out and then she'd go back to Millrise.

Chapter Four

Spencer sat at his kitchen table, staring out at the gloomy sky and waiting for dawn to break. His was a smaller, quieter drama, but it troubled him as much as Darcie's did her. It was good to finally be home, but in many ways it filled him with apprehension, and part of him couldn't wait to take off again and leave Honeybourne and its painful memories behind. In America he could pretend that he was someone else, and his new life allowed him no time to dwell on what had gone before. Here there was no escape, and the arrival of his parents would only make it all worse.

He cupped his hands around a coffee mug that was now only lukewarm. He didn't really want it, but hadn't known what else to do so early in the morning so had made it anyway. Tori was still sleeping in his bed. That was weird and alien in itself. They had separate apartments in Colorado, and although they often shared a bed, this felt different, like living together, and the feeling was compounded by the fact that they had both been too tired to make love, so had slept wrapped around one another with not a flicker of desire, like a couple who had been together for years. But that was normal, wasn't it? It was how things were supposed to progress. Surely it was a good thing that their relationship now felt as old and solid as his home?

Pushing himself up from the table, he went through into the living room and rummaged around in the old sideboard left to the family by his grandma. He pulled out a photo album and sat on the sofa with it.

Most of the photos in there were over ten years old. Nowadays, photos were taken on phones, tablets and digital cameras, and they felt somehow transient, less real, stored in virtual locations that couldn't be opened or held or touched. Even the memories themselves didn't feel solid, like the ones in his hands now. He smiled to himself as he flicked through. There was one of him on the back of an elephant in India aged ten. One on a protest march in London with his mum when he was twelve. She loved a good protest, and had dragged him along to so many things that he could barely remember what most of them were. As a child he had had even less of an idea what they actually meant, but he had always wanted to make her happy and proud, and knew how important these things were to her, so he had always gone. But then he had started to hang around with Dylan, who scoffed at the idea. Spencer had been so desperate to maintain the link to Jasmine that he had dropped all protest activity immediately. His mum had looked sad when he'd first refused to go with her, but she accepted it with quiet dignity, which had been almost more heart-breaking than if she'd been angry. After she went on the second and third without him, she stopped asking, though sometimes Spencer had wished that she would.

More photos: of family weddings and christenings, birthday parties, family friends who had come and gone, of school trips and summer fêtes. There he was, standing with his arm wrapped around Jasmine at a fancy dress party, Peter Pan and Wendy, their cheeks pressed together as they hugged and laughed for the camera. He was her best friend, and he had hoped, even assumed, that in time he would become more than that. But that battle had been lost and now Rich was the man who would hold her and keep all her secrets forever.

His mind went back to Tori, a knife of guilt in his heart, and he slammed the album shut, shoving it back into the cupboard. He loved Tori, didn't he? He'd proposed to her, was planning a life with her... For God's sake, she was about to meet his parents.

What the hell was wrong with him?

She had reached for him as daylight stole into the bedroom, and his side of the bed was cold and empty. Tori found Spencer asleep on the sofa, a blanket tucked tight under his chin. It made him look boyish and vulnerable, and even as her heart swelled, she recalled snippets of conversations they'd had in the pub the previous night. If there were old feelings to resolve, he wouldn't hide that from her, would he? He wouldn't let her say yes to marriage and consider moving thousands of miles to be with him if he wasn't certain himself, surely? She was filled with a sudden, desperate need for him, the urge to be sure of his love, and she bent to kiss him. He opened his eyes and gave her a bleary smile.

'What are you doing down here?' she asked. 'I don't take up that much room in the bed, do I?'

He sat up, patting the sofa for her to join him. Wrapping his arms around her he drew her close. 'I couldn't sleep, so I came down to get a drink, and I didn't want to disturb you getting back into bed with my freezing cold feet, so I decided to stay down here.'

'I wouldn't have minded your feet. You could have warmed them on my hot butt.'

'Your butt is hot,' he agreed, 'but I'm not sure foot warmer should be its primary function.'

Tori nuzzled into him. 'Come back to bed now and I'll warm the whole of you up.'

'I'd love to but I think I'd better get this place in order before my parents arrive.'

'It looks ok to me.'

'It's really not. I haven't been here for months so there must be inches of dust on everything.'

'But this is the last time we'll have the place to ourselves until after Christmas, so maybe the dust can wait just half an hour...'

Spencer pressed his mouth to hers. The doubts she had been harbouring melted. When they were together, everything felt right and it was hard to understand how she could ever feel otherwise. She believed he loved her, and when he kissed her she felt certain.

'Only half an hour?' he said. 'That's never enough with you.'

'I know,' she whispered, falling into the sea of his eyes as she reached to kiss him again. He was her future, and whatever was in his past, she had to let it go and believe that it would stay there. 'I was lying about that in the hope you'd forget about the cleaning once I got you in my clutches.'

'What the hell...' Spencer flipped her onto her back and rolled on top of her. 'Who needs a bed when we have the sofa right here?'

Jasmine shoved open the doors of the bakery, and as she lugged in the car seat along with Oscar's bags, Darcie ran from behind the counter to help her. It was snowing again and Jasmine shook the flurries from her hood as she handed the car seat with Oscar in it to Darcie. Millie had just given some change to one of her fans from the pub – Jim or Saul, Darcie still didn't know which was which

– and as he left the shop, Millie lifted Oscar from the car seat and hugged him close.

'Hey, my little man. Did you have a good time with Aunty Jasmine?' she crooned.

'He's been as good as gold,' Jasmine said. 'And you look like a different woman this morning,' she added with an approving nod.

'I feel like a different woman. I'd forgotten that night-time can be used for sleeping as well as feeding and burping. Was he ok with the expressed milk?'

'No problem at all.'

'Have you got time for a cup of tea?'

Jasmine looked at her watch. 'I have to get the triplets before lunch, but I should be ok for a quick one.' She took a seat at an empty table, and Millie started to hand Oscar back to her when Darcie interrupted.

'You sit down,' she said to Millie. 'We're quiet right now so I'll get the drinks.'

'Oh, you are an angel,' Millie smiled. 'You'll join us, won't you? Might as well if we've got nobody in. The pies for Colleen won't be ready for half an hour or so.'

Darcie nodded and went to make the coffees while Jasmine and Millie fussed over Oscar and Jasmine gave a detailed breakdown of how he'd been overnight. When Darcie returned, she found Millie shaking her head in some wonderment.

'How did you get him to be so calm?' she asked. 'It sounds like he was a dream.'

Jasmine smiled. 'I suppose it comes with practise. And it's so much easier when they're not your own. Even if he'd been crying all night I'd know that I was going to give him back at some point. Your mindset is different and it's a lot more stressful knowing that this is your life for the next few years.'

'Don't remind me,' Millie said. She kissed a now sleeping Oscar on the head as she cradled him in her arms. 'Dylan says the same thing, but it's hard not to feel like a failure.' She turned to Darcie with a smile as she put a cup of coffee in front of her. 'I don't know what I'd do without my wonderful cousin.'

Darcie sat next to her but didn't say a word. Her plan to leave after Christmas was still very much in her mind, but the guilt was already beginning to set in over her decision.

'So,' Millie asked, 'how was Rich this morning?'

Jasmine rolled her eyes. 'As grumpy as he usually is with a hangover.'

'But he was ok with having Oscar overnight?'

'I doubt he even noticed – he was more or less out cold as soon as he hit the pillow. I slept in Reuben's room with Oscar. There was a lot less snoring in there, I can tell you.'

'Oh, I bet. My little Oscar doesn't snore. He makes every other noise under the sun and he makes a few smells but he doesn't snore.'

'Just like his dad then,' Jasmine said, raising her eyebrows. She turned to Darcie. 'Have you recovered from your shift at the pub with my brother?'

'It was ok,' Darcie said carefully.

'So he didn't have you dancing on the bar with him when Slade came on the Christmas CD? It wouldn't be the first time the Dog and Hare has had that treat.'

'Oh no. He spent most of the night talking to Rich and Spencer.'

'I see... But Tori was there?'

'Oh, yes! But she mostly just watched them get drunk. She helped me a bit behind the bar, actually, towards the end of the night.'

'Sounds about right that someone would have to bail them out,' Jasmine snorted. 'But it was nice of Tori to do that. She's really lovely; I'm so happy for Spencer that he's found the right girl.'

Millie looked down into her coffee and Darcie was struck by the sudden heavy silence. Was there something she was missing?

'Anyway…' Jasmine rallied. 'Oscar was such a good boy that it got me thinking…'

Millie looked up. 'You'd have him again?'

'Of course. In fact, having him last night has made me realise how much I've missed a baby around the place. In fact, he's made me quite broody.'

Millie's eyes widened. 'You don't mean…'

'I want another.'

'But you already have three!' Darcie squeaked, unable to help herself.

'I do,' Jasmine laughed. 'But they're ten in a couple of months and already quite independent. Soon they're not going to need me at all. I think I'd like to have one more before I shrivel up into a barren husk of a woman.'

'One more with you might mean four more,' Millie said darkly.

'I know that too,' Jasmine replied. 'But I figure the likelihood of another multiple is quite small.'

'I'm not sure of the statistics but I think you might be persuading yourself of that fact more than anyone else.'

'Maybe,' Jasmine smiled.

'Have you mentioned it to Rich?' Millie asked.

Jasmine wrinkled her nose. 'Sort of, before I left to come over here.'

'And it didn't go down too well?'

'You could say that. What he actually said was something along the lines of over his dead body.'

'I suppose you do have your hands full already,' Millie mused.

'Don't side with him!' Jasmine laughed. 'You're supposed to back me up!'

'But I can see his point. Poor Rich doesn't cope well with stress.'

'We coped alright with three at once so I don't see how one more would push him over the edge.'

'He's got more work on now that his career is taking off. You too, come to think of it.'

'True, but we have a good support network, and I don't think we'd be the first working parents in the world. I'm sure we'd manage.'

Millie looked unconvinced. She blew out a long breath. 'What makes you think he'll back down?'

'He won't,' Jasmine said with a wicked grin. 'But we'll see how he holds out over Christmas when I refuse his conjugal rights.'

'Devious,' Millie said.

'I know…'

The conversation was interrupted by Dylan hauling a huge plastic tray through the front doors.

'How did it go?' Millie asked keenly.

He nodded, beating the snow from his coat. 'They seemed happy enough, but I suppose we'll really know when their customers have tried them.'

'A new pub in the next village,' Millie replied to Jasmine's questioning look. 'They're taking our steak pies on a month's trial but we're hoping they'll become a big customer.'

'That's brilliant,' Jasmine said.

'We certainly need them. It's been so quiet here the last couple of months, which has been good for motherhood, but not great for the business.'

'It's been cold, though,' Jasmine said, 'and people have been thinking of other things in the run-up to Christmas. Things will improve in the summer.'

'Well,' Dylan said as he sat down at their table, 'we have plenty of ideas if they don't. We won't be letting the bakery go without a fight. After all, if it wasn't for this place, I wouldn't have my beautiful girlfriend and very noisy baby.' He leaned in to place a passionate kiss on Millie's lips.

Darcie looked away to where snow was gathering in the corners of the window frame. She was sorry that she wouldn't be here in the summer to help get their business expansion plans off the ground, but it was better for everyone in the long run. And right now, with Dylan throwing loving looks in Millie's direction, it was almost more than she could bear. How could she carry on living this way? It was as if she was a time bomb, and any moment she might blow and tell them everything. Darcie couldn't risk the consequences of that – it might drive a wedge between her and Millie and she wouldn't allow that to happen no matter what else did.

'Nobody in Honeybourne would let this place go without a fight,' Jasmine said. 'That's how we work around here, we support each other.'

'I know.' Millie smiled at Darcie to indicate she was included in that support.

It added to Darcie's guilt, particularly as she recalled how little support she had offered Millie when her ex-boyfriend had died. She had been young at the time – at least she felt a lot younger than she did now – and she hadn't really understood what had happened, but she vividly remembered the day Millie had decided to leave their home town and how she hadn't tried to persuade her she shouldn't.

Things had worked out in the end, but it could have been a very different outcome. Perhaps that was part of the reason why she'd felt the urge to come down and help Millie at the bakery. But even that pure motive had been tainted by something she now felt ashamed of.

'So...' Dylan said, grabbing Millie's mug and taking a slurp. 'What were you all looking so sneaky about when I came in?'

Millie and Jasmine looked at each other and then burst into laughter. Dylan shot Darcie a bemused look. 'That good, eh?'

'Please stop pacing, you're making me nauseous.' Tori patted the sofa next to her. Spencer shook his head. The sun was up now, the snow lying in drifts in the garden and the sky heavy with more to come. Spencer and Tori had spent the morning cleaning and putting up Christmas decorations. Spencer had inherited most of them from his parents when they moved away, and although they were a little nibbled around the edges – the tinsel was torn and threadbare in places, baubles scratched and cracked, and the fairy had lost half a wing – he had smiled at the sight of them. It finally felt like Christmas, but not one he completely recognised. It was like Christmas was old and new, all at the same time: same old decorations, new and very different life.

'You're not getting me on that sofa again,' he replied. 'It'll end in filthiness and my parents have to sit on that in about ten minutes from now.'

'It won't end in filthiness if we only have ten minutes, will it?'

'I could manage filth in ten minutes and sitting next to you is too tempting. It wouldn't be any good, of course, but you might want to get used to the idea for when I'm old and can't manage more than ten minutes.'

Tori giggled. 'Please just sit down.'

'I can't.'

'I thought they were cool, your parents? Dylan told me they were.'

'They are. That's why I'm nervous about you meeting them. They're a bit *too* cool.'

'Is that even a thing? How can someone be too cool?'

'Believe me, it's possible.'

'Well, if they made you they can't be that bad.'

'You haven't met them yet. Save that opinion until later today.'

Spencer sat down next to her with a deep sigh. 'This is crazy, isn't it? We shouldn't be worrying about stuff like this, we should only have to care about what we feel for each other. Why are we getting worked up over it?'

Tori prodded him playfully in the chest. 'I'm not, buster. It's you having the nervous breakdown.'

'So you don't care if your parents like me or not? Honestly?'

'I didn't say that, but I only really care because you care.'

Spencer kissed her lightly on the nose. 'God, I wish I could be more chilled about it all. Things seemed so much easier when it was just you and me having fun before all this parent business, but this feels like the real world now.'

'It is the real world, dummy. It's always been the real world, we just kept it real small. But if we're serious – if *you're* serious – about us moving to the next phase, and we have been engaged for eight months now so I hope you are, then we have to do this. Right?'

Spencer nodded. 'You're right. But I won't say I told you so when you decide that my parents are so wacky and embarrassing that you don't want to marry me after all.'

'I like wacky and embarrassing. That's why I dated you.'

'Ha ha, very funny.'

There was a knock at the front door, and Spencer shot to his feet. 'They're here!'

'Yay!' Tori squeaked, getting up with him and grabbing him by the hand. 'Let's go meet the parents!'

Spencer couldn't help but laugh, even though his stomach was doing backflips. At least someone was excited to see his mum and dad. If anyone had asked, he wouldn't have even been able to articulate what his misgivings were, but whenever Lewis and Jenny Johns were around, he was always filled with some vague sense that he was a disappointment to them in some way. He wasn't exciting or daring or spontaneous like they were. He wasn't doing some crazily romantic astrophysics research job like his dad did in Barcelona, nor was he a successful freelance journalist and political activist like his mum. He didn't drive a mod scooter, nor did he flamenco dance three nights a week, or paint or sculpt or play the violin or do any of the amazing things they did. He was just a teacher in a village school. He was just Spencer. Somehow, it never felt like enough, no matter how many times they told him they were proud.

But when he and Tori opened the front door together, ready with smiles and hugs, they found not Spencer's parents but Ruth Evans on the doorstep.

'Ah…' Spencer said, not knowing what else to say.

Tori shot a quick glance at Spencer before smiling brightly at Ruth. 'What can we do for you?'

'Ooh, look at you, all cosy in the house like a married couple already,' Ruth said, nudging her way forwards as if trying to get across the threshold in a move so furtive that they might not even notice she was doing it until she was in.

'Oh no, not quite,' Spencer said, subtly blocking the doorway in a match to Ruth's stealth. 'We were expecting—'

'Lewis and Jenny,' Ruth interrupted. 'I know. Dylan Smith told me they were due to arrive any time now.'

Spencer stared at her. He couldn't help it. Ruth had some odd notions of boundaries, but this was a new level of impertinence, even for her. She knew his parents were due at any moment and that he hadn't seen them for God knew how long, and she still thought that was a good time to come round? Not only that, but she also knew that it was the first time they would be meeting his fiancée. The world had gone mad... Or maybe he'd gone mad for being surprised that Ruth was capable of such a misjudged social call.

And right on cue, a car bearing the logo of Countrywide Vehicle Hire pulled up, and out climbed his parents.

'SPENCER!' There was a squeal and a flurry of fabric, and Ruth was practically knocked over in Jenny's rush to get to her son. She threw her arms around him and pulled him close. 'I'm so happy to see you!'

'Hey, Mum!' Spencer cried, almost choking from the force of her hug. 'It's good to see you too.'

He gently prised her arms from his neck, smiling broadly. Looking up, he saw that his dad was smiling at Tori, but then he switched his attention as Spencer made eye contact.

'How are you, son?' he asked, clapping him on the back before pulling him into a manly hug. 'It's been too long.'

'It has, Dad.' Spencer stepped back and took Tori's hand.

'Mum, Dad...'

'This must be our future daughter-in-law!' Jenny squealed as she grabbed Tori to dish out the second overly violent hug of the day.

'I am,' Tori laughed, taken aback at the enthusiasm and familiarity of the greeting.

'Pleased to meet you,' Lewis said, grinning at her.

'Oh, Lewis,' Jenny said, appraising Tori at arm's length, 'she's every bit as lovely as her photos!'

'That she is,' Lewis nodded. 'We've heard so much about you, Tori, we feel like you're family already.'

Tori looked at Spencer with a bemused smile. 'You have?'

'Of course,' Spencer said with a sheepish grin. 'What else am I going to talk about when I phone my parents but the love of my life?'

From behind them Ruth cleared her throat loudly and they all turned to see her watching the exchange avidly.

'Oh, hello, Ruth,' Jenny said with rather less enthusiasm than she had shown Tori and Spencer. 'Long time no see. How are you?'

Spencer could barely contain the groan that formed in his throat. Had his mum really been away from Honeybourne so long that she had forgotten the first rule of any opening conversational gambit with Ruth Evans? You never asked how she was – not ever.

'Well...' Ruth began, but Spencer quickly cut her off.

'Mum, Dad, maybe we can catch up with Ruth properly at the Dog and Hare later? It's Frank Stephenson's turn to man the bar, and I think you're helping him, aren't you, Ruth?'

'Yes, I—'

'Wonderful!' Spencer said. 'That's all settled then. We'll be in around eight.'

Ushering his parents and Tori inside, he shut the door, leaving Ruth in the snow. Tori stared at him.

'I can't believe you left that poor old lady out there!' she said, half laughing but looking slightly shocked all the same.

'Trust me,' Lewis said with a chuckle, 'that old lady is tougher than she looks. She probably has enough whisky in her bloodstream to fight off hypothermia for days on end.'

Spencer nodded agreement. 'If you're going to live in Honeybourne there's a lot you need to learn about its residents or it'll drive you potty.'

As soon as he said it, he bit his lip, colouring as his gaze went to the floor. They had talked vaguely about where they were going to live when they got married, each scared to say something that would upset the other, but it was the first time he had said something that so obviously assumed they would end up in England. He'd done it completely unconsciously, but it was out of order and Tori would think so too. He realised there were going to be tears on one side or the other, because although she hadn't said it outright, he knew Tori wanted to stay in Colorado as much as he wanted to come back to England.

But whatever she was thinking, she offered no reply, clearly courteous enough towards his parents to wait until they were alone. Instead, she turned to them and smiled. 'How was your flight?'

'Boring,' Lewis said, 'as all flights are. When you step on a plane, the only thing you want to do is step off again as quickly as possible.'

'I couldn't agree more,' Tori said. 'When we came over from the States a couple of days ago I thought the flight was going to last forever. If I'd been handed a parachute, I think I would have happily used it.'

'Oh dear,' Jenny smiled. 'I'm glad they didn't give you a parachute or we'd have had a very strange Christmas. Have your parents arrived yet?'

'Not yet. They're flying in tomorrow and we're going to collect them – I thought it might be easier as they've never been to the UK before.'

'Wise,' Lewis said, 'public transport here when you're not used to it can be a baptism of fire. They'd never want to visit you again.'

Spencer winced inwardly. There it was again, the assumption that they'd settle in England, only this time his dad had put his foot in it. Lewis could hardly be blamed for the mistake, but it wasn't going to go down well with Tori or her parents if it kept happening. He resolved to have a quiet word with his mum and dad later when she was out of earshot and realised that he probably should have briefed them before. 'Let me take your bags to the bedroom,' he said, moving things into safer territory.

'I hope you haven't felt the need to give up your room for us,' Jenny said as they followed him through into the living room.

'Actually, we did think it would be nicer for you to have the bigger room,' Tori said.

'Which does happen to be mine... And used to be yours, of course,' Spencer added.

Jenny waved her hands. 'It's not necessary. When you've slept on the floor of a shanty in São Paulo you can cope with a small room in a perfectly nice cottage in England. It's really not necessary for you to worry about where we sleep.'

'Speak for yourself,' Lewis said. 'I've fallen asleep in far too many lab chairs this last couple of years to do my back any good. I'll take a bit of luxury and you can keep your shack in South America.'

Jenny slapped him on the arm, but it was done with a smile. 'Honestly. You'd take your only son's bed?'

'Yes,' Lewis grinned. 'Without hesitation.'

* * *

'Your cooking skills have definitely improved,' Jenny said, swallowing a forkful of the lasagne Spencer had set in front of them. He took a seat at the table with a broad grin as he reached for the pepper grinder.

'They couldn't have got worse. And I had Tori to help too, don't forget.'

'That would explain it,' Lewis laughed. He turned to Tori. 'Have you ever before met a man who could burn a tin of beans?'

'I didn't think I had,' Tori smiled.

'It was less about my lack of cooking skills and more about being distracted from the task,' Spencer protested. 'You would be telling me about some new supernova that had just been found or Mum would be showing me photos from whatever war-torn country she'd just got back from. It's no wonder I forgot about the beans in the pan. It wasn't easy growing up in a house full of genius.'

'Well I'm not going to apologise for giving you an interesting childhood,' Jenny said.

'I wouldn't have had it any other way…' Spencer dropped some salad onto his plate. 'But there were certainly a lot of normal skills that I had to wait to develop.'

'You took a long time to develop a lot of things,' Jenny said, winking at Lewis. Spencer looked up sharply, but she didn't say the thing he was afraid she had been about to say. Instead, she turned her attention to Tori. 'So, tell us something about yourself. We've heard Spencer's version, but what makes you tick?'

'I'm not all that complicated,' Tori laughed. 'I certainly didn't grow up in a house full of genius. My childhood was pretty conventional. My parents are both lawyers and I had a regular upbringing. They worked pretty long hours so I spent a lot of time with my grandma, but she passed away five years ago. They're good people and I was happy.' She shrugged. 'Not much else to tell, really.'

'There must be more to you than that,' Jenny insisted. 'What about you as a person? What are you into, what gets you excited, makes you mad? You must have hopes and dreams for the future.'

'I don't worry too much about the future. Right now I'm happy with Spencer, and I want to get married and settle down, maybe get a promotion at work, then we'll see where life wants to go from there.'

'A good philosophy.' Lewis nodded approvingly. 'You can map your life journey until the stars go out, but life will always have a way of forcing you to take a detour. The best you can do is be ready to go with the flow.'

'I suppose it will be a huge change coming to live in England as it is,' Jenny agreed, 'you don't want to create too many other complications just yet.'

Spencer choked on his wine. 'Mum!' he spluttered. 'We haven't really decided where we're going to live after we're married.'

'Oh? So you might not come to England?'

'We're still thinking it over,' Tori said.

'But…' Jenny glanced at Lewis. 'Colorado is so far away.'

Spencer stared at her. 'How can you say that when your job takes you much further away?'

'That's different. I don't live in those places.'

'You live in Spain! What difference does it make to you if I'm in England or not?'

'We're only in Spain until your dad's research project comes to an end, then we may well move again. And Spain is a lot closer to

England than it is to America. I'll want to visit my grandchildren, won't I?'

'Steady on! Nobody has mentioned kids yet!'

'Of course not,' Jenny said in an irritatingly level voice. 'But it will happen, won't it?'

'I suppose… But then Tori's parents will be just as keen to see their grandchildren. And we can't assume that it's ok for them to travel thousands of miles all the time.'

'I'm sure they would if they had to.'

'I'm sure they would too, but that's not really the point.' Spencer grabbed his wine glass and took a gulp. Why did conversations with his parents always end up with him feeling frustrated? He had wanted this to be a nice dinner where they could get to know Tori, and now it was turning into a battleground. Tori shot him a hopeless glance. She was clearly feeling the pressure of being in the middle of a stand-off and it wasn't fair to do this to her. He smoothed his features into a tight smile. 'So, Mum… Is your Spanish housekeeper managing to keep her clothes on these days?'

Jenny raised her eyebrows. 'Well, we haven't caught her cleaning in the nude for at least three months, but we suspect that's down to the temperature drop more than the telling off we give her when we catch her. I have no objections at all to naturists, but the only full moon I want to see after a hard day at work is the one in the sky.'

Tori's eyes widened. 'She cleans in the nude?'

'Only when she thinks we're not around. We laughed at first, but then it really started to get too much.'

'She said it was because she gets hot,' Lewis added, chewing serenely. 'But she's about ninety, so we think maybe she's doing it to be belligerent… Like that poem.'

Tori frowned and glanced at Spencer for clarification.

'You probably haven't heard it,' Jenny said, 'but it's something like when I am old I will wear purple and red and basically go out of my way to piss people off, just for the hell of it because I'm old.'

'Kind of like Ruth,' Spencer said with a grin.

Tori gave a bemused smile. 'No, I've never heard that poem. I'll be sure to look it up, though.'

'Anyway,' Jenny continued, 'I have a feeling Bonita has reached that stage of her life. But she does work bloody hard, and she's reliable, and I really wouldn't want to part with her, despite the occasional peep show.'

'If we ever employ a cleaner I'll be sure to check whether she's partial to taking her clothes off while she's got the hoover out,' Spencer smiled. 'I'm not sure I could be as forgiving about it as you.'

'Me neither,' Tori said, 'especially if she was young and hot. I wouldn't want her leading my husband astray.'

'I don't think you'd need to worry on that score,' Lewis said. 'Spencer's never been what you'd call a ladykiller.'

'Thanks, Dad,' Spencer frowned. 'Make me sound like a complete loser who couldn't get a girlfriend.'

Tori gave a little laugh, but she looked uncertain as to whether she should be laughing or not.

Jenny turned to her. 'For years we honestly thought he was gay.'

'Mum! Do we have to have this conversation? As you can see, I am quite straight so you needn't worry any longer.'

'I wouldn't have had a problem with it,' Jenny replied. 'As I told you on many occasions. I just wanted you to be open and honest with us.'

'And I told you on every occasion that I wasn't gay,' Spencer said, trying to keep his voice level.

'Yes… We realised that when you started following Jasmine Smith around like a lost puppy. You were so obviously smitten that we knew we'd been mistaken.'

Spencer shoved a forkful of lasagne into his mouth so he wouldn't have to reply, and hoped that Tori wouldn't work out that Jasmine Smith was now Jasmine Green. Not because he had anything to hide, but he'd somehow never got around to telling Tori the truth. The trouble was, he was beginning to realise that he would always have feelings for Jasmine, and sometimes he worried that it was a bit more obvious to onlookers than it should be.

'You never mentioned a girlfriend named Jasmine before,' Tori said, her eyes narrowing a little. Had she already worked it out?

'Oh no, he never went out with Jasmine – daft sod never asked her,' his mother helpfully chipped in. 'He was friends with her brother. They still live in the village.' She turned to Spencer, oblivious to the fact that his face was burning. 'I'm looking forward to seeing Dylan again. Who'd have thought he would have settled down and got himself a baby?'

Tori looked from one to the other but said nothing, clearly piecing together what she had just heard and arriving at the truth.

'But that's all in the past now,' Spencer said, forcing a laugh. 'I was a daft teenager. And she's been married for years.'

'Rich Green,' Jenny snorted. 'He's alright but I could never see what he had that you didn't.'

'Muscles, for a start,' Spencer said, hoping the attempt at humour would defuse the situation. What was Tori making of all this? Their relationship had yet to be tested in that way. He had no idea if she was the jealous type or not, but he didn't fancy finding out – and not so close to home when so many other problems could be raked up with it.

'Didn't you have a fight with Dylan Smith?' Lewis said, looking at Spencer thoughtfully.

Oh, God, not this as well!

'You had a fight?' Tori turned to him, her eyes wide now in genuine shock.

'It was over something and nothing and we're ok now,' Spencer said quickly.

'I just can't imagine you fighting.'

'Well, it wasn't so much a fight, because that implies that both parties were capable of fighting. It was more Dylan throwing a punch and me lying on the floor afterwards.'

'I can't imagine Dylan fighting either,' Tori said, shaking her head. 'He seems so sweet.'

'There's a lot more than meets the eye in this village,' Jenny said. 'It might look like a chocolate box place, but there've been scandals enough through the years to keep the longest running soap opera in scripts.'

'That's what everyone keeps telling me. Is that why you left?'

'Oh no,' Jenny laughed. 'Why would I leave that much fun behind? No, we moved when Lewis got handed this research project. I expect we'll come back one day soon.'

Spencer looked up at her over the rim of his glass. Only with the greatest sarcasm could he say he was looking forward to that prospect right now. Judging by the complications they had already caused him after being home for less than a day, married life in America was looking more appealing by the second.

Ruth sneezed again. It was far louder than it needed to be and Spencer knew that it was for his benefit. Ruth's memory wasn't what it had once been, but when it came to petty slights she was as sharp as one of Jasmine Green's put-downs. Spencer shot Tori and his parents an exasperated look as they stood at the bar of the Dog and Hare, apparently not a bit tired after their long day of travelling and embarrassing their son, and now ready for some hard drinking at the pub they fondly still referred to as their local, even though they now lived in a trendy, bar-filled suburb of Barcelona.

'Look,' Spencer said to Ruth again, 'I'm sorry about you being caught in the snowstorm. I would have asked you in but—'

'He forgot his manners,' Jenny said, firing a mischievous grin at her son. 'But we have given him a jolly good scolding and he won't do it again.'

Spencer bit back a grin. While he hadn't missed his mum and dad's sometimes embarrassing behaviour, he had missed their humour.

Ruth grunted as she polished a pint glass but offered no reply – which in itself was a weird occurrence. The glass didn't really need polishing, but presumably it made her feel as if she looked the part, which had been given to her only when Ruth had looked like she would burst into tears at being left off the emergency shift rota. There had been some mention of her age and health and she'd looked even more devastated. In the end, it had been easier to let her do it. Colleen was back on duty too, and seemed happier than she had done for days now that Doug was home. He was in no state to do work of any kind, but Spencer imagined that the pub must have felt vast and empty at night without him there. He could see why having him back would cheer her up. Doug was currently in the living quarters watching TV and probably feeling useless but at least calm and happy to be home. That might all change the next day, when Tori's parents would arrive to take the largest guest suite, because he had a feeling they were going to shake things up even more than his own parents had.

They were spared further grovelling to Ruth when Jasmine and Millie arrived, giggling like a couple of schoolgirls sneaking out and already drunk on their parents' stolen home brew. At the sight of Jenny and Lewis, Jasmine broke into a huge smile and flew at them with a squeal.

'Hey!' she cried in a flurry of pink curls and wool, throwing her arms around them both at the same time. 'I'm so happy to see you!'

After warm hugs and expressions of delight, Jasmine finally stepped back to appraise them both. 'You look really well,' she said with a tone of approval. 'In fact, you both look incredible. How do you manage to stay so young looking? Have you got a mysterious painting in the loft or something?'

'I wish,' Jenny laughed, smoothing a hand over her black leather jacket, clearly flattered but too modest to acknowledge the compliment. But with her elfin hair, healthy tan, and jeans and boots that accentuated her long, lean legs, she did look good for her age. Spencer smiled to himself – he knew that she probably thought that sort of vanity was intellectually beneath her.

'It must be all the sun,' Lewis said cheerfully, less reluctant to acknowledge that he had the sort of physique that would make most men his age green with envy. It was even more surprising when you considered that he spent a lot of his days locked away in a windowless lab or doing experiments with impossible to pronounce bits of atoms in darkened rooms. He turned to Millie. 'And you must be the goddess who managed to tame Dylan Smith.'

Millie blushed. Spencer couldn't decide whether it was the overt compliment, or the mention of Dylan's less than angelic past that made her face burn, but he guessed it might be a bit of both.

'I'm Millie,' she said, offering a handshake. He brushed her hand aside and pulled her into a hug.

'Very pleased to meet you, Millie. And here you are, out on your own. Don't tell me Dylan is at home holding the baby?'

'I've insisted it's the girls' night out tonight,' said Jasmine. 'So he didn't have a choice. He's at our house with Rich and the triplets. I thought Millie deserved it as she hasn't had a night out since Oscar was born.'

Lewis shot Spencer a grin. 'Now I really have seen everything. Are you sure Dylan hasn't been abducted by aliens and replaced with a replica?'

'You'd know about all that sort of stuff,' Jasmine laughed.

'Oh, now aliens aren't my territory at all. Dark matter and missing bits of the universe – they're more my thing. Though it doesn't mean I rule out the existence of life on other planets, I just don't worry about it as much as some of my colleagues do.'

'Speaking of life on other planets,' Jenny added, offering Millie a welcome hug of her own, 'how is Dylan finding fatherhood? If there was one man in this village I couldn't imagine settling down it was him. I don't know what you've got but you should bottle and sell it.'

'He just grew up,' Jasmine cut in, steering the conversation into safer waters.

Spencer smiled at Jasmine and as he did so became aware of eyes on him. He turned to see Tori watching him with a curious expression: thoughtful, questioning, calculating almost. The smile he gave her in return was less assured, and though he had nothing to feel ashamed of, guilt crept into it.

'So,' Jasmine said, turning to Tori and Spencer, 'have you settled into the breakneck pace of Honeybourne?'

'It's been interesting,' Tori replied, her features smoothed into a courteous smile.

'It got really interesting when the folks arrived,' said Spencer, laughing self-consciously.

'I hope that's in a good way,' said Jenny.

'Let me get a round in,' Jasmine said, 'and then I want to hear all about what everyone has been up to.'

While Jasmine took orders and then hopped behind the bar to get them all herself – Ruth was interrogating Frank Stephenson about something she had heard in the newsagent, Jenny and Lewis were distracted by some discrepancy with the cash in Lewis's wallet, and Colleen was busy with a meal order for Jim or Saul – Tori's smile faded. She turned to Spencer, her expression asking for some reassurance.

He took her in his arms and kissed her briefly, pulling back to study her face. 'How are you holding up?' he asked in a low voice. 'Want to go running for the hills of home yet?'

'Not yet.' She shook her head, and her gaze swept the rich wooden interior of the pub, where the old Christmas decorations glinted in the orange lamplight and the quiz machine whirred and pulsed in the corner while old friends chatted and laughed at tables. 'Maybe it wouldn't be so bad here.'

'What does that mean?'

'If it means so much to you to live here when we're married, then I guess we could try it. You already have a house here, so it makes sense in many ways. Jobs might be a problem, but the citizenship won't be with my Irish ancestry and—'

'You really mean that? You'd come here?' Spencer's eyes widened.

'Sure. I don't mean that we couldn't review the situation in a year or so, but—'

Spencer pressed his lips to hers. 'You'd do that for me? I don't know what to say.'

'Just don't expect me to back down over everything.'

'I would never do that.'

'I know. But don't get tempted to forget it.'

Spencer kissed her again. But then he broke off with a broad grin at the sound of a voice behind them.

'Couldn't you two save that for later? I'm sure it's very enjoyable but we have serious drinking to do.' Lewis was holding up his pint glass with a look of satisfaction, while Jasmine placed two more glasses on the bar next to Spencer and Tori.

Tori looked at Spencer with a faint smile. 'Would living here mean having to get drunk every night?' she asked. 'Because I'm not sure my liver will take it.'

'Living here would mean anything you wanted,' Spencer replied. 'Just so long as we were together.'

She lowered her voice as the others returned to a conversation about Lewis's research project. 'Tell me one thing,' she asked. 'Tell me the truth and I won't ask again. I'd be laying a lot on the line coming here... There's no unfinished business I need to know about, is there? Tell me you won't ever let me down.'

Spencer's eyes flicked involuntarily to Jasmine, who was giggling uncontrollably at something his dad had said, the apples of her cheeks framed by her curls and her eyes bright with intelligent humour. The look was so quick that anybody else might not have noticed it. He turned his attention back to Tori, the look in her eyes telling him that she had to be sure. She was giving her heart, giving up her home and the life she knew for him, and his promise was the least she deserved. He could keep his stupid feelings for Jasmine in check for her, couldn't he? After all, it wasn't like they were going to get him any-where. Jasmine belonged with Rich – always had and always would, so there was no point in having feelings for her. And he did love Tori. He didn't know if it was possible to love two people, but he knew that what he felt for Tori was real.

He stroked her hair back behind her ear and smiled down at her. 'There's nothing for you to worry about. I'm with you now, and I love you, and if you're happy with that, it's all we need.'

She nodded. 'Ok. That's good enough for me.'

Chapter Five

Snow lay hard on the ground, piled up in alleyways and packed against the sides of buildings like mini glaciers, but the pavements were clear and a low sun skimmed the rooftops, blazing brightly at an angle so that Darcie had to squint against it. She should have worn sunglasses, but as it was the middle of winter it felt like a ridiculous thing to do and they had stayed in the drawer back at the bakery. She was squinting now through the window of the bus as the spire of Salisbury Cathedral appeared on the horizon.

Dylan had rolled in at around eleven the previous night with Oscar in his car seat, followed not long after by Millie, accompanied by Spencer, Tori, Jenny and Lewis. A tipsy Millie had insisted that Darcie take the day off, rambling on about how she was too quiet and serious for a girl of her age and ought to be out shopping and getting excited about Santa hats and singing reindeer at this time of year like everyone else, and that it had to be a town of a normal size, not a one-horse place like Honeybourne. Darcie couldn't imagine that Millie had ever got excited about Santa hats and singing reindeer, but Dylan had been in total agreement, telling Darcie that she needed to take some time for herself because she really hadn't been herself. So even though she wasn't that keen to wander alone around a town she didn't know, she had agreed to take a trip out to Salisbury on the bus to have a look. She'd left the bakery in full swing, despite the earliness of the hour, her arguments of how they needed help with Oscar and couldn't get all the stock out in time falling on deaf ears.

The bus juddered to a halt, some passengers getting off but more getting on. There were too many people on it already for Darcie's liking, and the bodies packed around her added to the hot fug created by the heaters pumping out at her feet. She sweated in her heavy coat, and was just about to take it off when the empty seat next to her was taken by a boy, which now made it far more difficult to get her arms out of her sleeves without actually hitting him in the face. He nodded briefly at her, adding a quick smile, and she took a moment to appraise him. He looked around her age – maybe twenty-two or so – with sandy hair and intelligent hazel eyes that reminded her of Dylan. God, everything seemed to remind her of Dylan lately and that wasn't what she wanted at all.

'Hot in here, isn't it?' he said.

Darcie turned to him, surprised to find that he was addressing her.

'A bit,' she replied, turning her face to the window again.

'You going to Salisbury?' he asked.

She turned back with a brief nod.

'Thought so,' he said. 'You live there?'

'No.'

'Right. You live nearby?'

'Not really.'

'Don't worry,' he said, 'I won't talk to you if you don't want to. I just thought…'

Darcie found herself blushing. She would have blamed it on the heat but she realised it was because, now that she looked properly, he was actually very attractive. And it wasn't like her to be so rude; she was suddenly embarrassed at the thought of her terse replies.

'It's ok... I'm sorry, I was just thinking about stuff I had to do today.'

'You Christmas shopping?'

'Probably... Not really. To be honest, I just needed a day on my own.'

'I get that. Sometimes I could just run away.'

'Do you live with your parents?'

He shook his head. 'That would be a lot easier. I live with five other guys in a student let.'

'Nearby?'

'In Winchester. I'm just off to visit my parents who live in Salisbury.'

'Do you like living there?'

'The city is alright. The student flat... Well, let's just say if you want privacy and sanitary conditions, it's not the place to be.'

'It sounds like fun.'

'There's always something going on – day or night. It's ok sometimes but sometimes you want to punch someone, and it's terrible for revising. What about you? Do you live with your parents?'

'No, my cousin.'

'Right. That must be fun. But you're not local – at least, your accent isn't.'

'I'm from Staffordshire originally. My cousin bought a bakery in Honeybourne and I'm helping her run it.'

'Sounds cool.'

'It's really not. Your life sounds way more fun.'

'You didn't go to uni, then?'

'Never seemed to get the chance. I'm not sure I'd be bright enough anyway.'

He shrugged and gave her a warm smile. 'You never know until you try. Didn't you ever fancy it?'

'I hadn't really thought about it before. Nobody in my family went to university, so it just didn't come up in the scheme of potential life plans.'

'My parents would have disowned me if I hadn't gone. But I stayed pretty close to home – that way I can take my washing for my mum to do and get a decent meal once a week.'

Darcie couldn't help but smile at his honesty. 'I'm sure she loves getting your smelly socks once a week.'

'They smell good, actually. Like rose petals.'

'Is that before or after she washes them?'

'Before – obviously.'

'What do you study?'

'Law. And pratting about. It's hard work but it's ok.'

'The pratting about or the law?'

'Both.' He grinned. 'So you're not Christmas shopping today?'

'No, I have everything I need.'

'That means you're totally free then… Today, I mean. If you're not shopping and you're not meeting anyone, then you're free.'

'How do you know I'm not meeting anyone?'

'I just guessed. You have the air of someone who's not meeting anyone today.'

'That's some guesswork.'

'It's my incisive lawyer's intuition.'

The bus stopped, and the passenger dance repeated itself as some got off and more got on. It seemed that every stop closer to the town made the bus busier. But the man remained.

'You still haven't told me your name,' he said as the bus lumbered away from the stop again.

'That's because I've only just met you.'

'You won't tell me? How about I guess?'

Darcie smiled and waited, arms folded and eyebrow cocked. He was cheeky, this one, some would say even cocky, and he was presumptuous, but underneath it all she had a feeling he was sweet. She was beginning to enjoy their flirting game, because she recognised the exchange now for what it was. And it felt nice.

'Right…' He narrowed his eyes and screwed his face in concentration, like an old-fashioned conjurer doing a mind-reading act. 'Alice?'

Darcie shook her head.

'Fearne… Rachel… Mia?'

'Nope. Nowhere near.'

'Oh… More exotic? Ok… Alexandretta?'

She shook her head.

'Peony?'

Darcie burst into a loud giggle. 'No way.'

'More traditional? Mary?'

'No.'

'Eleanor?'

'No.'

'Englebert!'

Darcie snorted. 'Don't be silly!'

'It would have been hilarious if it was, though.'

'I can assure you it's not Englebert. Who is even called Englebert?'

'Come on then, put me out of my misery. It's nearly Christmas, you clearly aren't going to meet me for coffee later today, and you probably won't call me when I hand you my phone number in a minute, so at least tell me the name I can cry myself to sleep over.'

She couldn't help her broad smile and though, at the back of her mind, she wondered whether it was wise to get this friendly, she gave him his answer. 'Darcie.'

'Darcie? Cute.'

'Thanks. Now it's your turn.'

'You want to guess?'

She shook her head. 'I'm terrible at guessing and we'd be here all day.'

'Nathan.'

'Ok. Hello Nathan.'

'So... Was I right about the other stuff?'

'What stuff?'

'You know... That you won't meet me for a drink and you won't call when I give you my phone number.'

'Why do you say that?'

He shrugged. 'Just a feeling. I've got previous.'

'We're not all the same.'

'That's what I'm banking on.' He took an envelope from his coat pocket and tore off a corner. 'I don't suppose you have a pen? I'm afraid my phone battery's pretty much kaput so I'll have to do my flirting the old-fashioned way.'

'It's a good thing you can remember your number without looking at it on your phone. I couldn't.' Darcie rifled in her bag and produced a pen, which he took with a grin.

'See, that's serendipitous already,' he said.

'What is?'

'That you had a pen when I asked for one and I could remember my phone number without looking it up.'

'I've always got a pen.'

'A girl who's ready for anything – I'm in love already.' He handed her the slip of paper and pen back. On the paper he'd scribbled his name and mobile number. He glanced up at the window. 'This is my stop.'

Darcie nodded. She hadn't wanted the conversation at first, and she hadn't wanted the company, but now she was quite sorry to see him leave. She gripped the telephone number and smiled as the bus halted and he stood up.

'Don't lose that number, will you?' he said. 'You might need it later if you decide I'm worth taking a chance on.'

'I won't lose it,' she said. And then he threw her a last smile before he got off the bus.

Spencer had forgotten how raucous his parents could be, and he had never really tried to keep up with their drinking before. This morning he certainly knew about it. The pub had got fuller, everyone's spirits high as more and more people came to welcome Mr and Mrs Johns back, and Spencer had lost track of what he was drinking. He only knew that various glasses kept appearing in front of him and eventually he had stopped worrying about where they had come from and had happily drunk them anyway.

He gazed around the tiny spare bedroom, every available space stacked with boxes and black bin liners full of old belongings that he really ought to have sorted long ago but never seemed to find the time for. There was a faint sigh next to him as Tori turned in her sleep and buried her face in his shoulder. He stroked an errant lock of hair from her cheek and kissed her gently, so gently that she didn't wake, and smiled. It didn't matter that her breath would have made the hardiest wino proud, or that her mascara was smudged down her face because she had been too drunk to take it off before bed – to him she was the most beautiful sight to wake up to that he could imagine. His parents seemed taken with her too, so now there was just the one set to win over, albeit the toughest set by far. Today was D-Day: Tori had done her bit, and now it was time for Spencer to step up to the plate.

He curled an arm around her and closed his eyes again to drift back off. But they hadn't been closed for long before he heard footsteps thudding across the landing, followed by the sounds of someone vomiting into the toilet bowl. It sounded like at least one of his parents was reaping the rewards of their night out. At least he wasn't hurling, which could only be a good thing with just one bathroom to share.

'Somebody can't hold their liquor,' Tori mumbled. Spencer grinned.

'Sounds that way.'

'It can't be you, then, as you're here talking to me.'

'Nope. But I have a feeling Mum and Dad drank a lot more than we did. It was all those freebies.'

'Nobody drank as much as Ruth. That woman is a tank.'

'I'll bet she doesn't even have so much as a headache today either.'

'Her liver must be pickled.'

'It's all those tonics she gets from Millie. Maybe I should get some for Mum and Dad.'

'Don't encourage them...' Tori opened her eyes, bluer than the frosted sky outside their window, and smiled up at him. 'We need them sober today.'

His own smile faded. He didn't need to be reminded of the impending meeting of the parents, and it seemed that last night had only served to spell out to Tori, who now knew both sets, that it was going to be a stressful time. It was something Spencer had already worked out for himself, though he had tried not to dwell on it, but Tori's own unconscious admission had just brought all those anxieties right out to laugh in his face.

'What time is the plane landing?' he asked.

'Not until late afternoon. We have plenty of time to sober your folks up.'

'I was wondering how much time I had to stick my head in an oven.'

Tori nuzzled closer. 'It'll be fine – stop worrying.'

'Do you think? Don't forget that I'm not Hunter Ford… I'm just a primary school teacher.'

'So am I. And I'm very glad you're not Hunter Ford.'

'And you're always telling me how disappointed they are.'

'They're not disappointed. At least, not with the lifestyle or the job I chose, even if they're pissed off about Hunter. They just imagined me going into something more…'

'Better paid and much sexier?' Spencer finished for her.

'Something like that. But you're always telling me that it's like that with you and your parents too.'

'Yeah, I suppose so.'

'I guess that has a lot to do with why we click.'

'The difference is that we can put a bottle of wine in front of my mum and dad and they'll forget any disappointment in their only son and have a good time. Yours don't drink, so what do we do?'

'What I've always done – live my life the way I choose and to hell with what they think. They can accept it or they can get worked up, but I won't get worked up.'

Spencer sighed. 'I wish I could think like that. But this afternoon I'll have two sets of parents disappointed in me.'

Tori kissed him. 'You're taking this way too seriously.'

'It matters. It's our future.'

'Exactly. It's *our* future, nobody else's. As long as we stay strong, that's all I care about.'

'You're amazing, you know that?'

'Kinda... So are you going to kiss me or what?'

'My parents are in the next room.'

'So that means you can't kiss me?'

'A kiss won't be enough.'

'Damn straight.' Tori reached beneath the sheets and he stiffened against her hand.

'Tori!' he squeaked.

'Tell me you don't want to,' she breathed.

'Of course I do.'

'Then what's the problem?'

She kissed him, and he rolled her onto her back, gazing into her eyes. He wanted her, and it was like he had never wanted her so badly, almost as if he knew that troubles were coming and this would be the last time. 'It's the next room. They'll hear...' he said.

'We'll just have to be really quiet then, won't we?'

It was underhand, he knew that, but Spencer had enlisted his mother's help in getting Tori out of the way while he went to see Millie. Ostensibly, he wanted one of the wonderful potions she created, something to bring his stress down to a level he could cope with. But he wanted to talk too, and Millie – and sometimes even Dylan, when the mood took him to be serious – was a good listener. At Spencer's request, Jenny had insisted that Tori accompany her to the supermarket outside the village so that they could get in Christmas supplies and also get to know each other a little better, and despite the motivations for this, Spencer didn't think it was a bad thing. Lewis had been overjoyed to rediscover the scooter he had left in the garage still started up, despite Spencer not being around for the last year to keep it running for him, and he had thrown himself into delighted tinkering with it that lasted well into the afternoon. Whoever the culprit of the early morning vomiting session was, Spencer didn't ask, but as they both looked as fresh as the clear morning that greeted them, he guessed they'd recovered pretty quickly.

Now Spencer found himself pushing open the door of the Old Bakery to find Ruth behind the counter with Millie instead of Darcie, while Dylan was out back wrestling with a batch of soda bread.

'Spencer!' Millie smiled, Oscar strapped in a baby carrier at her front. 'On your own today? I heard it was a heavy night after I left… I suppose they're all hungover at your place?'

'Actually, they're not bad. Mum has taken Tori shopping and Dad is tinkering with his bike.' He looked at Ruth. 'You don't look too bad either, and I'm sure you drank us all under the table.'

Ruth grinned. 'Once you've shared a bottle of Navy rum and lived to tell the tale you can drink anything the Dog and Hare has to offer.'

'What can we get you?' Millie asked brightly.

Spencer paused, glancing at Ruth, who watched with a bit too much interest. He needed to talk to Millie, alone, and he had gone to all this trouble because Millie would know exactly the right thing to say and do to ease his mind. She seemed to understand his current predicament too, because she turned to Ruth.

'Would it be a huge problem to call at the Dog and Hare for me? I think we delivered short on their order this morning and I don't want to leave Colleen in the lurch for the lunchtime trade, so I could do with you taking half a dozen pies over.'

Ruth looked as though she wanted to argue, but then she nodded. 'I'll be back before you can say steak and kidney.'

'If you pop in and see Dylan he'll sort you out with the stuff to take. Just let him know that he needs to do it because I'm serving Spencer and I might as well feed Oscar at the same time.'

Ruth headed for the kitchens out back and Millie turned to Spencer. 'I can always tell when something isn't right with you. So, come on, what is it?'

'I know. That's why I wanted to come and talk… I mean, I know you're busy and I used to be able to talk to Jasmine but…'

'Of course. Sit down and I'll get us a drink.'

'No.' Spencer shook his head. 'I don't want to put you to a load of trouble. I just want…' He hesitated.

'What?'

Spencer lowered his voice. 'I know that you don't always agree with people's reliance on your herbal mixes but… God, Millie, I could really do with something to calm me down right now.'

'My tonics?' Millie smiled. 'If you're asking for one of those, then I know you're serious. You're not like Ruth, asking for them every day for everything from wrinkle repair to making the postman fall in love with her. You're really that stressed? I don't know that a potion would be anymore use to you than a nice cup of chamomile tea and a chat, if I'm honest, and that's not me trying to get out of making one for you, because you know I will do whatever you ask if I think it will help.'

Spencer took a seat at an empty table and Millie joined him. 'My mum and dad are here, and that's bad enough, but Tori's are arriving later today, and I feel as if I'm going to explode with the stress.'

Millie frowned. 'Why? It might be a bit nerve-wracking because they're your future in-laws, but you've met them before and you don't usually have any social hang-ups. Just be your wonderful self and it'll be fine.'

'They don't like me one bit – Tori's parents. I don't know if I mentioned it before. They wanted her to marry some son of a family friend. He's everything I'm not, of course, so why wouldn't they?'

'But Tori has told them you're the one? And they know you're engaged?'

'Yes. At least, I think so.'

'Surely they'll make an effort to get along with you now that they know all this?'

'Yes, but…' Spencer stopped. What exactly was he trying to say here? Millie was right, there was no logic in him feeling so worked up. The stress was coming from somewhere else, somewhere within himself, but he couldn't put a name on what it was.

'Have you tried telling Tori how you feel?'

'Not really. I don't even know where to begin.'

'There's not a lot you can do to fix things if you can't even talk to her.'

'Oh, I can talk to her. I mean, she's amazing, of course she is and we can talk about almost anything…'

'Then I don't understand the problem.'

'I can talk to her about almost everything. Just not this.'

Millie frowned. 'I'm sorry, Spencer, but you're not making a lot of sense. Perhaps you can work through the thing that you want to say to her with me? Saying it here might help you make some sense of it all, get your thoughts in order, help to turn it into something you can articulate to her when you see her...'

Spencer gave her a tight smile. Millie was so patient and understanding, it was no wonder Dylan had been tamed by her. She had a way of being able to look into a soul and see only the good in there. And whatever was broken, she could fix. It was a strange but wonderful quality to have. He took a deep breath. He could trust Millie, and perhaps it would be good to air his feelings, vague and difficult to express though they were.

'I have this awful feeling of foreboding,' he said slowly, 'and how I don't know whether I see us staying the course...'

Millie's eyes widened. 'Is that really how you feel?'

He sighed. 'I don't know. I love Tori, but I'm not sure about any of this. Somewhere along the line I'll hurt her, or I won't be good enough, or she'll wish she'd married that smug bastard her parents are so keen on her getting with. I don't even know what's going on in my own head and it scares the hell out of me. That makes me an annoying git, doesn't it?'

'No,' Millie smiled. 'It makes you a good person who understands what a huge commitment marriage is and takes that seriously. You just want to be right, and more people should be like that before they leap into marriages that are doomed from the start. But you need to tell Tori how you feel.'

He shook his head. 'She wouldn't understand like you do. She'd take it personally, and she'd probably dump me. Not to mention that her parents would be throwing a party at the first sniff of trouble.'

'Do you know that for certain? How about you just broach the subject of putting the wedding off for a little while? I know you said

July when I pushed you the other day, but it was sort of on a whim, wasn't it?'

'She'd see that the same way, and I wouldn't blame her. The thing is…' He ran a hand through his hair and glanced towards the kitchen doors. 'I thought everything was rock solid myself until I came back.'

'To Honeybourne? But it's not the first time you've been back since you and Tori got together. You came back for the bakery opening and—'

'I know. But I didn't stay. I didn't have time to really see…'

'Jasmine.' Millie stroked a hand over Oscar's head to quiet him. 'I had wondered.'

'You could tell? You could see it?'

'Not really. But those sorts of feelings are hard to just forget about and I know how much you cared about her. Do you think that's really the issue here, though? Or is she just an excuse to explain your own doubts and fears that have more to do with commitment than with old flames?'

He shrugged. 'I wish I knew the answer to that. I've never thought of myself as a commitment-phobe before.' He smiled slightly. 'That was always Dylan's territory.'

'Quite. It's funny how life can turn things on their head. Would you like me to talk to Tori? Or Jasmine?'

'And say what? I'd sound like a bastard and they'd be right to think it – I feel like one for even having this conversation or these thoughts. Tori is an incredible girl, more than I could have hoped for or deserve, and I ought to get her down the aisle as quick as I can. You're the only person I could say all this to and know that I wouldn't be judged.'

'There is your first problem. You think that you don't deserve happiness, and if you're not careful, that will become a self-fulfilling prophecy. I know this because it very nearly happened to me when I first arrived in Honeybourne. It was you who saved me – with your wisdom and understanding and your support. You showed me that everyone who tries to give happiness deserves to get it back. You should spare a bit of that for yourself. If anyone deserves happiness, it's you, Spencer, and maybe when you start to believe that, you won't be programmed to self-destruct at the first sign of it.'

Spencer was quiet for a moment as he gazed out of the window.

'Do you love Tori?' Millie asked gently.

He turned to her and nodded.

'Then love her. Nothing else will matter in the end if you hold on to that.'

Spencer's reply was cut short by Ruth and Dylan coming through to the main shop.

'I've been through the order sheet for the Dog and Hare,' Dylan began as he strode over to the table, Ruth waddling behind in his wake, 'but I can't see that anything was missing. At least, Colleen ticked it all off as received.'

'Oh…' Millie smiled absently. 'My mistake then.'

Dylan glanced between her and Spencer, frowning for a moment, and then gave a brief nod of understanding. 'Alright, Spence?'

'We were just talking about the arrival of Tori's parents,' Millie said. 'I think Spencer wants to know if he can hide out here until Christmas is over.'

'I wouldn't blame you, mate,' Dylan said, clapping him on the back with a grin. 'Christmas makes me feel like that full stop.' With another nod, Dylan went back through to the kitchens. Ruth stood next to the table with an expectant expression. And then Oscar began to cry.

Millie gave Spencer an apologetic smile. 'I'd better feed him before the slates fall off the roof with the volume.' She turned to Ruth. 'Could you manage the counter for half an hour on your own?'

Ruth trotted off and Millie faced Spencer again. 'Do you still feel you need the thing we talked about?' she asked in a low voice as she watched Ruth get organised at the counter. 'I could sort you one later.'

Spencer shook his head slowly. 'I think you're right. It's my head I need to sort out and it's probably not something that a potion can do.'

'I think so. But stop letting your head tell you what to do and follow your heart. Sometimes your instincts are your best guide.'

Spencer stood up. 'Thanks, Millie. I don't know what I ever did without you.'

'Any time,' she smiled. 'See you later. And good luck.'

Jenny cursed as the gear slipped out again. 'Sorry,' she said, throwing a glance at Tori who was sitting next to her. 'I'm not used to right-hand drive cars now, and I haven't driven in the snow for years.'

'I don't mind a little coarse language,' Tori smiled.

'That's lucky, because you might hear quite a bit today. It probably would have been safer for us to hop onto Lewis's scooter than me drive this thing.'

'You're doing ok,' Tori said. 'Everyone gets nervous driving in snow. We're used to it back home but even I don't take the car out unless I have to.'

'Bless you for being so polite,' Jenny said, peering at the road ahead, 'but I know that's all it is. I'm a disgrace to women drivers everywhere today. So much for my principles of women's lib.'

'How far is it to the store?'

'Damned if I know. It wasn't even built when we left Honey-bourne. I think Spencer said it was about three miles out, and this is a straight road. I doubt they've covered it in trees to make it sit sympathetically with the surrounding countryside so we would be pretty dim if we missed it.'

'Depends on how much snow has been dumped on it,' Tori said mildly.

'Good point,' Jenny laughed. 'Now I know we're on the same wavelength. Let's turn around and get the boys to come shopping and they can look for it in the snow.'

'What do we need to buy today?'

'I forget... There's a list somewhere in my bag.'

'It's just that, well, it seems a bit silly to come all this way unless it's for something really essential. I don't suppose Spencer has put you up to this? A way to make us be friends?'

Jenny fired a grin at her. 'You're not daft, are you? He just wants everyone to get along – it means a lot to him.'

'Oh, I don't mind. It's just the sort of thing he'd do.'

'He always was the first person calling for harmony – hated fighting and confrontation, even as a child.'

'What was he like?'

'As a boy?'

Tori nodded.

'Quiet, thoughtful... more likely to have his head in a book than be up a tree. He was a bit more outgoing after he made friends with Dylan. Not that I had any problems with him reading books.'

'There's an age gap of a couple of years between them, isn't there? Spencer says he's older than Dylan. How did they become such good friends? I know from teaching the kids at Riversmeet Elementary that the year groups don't often mix to that extent.'

Jenny shrugged. 'To be honest I don't know. Lewis and I thought it was an odd friendship at first but it brought Spencer out of his shell so it was obviously a good one in the end.'

'But they fought… What was that over?'

'Spencer wouldn't say at the time and he's never said since.'

'Does he usually tell you everything?'

Jenny was silent for a moment. 'I suppose he does really.'

'So that's odd, right?'

'A little,' Jenny conceded.

'Don't you wonder why he doesn't tell you?'

'It's his business. I've never been the prying type of mother. It wasn't like he was a little boy when it happened – they were both grown men and old enough to sort it for themselves. When he's ready Spencer will tell me. If he doesn't then maybe I don't need to know anyway.'

Tori fell silent as she mulled over Jenny's statement. Knowing how her own mother would have reacted to such a situation, she couldn't quite believe that Jenny would be content to let it slide without demanding so much as a word of explanation. Didn't she care about Spencer? Didn't she want to know what had driven him and his supposed best friend to fight – a fight that, by all accounts, had meant they hadn't spoken for years afterwards?

'I think I can see the corporate hellhole up ahead,' Jenny said, nodding towards a vast, flat-roofed building on the horizon.

'The what?'

'Supermarket,' Jenny replied.

'I guess you don't much like shopping.'

'It's a necessary evil. I like independent shops, though, not these monsters of mediocrity. There are some lovely ones in Barcelona where I get my food whenever I can.'

'I've always wanted to go to Spain,' Tori said, sensing a change of subject might be in order. 'I've barely travelled anywhere outside the US at all.'

'I suppose you're a long way from everything,' Jenny said as she swung into the giant car park of the supermarket. 'A lot of Americans don't get to travel much outside their native country, or so I believe.'

'America is so big that most of them will probably never even manage to see the whole of their own country,' Tori agreed, climbing from the passenger door.

Jenny shot her a sideways look as she locked the car. 'It's an incredible country. I suppose it would be quite a wrench to leave it... If you choose to come to England once you're married, that is.'

Tori looked up at the store, neon lights announcing the wealth of goods inside. This wasn't a conversation she wanted to have with Jenny, at least not until she was certain of things herself. The more she heard about Spencer's past, the more she felt that living in America, away from reminders of that, might be the best decision for their future. She was quickly beginning to realise that the man she had been dating there was a different one to the man she had seen in his home village. Perhaps there was too much history here. But she also realised that he was bound to Honeybourne in the same way she was to her home, and it would be a wrench for him to say goodbye to it forever, just as it would be for her. She could talk to him, persuade him of the sense of her argument, and he would undoubtedly compromise for her – but was that fair to him?

'It looks busy in there,' she said, looking towards the store.

'You wouldn't think anyone would be daft enough to come out in this weather to shop. I've travelled the world and seen dictatorships, poverty, incredible displays of courage, selfless acts of love, some of the strangest customs from the furthest reaches of the globe first-hand… but the British propensity to shop still never fails to surprise me. If the end of the world was announced right now, there'd be a queue for cut-price televisions.'

Tori laughed. She liked Jenny and Lewis a lot. They had clearly made Spencer the man he was, but in so many ways they were very different from him – they were more outspoken, freer with opinions, less empathic. But they were witty and intelligent and curious about the world, just like Spencer. She wasn't sure what her parents would make of Jenny and Lewis, though, and that might just present a huge problem.

The garage door was wide open, The Who blasting from an old CD player as Lewis worked on his moped.

'It's like you were never away,' Spencer said, smiling as he leaned on the doorframe.

'I wish I could say the same to you,' Lewis replied, blowing dust from a large nut. 'My poor scooter has almost seized up with nobody riding it.'

'I wouldn't have ridden it if I'd been at home.'

'But you would have started it up occasionally.'

Spencer frowned, but said nothing.

Lewis straightened up. 'Never mind,' he said. 'I know you've got more important things to worry about.'

'Don't remind me. Is Mum back with Tori yet?'

'Not yet. Your mum is very vocal about how much she hates chain shops, but get her in one and the transformation is incredible. She's quickly seduced by all those materialistic things she says she doesn't need – she'll probably come back with armfuls of very unethical toiletries and Jammie Dodgers.'

'Probably,' Spencer laughed. 'Although I can help her out with the biscuits if she does.' He rubbed his hands together. 'It's perishing in here. Don't you want the heater on? I can fetch it out and put some oil in.'

'I'm ok – worked up a good sweat on this bike.' He wiped his hands on a rag, silently appraising his son for a moment.

'What?' Spencer asked, suddenly feeling uncomfortable under the scrutiny.

'Your mum thinks you're having doubts.'

Spencer blinked. 'About what?'

'About Tori.'

'She said that?'

'Yep.'

'Of course I'm not. That's ridiculous!'

Lewis scratched his head. 'See, you say that, but women are good at spotting these things. We Neanderthals lumber about the place pointing at shiny objects and grunting, but the women… they're taking it all in. A woman would probably know it before you did, and your mother in particular is rarely wrong.'

'She's wrong this time.'

'If you say so.'

'Dad…' Spencer warned.

Lewis held his hands up in a gesture of defeat. 'I'm only telling you what she said – don't shoot the messenger. If you say it's all good then it's all good. We just wanted you to know that if you need to talk then we're here for you.'

Spencer's mind went back to all the times during the last couple of years when he had needed to talk and they weren't there. What about those times? But it seemed churlish to say it, and perhaps it was as much his fault – with his innate need to bottle things up and spare others from what he viewed as an imposition – as it was theirs for being in another country. If he had asked, they probably would have helped.

'So, this date for the wedding,' Lewis continued, 'it's a definite?'

'Sort of… I suppose so.'

'You don't sound sure of that.'

'It's just that we haven't really made any concrete plans yet.'

'Well, when you do, don't forget to whistle if you need some cash to make it happen. I know it's traditional for the bride's family to pay but it's all bollocks if you ask me.'

'Thanks, Dad. I missed you and Mum, you know that?'

'I expect you did.' Lewis turned his attention back to the bike. 'You'll miss us a heck of a lot more if you're in America for good.'

'Tori's close to her parents too. She'd find it just as hard to leave them, and I'm already used to being without you. I'd miss you, but I never said I couldn't cope.'

'And you think she wouldn't be able to cope without her parents?'

'She's never had to – that's what I'm saying.'

Lewis nodded to himself as he ran a cloth over the mudguards. 'You know how to make a man feel guilty, don't you? That's one trick you picked up from your mother.'

'Don't be daft. I'm just stating facts. Your science brain loves facts, remember?'

Lewis looked up with a grin. 'Got me there. So I can tell your mum that you're happy and sure and this is all going to happen?'

'Yes, absolutely,' Spencer replied, with more conviction than he felt. Maybe if he said it enough times, and with enough feeling, it might become the truth.

In the end, there hadn't seemed much point in staying in Salisbury. Darcie had already finished her Christmas shopping a week before, such as it was, and she didn't have a lot of money to spend on anything else. The wooden stalls of a continental market lined the streets, selling hand-knitted woollen gifts and home-made toys, roasted chestnuts, sugared doughnuts, hog roast sandwiches and fragrant mulled wine, and while they made Darcie feel more festive than she had done so far this year, there hadn't been a lot she needed from any of them. She'd been true to her promise to Millie and Dylan and done her best to make the most of the time off she'd been granted: she'd mooched around the shops for an hour or so, gone to see the cathedral and the river, but then she just wanted to get back to the bakery.

Part of her had hoped she'd see Nathan again in town, even though he'd got off the bus a couple of stops before the city centre, but she didn't. That hardly stopped her thoughts straying to him every once in a while, though. The more she pictured his cute smile and the way his hair flopped cheekily over one eye, so that he had developed an adorable habit of blowing it out of his way, the more she wanted to call that phone number. It wasn't as simple as that though – it never was with her. The idea, despite being appealing, also made her feel nervous and flustered. She wasn't good in social situations, especially with people she didn't know, and she always seemed to do and say the wrong things. He was a law student, he was smart and educated… What would he want from a girl like her who had no education, no decent job and no real knowledge of the world? She had nothing to offer in the long term, and anything short-term she wasn't interested in giving. One-night stands, even short-term flings, weren't her style. She was looking for commitment. Would she get that from someone like Nathan?

As she sat on the bus, just after lunchtime, she pulled out the scrap of paper with his phone number on it. The sunshine of the morning had quickly been swallowed by cloud and it had started to snow again, so fine that it was hardly more than rain, but the sky promised more to come. The town flashed by, a festive whirl of coloured lights and bright shop displays, people hurrying to and fro, making last-minute preparations so that Christmas Eve could come and they'd be able to sit with their friends and family, wine on the table and carols on the CD player, and know that everything was as perfect as it could be. The bus stopped and a woman with a toddler climbed on and sat in the seat in front of Darcie. The child was eating hot doughnuts, and Darcie could smell the sugar on the air. She smiled awkwardly as the little boy leaned over the seat and grinned at her, his face covered.

'Hello… Are those doughnuts nice?'

'Sit down,' the woman scolded, and pulled him back onto his seat.

Darcie turned her attention back to the window. Then she looked at the phone number in her hand again. Without another thought, she keyed it into her phone, saved the contact, and then sent a text.

After some discussion on the phone about the current weather in England and the fact that the British authorities just didn't seem able to make even the largest roads traversable when faced with a flake of snow, Tori's parents had decided that they would make their own way to Honeybourne from the airport to save her and Spencer driving in potentially treacherous conditions. Spencer wasn't sure whether this made things better or worse for him, but at least it saved them a long and awkward car journey together, even if it did mean his stomach churned as he sat around waiting for them, suddenly with a lot more time to dwell on what could go wrong and not a lot to take his mind off it. They were currently in the Dog and Hare, having checked on the room they'd asked Colleen to reserve for the Dempseys at least four times now.

Tori's phone bleeped. She looked up at Spencer and then opened the text. 'The taxi has just pulled into Honeybourne!' she squealed.

Spencer looked over the coffee cup he was holding. It felt weird drinking coffee in the Dog and Hare, but it seemed sensible to lay off the booze, at least until he'd had another crack at Tori's parents and persuaded them he wasn't a complete loser, which he was pretty sure holding a pint of beer as they arrived wouldn't do. It had seemed easier to meet them here too, as this was where they'd be staying until after Christmas and, just for now, his own parents had stayed at his house to give them a bit of breathing space before complicating things further. Thankfully, the pub was quiet. He wasn't sure that a couple of teetotal lawyers would have been quite so keen to stay there had they seen it the previous night. And if it got rowdy again tonight… well, it wasn't worth thinking about just yet. He'd have to have a word with his mum and dad about it, that was for certain, as they'd instigated most of the rowdiness in the first place.

'That's brilliant,' he said, trying to sound more enthusiastic than he felt, which wasn't very difficult under the circumstances. 'They made good time on the motorway then.'

Tori leapt up from her seat and went to the window, hugging herself as she gazed out.

'Have you heard from them?' Colleen shouted from across the bar where she was wiping down the beer taps.

'Yes!' Tori said, spinning around to face her. 'Nearly here!' She flipped around to watch the window again.

Spencer shot Colleen a helpless smile, and she sent one back that was rather more vague and less loaded with subtext. He took a deep breath, wishing now that he had taken one of Millie's potions away. At least he might have been fooled into being calmer, even if it was all hokum, as some believed. Instead, he only felt sick, and chanced a glance at the cigarette machine as he wondered if this was a good time to start smoking.

Ten minutes later, Tori ran for the door. She yanked it open and threw herself into the arms of a tall, greying man, immaculately dressed in suit and tie with navy woollen coat, looking for all the world like he was on his way to a business meeting despite the fact that he was on holiday.

'Daddy!' she cried.

She'd seen her parents quite recently back in Boulder, and Spencer wondered vaguely at the enthusiasm of the greeting. Perhaps she was as nervous about the visit as he was, but where he was all edginess, her nerves manifested as unreasonable excitement.

The greeting was followed by 'Mommy!' and a similar hurling of herself at a woman every bit as distinguished as her husband – a stately blonde who looked as though she was no stranger to the Botox needle and also dressed in a long woollen coat, a white blouse and pencil skirt beneath.

'I'm so happy you could both come!' Tori squeaked breathlessly. 'I just know you're going to love England!'

The way they both looked around the pub, it seemed very much as if they had already decided they weren't going to like England one bit. And then they turned as one as Spencer stood from his seat and made his way over. The grin was stapled to his face, and it felt as though it might crack if he didn't hold it still. If they had looked disappointed in the pub, they looked positively devastated to lay eyes on him as Spencer held out his hand to shake.

'Mr and Mrs Dempsey,' he said, 'a pleasure to meet you again.'

With a great deal of formality, they both shook hands with Spencer. It was a world away from the warm greeting his parents had afforded Tori the day before.

'This is where we're staying?' Mr Dempsey asked as he gave the pub another once-over.

'Isn't it quaint?' Tori asked. 'It's the only place in the village, you know.'

'I know,' said Mrs Dempsey. 'I checked. The nearest good hotel is miles away.'

There was a tone of derision in her voice that got Spencer's hackles rising. They had just arrived and within a matter of seconds had managed to make clear their dislike of not only him, but also his home, which hurt a lot more. The nearest *good hotel* might be miles away, but right now he was very tempted to drive them straight to it and dump them there. If they were unhappy now, they were going to be livid when they found out it was Spencer's turn on the bar that night.

Colleen wandered over, seemingly oblivious to the disapproval of her pub. She gave them a warm smile. 'Hello, welcome to Honeybourne. I'm the landlady and I'm here all the time, so if you need anything, night or day, just let me know. Would you like to see your room?'

'Where are the suitcases?' Spencer asked, looking around.

'The rudest cab driver ever refused to bring them in,' Mrs Dempsey said. 'They're out there on the sidewalk, and I had to beg him to even get them out of the trunk for us.'

'That's British hospitality for you,' Spencer said, doing his best to smile in what he thought might be a relaxed and jovial manner, but nobody else seemed to get the joke. He let out a small sigh. 'I'll get the cases in.'

First there were too many stairs and no lift, then their room wasn't big enough, then the shower was too small, then there was too much noise from downstairs. Spencer wondered when the Dempseys were ever going to stop complaining and find something nice to say about their accommodation. It wasn't exactly the Hilton, but they could have been a lot worse off, and at least it was homely and friendly – two things that Spencer valued quite highly if he was staying in a new place. Colleen bore it all with impressive fortitude and grace, and Doug even got called from his sick bed to pitch in as best he could with entertaining their guests. By the time Spencer had left them to settle in and have a few hours alone with Tori, he was gladder than he could say to no longer hear their whining voices in his ear. If they had turned around and demanded to be taken straight back to the airport, he would have quite happily obliged. Though he would be forced to spend the evening in their company, at least he would have the distraction of serving behind the bar at the Dog and Hare. He hoped that trade would be brisk so he could escape them as often as possible.

'Have they arrived?' Jenny asked as Spencer shuffled into the living room and dropped into an armchair. He blew out a long breath and raised his eyebrows at his mum. 'That bad?' she asked with a faint smile.

'I'd been prepared for them to be a bit... disorientated,' he replied, trying to be as tactful as possible. 'But they're, well, "high maintenance" is maybe the phrase I'm looking for.'

'Pains in the arse is what you mean,' Lewis cut in as he emerged from the kitchen with two mugs. 'I've just made a cup of tea – do you want one?'

Spencer nodded gratefully. 'That sounds amazing. How about a padded cell too while you're at it? Or some earplugs?'

'I suppose it's all a bit different from what they know at home,' Jenny said as her husband handed her a mug and then disappeared back into the kitchen. 'Honeybourne must be a bit of a culture shock.'

'That doesn't give them the right to be rude about everything.'

It was Jenny's turn to raise her eyebrows.

'Yes,' Spencer confirmed her silent question. 'They're pretty obnoxious, and being away from home hasn't improved that. Fabulous in-law material. I don't know how the hell they managed to produce a girl as sweet as Tori.'

'Do you think this might have some bearing on your decision to move to America?' Jenny blew on her tea before taking a sip.

'Mum, I haven't decided to move to America.'

'It sounded that way earlier darling.'

'Well, I'm sorry if it did, but nothing has been decided yet.'

'I sense some friction over it... and I'm guessing that Tori will win, because you're a people pleaser and you always back down.'

'There's no winning or losing, Mum. We need to work out what's best for us in the long run, and I'm trying not to be swayed by my feelings too much. I think Tori will do the same. We'll look at the finances, and the possibilities of where our kids will grow up if we have any, and what that will mean for their futures—'

'Tori will win,' Jenny repeated.

Spencer held back a scowl. Why did everyone feel the need to interfere? And why did they all think they knew what was best?

'Especially if her parents are the nightmare you say they are,' she added.

Lewis came back in and handed Spencer a mug. 'Maybe they're just being like that because they feel uncomfortable in their surroundings? Fish out of water. Perhaps they'll be more reasonable once they settle in a bit. Life in a small village in England will take some adjusting to compared with what they're used to – particularly this village.'

'Maybe,' Spencer said thoughtfully. His dad settled on the sofa next to his mum and took a satisfied sip of his drink. This was like home for them, so it was easy for them to be relaxed and themselves as soon as they arrived.

Perhaps his dad had a point. Maybe once the Dempseys felt more relaxed in their surroundings they would be a bit more receptive to him and to the fact that Tori might decide to choose life here over her old one. He wondered if his mum and dad would mind swapping accommodation, and he felt sure that if he explained the reasons why they would say yes, so that Tori's parents could stay at his house and away from the pub. They might feel much more settled in his house. But then he thought about the scorn with which they had viewed the pub, and how they might show the same kind of distaste for his house, and he wasn't sure he wanted them there after all. There would be no escape from the onslaught either, and Spencer – though he rarely lost his temper – was certain that Christmas would end up being ruined by an outburst he wouldn't be able to contain. That would make things even more difficult for him and Tori than they already were, and he didn't want to be the cause of that ill feeling.

'There's not really anywhere else they can stay,' he said. 'Not close by, anyway.'

'I think there's a Premier Inn on the motorway,' Lewis said. 'That might not be too far away for them.'

Spencer thought that a Premier Inn on the moon wouldn't be far enough, but he shook his head. 'It'll seem as though we're pushing them out if we put them there. And I can't imagine they'd be much happier there anyway – they're more like exclusive, boutique hotel kind of people. Club class, that sort of level of comfort. They're used to the best.'

'There's nothing wrong with a Premier Inn,' Lewis retorted, looking slightly offended. 'It's always been good enough for me and your mother.'

'Yes, but Mum is quite happy sleeping on a rock in the Kalahari, while you find your lab chair just as comfy. They're not like that.'

'They sound like stuck-up arses to me,' Jenny said.

'Mum…' Spencer warned.

'I know!' She held up a hand. 'I'm not going to say anything when I meet them later. I'll be impeccably behaved.'

What Spencer wanted to ask was that they just refrained from being themselves for a couple of nights, because he knew very well how much they'd clash with the Dempseys' conservative sensibilities. But he loved all that his parents were, despite sometimes being overwhelmed by it, and why should he ask them to be different people just for a little peace? If Tori's parents didn't like them, wasn't that their problem? And if his parents had to make an effort, then Tori's should too, and he hadn't seen them trying very hard so far. 'I'd appreciate it,' was all he said in return, and it was the most he could ask of them. He drained the last of his tea and pushed himself up from the armchair. 'I'd better shower and get changed. It's my turn on the bar tonight.'

'We could do that,' Jenny said. She looked at Lewis who nodded agreement.

'No… Thanks anyway,' Spencer said. 'You need to be getting to know Tori's parents.'

'If all that you've just said is true, then I'd rather be working,' Jenny said darkly.

'I know,' Spencer smiled. 'But it's important to me and to Tori. You can do this for me, can't you? If anyone can put them at ease, it's you.'

'Don't think I can't recognise buttering up when I see it,' she replied with a half-smile.

'But is it working?' Spencer asked as he made his way to the kitchen door with his empty mug.

'Maybe a little…'

'Good!' Spencer laughed. 'You know I'll love you forever if you can break the ice with those two. Maybe you'll do a better job than I have so far.'

He stepped into the kitchen and dumped his mug in the sink. He could only hope they'd do a better job than him, though judging by the way the Dempseys had looked at him all afternoon, they could hardly do much worse.

'I'm sorry,' Darcie said again. She'd apologised at least five times now, and every time Millie had patiently told her that there was no need, and that the bakery would survive for a few hours without her, particularly as it would be closed by the time she left for her party anyway.

'You look lovely,' Millie said as she paced the bedroom, Oscar slung sleepily over her shoulder as she tried to get his wind up. 'The shoes are just in the bottom of the wardrobe if you want to borrow them. Lucky we're the same size.'

'Are you sure you don't mind?' Darcie asked as she rooted for them.

'Of course I don't! I wouldn't have offered otherwise, and they really go with your dress.'

Darcie looked down at herself. It was an old dress, short and simple and very flattering of her curves, and she liked it well enough usually. But now she was beginning to regret not getting back on the bus and heading into Salisbury again to buy a new one after getting Nathan's invite. After her text, he had called her straight up and begged her to come to the Christmas party he was throwing with his housemates. She had protested that it was too short notice, and that she wouldn't know anyone, but he had been so persuasive that in the end, much to her own surprise as anyone else's, she had found herself agreeing to go.

'Stop worrying,' Millie smiled. 'It's about time you let your hair down. You're always here, running about for us and never doing anything for yourself, which is why we wanted you to take a day off and get out to see a bit of the county. And look what happened – you get hit on straight away! It just goes to show that we're holding you back keeping you cooped up here.'

'I don't feel cooped up,' Darcie said. 'I like being around here with you.'

'I know, but it doesn't seem right all the time. When I was your age I was always out.'

'You make it sound like you're ancient,' Darcie said. 'You're only thirty…' She stopped and frowned. 'Thirty-something…'

'I feel ancient some days, so it's best that you forget exactly how much older than thirty I am.' Millie laughed. 'It's a national secret anyway so if you remember I'll have to kill you.'

Darcie slipped Millie's shoes on and checked her reflection in the full-length mirror. She didn't feel like a million dollars, but it would have to do. She had no idea what kind of clothes she should wear to a party at a student house anyway. In fact, the closer it got, the more worried she felt that she was going to make a total ass of herself. Would it be all witty and clever conversation that she couldn't join in with? Or would it be so drunken and raucous that she'd find herself feeling like she was in the middle of a riot? She only hoped that Nathan would keep his word about looking after her. And that was another worry – she'd only met him on the bus today, and now she was going to a party at his house. Other than what he had told her during that brief encounter she didn't know a thing about him.

'Dylan says he'll stay nearby so that you can call him the minute you want to leave and he'll be there in a flash to get you. So if you're not having a good time, or you've just had enough, or whatever, you can phone his mobile,' Millie said. Darcie smiled. It was funny how Millie always seemed to know what she was thinking, and always knew the right thing to say to make her feel better. There was no doubt in her mind that Dylan would be there for her. He'd probably sit outside in his car like an anxious father, but that didn't bother Darcie, it made her feel safe. Dylan made her feel safe… At least sometimes. That was probably a large part of the problem.

'I feel as if I'm really putting you out… Sorry.'

'Will you stop saying sorry?' Millie laughed. 'We're family, and you do enough for us. It's about time we did you a favour in return.'

Darcie took a deep breath. 'Do I look ok?'

'You look lovely. This Nathan guy had better be worthy of you, that's all I can say.' She kissed Darcie on the head.

Sometimes, Millie felt more like a mother to Darcie than a cousin, and this was one of those times. Not that Darcie minded one bit – it was Millie's default setting to care about everyone as if they were her own, and the world would be a strange upside-down place if that ever stopped.

Dylan poked his head around the bedroom door. 'Am I allowed into this surreal women's universe of matching shoes and feminine wiles?'

'Idiot!' Millie giggled. 'Come in, we're done, I think.'

He wore a grin as he wolf-whistled Darcie. 'Looking good! I might need to come on heavy to this student now, be your bodyguard, because he will be thinking terrible thoughts.'

Darcie blushed, her gaze going to her feet.

'Don't be daft,' Millie said. 'Darcie knows how to take care of herself. Did you call Bony?'

'Yeah, he's up for a quick game of cards so I'll stay at his house for the evening and only be about twenty minutes away if you need me, Darcie.'

'All evening, and that's a quick game of cards?' Millie asked.

'You should have seen the all-night sessions we had before I met you. Not that I miss them or anything. No poker game is any replacement for the joy of hearing your firstborn scream the place down all night as he battles his colic.'

'Thank goodness he doesn't seem too bad tonight,' Millie said, kissing Oscar's head.

'You'll be alright, though?'

Millie nodded. 'Jasmine said she'd call over.'

Dylan narrowed his eyes slightly. 'She's been over a lot… Not that I mind but—'

'Yes, she is very broody,' Millie replied, acknowledging what she guessed was on his mind. 'And I expect Rich is having his ear bent a lot about another baby.'

Dylan pulled a face. 'God, I wouldn't like to be Rich right now. Once Jas gets an idea in her head, she doesn't get it out again.'

'I'm sure they'll work it out.'

'So long as they don't get another set of triplets.'

'I think that might be the issue for Rich too,' Millie said, and then angled her head subtly in Darcie's direction, who was watching patiently.

Dylan frowned, and then he seemed enlightened as he looked at Darcie. 'Are you ready, Cinders? Your pumpkin awaits!'

Dylan had navigated the suburbs of Winchester with ease and Darcie wondered at his confidence. He had chatted and joked, where Darcie had stared – sometimes at him, and then when she remembered that she shouldn't be staring at him, out of the window. Every street looked the same to her, and she was glad he knew where he was going, and that he was coming back to get her.

Eventually they pulled up at a large, turn-of-the-century town-house, eaves decorated with faux-Tudor beams, and grubby plastic windows and front door that seemed oddly out of place with the architecture.

Darcie threw Dylan a questioning look.

'This is the road,' Dylan said.

Darcie turned her gaze back to the house. Every tree in the front garden was strung with lights. None of them matched, and some of the bulbs had blown, but it looked festive, she supposed, if your idea of festive was a sort of drunken Blackpool Illuminations. Huge inflatable reindeer stood sentry at the front door and a sprig of mistletoe hung from the frame – actually, not so much a sprig as a whole branch snapped on the run from whatever nearby tree it happened to be clinging to. Music was already pumping from the open windows, along with the sound of raucous laughter, and it was barely eight o'clock.

Dylan sat in the passenger seat surveying the scene before turning to Darcie. 'I must be getting old,' he said with a slight grin. 'A couple of years ago I'd have been in there with you, but now I'm quite concerned about the thought of you going in there at all.'

'Did you want to come in?' Darcie asked. 'I'm sure—'

'God no!' Dylan laughed. 'I wouldn't want to cramp your style. Do you want to text your fella and tell him you're here? It might be easier than walking in alone.'

'Good idea,' Darcie said, thankful that he hadn't suggested walking her in, because that would have felt too weird. She tapped out a message, and after a few silent moments, her phone bleeped a reply: *'Coming out now.'*

Darcie looked up to see Nathan jog down the path wearing a huge grin. He had on jeans, trainers, and a Christmas sweater depicting a tree complete with flashing lights that intermittently lit up his face in a rather unsettling manner. Darcie hoped that he would take it off at some point, because it was giving her a headache already and she certainly couldn't kiss him and keep a straight face while he was wearing it.

'See you later,' Dylan said as Darcie got out of the car. 'Don't forget,' he added, a serious note to his voice now, 'any time you need me to come and get you, just holler, ok?'

'Ok.'

'You look great,' Nathan said, as Darcie watched Dylan's car pull away from the kerb, suddenly wishing she was in it. 'I was beginning to think you wouldn't come.'

'Huh?' She turned around.

'I said you look great,' he repeated. 'Who's that?' he added, angling his head in the direction Dylan's car had just taken.

'My cousin's boyfriend. I live with them both.'

'That's got to be awkward,' he commented as they made their way back to the house.

'Not really. I have a bit of my own at the back where I sleep and I don't hear much from there.'

'You're lucky then. Because in this house, I can hear *everything* that goes on… if you know what I mean. I've got no objections to the others bringing girls or boys back, but I don't want to hear all the sordid details.'

'Oh…' Darcie felt herself blush and wished she could stop it. Seriously, she was twenty-two and far too old to be turning tomato all the time, but she couldn't help it and she couldn't think of a way to stop doing it. She only knew that it made her look very silly and young.

'Anyway,' Nathan continued, 'enough of that. How about I get you a drink while we can still get near the booze in the kitchen?'

Darcie gave him an awkward smile. A drink sounded good – perhaps it would relax her, because she felt anything but relaxed, and she didn't want to come across as the uptight wallflower that she was sure she looked like right now. Once again she had to wonder what on earth a boy like Nathan had seen in her that made him want to pursue her. There must be plenty of pretty students at his university more suited to him, so why her, a girl he just met on the bus? But she followed him anyway. Even though the party had barely started, the hallway was lined with people, which led Darcie to believe that every room would be just as packed with strangers. She could smell cigarette smoke, a heady mix of various perfumes and deodorants, and a hint of fried food and canned pine fragrance spray. The whole effect was more than a little disconcerting. As they made their way through the house, he drew a packet of cigarettes from his back pocket. He took one for himself, and then offered her the open pack.

'I don't smoke,' Darcie said.

'I wish I didn't,' he replied, putting the pack away before lighting his own. 'It costs a fortune and my mouth tastes like shit after a night out.'

'Why don't you quit then?'

He shrugged. 'Once I've had a couple of drinks I can't say no.' He stopped at a kitchen worktop loaded with coloured bottles and towers of plastic glasses. Standing next to it were four guys, who turned as one and regarded Darcie with interest. She glanced at Nathan, who simply grinned and waved a hand towards each in turn. 'My house-mates... Will, Iqbal, Jay and Lee.'

'Hi,' Darcie said with a shy smile.

'So you're the girl on the bus?' one of them said. He looked at Nathan. 'Good work!'

'Yeah, so you can keep away from her,' Nathan laughed, 'everyone knows what a perv you are, Jay.'

Jay held his hands up and pulled an exaggerated face of innocence. 'I would never!'

'Come on,' Nathan said, taking Darcie's hand. 'What can I get you? Beer, spirits, weird dayglo alcopop thing?'

'Beer is fine,' Darcie smiled.

'That's probably a wise choice,' he said, picking up one of the coloured bottles and holding it up to the light, 'because I have no idea what kind of weird shit might be in one of these.' He cracked open a bottle of Beck's and handed it to her. 'You want me to put your coat in the cloakroom?'

'You have a cloakroom?' Darcie asked, taking the drink from him.

'No, we have a bed, but it serves the same function.'

Darcie silently wondered whose bed it was and how many couples might end up beneath or even on top of those coats during the course of the night, but she didn't want to seem rude, so she shrugged off her jacket and handed it to him.

He strode to a door off the hallway, and threw her jacket in the room beyond before slamming it shut again and returning.

'Oh,' Darcie said. 'The bedroom is downstairs?'

'Every spare room is a bedroom in student houses – maximum profit and all that. It makes for interesting times.' Snapping the top off a bottle of beer for himself, he took a gulp before nodding towards the hallway. 'How about we go and mingle. I can introduce you to student life, and maybe you'll like it.'

Darcie gave the brightest smile she could muster as she fingered the mobile phone in her shoulder bag and wondered how far away Dylan was.

* * *

Spencer arrived at the Dog and Hare around six so he could help Colleen set up, leaving his parents to follow on when they were ready. He got there to find that Tori had taken her parents to the Old Bakery for coffee and cake. Millie wouldn't have been open at that hour, but Colleen said that Tori had called her and she had agreed to open up for them especially. Spencer couldn't help a small smile at the thought. It was just like Millie to put herself out to help a friend in need, and after their chat earlier that day she probably understood the situation perfectly. He only hoped the Dempseys' scathing opinions of everything else in Honeybourne wouldn't be extended to Millie's pride and joy when she had gone to so much trouble to make them welcome.

He was humming along to 'Merry Christmas Everyone' as he wiped down the top of the bar, more relaxed than he had been in some time, when Colleen unlocked the doors of the Dog and Hare. For the first time since he had arrived home, it really was beginning to feel like Christmas. Maybe it wouldn't be so bad. Perhaps his nerves had made him overreact to things that had been said today, and tomorrow, when their jet lag had worn off and he was more himself again, he would be able to get on better with Tori's parents. They might even grow to like him and Honeybourne a little before they went back home. After all, it was Christmas, the time of goodwill and miracles… Although it might take a miracle and a half to get them to like him if their last couple of meetings was anything to go by. He wasn't the catch of the century, he knew that, but he wasn't a serial killer or the village idiot, and he deserved a chance, surely. Well, tonight, he was going to show them that they were wrong, and that he was the man to make Tori happy.

Ruth was the first person to totter in shortly after Colleen had opened up. Spencer gave her a smile.

'What can I get you, Ruth?'

'I've just seen your girlfriend's parents,' she said, ignoring his question. 'They're very posh, aren't they?'

'A bit,' Spencer replied warily. 'Where were they?'

'Coming out of the bakery. They were with Millie.'

'Oh? And how did they look?'

Ruth frowned. 'Very boring clothes – his and hers matching coats.'

'No,' Spencer laughed, 'I mean did they seem as if they were enjoying themselves?'

'Well—,' Ruth began, but was cut short as the doors of the pub opened.

They both turned to look, and Tori came in, followed by her parents. They were smiling and laughing; whatever Millie had done, it seemed she'd put them in a much better mood.

'Perfectly lovely…' Spencer heard Mrs Dempsey say. 'And her husband too—'

'Her boyfriend,' Tori corrected.

Mrs Dempsey waved her hand dismissively. 'Husband in all but name…'

'It's a shame we had to cut the visit short,' Mr Dempsey said.

'Well, Dylan did have to run Darcie to her party,' Tori said. 'And Millie had to feed Oscar. But I'm sure we can do it again if they're free before you go home.'

'Oh, I'd love some more of that divine… what was that cake called again? The strange one I really liked?' Mrs Dempsey asked.

'I think it was bread and butter pudding,' Tori said. 'But I might be getting mixed up – she got so many out.' She looked up and gave Spencer a dazzling smile. 'Hey, Popsicle, how was your afternoon?'

'Not as good as yours by the sounds of it,' Spencer replied as she leaned over the bar to kiss him. 'They sound a lot happier,' he added in a whisper.

Tori frowned. 'They were happy before.'

'Oh...' Spencer pulled away and caught their expressions darken as they turned their attention to him. If they'd been happy all along, he wouldn't fancy seeing them in a really bad mood. 'Can I get you all a drink?' he asked.

Ruth cleared her throat. 'I think you were serving me.'

'But I asked you and you didn't order,' Spencer replied.

'That doesn't mean I don't want anything,' Ruth huffed. 'I just hadn't made up my mind what I wanted.' She tutted as she pulled out her purse. 'This place is going to the dogs without Doug in charge...' she muttered.

Spencer gave Tori and her parents an apologetic shrug. 'I'll get you that drink once I've sorted Ruth out.'

'Well, she was already waiting,' Mr Dempsey said.

'Thank you!' Ruth turned to him and almost curtsied in the most comical way. 'I had been waiting...' She gave a theatrical sigh. 'Young people today are so impatient.'

'They are,' Mrs Dempsey agreed. 'It's all instant gratification these days.'

'Yes,' Ruth said, although Spencer was pretty sure that the conversation was already losing her as she returned her attention back to her purse, peering in and then counting out coins onto the bar.

'Maybe you'd like to sit down, I'll come and take an order from you,' Spencer said to the Dempseys. He was quite sure that whatever he said or did was going to be wrong so it was better to stay silent on the subject of Ruth and how awkward she was capable of being, not to mention her terrible memory. She might well have come into the pub intending to buy a drink, but it would take her another twenty minutes to remember what it was she had wanted, if it even was what she had come in for at all. Maybe it was better just to shove Tori's parents into a corner and hope they stayed out of the way for the rest of the evening.

'Good idea,' Tori said, ushering her parents to a free table.

As he had predicted, Ruth stood staring vacantly at the row of optics on the back shelf, while Spencer drummed on the bar with his fingers and waited. He glanced up to see Mrs Dempsey grimace as she put her hand on the table, and heard her say something about it being sticky. He let out a sigh. Colleen wasn't quite keeping the pub as spick and span as she usually would, but she was doing her best and he felt sorry for her having this added burden now. Besides, what was an English pub without a bit of spilled beer on the tables from time to time? If they wanted authenticity, you didn't get more authentic than that.

'I think I'll have a nice brandy and lemonade,' Ruth said, shaking him from his thoughts. She nudged a small pile of loose change across the bar towards him. 'I believe that should be the correct amount.'

Spencer turned to prepare the drink. When he turned back, Ruth had gone over to the table where Tori was sitting with her parents and had made herself comfortable. Spencer could hardly contain his groan. Ruth would drive them insane within half an hour and that wasn't the mood he wanted them in. He scraped the coins from the bar and dropped them into the till before taking her drink over.

'One brandy and lemonade…' He looked at Tori and her parents. 'Can I get you anything? A pint of bitter, perhaps? Sample the local brew?'

'My parents don't drink,' Tori said awkwardly. 'I'm pretty sure I mentioned that a few times before.'

'No... um, I mean, maybe you did...' Spencer said, shoving a hand through his hair and wishing he could rewind. 'I forgot, I'm sorry.'

'Three coffees will be just fine,' Mr Dempsey said.

Spencer glanced at Tori, who had been drinking like the proverbial fish the previous night. But she didn't correct the order, so Spencer guessed that she was being on her best behaviour tonight. 'Three coffees,' he repeated, and then went off to find Colleen, who was in the kitchen, to see if she could assist as there were no hot drink facilities on the bar. As he left he could hear Ruth launch into full gossip mode. God only knew what she would tell them but there wasn't much he could do except grin and bear it.

Colleen set straight to work on the drinks without a bit of fuss, and as Spencer returned to the bar, Frank Stephenson greeted him with an order for a pint of bitter. Shortly afterwards the owners of the newsagent arrived, followed by Saul and Jim (who were never seen apart) and then Jasmine, who called for a bottle of wine to take out to Millie's as she was sitting with her while Dylan and Darcie were out for the evening. The pub filled in this manner for the next hour or so and Spencer was kept busy enough to avoid having to answer the complaints that he could see, every time he looked over, were coming from the Dempseys' table. He saw Mrs Dempsey grimace at the coffee, and then Mr Dempsey wobble the table violently (presumably to demonstrate its poor condition) and Tori's body language as she tried desperately to get rid of Ruth. Colleen came through from the kitchen to turn up the Christmas music and to switch on the quiz machine, so that it began to whirr and bleep from the back of the room, and Spencer looked across to see Mrs Dempsey roll her eyes at the increased noise. Doug made an appearance in the bar in his wheelchair, and made a point of going to speak to them, which seemed to make them look a little happier as they chatted away.

But then Spencer's parents arrived. He flung open the hatch to get out from behind the bar and sprinted over to them before they could spot Tori.

'Mum, Dad – they're here, but they're still grumpy,' he hissed.

'But we have to go and talk to them,' Jenny replied, looking confused.

'I know but…' How could he ask them to be a little bit less… *them*? 'They're teetotal. I don't suppose you and Dad could lay off the sauce a bit tonight?'

Jenny stared at him. 'You make it sound like we're a couple of alcoholics!'

'I didn't mean that. I'm sorry, ignore me, I'm a wreck.'

'You are,' Lewis said, 'and you need to get it together! Surely four adults can get along for a few hours for the sake of our kids and accept each other, warts and all.'

'It's not the warts I'm worried about,' Spencer said.

'You're fretting too much, it'll be fine.' Lewis clapped him on the back. 'Come on, take us over and introduce us and I'm sure we can do the rest.'

Spencer nodded and they followed him to the table where Ruth could be heard sharing rather intimate details of thirty-year-old village scandals. Spencer gave a polite cough and she spun around.

'Oh, hello!' she said, grinning at Lewis and Jenny. 'Come to join us?'

'We have,' Lewis smiled.

'Although Colleen did say she needed some extra help in the kitchen earlier,' Spencer added. 'And I don't know who can help because I'm rushed off my feet behind the bar—'

Ruth leapt up. 'Why didn't you say so? I'll go and see what she needs. I don't know why people just don't ask...' she continued as she hurried off to the kitchens.

'That was a masterstroke,' Tori said, throwing Spencer a smile.

He shrugged. 'I figured you needed a break. And by the time she's worked out that Colleen doesn't need her after all, she'll have forgotten who she was talking to.'

'That seems a bit mean,' Mrs Dempsey said.

'Oh, you don't know Ruth Evans,' Lewis replied. 'She won't be bothered one bit, and she can always find her entertainment elsewhere.' He stuck out his hand. 'Lewis Johns...'

'Todd Dempsey,' Tori's father replied, shaking hands. 'And my wife, Adrienne.'

'Pleased to meet you,' Lewis replied, shaking hers too.

'And I'm Jenny,' Spencer's mother added, greeting them both in the same way.

Spencer glanced at the bar where Frank Stephenson was waiting with an empty glass. He looked back at the table full of parents. It all seemed very civil as they smiled at each other. Maybe it would be ok after all. It would have to be for now anyway, as his pint-pulling services were needed.

Darcie stood with her back against the wall of the living room, clutching her third beer of the night and wondering where Nathan had disappeared to. She watched as the room bounced to a dance tune she'd never heard before, people's drinks splashing as they danced. The floor was littered with broken crisps and crumbs, and an upturned biscuit tin lid sat on a shelf, full of cigarette butts. To her right a boy had his hand up a girl's top and his tongue down her throat. To her left, two girls had their hands in each other's bras and tongues down each other's throats. Why had Darcie thought this was a good idea? She was a stick in the mud, but tonight she had tried, and for a while she had even enjoyed herself. Nathan was fun, and he was cute, and his friends were funny and entertaining, but it seemed they had all soon got bored of keeping the new girl company and had drifted off to more familiar companions – even Nathan. He had spotted a friend, told Darcie he would be right back, and she hadn't seen him since. That was half an hour ago. It wasn't that she was particularly needy, but his company would be nice and infinitely better than being the loser in the corner nobody wanted to talk to.

She pulled her phone from her bag and checked the display. No calls or texts. Not that she expected any, but she had wondered whether Millie or Dylan would have checked up on her. She supposed that they had assumed she needed space, and she would call if she wanted them. Her finger hovered over the home button. She could call, and Dylan would come and get her, right now if she asked. But she didn't want to be that pathetic.

Suddenly, above the music and cheering, she heard a screech. And then Nathan's voice. He sounded angry, and he must have been considering the volume of his shout. She turned to search for him, and saw a girl grab his arm and yank him back into the hallway as he tried to get through the living room door.

'I didn't say we were finished!' she screamed.

'You're making yourself look like a twat,' Nathan shouted in reply. He shook his arm free, and as he made eye contact with Darcie, his face tried to convey some sort of apology, but Darcie wasn't fooled. It was clear there was history here and she'd been dragged right into the middle of it. She could have slapped herself for being so stupid. Now seemed like a good time to get her coat and make that call to Dylan.

Without another thought, she made her way to the doorway with the intention of slipping past them both while they were preoccupied with their argument, getting her coat and leaving as quickly and quietly as possible.

'Darcie...' Nathan called as she squeezed past them. 'Darcie, you're not going?'

'I think it's best,' she replied.

'*Darcie*!' the girl mimicked. 'Ooh, what a perfectly cute name! You don't look like Nathan's usual type to me.'

'Back off, Carly!' Nathan warned.

'Or what?' Carly shoved him hard and, taken by surprise, he was thrown off balance onto the floor. 'I need a word with Darcie, because she needs to learn to keep her filthy paws off men who don't belong to her.'

Nathan scrambled to his feet, but too late – Carly slammed into Darcie and pinned her against the wall. Darcie grimaced at the stink of alcohol and stale cigarettes on her breath. It was strange, the thoughts that whirled through Darcie's head at this point, and the overwhelming one was that this girl could have been pretty if her face hadn't been painted with far too much make-up and twisted with loathing and bitterness.

'Nathan belongs to me,' Carly hissed, 'and no chubby little tart is going to take him... alright?'

'I wasn't trying to—' Darcie began, but Nathan dragged Carly away.

'Get off her you nutjob!' he shouted. 'We are finished! Why can't you get that through your thick head?'

'Come off it, Nathan,' Carly sneered. 'The only reason this sad specimen is here is to try and make me jealous and you know it. Although you didn't really think I'd be worried by this…' She waved a dismissive hand up and down at Darcie. 'Please. You've never been into fat girls so you obviously just invited someone who was desperate enough to say yes.'

Darcie stared at them, her eyes filling with tears. She had known it all along. Of course a boy like Nathan wouldn't have ever noticed a girl like her, not in a million years. She was chubby and plain and boring – she wasn't even clever or in a good job. She was nobody, and she always would be. No wonder all her relationships had failed.

'Darcie…' Nathan began, but she shook her head forcefully.

'It's fine,' she said, rubbing a hand over her eyes and drawing herself up to her full height. 'I see how things are.'

'No, you don't!' Nathan pleaded. 'Just give me a chance to explain!'

Darcie looked at him, and then she caught the sneering grin stretched across Carly's face. Whether Nathan had intended this or not, she wasn't staying to be humiliated any longer. She may be chubby and boring, but that didn't give anyone the right to treat her with such contempt.

'He's all yours,' she said quietly, before pushing past them and out of the front door.

Once she was out of the garden, Darcie started to run. Nobody came after her, and she supposed that Nathan had either been prevented by

Carly or that he didn't care enough to try and catch up to explain. It didn't matter in the end because all Darcie wanted to do was get away. She hadn't even picked up her coat, but she wasn't going back in and would just have to consider it lost now. If that was the worst outcome of the evening then it was a small sacrifice. The streets around her blurred with her tears; even if she had known them, she wouldn't have had a clue where she was going. All she knew was she had to walk and, as her breath came in stuttering gasps, she needed to calm down. The evening's events weren't something she wanted to drag Millie and Dylan into, and Dylan finding her a sodden mess would lead to awkward questions with possibly awkward consequences.

But as she continued to walk, she realised that she was hopelessly lost. And she was freezing too. She wrapped her arms tight around herself in a bid to stop the shivering, her toes burning with the cold in Millie's unsuitable shoes. Forced to admit defeat, she pulled her phone from her bag and dialled Dylan's number.

'Had enough already?' His warm tones came from down the line and it was all Darcie could do not to break down.

'Yes, please come and get me,' she said, biting back the tears. 'But I'm not at the house anymore.'

'You're not?' Dylan asked, now alert. 'What happened?'

'Nothing... nothing happened.'

'Then where are you?'

'I'm...' Darcie looked around. How could Dylan come and get her if she didn't have a clue where she was?

'Darcie?'

'I'm... hang on...' She began to jog, as best as she could on the icy pavements and in her high shoes, to the nearest street corner. 'I'm on Hardy Street.'

'I know that. Stay there and I'll be with you in ten.'

Darcie's reply was cut short as Dylan hung up. She put her phone away and glanced up and down the street. It was a quiet suburban road much like any other – most of the houses were probably owned by families and couples, not like the street where Nathan's was. His street felt very much like a student area, almost every window displaying empty bottles, haphazard piles of books or music posters. Here, the gardens were neat and well-tended, Christmas trees twinkling in many of them, the windows dressed with slick blinds or trendy curtains. Coloured fairy lights bordered some, and the glow of televisions flickered from within others. It would be nice to be inside one of them now, loved ones sitting around, perhaps watching a film together, and a casserole in the oven. All Darcie wanted was her happy ending – was that too much to ask for? She didn't want to be rich or clever or stick thin; she just wanted to be accepted and loved for who she was. Her heart had told her to take a chance on Nathan, and her heart had been very wrong. It seemed as though her heart was wrong about everything lately.

The cold was getting unbearable and Darcie was on the verge of running back to try and find Nathan's house to get her coat when she saw Dylan's car turn the corner of the road. Relief flooded through her, and she had the passenger door open almost before it had stopped.

'What happened?' Dylan asked, his voice tense.

'Nothing,' Darcie replied, trying to stop the shivering.

'I'm not stupid. Where's your coat?'

'I forgot it.'

'And you couldn't go back to get it? Why would you leave without it and be afraid to go and get it?'

Darcie bit her lip. 'Can we just go home, please?'

'Did he try to force himself on you? Because if he did—'

'No!' Darcie squeaked. 'No, he's not like that!'

'Then why are you in this state?'

'I'm not in a state.'

Darcie stared straight ahead, watching the lights twinkle in the darkened street. It was nearly Christmas, wasn't everyone supposed to be happy now? What had she done wrong? Silently, she willed Dylan to pull the handbrake off and take her home. But there was a stubborn silence, and she turned to find him watching her intently.

'I'm not stupid, Darcie.'

'I didn't say that!'

'Then why can't you tell me what happened?'

'Please… I just want to forget about it.'

Dylan faced forwards, gripping the steering wheel as he clenched his jaw. 'We'd better go and get your coat.'

'No!' Darcie hugged herself tighter. 'No,' she repeated, trying to control the panic in her voice.

'It won't take ten minutes,' Dylan insisted. 'If you don't want to go in you can stay in the car and I'll go and get it—'

'Please!' Darcie sobbed, unable to hold it back any longer. 'I don't want to think about it and I don't want to see that house again!'

'Hey, hey…' Dylan's tone was softer now as he turned to her. 'I didn't mean to make you cry.'

'You didn't make me cry,' Darcie sniffed. 'The whole night made me cry. I'm an idiot.'

'Of course you're not. Why do you say that?'

'Because I thought Nathan liked me, but he didn't at all. He just wanted me at his party to make some girl jealous.'

'Who told you that?'

'The girl did.'

'And was he there at the time?'

'Yes. He denied it but it's obvious. Why else would he ask a girl he only met on the bus that day to his party?'

'Because he liked you?'

Darcie shook her head.

Dylan was thoughtful for a moment. 'Things aren't always what they seem. Trust me, I know it better than anyone.'

'He didn't like me, he just needed me.'

'He could have used any girl at the party to do that.'

'They might have all known about Carly.' Darcie sighed as she dried her eyes on a ragged bit of tissue from the bottom of her bag. 'I know what I saw and I just want to forget about it. If I lose a coat, at least I'll have kept a shred of dignity. It's about all I have left.'

Dylan nudged her with an encouraging smile. 'You still have us – me and Millie. Even Oscar is quite partial to you.'

Darcie's eyes watered again. Why did he have to be so caring and considerate and so… *perfect*? She had only said yes to Nathan because she wanted to get Dylan out of her head, and now the situation had thrown her right back into his path, but with more pain than ever before. Now she had been hurt by Nathan and Dylan was the man making her feel better, but that wasn't what she needed at all, because in the end it would only make her love him more.

'Darcie, it's no bother for me to go back,' he said gently. 'There might be an explanation you want to hear, and if there isn't, we have the excuse of getting your coat. Or if you want to wait in the car parked around the corner, I can go in and have a word.'

'I don't care about the stupid coat!' she cried. 'And I don't care about Nathan!'

'Right,' Dylan said quietly as he turned his eyes to the road.

Darcie wished that the seat would swallow her. 'I'm sorry,' she said.

'It's ok. I understand you've had a stressful night. I'll take you back now and we won't talk about it if you don't want to.'

She nodded, the lump in her throat choking her reply. She just wanted this night to be over and she never wanted to think about it again.

Chapter Six

Once the kitchen had closed for the evening, Colleen came out to the bar to help Spencer. She looked fondly at Doug, who was sitting in his wheelchair and laughing with Frank Stephenson. 'He's so much better than he's been for ages,' she said. 'It's done him the world of good to come into the pub for a bit instead of moping in our living quarters. He really misses being at work and he loves this place.'

'He does look cheerful,' Spencer agreed, but his gaze, as it had done many times that night, went to the table where his parents and Tori's were talking. He wanted to be able to say that they looked cheerful too, but as the night progressed he saw hand flapping, frowning and head shaking – a few too many worrying signs that they were disagreeing on a lot of things. His parents had come over for a few drinks, and when he had asked them how things were going they told him not to worry. Tori had come over for coffees and she had told him the same, though her face said a different story. He had gone over as often as he could – though not often enough – and everyone had smiled tensely at him, though he wasn't fooled.

The room had got louder and hotter, and spirits had been high. It was hard not to be affected by the atmosphere, and Spencer had almost been enjoying it, despite the worries about the table where his parents sat, but that was all wiped out in an instant as he saw Tori march towards him. He could tell by her face she wasn't happy.

'How's it going?' he asked for the fourth or fifth time that night.

'You need to talk to your parents,' she said briskly. 'Can't you stop serving them alcohol?'

Spencer's mouth dropped open. 'They haven't had that much!' And true to their word, though they had ordered a few drinks, compared to what they'd usually have it was practically teetotal.

'You think?' Tori's hands went to her hips. 'Well, they seem pretty drunk to me. Unless they naturally insult people all the time.'

'What do you mean? I thought everything was ok.'

'It was, until they started talking politics.'

'But you know my mum is a political correspondent.'

'Yeah, and you know my mom and dad are Republican. So your mom is spouting a lot of stuff that they don't like and she's practically telling them that their political beliefs are bullcrap.'

'She's entitled to her opinion,' he replied, suddenly feeling defensive on his mum's behalf.

'Not when she's pissing them off!'

Spencer's brow furrowed. 'So you're saying that my mum and dad can't have opinions, but yours can? What makes their opinions more valid? My mum happens to know a lot about it.'

'Yeah, well so does mine and she doesn't back down in a fight.'

'So my mum should? How is that fair?'

'Fair doesn't come into it!' Tori hissed. 'We want them to get along! And it's not helping that they want to go up to their room now but there's all this noise down here so they won't be able to sleep. And you've been missing all night when you should have been talking to them to get them to like you!'

'It's a pub, for God's sake! It's going to be noisy and, in case you missed that part, I'm stuck behind this bar to help out someone in need!' He paused as Tori scowled at him. 'You're saying they're not getting along? Earlier you said it was fine.'

'Earlier I was trying to make you feel better. Now I don't feel like doing that.'

'How is this my fault?'

'You should have talked to your parents and told them what *not* to say.'

'You could have talked to yours and done the same!'

'So are you going to go and tell them now?'

'Tell them what?' Spencer asked, knowing exactly what she meant. Confrontation didn't sit well with him, and neither did arguing with Tori, but she was in the wrong. He had been afraid that their parents wouldn't get along, but he had never expected to get the blame for it.

'That they need to stop drinking and they need to keep their stupid opinions to themselves.'

'Their opinions are stupid? Then so are mine, because they made me!'

'Now *you're* being pretty stupid! If your parents love drinking so much, why aren't they staying in the room above the pub? My parents would be far happier in your house than here.'

'Oh, would they? In *my* house, where *I* live… the man they hate, apparently? That's a fabulous idea!' Spencer glared at her. He had never been this angry with her before, and it made him feel odd and sick to his stomach, but he couldn't help it. He had been all set to suggest to his parents that they swap accommodation with the Dempseys earlier that day, but now it was the last thing he would ever do, simply because Tori's assumption that he should do it made him want to dig his heels in. 'That house belonged to my parents, why shouldn't they stay there when they come to visit?'

'It doesn't belong to them now.'

Spencer was suddenly aware of the volume of their argument rising. He glanced around the bar before leaning into Tori and lowering his voice. 'Exactly right, it belongs to me and I say who stays there. If my life depended on it, I wouldn't have your stuck-up parents there after this!'

Tori was silent for a moment as she stared him down. 'Not even if our relationship depended on it?' she asked quietly, reducing her volume to match his but with no less belligerence in her tone.

Spencer shook his head. 'That's below the belt.'

'Is it?'

'I can't and I won't ask my parents to leave.'

Tori said something, but Spencer didn't hear what it was. His attention was caught by the door of the pub opening, and a pink-haired figure making her way to the bar with a huge smile on her face. Tori frowned, and then she turned to see Jasmine too. She looked at Spencer, her eyes filling with tears.

'Ok... I see how it is.'

And as she walked away, Spencer was suddenly engulfed by panic. Was she talking about their argument, or the fact that all his anger had just melted away at the sight of Jasmine? He wanted to call her back, but the words wouldn't come. Instead, he watched as Tori's parents got up from the table, said stiff goodbyes to his own, and left to go to their room, Tori going with them. It seemed pointless to follow them. The mood Tori was in, there was no way she was going to talk this out, and besides, he still had a bar to man.

'Martini...' said Jasmine in her best James Bond voice as she approached the bar. 'Shaken, not stirred.'

'Hey,' Spencer said in a dull voice.

Jasmine narrowed her eyes. 'Everything ok?'

'Yes, fine…' Spencer said, forcing a brief smile. 'I thought you were sitting with Millie tonight while Darcie and Dylan were out.'

'I was, but they came back early. I don't think Darcie's date went well and Dylan went to fetch her, so they're all going to get an early night. Me, though… Well, I'm not going to throw away a night off by going home early, so I thought I'd come and see what was going on in the hippest nightspot in Honeybourne.'

'Won't Rich be missing you?' Spencer asked.

It was odd that she didn't want to go home to him, and even odder to find her drinking in here alone… Not that she would be alone for long, but she hadn't known that when she arrived. She usually loved nights in with Rich.

She shrugged. 'I'm not in the mood to care tonight. Have you got a nice house red for me? Big glass…'

'You want to talk about it?' Spencer asked as he poured her wine.

'Not really. I'm sure it will all blow over soon enough and it's not the first row we've had.'

So she'd had an argument with Rich? There seemed to be something in the air tonight. Maybe it was the stress of Christmas getting to people.

'You don't look much happier,' she said as he took the money from her and dropped it in the till. 'What was going on with you and Tori when I came in?'

'Parent trouble. They don't seem to be getting on.'

'Well, you could have seen that coming a mile off,' Jasmine laughed. Spencer couldn't help a smile.

'I did. But I was hoping I'd be proved wrong, or that they could at least keep a lid on it for a few days. Seems it was too much to ask.'

'Want me to go and talk to Jenny and Lewis? Ask them to cut you a bit of slack?'

Spencer's expression darkened. 'I don't think it's them who needs talking to. Tori's parents are so up themselves it's untrue. They complain constantly about everything, and everybody has to agree with everything they say. It makes me wonder sometimes if Tori won't turn out like that in the end.'

Jasmine's eyes widened. 'You really feel that way?'

He sighed. 'I don't suppose so. We've just had the most humungous bust-up though, and she's probably not even going to come back to the house tonight... She's just disappeared upstairs with the Borgias.'

Jasmine giggled. 'You can't call them that!'

'No? How about Mr and Mrs Hitler?'

'That's even worse! They can't be that bad.'

'Yeah, they can.'

Lewis ambled over to the bar. 'Hi, Jasmine,' he said, giving her a hug. He shot a rueful look at Spencer. 'Did we blow it?'

'God no, Dad!' Spencer said. 'You and Mum did nothing wrong.'

'They disappeared pretty sharpish after we got onto your mum's favourite subject...'

'They were probably tired – jet-lagged, you know?'

'Tori too?'

'She wants to spend time with them. It's understandable,' Spencer lied, knowing that his father wasn't swallowing one bit of it. But Lewis merely smiled amiably. 'I suppose we're allowed to have a drink now?'

'You could have had one before – in fact, you *were* having drinks before,' Spencer said.

'Yes, but we were… How did you put it earlier? *Laying off the sauce…*'

Spencer gave him a sheepish grin. 'Sorry about that. I had no right to tell you what to do.'

'Love does strange things to us,' Lewis replied as he turned his attention to the various beers on offer across the bar.

Spencer glanced at Jasmine, and then his thoughts turned to the people in a room above his head. Love really did do strange things to him. He only wished love would give it a rest because he'd had just about enough.

'Who's the girl who came in as we left to come back to the room?' Tori's mum asked as she handed Tori a crisp cotton handkerchief.

Tori blew her nose and offered her a grateful smile. 'Which one?'

'Crazy hair, crazy coat, just a little bit of crazy everywhere – like everything and everyone else in this place.'

'You mean pink hair?'

Mrs Dempsey nodded.

'Jasmine.' Tori almost spat the name out.

'She looks ridiculous.'

'Not if you're Spencer she doesn't.'

Mrs Dempsey looked sharply at her and Tori wished she hadn't been quite as keen to share her feelings right at that moment. But she was hurt and she was angry, and it had just slipped out. It wouldn't take long for her mother to pick it up and run with it though.

'What does that mean?'

'Nothing. It doesn't matter.'

'Is she an old flame?'

'No.'

'Then what did you mean by your comment?'

'They're friends.'

Tori's father came in from the bathroom, massaging lotion into his hands. 'How's my little girl?' he asked. 'Feeling better now?'

Mrs Dempsey waved him away. 'Not now, Todd. Go and watch TV or something for a while.'

'But there's nothing on I want to see.'

'Read a book or something then!'

With a grunt, he disappeared into the small bedroom off the main suite. Mrs Dempsey sat next to Tori on the sofa and pulled her into a hug.

'It's not too late to fix this,' she said.

Tori pulled away to look at her. 'Fix what?'

'This mess with Spencer.'

'I don't get it.'

'It's clearly a huge mistake, and it's better you find out now than when you're married and stuck with him.'

'But I love him!'

'Do you? And can you be sure he loves you? The evidence is there right in front of your eyes – you just said it yourself. If he's looking at other women now, and you're not even married, then imagine what you might be dealing with once the ring is on your finger.'

'Spencer is not like that.'

'*All* men are like that.'

Tori stared at her. 'How can you say that? What about Daddy?'

'Because it's true. The best you can hope for is one you can keep in check, or one who can fund the kind of lifestyle that will make the bitterness of the pill a little easier to take.'

'That's crazy!'

'That's life. Take it from someone who has age and wisdom on her side.'

Tori frowned. 'And I suppose you think the ideal candidate is Hunter Ford?'

'There are worse out there. He'd give you a good life.'

'Spencer will give me a good life.'

'Spencer will let you down! His parents are simply dreadful and this village is… well, there isn't enough here for an intelligent young woman like you.'

'Shouldn't I be able to make that call? I like it here and I like his parents.'

'What about Jasmine?'

'She's great too,' Tori replied carefully.

'If there's the slightest doubt, walk away. You might be in love now, and it might hurt like hell, but it's the sensible thing to do.'

Tori shook her head. 'That's the problem with you – everything has to be sensible. Love isn't sensible and I don't want it to be any other way.'

'Then you'll get hurt. Hunter will be married off to some other eligible woman and you'll have nothing. And don't think your father and I will be around to pick up the pieces when that happens.'

'Spencer won't hurt me. He's a good man and he'll make me happy.'

'Then why are you sitting here? Go down and ruin your life if you're so certain he's the right one.' Mrs Dempsey folded her arms and stared. Tori fiddled with the hem of her sweatshirt. Spencer was the one, wasn't he? He loved her and would never hurt her; she wanted to believe that more than anything. But right now he was working in the bar, probably laughing and joking with Jasmine and his parents and not giving her a second thought. If she was so sure of him, why couldn't she bring herself to go downstairs right now and see for herself?

Chapter Seven

Millie was already moving around downstairs in the kitchens when Darcie's alarm went off. She'd probably been up for hours already with Oscar and hadn't bothered going back to bed, which was a regular thing these days. Darcie slammed her hand down on the clock to switch the bleeping off and rolled onto her back, staring up at the ceiling. Though she hadn't imagined for a minute she would get any sleep the previous night, she had been so emotionally drained that she'd passed out as soon as she tucked her legs under the covers. But now, instantly awake, her mind went back to the events of Nathan's party, and the way she had spoken to Dylan afterwards. God, she was an idiot, and she didn't think that any number of years on the planet was ever going to change that. The best thing now, though, was to look forward, forget it ever happened and try to get on with the here and now, at least until after Christmas when she would break the news to Millie that she was returning to Millrise. What she would do once she was back home, she had no clue, but at least she would be away from temptation and trouble.

Her breath curled into the air, caught in the lamplight that illuminated a room not yet touched by daylight. The heating had only just clicked on and it was still chilly; there was no birdsong and no sounds of daily life outside the bakery, so it still felt very much like the middle of the night, despite the fact that she was about to start work for the day. Even though some mornings it felt like a form of medieval torture, Darcie would miss this life. She had grown to love the peace of Honeybourne, the closeness and community spirit of its residents; a simpler, slower pace of life that some might find dull but that made Darcie feel safe. If it hadn't been for Dylan... Well, there was no point in dwelling on that now. There was Dylan, and that was a fight she knew she was losing. The only option left now was to go home.

She got out of bed and was about to rush into the shower when there was a tap at the door.

'Darcie?' Millie called softly. 'Are you up?'

'Come in. I'm decent.'

Millie smiled as she opened the door. 'I wanted to ask you about last night. Dylan told me what happened – at least, what he knows. I didn't want to mention it before you'd had time to sleep on things, put a bit of distance between you and what happened.'

Darcie tried not to groan. Of course Dylan had told Millie about it. What else was he going to do?

'He said you didn't want to talk about it,' Millie continued, 'and I understand that, but I've always felt that we can share things, like sisters. So I wondered if it would be easier to talk to me. And it might help you feel better to get it off your chest.'

Darcie sat on the bed and pulled her dressing gown tighter. 'I was just caught in the middle of some unfinished business, that's all. I don't know whether Nathan had intended what happened, or whether it was an accident or just bad timing. All I know is that he has history with a girl who hasn't let go yet.'

'Is he still seeing her?'

'I don't know. He said not, but she said he was. She said I was just a ploy to make her jealous and that he didn't like me at all. She said I wasn't even his type.' Darcie gave a tiny shrug. 'Looking at her that was probably true. She was like a model – stick thin, all legs and hair and very pretty.'

'You're pretty,' Millie frowned. 'Don't you forget that!'

'I'm ordinary. She was beautiful.'

Millie frowned and Darcie could see that she wanted to argue the point, but she let it go. 'So what happened?'

'She told me he was using me and that he wasn't interested, then she got personal and insulted me. Nathan didn't do much to make me believe that he was genuine, and he certainly didn't stick up for me. So I left. That's it.'

'Dylan said you were very upset when he picked you up. I didn't realise it had been that bad. When you came in last night you seemed disappointed but not distressed…'

'I was upset, but I'm over it. I'd had a bit to drink and I wasn't thinking straight. I'm fine this morning and I don't want to dwell on it anymore.'

'You won't be seeing him again?'

'Not if I can help it. I've deleted his number from my phone and I'm never accepting numbers from boys I meet on buses ever again. And if I never see Salisbury again it will be too soon.'

Millie sat next to her and smoothed a hand over her hair. 'It's hardly Salisbury's fault.'

Darcie gave her a thin smile. 'I know. I just wish I hadn't gone on the bus at that particular time on that particular day and then I would never have met him.'

'You really liked him, didn't you?'

Darcie looked at her. She had liked Nathan enough, but that wasn't the reason she had agreed to go to the party. The real reason was one she could never tell Millie, and she felt the increasing burden of her treacherous heart with every kindness Millie showed her. Millie pulled her into a hug, clearly taking her silence as a confirmation that she was right, and Darcie let her. If Millie believed that she was broken-hearted over Nathan, then that was probably for the best.

After his shift the previous night, Spencer had gone upstairs to see if Tori was coming back home with him only to be told by a stern Mr Dempsey that she was asleep in their room and would be staying the night. Spencer had walked back without her, deep in thought and feeling wretched as he and his parents walked Jasmine home safely. Along the way they shared theories about why Tori's parents were so determined to make themselves as unlikeable as they could. Jasmine concluded that it was simply a case of not wanting their daughter to relocate, and Jenny agreed, while Lewis aired the opinion that they were a pair of pompous twats and if he never saw them again it would be too soon. Spencer was the only person who stayed silent on the subject, listening absently as they trudged through the snow. He had played the argument with Tori over and over in his head, wondering what he could have done and said differently so that she would be walking with them now, her hand in his as they gazed up at the frosted stars and the twinkling Christmas lights draped over every tree on the route.

At Jasmine's door, she had looked up at her own house and sighed. 'It looks like Rich's gone to bed.'

Spencer's mind had gone back to her arrival, and the hint that they'd had a major bust-up too. It was nothing new for Jasmine and Rich, as everyone knew.

She had pulled each of them into a warm hug, and Spencer's had been the longest and warmest of all. He savoured her scent, her softness, the feeling of being at home in her arms. Why did she have to be so right when it was all so wrong? And what did that mean for his relationship with Tori?

'You'll make it up, don't worry,' Jasmine had said in his ear. 'I can tell by the way she looks at you that she's head over heels.'

Spencer had smiled thinly. 'I wish I could say the same for her parents. Are you sure you'll be alright?'

'Me? Of course. I can handle grumpy-pants in there. Go to Tori and sort it out. Don't lose her, because love like that doesn't come around very often.'

He had watched Jasmine let herself into the house and had carried her words and her scent home with him.

As he woke now on Christmas Eve morning, his arm swept the bed and then he remembered that the other side was empty because Tori hadn't come home with him and it was all his fault. He rolled over and checked the phone on the bedside table. No messages and no missed calls. Not that he expected any and he certainly didn't deserve them, but there had been the slimmest hope she might have relented overnight. He rolled onto his back and stared at the ceiling. Was this it? Had he blown it for good?

It was difficult to know exactly when the situation had gone past saving. Was it when she'd disappeared with her parents? Or was it because he hadn't insisted on being let in to see Tori, despite Todd Dempsey's dismissal? Or was it even when Jasmine had arrived at the pub and his attention had so obviously been caught by her when it should have been on Tori and nobody else? Whenever it was, he had made the mistake of staying downstairs on the bar, feeling wretched and angry and drinking too much, when he should have been upstairs talking to Tori. And then he had made things worse by going home without her instead of fighting for her like he should have done. On reflection, he probably didn't deserve her.

He reached for his phone again and sent Tori a text. It was early and he didn't want to piss them all off even more by waking them with a phone call. It just said one word: *'Sorry.'* There wasn't anything else to say, and he could only apologise for his part in what had happened – the rest their parents would have to get together and thrash out.

Tori's reply came through almost immediately: *'Me too.'*

Spencer smiled, relief flooding through him. It was a start, and at least she sounded willing to talk. He tapped out a reply.

'Can I see you?'

'Sure, give me an hour.'

'We need some privacy.'

'Churchyard?'

'Good thinking. At the churchyard in an hour then. I'll carry a newspaper and wear a pink carnation in my buttonhole.'

'You're such a goofball! X'

Spencer put the phone down and got out of bed. He needed a shower and some breakfast, and he somehow needed to talk to his parents in order to avoid a repeat of last night's stand-off. But as he passed the door to their room, he heard the tandem snoring that told him they were both still out for the count and not likely to rouse any time soon. He'd have to try and grab them later – after he'd made things up with Tori but before they all met again at the carol service that night.

His parents went to the carol service every Christmas Eve when they were in Honeybourne, though they were far from religious and made a point of telling everyone who would listen that they didn't go to hear about God, but to join in the singalong and feel like part of the village tradition. Tori's parents, on the other hand, were keen to go because they were deeply involved in the church at home. It didn't take a genius to see where this was headed unless he had a quiet word first, and he really didn't fancy a repeat performance of the doomed politics debate.

Fifty minutes later Spencer was walking the road to the churchyard. He was surprised that Tori had memorised its whereabouts so well, but he had to smile at the possibility that she had taken particular note of it as a contender for the wedding venue, and had secretly stored the information for a later discussion. He felt a pang of guilt that this conversation hadn't already happened. While they had been engaged since the spring, it had been something of an empty promise in many ways because they were no nearer to organising it than they had been at the start. They had both stalled – they'd been busy at work, not had the money, a million different excuses – and it seemed as if they had all the time in the world. But his exchange programme was due to finish in the summer, and then he would have no reason to stay in America, and it suddenly struck him, after he had come so close to losing her, that perhaps this was a good time to start doing something about it.

As he waited for Tori, he wandered the churchyard for a while. It had started to snow, only gently, but it fell on the frozen chunks of ice still lining the paths from the last snow, settling on the weathered old headstones like a sprinkling of flour.

As he looked up, he saw Tori's petite figure skirting the outside wall and ran to the gates to meet her. She flung herself into his arms and pulled him into a passionate kiss.

'I'm so sorry!' they both said together, and Spencer kissed her again, holding her close and breathing her in.

'Let's never do that again,' he whispered.

'Deal,' Tori replied. 'But we do need to talk.'

Spencer pulled away and gazed at her. 'I know. Let's walk so we don't freeze to death.' He took her hand and led her along the path closest to the church.

'This place must be really old,' Tori said, looking up at the opulent stained glass windows and weather-worn architecture.

'I think it dates back to Norman times.'

'It's beautiful.'

They were silent for a moment, Tori captivated by her surroundings until Spencer broke it. 'I'm really sorry about last night.'

'It sucked.'

'Just a bit. What are we going to do?'

'I think we might need to keep them apart as much as we can,' Tori ventured. She looked up at Spencer for a reply, but he just nodded thoughtfully.

It seemed that the problem was much deeper than that, and he wondered if either of them would be brave enough to say it. While the parents were a huge issue, their discord seemed to be just a representation of the things that Tori and Spencer needed to say to each other about their relationship and where it was going, and while they remained unsaid, the two of them would remain stuck. Spencer couldn't understand the reasons for this, but he knew that he needed to work it out, and soon, if they stood a chance of a future together.

'I think that's going to be difficult, to be honest. Tonight we have the carol service and there is no way any of them will miss that. To-morrow they have to eat Christmas dinner together. By Boxing Day, they might have killed each other.'

'Or we might,' Tori said with a wry smile.

Spencer gave her hand a squeeze. 'I hope not.'

'Look… I know that my parents can be difficult, and they can be a bit scary, but they just want what's best for me. You can understand that, can't you?'

Spencer nodded. 'And the same goes for mine – apart from the difficult and scary bit.'

'They're scary when they won't shut up.'

'True. But they're entitled to say what they think just like everyone else is.'

Tori frowned. 'But sometimes we have to keep our opinions to ourselves to keep the peace… And if they loved you they'd do that for you.'

'They do love me!'

'I know, it's just…' She let out a deep sigh.

'Let's not get into that same argument we had last night, eh?' Spencer said.

'Exactly. It's not getting us anywhere. We're just going to have to ac-cept that they're never going to be bosom buddies. But if they could be in the same room without World War Three, it would be pretty good.'

'And probably the best we could hope for.'

'You talk to yours, and I'll talk to mine. Maybe we can pull this off if they're willing to put their differences aside for a couple of days.'

'Ok.' Spencer bent to kiss her. 'And I'm sorry I didn't come up to get you last night straight away when you left the bar. I was an idiot.'

'You didn't come up at all.'

'Your dad said you were asleep and…'

Tori grinned. 'The sly old fox!'

'So you weren't asleep?'

'No. I was watching TV with Mom. You should have come up, but I know you were working, so it's ok I guess.' She paused, looked straight ahead, and asked her next question in a careless tone that masked something much more. 'So Jasmine came in pretty late and by herself…'

'Yeah. She'd been with Millie while Darcie was out, but Darcie came home early and I think Jas had an argument with Rich or something before going out so she didn't want to go straight home.'

'Do they argue a lot?'

Spencer looked sharply at her. 'What makes you ask?'

Tori shrugged. 'Just stuff I heard.'

'From Ruth, by any chance?'

'Your mom too.'

'Don't put too much stock in the gossip you hear in these parts – even from my mother.'

'That's what I figured. But you left with her last night when you'd finished working…'

'After I'd come up to find you and had been turned away. I walked her home – with my mum and dad. Who told you?'

'Colleen.'

'Of course… Do you have a problem with Jas?'

'Should I?'

'We're just old friends.'

'If that's what you say, then I believe you.'

'It is.'

'But you used to be in love with her?'

Spencer stopped on the path. 'Tori, what is this?'

'You're not denying it.'

'I love you.'

'You still maybe love her a little? It's ok, I just need to know what I'm up against.'

He took her into his arms and pulled her into his embrace. 'I love *you*. Jasmine and I... we never got that far, and despite all the rows, she's crazy about Rich – always has been. So you don't need to worry.'

'You say that but you still haven't denied that you love her too.'

'Love is a very strong word. I had feelings for her, but if they weren't reciprocated then it couldn't really have been love, could it?' Spencer replied, but he wondered if he was trying to convince himself more than Tori.

'I don't know,' Tori said, her eyes watering. 'I just need to be sure, and right now I'm not sure of anything.'

'I want to marry you – not Jasmine. Isn't that enough? Jas and I are friends, and we were once very close... I'll always be fond of her, but my heart... that's yours.'

'You mean that?'

'Yes, of course I do.'

'Because I don't think I could live in this village with her here knowing that you still had feelings for her.'

Spencer blinked. 'Wait... You mean you're still considering Honeybourne, even though all this shit has happened here over the last couple of days?'

She shrugged. 'We gotta live somewhere, and I quite like it here.'

He picked her up and swung her around as she laughed. 'You'd do that for me? You'd move here?'

'I'm saying maybe, but let's not get ahead of ourselves. There's a lot more to talk about first.'

Spencer grinned. 'I'm all ears.'

It didn't feel like Christmas Eve. In fact, as far as the bakery was concerned, it was just another day, and busier than it had been for a while, with people calling in for last-minute treats to grace their Christmas tables. Millie had promised Dylan that they would close early, but as things were, it was quite possible they would close a lot later than usual. But Millie had said (and Dylan and Darcie both agreed) that the money was needed and if they had a busy day, they would just have to make the most of the respite that Christmas Day would afford them.

Millie had just seen Saul and Jim out with an armful of pies that quite possibly represented their Christmas dinner when a sandy-haired youth entered with a coat draped over his arm and an anxious expression.

'Darcie...' Millie called as her gaze fell on the coat and a look of recognition illuminated her features.

Darcie came through from the kitchens with a tray of bread pudding. She almost dropped the tray, and then stopped and stared.

'Nathan!'

He shuffled awkwardly over to the counter. 'I wanted to return your coat... I think it's yours, right? There were so many unclaimed at the end of the night it was hard to tell.' He glanced at Millie, who was watching intently with her arms folded across her chest, then back at

Darcie. 'I don't suppose we can go somewhere to talk,' he added in a
low voice.

'How did you find me?' Darcie asked, still clinging onto the tray.
Millie stepped forward and took it gently from her.

'If you need ten minutes—' Millie began, but Darcie stopped her.

'It's ok. I don't think we'll be long.' She turned back to Nathan
and waited.

He looked sheepish. 'I remembered the village you said you were
living in, and as there's only one bakery here…'

Even as she resolved not to give him a second chance, Darcie felt
that resolve melting away. He had come to find her, all that way on
Christmas Eve, when he didn't need to at all. He could have called
her to collect her coat, put it in the bin, sent it to charity, left it to
rot where it fell… But he came to bring it back and she felt sure that
wasn't the only reason he had come. But she couldn't risk getting as
hurt as she had been the night before – she didn't think her heart
could take a second pounding like that.

He pulled her to one side as Ruth Evans came in to distract Millie.
'Please, just let me explain about last night.'

'I don't need an explanation… I understand it must be difficult
and you've just broken up with Carly—'

'That's just it – we haven't only just broken up. We broke up
months ago, and she just keeps turning up to ruin my life because she
can't let go. I swear, she means nothing to me.'

'How did she know about the party?'

'Come on – it's not that hard to find out about student parties.
The campus is a smaller place than you think and word gets round
quick, especially when there's a possibility of free booze or a shag.
Not that I was after a shag with you,' he added quickly, 'although that

doesn't mean I don't fancy you and one day I would... well, you know what I mean...'

Darcie couldn't help but smile at his blushes. It was sweet, and she still felt he was sweet too beneath that street-cool exterior.

'So you're going to give me another chance? Your smile tells me you want to...' he said, giving her a small, hopeful grin.

Darcie chewed on a nail, and glanced around the room. Millie was still being held captive by Ruth, though she kept throwing meaningful looks across at her and Nathan, as if to say to Darcie that she was there the moment the SOS came through and she needed to get rid of an unwanted visitor. Dylan was nowhere to be seen, presumably somewhere out back with Oscar or in the kitchens.

'I don't know,' Darcie replied finally. 'Your world is so different from mine. I don't really like parties and I'm pretty boring.'

'We don't have to do parties, we can just hang out and, well, whatever. And if you saw me with my Xbox, you'd see that I'm pretty boring too most of the time. But you have to throw a party or two at Christmas, don't you?' He pulled his mobile phone from his pocket. 'I bet you've deleted my number... Let me give it to you again and you can think about it.'

'What about Carly?'

'What about her? We're not going out anymore.'

'That's not what she thinks. And I only have your word for it. I can't stop thinking about what she said last night – that you were only trying to make her jealous.'

He raised his eyebrows. 'Would I have come all this way with your coat just to talk to you if I was trying to make her jealous? She's not here, so what am I gaining other than a second chance with you?'

'My phone is in the back. I can't get it right now.'

'It doesn't matter. I still have your number so I'll phone it and you can store the number from the missed call if you decide to. I won't pressure you, but I do want to see you again if you can get past what happened at the party last night.'

Darcie was about to reply when she heard Dylan's voice behind them. 'Is everything alright, Darcie?' She turned to see him looming over Nathan as best he could, though it was hard to look scary with a baby strapped to your front. If the situation hadn't been quite so emotionally tense, Darcie would have laughed out loud to see it.

'Yes,' she said, glancing between him and Nathan, who did seem to shrink away, despite the baby-hampered offensive.

'Are you sure? Because you don't look ok… Is this him?'

Darcie nodded, and she wondered what Dylan was going to do, but he simply aimed his coldest stare at Nathan. 'Darcie is like family to us, and I don't take kindly to people hurting my family. You understand?'

Watching him warning off Nathan with Oscar strapped to him, Darcie realised suddenly how much of a dad he was, and how he clearly viewed her in the same way he saw Oscar, and it was like a bolt of illumination. She had loved Dylan all this time, and he had only ever seen her in the way he saw Oscar – someone under his protection, someone he needed to care for like a child. It was difficult to comprehend how this made her feel, she only wondered how she hadn't seen it before. Dylan would never have loved her in the way she loved him, even without Millie. How could he when he saw her as a little sister, or even a daughter? The idea was going to take some getting her head around, but perhaps it would be a turning point.

Nathan nodded uncertainly. 'I didn't mean any of what happened last night and I came to set things straight – that's all.'

'That's good then. So consider things straight. You can be on your way and not bother her again. And if I see you around this village I'll want a damn good reason not to smash your face in.'

'Dylan!' Darcie squeaked. She wasn't sure she liked this heavy-handed approach and she wasn't sure she liked this Dylan either.

'I think Nathan understands me,' Dylan said grimly.

'Yeah, I understand.' Nathan turned to Darcie. 'Don't forget what I said… Think about it, yeah?'

She nodded. And then Nathan handed her the coat before turning to leave. They watched him go, and then Dylan looked at Darcie.

'You're not seriously giving that loser another try, are you?'

'He wanted to give me his number again—'

'Darcie! Have you forgotten what he did last night?'

'No, but—'

'Believe me, I've seen his type before… I *was* his type before! And I know he'll mess you around if you let him get under your skin.'

'But you're not like that now,' Darcie protested, feeling more than a little confused. The previous night he had told her there must be a reasonable explanation for what had happened. Now he was like an overprotective uncle, unable to listen to reason. Perhaps something about the way Nathan looked had put him on his guard, or maybe it was something Millie had said after talking to Darcie. Maybe last night he had simply been trying to make her feel better when she'd been at her lowest. Whatever it was, Dylan wasn't happy and was rather less inclined to give him the benefit of the doubt in the cold light of day.

But then he turned to look at Millie, who was still trying to get rid of Ruth as more customers appeared behind her, and his expression softened instantly. 'Only because of one extraordinary woman.'

Darcie's heart sank. Millie was extraordinary, and she was very ordinary indeed. Maybe Dylan had a point. Maybe she was asking for trouble by giving Nathan another chance, but she couldn't help but believe his promises and she wanted to believe that he really did like her, that he thought she was special. And his excuse was plausible. Now that she thought about the events of the previous night, his explanation did make sense. The way he was with Carly certainly didn't look like the behaviour of someone in love. He'd looked as shocked at the way things turned out as Darcie. He'd also gone to a lot of effort to come and apologise, and like he said, why would he do that if he didn't really like Darcie? He wasn't going to make Carly jealous in Honeybourne when she probably had no idea that the village even existed.

What Carly had said also played on her mind. Darcie didn't have model looks like Carly did, and if Nathan had wanted to make her jealous he could have chosen a stunning girl to do it with, not someone as ordinary as Darcie. So whatever weird reason he might have had to give Darcie his number, there must have been a bit of genuine attraction… Though she found it hard to believe, it was easier now to believe than Carly's version.

'Give him a wide berth,' Dylan said, breaking into her thoughts. 'You deserve better.'

Darcie looked up at him, cradling and kissing Oscar's head as he spoke. She may have deserved better, but he wasn't available and never would be.

'You're cold?' Spencer asked. He and Tori had wandered around the churchyard for over an hour, so wrapped up in the things they needed to say that they had hardly noticed the snow getting steadily worse until it forced them to take shelter in the doorway of the church. He hugged her close, trying to warm her up.

'I'm fine,' she said. 'Nothing that a little hot chocolate wouldn't put right.'

'I happen to know just the place to get the best hot chocolate in town… and it's not the Dog and Hare.'

Tori smiled, but then it faded. 'I should get back. Mom and Dad will be missing me.'

'But they know where you are?'

'They know I'm with you, but they'll worry – I've been out for so long.'

'You mean they'll be annoyed at being left for so long?'

'Yeah… I guess so,' Tori said with a sheepish grin.

'Stuff 'em! And I mean that in the best possible way. They can manage without you for another hour, and we have a future to plan.'

'And might that future involve a fairy-tale wedding in a pretty English church?'

'It might…' Spencer said, kissing her.

The doors of the church opened and they leapt apart.

'Don't mind me,' the man said as he went to a poster frame to put up details of the carol service. Spencer took in the long garments of office and frowned.

'You're the vicar?' he asked with a look of confusion.

'Last time I checked,' the man replied with a white-toothed grin that could dazzle birds from the sky. He looked young – early thirties at most – and he was handsome. Spencer detected an accent that sounded like it originated from somewhere in Africa.

'I'm sorry,' Spencer explained, 'it's just that last time I was here Clive was the vicar.'

'Oh…' The man wiped his hands on his cassock and held one out for Spencer to shake. 'You're from Honeybourne? I haven't seen you around.'

'I've been working in America. Just come home for Christmas. This is my girlfriend, Tori.'

'I should think so,' the vicar said cheerfully. 'I would hope you don't kiss all the girls you meet like that. And you're?'

'Spencer Johns. I used to teach at the school here. Well, I suppose I still do, technically, although I'm on an exchange programme at the moment.'

'Ah, I have heard your name before. Tristan Okonjo… That's me, in case you were wondering. I'm very pleased to meet you. And might you be joining us for the carol service tonight?'

'We're planning to,' Tori put in.

'That's wonderful. Extra voices are always welcome.'

Spencer was suddenly gripped by a wild and crazy idea. 'How quickly can you get a wedding arranged?'

Tori stared at him, but he simply smiled and took her hand. 'You're not getting away,' he said. 'Not again.'

Tristan threw back his head and laughed. 'Don't let Mr Policeman hear you say it like that!' He held his sides as if to show that they were splitting. 'I certainly can't marry you today, if that's what you're thinking.'

'When?'

Tristan shook his head. 'You'll have to come and see me next week to talk it over.'

'But we'll be on our way back to America next week.'

'Mr Johns…' Tristan clapped him on the back. 'If you love her and she loves you, then it will happen. There is no need to rush the course of true love.'

'It's a lovely idea,' Tori said, nudging Spencer, 'but Tristan is right. We should do it properly. Besides, my parents would kill me if we did it this way.'

'Being killed by one's parents is not a good way to start married life,' Tristan agreed, his face stretched into a broad grin. Spencer wondered vaguely whether he ever stopped grinning. 'Come and see me by all means before you go overseas, and we can talk about dates and other things if you want to marry here.' He gave them an amiable nod. 'Now you must excuse me – I have a lot to do before the service later.'

'It was lovely to meet you,' Tori called after him, and he waved a huge hand behind him as he walked back into the church. She turned to Spencer. 'That was so romantic... Thank you for trying.'

'It's a shame it didn't work out, though. It would have been quite nice to come and marry in secret, and nobody would have been able to stick their noses in to tell us how we should do it.'

'Oh...' Tori said. 'I hadn't thought about all that.'

'Trust me, I did. And I wasn't very keen on the idea. But, it looks as though we'll have to rethink the whole thing... Now, where were we?' He moved in for another kiss, but Tori pushed him off with a giggle.

'The vicar will come back out and have us arrested if we keep making out on the steps of the house of God.'

'I don't think God has any particular issues with making out,' Spencer replied impishly. 'In fact, I think he's quite a supporter of the old making-out business. After all, making out often leads to other things, and that's how he gets new fans...'

'We have to get back!' Tori snorted as she pushed him off again.

'Ok, I know when I'm beaten.' Spencer let go and dug his hands in his pockets, turning his attention to the snow. 'So are we getting that hot chocolate at the bakery or not?'

'Maybe just one,' Tori said, 'but then we have to get back or my parents will be calling in the FBI to look for me.'

'It wouldn't take them long to search Honeybourne, but if you're that adamant then I suppose I'd better keep my word.' He offered his hand and they walked out into the snow together.

The air of the bakery was warm and filled with the scents of cinnamon, coffee and sugar. It was busier than Spencer had seen it since arriving home for the Christmas break, apart from Colleen's emergency meeting. As they walked in, they passed a sandy-haired youth leaving, Dylan and Darcie watching him go and looking quite serious about it. Spencer led Tori to a table and went over to the counter to order.

'What was all that about?' he asked as Millie greeted him.

'What?'

Spencer nodded his head at Dylan and Darcie, who were now deep in conversation. 'They just watched a guy leave and Dylan looked like… well, it wasn't a look I want to be on the receiving end of again.'

'Oh, that!' She lowered her voice. 'That was the boy Darcie was meeting yesterday at the party. It didn't go well.'

'I heard that,' Spencer said. 'Jasmine called at the pub last night and said it had ended much earlier than expected.'

'Yes. I don't think she's telling us everything, but she was pretty upset.'

'So what did he want today?'

'He came to see her I think. Wanted to explain.'

'Wow, he's brave. If Dylan was looking at me like that I'd have been straight out the door again.'

Millie leaned over the counter with a conspiratorial air. 'Lucky for Darcie, Dylan wasn't in here when he arrived. I wouldn't have wanted to tackle him either. Poor Darcie will never get a boyfriend while she's under this roof if he deals with them all like that. I think he's considering the purchase of a shotgun for the next one.'

'He's just looking out for her,' Spencer replied gently.

'I know. And I love him for it. God knows she needs it.'

'Maybe she's tougher than you think.'

'Maybe. But I worry about her. She doesn't seem herself, but I know that even if she wants to go home, she feels guilty about leaving us to run this place. Not that there's much more for her there. But I've told her that we'll manage and she needs to do what's best for her.'

'Do you think she'll go home?'

'I don't know. Dylan told her to wait it out until after Christmas and then see how she feels. She says she'll do that, so I suppose time will tell.' She straightened up again and waved across to Tori, who waved back as she peeled off her outside layers. 'What can I get you lovebirds?'

'Hot chocolates. It's freezing out there and we need thawing out.'

Millie laughed as she turned away to prepare the drinks. 'So you saw Jasmine at the pub last night?' she called over her shoulder.

'She came by later on, after she'd left you.'

'On her own?'

'Yes. I suppose Rich was with the kids.'

'Hmm...' Millie said as she poured some milk into a jug.

'What does that mean?'

Mille turned to face him. 'I think they'd had words again. I feel as if it's my fault really.'

'How can it be your fault?'

'Well, it's this baby business. Ever since Oscar arrived she's been broody, and I don't think Rich wants to play ball.'

'I can't say I blame him,' Spencer said.

'I don't think it's that he says no, I think it's the absolute refusal to even discuss it that's making her angry. You know how stubborn they can both be.'

Spencer gave a thin smile. He knew that only too well, and it had nearly cost him everything last time he got in the middle of it. 'So what happened between them last night to get her so riled?'

Millie angled her head towards where Spencer had left Tori. 'You can ask her yourself – she's just sat down at your table with the kids.'

Spencer swung around and his stomach lurched. Considering the conversation he and Tori had had just an hour or so ago, Jasmine was probably the last person he wanted to see – which was a novel concept in itself. But he had just fixed things with Tori and Jasmine would only serve to remind her of all the things she was uncertain of in their relationship. If he was honest, it did the same to him too. When Jasmine was around, his feelings for Tori became clouded, and he couldn't see the truth of them anymore.

'Go over,' Millie said. 'I can bring your drinks when they're done.'

'Thanks.'

Spencer strode back to the table. Jasmine and all three of the triplets looked up at him with broad smiles.

'Mr Johns!' Rachel said. 'Are you coming to the carols tonight?'

'I think so,' Spencer said, smiling, but his glance wandering to Tori, trying to gauge her mood.

'Tori was just telling me you met the new vicar,' Jasmine said.

'He's quite a cutie, isn't he?' said Tori.

'Well, it's not for me to notice these things,' Spencer replied. 'He does seem a bit eccentric.'

'He's lovely,' Jasmine said. 'Almost enough to make me want to get up for church on a Sunday.'

'Steady on,' Spencer laughed, but then stopped short, looking at Tori again. If the situation was bothering her, she didn't show it. She simply smiled.

'Hop off the chair, Reuben,' Jasmine said, motioning towards her lap for her son to sit. 'Let Spencer have a seat.'

Spencer sat down just in time for Millie to bring over their drinks.

'Ooh...' Reuben looked at them, and then at Jasmine, his face alight with expectation.

'Sorry, pumpkin, we haven't got time to stop for drinks today – we've got a lot to do to get ready for Santa.'

'Do you want to take your order with you now?' Millie asked Jasmine.

She nodded. 'I'll be over in a minute for it.'

Millie went off to get the food order ready while Jasmine turned back to Tori and Spencer. 'What are you all doing after the carol service? I was thinking you might like to come to ours for drinks and nibbles.'

'That sounds—' Spencer began, but Tori cut him off.

'My folks are still a little jet-lagged and they'll probably be exhausted after that. It's lovely of you to offer but I think we'll probably have a quiet night.'

Spencer shot her a sideways glance. He wondered, exactly, where this quiet night was going to be. Christmas Eve was likely to be one of the pub's busiest nights and if they had found the previous night too much they'd be having breakdowns by the end of tonight. Or was she assuming that her parents would be invited to stay at his house after all? There wasn't enough room for all of them and he had made that clear before. Perhaps it was simply the idea of spending time with Jasmine that was worrying her, despite Spencer's attempts at reassurance. It was obviously something they were going to have to discuss.

Jasmine smiled. 'Not to worry. Maybe we'll make another night before you all leave.' She got up. 'Come on, kids, let's go and grab Uncle Dylan before we go, see if we can't get a cuddle from Oscar.' She turned back to Tori and Spencer. 'See you later at the carol service.'

'See you later,' Tori returned. She looked at her mug, which was piled with whipped cream and marshmallows. 'This looks amazing.'

'Why did you tell her no?' Spencer asked.

'I didn't think it was a very good idea. There's enough friction in the air without adding theirs to it – you said yourself they're not getting on.'

Spencer paused, waiting for Tori to add something about not wanting to spend time with Jasmine. But if she had a motive other than the one she had stated, she wasn't sharing it. He wasn't sure if that made him feel better or worse.

'I'm sure they wouldn't have a blazing row with visitors there,' he said. 'They can show some restraint sometimes.'

'Unlike your parents.'

Spencer frowned. 'Really? Do we have to do this again?'

'I'm sorry – you're right. I don't know what's wrong with me. Let's just have an evening at your place, huh? Maybe get some food and talk?'

'All of us? That's asking for trouble.'

Tori reached for his hand. 'We can do this. Let's not freak out, ok?'

'Ok,' he said, suddenly struck by an idea, 'how about we drive out somewhere a bit more neutral? A nice restaurant somewhere a bit posh?'

'Just us or with the parents?'

'Sadly with the parents. But it might be somewhere that suits everyone more than my house or the pub. And if we take our time over it, go somewhere with a classy bar as well, we might just stay away long enough to miss most of the action at the Dog and Hare.'

'Action?'

'Tori... I don't know how to break this to you, but you're in Britain and it's Christmas Eve. It's the season of goodwill to all men and huge drunken queues in Accident and Emergency.'

'Oh. Ok then, let's give it a shot. But I think my folks will want to do the carol thing first.'

'Mine too. They never miss it when they're home, though I have no idea why they go. I think it's to taunt the vicar.'

'I think they'll have met their match in the new one.'

'Mum will probably fall in love with him,' Spencer grinned. 'Before the night is out she might have been converted from staunch atheist to certified God-botherer.'

'Shhh!' Tori hissed. 'Please don't use that phrase in front of my parents!'

'Oh hell, I'm sorry, I forgot. They're God-botherers too, aren't they?'

'Stop it!' Tori giggled.

'I mean, I've got nothing against God, and He's done a lot for me, especially finding me a hot American chick, I just don't feel the need to bother Him on a weekly basis to ask for more stuff...'

'Spencer!'

'Ok, ok... no more jokes. I'll be on my best behaviour, I swear.'

'Good. Do you think Millie will mind me using her Wi-Fi? We can check on my phone for a restaurant that's not too far away.'

'Why don't you go and ask her for the password?' Spencer suggested. 'I can't imagine she'd mind at all.'

Tori kissed him briefly and then made her way to the counter. Spencer watched her go, thinking that if he could have punched himself in the face he would have. Why would he doubt what he had with her? She was an incredible woman and he was lucky to have her. He needed to stop being an idiot before he blew everything.

He looked around to see Jasmine smile and wave as she left the bakery with her brood in tow. Suddenly, with her gone, the air felt clearer again and his mood lighter. Secretly, he was glad Tori had answered for him when Jasmine had invited them over. Much as he loved Jasmine, it wasn't a wise idea, but he would have found himself accepting the invitation against his better judgement. If he and Tori did decide to move to Honeybourne after they were married, the issue was one he was going to have to address and sort out once and for all, because he couldn't go on like this.

As his gaze swept the room, it fell on Darcie and Dylan again. Dylan gave him a brief nod of recognition, and then went off to the back of the shop with a crying Oscar, while Darcie watched with an expression of yearning Spencer recognised only too well. It looked as though he wasn't the only one fighting with his emotions right now. He felt a sudden pull to talk to her – maybe it would help. But even if he could get her alone, how do you start a conversation like that? It looked as though, for now, she was going to have to work things out for herself, just like he was doing. He only hoped she was doing a better job than he was.

Darcie watched Dylan go through to the back room with Oscar. Then she looked across to the counter to see that Millie had gone over to talk to her friend, Spencer, while Ruth Evans dithered at the entrance before turning and heading back to the counter.

'I'll get some pork pies if you have any left,' she said as Darcie painted on a smile for her.

'How many do you want?'

'Two should do it. I won't need much food if I'm not eating at home tomorrow.'

'Oh,' Darcie said as she bagged them up, doing her best to feign interest though she couldn't have cared less about the reasons Ruth wasn't eating at home. She had to be civil, of course, because Ruth was a customer and for some strange reason Millie had a real soft spot for the old lady. As far as Darcie could tell she was an annoying busybody who drove everyone insane, but Millie always made time for her. Which was probably why Ruth insisted on hanging around the bakery like a gnat around a tree.

'Hasn't Millie told you?' Ruth asked as she placed the pies on top of her shopping bag.

'Told me what?'

'She's invited me to have Christmas dinner here tomorrow.'

Darcie looked up sharply from the till. 'Here?'

'So I'll be seeing you tomorrow,' Ruth said, oblivious to Darcie's sudden change of tone. 'Unless I see you before at the carol service.' Without waiting for a reply, she tottered out of the shop.

Darcie looked across at Millie again, who was sitting laughing with Spencer and his girlfriend. She had hoped that she could have a nice quiet Christmas Day, most of it doing as she pleased in her own little wing of the building, perhaps only popping up for lunch and a bit of telly later. But now she would be expected to endure Ruth's endless digging for information about her life and gossip about everyone else's. Not really her idea of a happy Christmas, but then it wasn't shaping up to be one of those anyway. She checked her watch; closing time was fast approaching and they didn't look close to closing at all. At this rate they wouldn't make it to the carol service, but perhaps that was a small mercy if Ruth was going to be there.

During a brief lull in customers, Darcie dashed out back to find her handbag and fished out her phone. There was one missed call – an unlabelled mobile phone number. It had to be Nathan, and she quickly stored the contact. She stared at it. She could call now, maybe fix something up with him for the next few days. It would get her out, away from temptation, and she would probably have a good time if it was just the two of them, with no crazy ex or wild parties in the mix. She was about to dial it when Dylan's voice came from behind her.

'I've just got Oscar down. Little bugger was desperate for a sleep but he wouldn't drop off. Anyway, have you had a break yet?'

Darcie whizzed around to face him, her cheeks burning.

'What's the matter?' Dylan asked, and then he saw the phone in her hand, Nathan's name in bright letters on the screen. 'Oh, Darcie, please tell me you're not going to call him.'

'I was… I was just thinking I might.'

'What for?'

She shrugged. 'I like him. And I think he meant what he said today.'

'He might have thought he meant it, but that doesn't mean he won't break your heart further down the line.'

Darcie was silent for a moment, and then she locked her phone and put it away.

'Listen,' Dylan said, 'I can't tell you what to do and I don't want to. If you want to see him then of course you should and it's nothing to do with me but… well, I think of you like a little sister, and I don't want to see you get hurt.'

There it was again – the way he saw her was nothing like the way she looked at him. *A little sister.* He couldn't have hurt her more if he'd plunged a bread knife into her chest, and he didn't have a clue he was doing it.

'I know,' she said quietly. 'And I'll be careful.'

Dylan patted her arm. 'I'm sorry if I've come over all dad on you.'

'It's ok.'

'So…' He tilted his head in the direction of the café. 'Are we going to see about kicking some of these reprobates out so we can close? It is Christmas Eve, after all, and I've got presents I still haven't wrapped.'

Chapter Eight

The trees of the churchyard were strung with lights, twinkling fireflies dancing on their bare branches and piercing the gloom. The rich tones of the organ rang out through the frosty night, calling the people of Honeybourne in to celebrate that Christmas had finally arrived. Spencer and Tori picked their way along the snowy path hand in hand, noses frozen and cheeks rosy with the cold. Lewis and Jenny walked ahead in matching Santa hats while the Dempseys brought up the rear looking about as festive as an undertakers' convention. Ruth walked alongside them, trying her best to engage them in a conversation they clearly weren't interested in having, while Jasmine and Rich followed with their triplets; Rich scowling like a sulking toddler over something but Jasmine unconcerned and chatting to Millie and Dylan who had left baby Oscar at home, not wanting to expose him to the biting cold or, indeed, the congregation to his mighty lungs. There was nothing more contrary to the sentiment of 'Silent Night' than the cries of a colicky baby, and once he got started, it was quite possible that nobody would be able to hear it anyway.

At the doors to the church, where the light from within spilled out over the steps, Frank Stephenson was handing out plastic cups filled with mulled wine – a particularly potent recipe to rival his infamous scrumpy – and hot Ribena for the kids, while Tristan the vicar greeted everyone with tones warm enough to melt the snow and a smile on his face bright enough to rival the lights strung across the ancient trees.

Mrs Dempsey grimaced as Frank tried to give her a cup of his brew.

'It's mulled wine,' Spencer said, 'kind of a Christmas tradition at the service – everyone gets a glass to warm the vocal cords up.'

Mrs Dempsey sniffed at it and her top lip curled up like a dog trying to eat a toffee. Spencer glanced at Tori and she gave a tiny shrug.

'Is it alcohol?' Mrs Dempsey asked.

'The clue is kinda in the name,' Tori laughed.

Tori's mother handed the cup back to Frank, who looked so shocked by the action that someone could have prodded him and he'd have fallen backwards.

'We don't drink,' she said, and Frank's eyes – if it were possible – grew even wider.

'How about some of the Ribena?' Spencer asked. 'Blackcurrant juice,' he added at her questioning frown. He could have added that it was what all the children were drinking but he wondered whether that might sound a bit patronising, although he was tempted, if only to make it clear that he thought she was making quite a lot of fuss over nothing. The whole village was trying hard to welcome this couple, and everywhere they went they did nothing to return it. Apart from with Millie, who seemed to be inexplicably golden in their eyes. Spencer made a note to ask her later for some of whatever secret potion she had slipped either them or herself to make that happen, because he didn't see how else she'd pulled it off.

'I'll leave the drink,' she replied, and gave her husband a look that said he would be doing the same whether he liked it or not. She turned to Tristan, who beamed at her with his megawatt smile.

'Welcome!' he boomed. 'It is always wonderful to see new faces at our church.'

'Thank you.' Mrs Dempsey gave the most genuine smile Spencer had seen on her since she arrived. 'I'm looking forward to the evening.'

'I am glad.' He shook her hand, and then reached for Mr Dempsey to shake his. Then he turned to Tori and Spencer. 'So, from the accent I must deduce that this is your lovely daughter and her boyfriend. Did you manage to warm up after being out in the snow earlier?'

Mrs Dempsey looked at them both sharply, and Spencer had the distinct feeling he was about to get his bottom spanked – and not in a kinky way. At the very least it would be bed with no supper.

'We took a walk around here this morning,' Tori said. 'We had a few things to discuss.'

Tristan nodded and tapped a finger on the side of his nose. 'Don't forget to come and see me when you've decided.'

Mrs Dempsey now looked at Tori so intently that she might have been trying to extract from her daughter's mind the contents of said discussion with the vicar through sheer willpower. But Tori simply smiled sweetly.

'We will,' she said.

Tristan treated them to one last incredible smile and then he turned his full beam onto Jenny and Lewis, who stopped for a short chat as Spencer went with the others to find a seat.

'We'd better save a couple of seats for Mum and Dad,' he said, not really convinced that it was the best idea for them to sit together but knowing he didn't have a lot of choice.

'What's eating them?' Tori whispered as Jasmine and Rich sat in the row of seats across the aisle, not speaking to each other and clearly not their usual selves.

'They do that from time to time,' Spencer said carefully.

Tori gave them another look, and then seemed to think better of pursuing the conversation. Instead, she turned to her parents. 'Isn't it just the most adorable place?' she asked, glancing around at the stone pillars, lanterns throwing flickering shadows across the intricate figures and patterns carved into them, the stained glass windows dulled by the night sky but no less beautiful, and the tiny choir of village children (and some borrowed from neighbouring parishes to make up the numbers) ready and waiting in their crisp white robes, their faces expectant. The scene was lifted straight from a Christmas card, and if people hadn't been feeling festive before, even the most hardened humbug couldn't fail to get in the mood being here.

'It's cold,' Mrs Dempsey said. 'Don't they have heating in England?'

'It's a huge stone building, Mom. The doors are still open too. It'll be better when we get started.'

'And the roof has never been without holes since I was a boy,' Spencer put in amiably. 'So it's bound to lose a lot of heat.'

Mrs Dempsey didn't smile or laugh or even acknowledge the joke. She just rubbed her hands together and eyed up the rest of the congregation.

'It must be real old,' Mr Dempsey said.

'I think you said it was Norman, didn't you?' Tori turned to Spencer, who nodded.

'Norman?' Mr Dempsey said. 'What's that, about two hundred years?'

Tori giggled. 'Daddy! You're not great on English history, are you? But if we're going to be part of an English family then maybe we all ought to learn some.'

'I know about the Constitution and the Bill of Rights and that's all I need to know,' he smiled. 'But if your Spencer wants to give us a little history lesson later I'll be all ears.'

Spencer smiled broadly. It was the first real encouragement he'd had from either of the Dempseys. Maybe he was making more head-way than he thought. Though when he looked across at Tori's mother again he wasn't quite so sure of that after all. She looked as though a history lesson from him was the last thing she wanted, unless it ended with a real-life demonstration of the guillotine with him as the victim.

'I'd be happy to,' he said. 'I'm no authority but I know a little. Maybe, before you go home, I could take you for a drive – see some sights? Stonehenge isn't too far away and that's always impressive.'

'That sounds great.' Mr Dempsey leaned across to his wife and touched her on the arm. 'Wouldn't that be great, honey?'

'Yes,' she replied stiffly, although Spencer suspected that she'd rather boil her own head than go out sightseeing with him. But at least it was progress of sorts and he'd take it where he could.

Lewis and Jenny made their way down the aisle, and Spencer waved them over to the seat he had saved next to him.

'Tristan is lovely,' Jenny said looking quite star-struck. 'I might have been tempted to find God if he'd been holding up the signpost.'

Tori laughed. 'You're so funny.'

Lewis patted Jenny's hand. 'You're far too sensible to find God.'

'What does that mean?' Mrs Dempsey asked sharply.

Spencer sensed the sea change in the atmosphere, and suddenly, the church wasn't the only thing that was cold.

Lewis waved a careless hand. 'Don't pay any attention to me,' he laughed. 'I'm a grizzled old scientist and it's hard to fit the notion of an omnipotent, omnipresent being in with scientific theories. I'm sure it works out just fine for people who want to believe, but for me... well, I find it difficult to swallow.'

'But you're here now,' Mrs Dempsey replied, 'in the house of the Lord.'

'We're here now because it's a village tradition which we happen to enjoy. It's a way of being closer to the community as a whole, at least once a year – or a lot longer for us as we haven't been back in a while...' He glanced at Spencer. 'And we're also here for our son, who asked us to come.'

'And look – we're almost ready to begin I think!' Spencer said with forced brightness, desperately trying to steer the conversation away from dangerous waters.

Tori gripped his hand and gave it a reassuring squeeze. He returned it with a helpless look. They had already arranged to take the parents out to a Chinese restaurant on the Winchester road later that evening in the hope that a relaxed atmosphere and good food would get them talking in a friendlier way, but if things were strained this early in the night, it was going to be a tough few hours. It was almost as if they were all actively putting up barriers so that they didn't get along, even if they did have some common ground, which Spencer reasoned must exist somewhere. After all, they were four well-educated westerners whose children happened to be engaged to one another – if they couldn't find anything in common from all that then the venture was truly doomed. It was beginning to irk him somewhat that none of them seemed interested in trying. The Dempseys were downright frosty, despite Tori having made it clear that she would be

marrying Spencer and not Hunter bloody Ford, but his own parents
– jovial and bohemian as they appeared to be – were doing a pretty
good job of rubbing Tori's up the wrong way, and even they couldn't
be so obtuse not to realise when to air their opinions and when to
keep them close for the sake of a little harmony. At some point he was
going to have to take his mum and dad aside and have a good talk to
them, and Tori would have to do the same with her parents; it was the
only solution if things didn't improve. But that was going to be very
difficult with Christmas Day just around the corner, and with all the
distractions that day would bring, and he had a horrible feeling things
might blow up before then.

Tristan made his way to the front of the congregation, his joyous
expression never faltering, as if simply breathing made him deliri-
ously happy. It probably did, Spencer thought, because he didn't have
two warring sets of parents at his side and very likely would be going
home to his snug little vicarage at the end of the night to sit with his
lovely wife, a hot toddy and perhaps a cute dog or two. And Christmas was the time when he was more popular than he would be all
year. Christmas Eve for him was probably like the last day of term
for Spencer when everyone – kids and teachers alike – shared excited
anticipation for the summer break to come.

He said a few words of welcome and smiled directly at Jenny in a
way that made her as flustered as Spencer had ever seen her – flicking
her hair back and almost panting. It was oddly disconcerting to see
one's mother flirt with a vicar in such an obvious way, and Spencer
was wishing he could switch some sort of filter on in his brain so it
wouldn't appear quite so obvious to him. He glanced at his dad. If
Lewis was worried he certainly didn't show it, watching proceedings
with a mildly entertained expression. In fact, he seemed almost as

much in awe of the charismatic new vicar as his wife was, only without the hair flicking and drooling. And then everyone stood, and the church echoed with the voices of choir and congregation alike in a heartfelt rendition of 'Away in a Manger'.

Tori's hand remained clasped in Spencer's, and as the music filled him, he could feel it lifting his mood. He looked down at her and smiled. If they stuck together, they could weather any storm, he was sure. He just needed to know that she was willing to go the distance too, no matter what came their way.

Oscar was finally dozing in Darcie's arms. Millie had been reluctant to leave them at first, and though Darcie had insisted she was capable, it had taken Dylan's persuasion to make Millie agree to go to the carol service without her baby. Oscar had been cranky for a while, but Darcie had found she had surprising patience with him and his crying didn't bother her as much as usual. Perhaps it was because he wasn't her child that she could stay detached enough not to get stressed by it. Whatever the reason, she had fed him with the milk Millie had left and walked the floor of the bedroom with him until his eyes had started to droop.

She laid him in his cot as carefully as she could and covered him with his fleece blanket. After switching the baby monitor on she tiptoed downstairs to look for her phone.

There was already a text from Nathan. She had messaged him as soon as Dylan and Millie had left to say that she was willing to give things another go, and it hadn't taken him long to reply.

I'm glad. I won't mess up again, promise.'

'We could meet after Christmas.'

'Great. I know a good pub.'

'No pubs. Somewhere quiet?'

'Ok. You like Thai food?'

'Never had it.'

'You're in for a treat then!'

Darcie smiled at the phone. Maybe she could give him a quick call while Oscar was quiet and while she had the place to herself. She was an adult, and she could call or see whoever she liked, but she still felt strangely guilty about the idea that she had ignored Dylan's warnings over Nathan. She was about to dial the number when there was a crash from outside. Darcie's head flicked up, and she ran to the front window of the café to investigate.

The street outside was blanketed in fresh snow, the streetlights giving it a strange orange glow, but it was deserted. Most of the village was at the church for the service, though Darcie hadn't fancied it and had been only too happy to use Oscar as an excuse to stay home. Despite her months at the bakery, she still didn't really feel a part of Honeybourne; she didn't fit in the way Millie now did. She wondered if she was just too shy to make friends, not that the pool of prospective friends her own age was very big anyway in such a small village, and without that it would always be hard to make the leap from outsider to someone who was accepted as part of the community.

Still perturbed and more than a little rattled by the noise, she went through to the back of the building. The tiny yard was swathed in velvet blackness and when she pressed her face to the glass to get a better look she still couldn't see anything but the faint outline of the metal bins. She could unlock the door and go out, but Oscar was asleep upstairs and she was home alone; the idea of going out to investigate when there was no help or protection in the house was not an appealing one. Maybe it was a fox or some other curious scavenger, but if it was something else, Darcie wouldn't be able to do much to fend it off. Perhaps the best policy was to stay in and mention it to Dylan when he got home.

But then she heard another noise – something bumping against the back door – and this time she was gripped by panic. Her thoughts went to Oscar. If anyone got in, if anything happened to Millie's baby, she would never forgive herself. Shaking, she raced back to where she had left her phone and dialled Dylan's number. It went straight to voicemail. He must have turned it off for church. Next she dialled Millie's number, certain that Millie would never switch hers off when she might be needed for Oscar, but although it rang out for a while, Millie didn't pick up.

Darcie went through to the back door again and leaned her ear against it, listening hard. All was silent now, but she felt certain, in a way she couldn't explain, that someone was out there. It was cold and it was Christmas Eve. Would a burglar be out on a night like this? Didn't burglars have nights off at Christmas too? And why would they be snooping around so early in the evening? Unless… Unless they thought everyone would be at the carol service…

And then the thought struck her. Nathan knew where she lived – maybe he had hopped on a bus hoping to surprise her? She unlocked her phone.

'This might sound silly, but are you here?'

'Weird. Why do you ask?'

'No reason. Just asking.'

'No, stuck at home with the parents. Wrapping a mountain of presents. Do you want me to be there?'

'Better not, I'm babysitting and my cousin will be back soon.'

'With her huge scary boyfriend?'

'Dylan? Is he scary?'

'He is if you're me.'

Darcie couldn't help but smile. She supposed Dylan had come over a bit heavy earlier that day, but she knew why and that made her smile a little wider still.

'I'll call you on Boxing Day. Maybe we can meet up. Happy Christmas.'

'Great! Back at ya!'

Darcie locked her phone. So Nathan wasn't lurking outside. Perhaps she was overreacting. It sounded quiet enough now, and there were a lot of foxes around these parts, probably finding it hard to track food because it was so cold and snowy. Though she was pretty sure that Dylan had taken all the rubbish to a nearby tip in anticipation of the bins being filled to the brim again over Christmas, so she wasn't sure what a poor hungry fox would find out there. She wasn't about to open the door to find out, and she had just decided to switch the lights out and ignore whatever was out there in the hope it would go away when a face appeared at the window.

Chapter Nine

'Spencer!' Millie called as he and Tori left the church. 'Wait a second!'

Spencer turned and smiled. 'I wasn't going to go without saying Merry Christmas.'

Millie followed him out of the doors, Dylan close behind. 'I know, I just wanted to ask you something. About Christmas lunch tomorrow.'

'I'd invite you but...' He lowered his voice with a grin. 'My mum's cooking is terrible and we can't tell her that so we're going to have to eat it anyway. I wouldn't subject you to that.'

'Don't be daft!' Millie laughed. 'I was actually going to invite you to ours. Ruth is coming, and I don't think Darcie is all that happy, so I figured lots of people around the table will help distract her. We'll have tons of room as we're going to push some of the tables together in the café and eat there. It might take some of the pressure off you and Tori too – I presume you're having both sets of parents over to yours? I mean, you can say no, of course, but it was just a suggestion that I thought of earlier... I couldn't help overhearing that they weren't exactly getting on like a house on fire.'

'You could say that,' Spencer replied. 'It's lovely of you to offer but isn't it a bit late to get more supplies?'

'We've got tons. Dylan bought a turkey at the same time as I did without either of us realising the other was getting it! And I expect you've got extra you could bring over in the morning? Please say yes – I think Darcie would really like to have a few more people around; I think she gets fed up sometimes with just me and Dylan.'

'Surely she can't get fed up with having me around,' Dylan said with a wide grin. 'I mean, is that a thing you have to take tablets for or something?'

Spencer put a hand on his shoulder. 'I can imagine how that's a difficult concept to grasp, mate. It must be so hard being awesome day and night.'

Dylan shook his head dramatically. 'Nobody can know my pain…'

Millie nudged him. 'Don't encourage him, Spencer, he's bad enough as it is.'

Spencer looked at Tori. 'What do you think?'

'I think it sounds like a great idea. We can spend Christmas morning together, and if Millie and Dylan are ok with it, we can go over to their place in the afternoon. I think my parents really enjoyed their time at the bakery and I'm sure they'd love to be your guests for dinner.'

'Do you want to run it by them?' Millie asked, scanning the crowds now spilling from the church. 'Where are they anyway?'

'I think my mom and dad are looking at the windows.'

Millie raised her eyebrows in a silent question and Tori smiled. 'Long story, but Spencer has stirred up some curiosity about old buildings that I never knew they had before. I think this is pretty much the oldest building they've ever been in.'

'My parents are chatting up the new vicar,' Spencer said. 'At least, Mum is, and Dad is there as backup to prevent his escape. I expect they'll be out in a couple of minutes so we can ask then.'

Millie checked her watch. 'We should get back,' she said to Dylan. She turned to Spencer. 'How about you let me know when you've checked with them and we can make some arrangements?'

'Sounds great,' Spencer said. 'Thank you... You know, for...'

'I know,' Millie smiled. 'A friend in need and all that. You'd do the same for me.'

'See you later,' Dylan said, nodding at them both before he and Millie set off down the path and into the night.

Spencer looked at Tori. 'If they ever get out of this church, do you still want to go and hit that Chinese restaurant?'

'Sure!' Tori smiled. 'For egg foo yung I'll drag them out of the church myself!'

Darcie hadn't realised she was holding her breath until she started to feel dizzy. She let it out and stared at the window. As quickly as it had appeared, the face had gone again, but she wasn't going mad – she had definitely seen it and it wasn't Nathan. Her heart thudded through her chest as she watched and waited, hardly daring to move. She needed to get help... She needed to grab something to defend herself should the man try to get in... She needed to protect Oscar... But she could do none of these things because her limbs refused to move. Instead, she stood clutching her phone and staring at the window in the darkened room, dreading to see the face again but needing to know if it was really there at all.

The sound of the key in the lock at the front of the bakery had her spinning around so fast she nearly lost her footing. She dashed into the main room, half expecting to see some stranger wielding a knife and coming to kill her.

'Darcie?' Millie asked in a tense voice. 'I've just seen your missed call, is everything alright?'

Darcie flung herself into Dylan's arms. 'There's someone outside!'

Dylan held her at arm's length. 'What do you mean there's someone outside?' he asked with a stony expression. 'Where outside? Trying to get in? Did they hurt you?'

Darcie shook her head. 'I saw someone out in the backyard. A face in the window, just for a second, but I know they were there.'

Dylan shot Millie a determined look. 'I'll go and check it out.'

'No!' Millie cried. 'What if he's armed? What if it's someone who's unstable?'

'He won't be stable when I've finished with him.' Dylan strode off to a cupboard and pulled out a broom.

Millie chased him and grabbed his arm. 'I can't let you go out there – Darcie, call the police.'

'I can deal with this!' Dylan said. 'There's no need to get the police and they won't thank us for coming all this way if it turns out to be a false alarm. At least let me check out there first.' He put a gentle hand on Millie's arm. 'I'll be fine. You worry too much.'

'Only because I love you.'

'I love you too.' He kissed her lightly on the head and headed for the back of the bakery. Darcie and Millie stood and watched with wide eyes.

The back door was opened, and then there was a scuffle, followed by shouting. A few moments later Dylan was dragging a young man in. He sat him on a chair and loomed over him.

'You don't move until I say so… Darcie, *now* you can call the police.'

'Wait!' the man cried. 'Please… I'm sorry, I didn't mean to startle you. I'm just… I was freezing out there. I wanted to get a quick warm, that was all, so I didn't freeze to death. I'll be on my way now, I swear, and you'll never see me again.'

'Too late, buddy, I've seen you this time and you don't get another chance to terrorise my family.'

'I wasn't trying to – I swear! I was hoping… It doesn't matter. Please, let me go.'

Darcie looked at him. He was young – perhaps late teens or early twenties, with black hair and dark skin, and he was in full army gear. Weren't there army bases nearby? She was certain she'd passed at least two on the roads that led into the village since she'd arrived in Honeybourne. What was most striking – more than how young and vulnerable he looked, more than the deep brown eyes that pleaded for mercy in a way that could only be genuine, and the way he was shivering with the cold – was that he looked terrified and very, very lost. It was the look of someone who was not only lost geographically, but in life, and she knew it because it was what she saw in the mirror every day.

'Why do you have an army uniform on?' she asked quietly.

Dylan and Millie stared at her.

'It's not such a strange question,' Darcie said with a slight shrug.

'No,' Millie said thoughtfully. 'I didn't think it was. It's a very good question.' She turned to the man. 'Why are you in uniform?'

Dylan folded his arms, the broom handle tucked inside them. 'Larkhill or Tidworth?' he asked the man, who swallowed hard.

'I'm already in so much trouble,' he replied. 'Please, just let me go… I'll disappear.'

'I can't do that,' Dylan said. 'Wherever it is you've run from you have to go back. You know that as well as I do.'

'Where has he run from?' Millie asked, looking from one to the other with a puzzled expression.

'AWOL,' Dylan said. He looked at the man. 'I'm right, aren't I?'

'What does that mean?' Darcie asked.

'It means…' Dylan turned to her, 'that he's on the run from one of the army camps. Absent without leave.' His attention went back to the man. 'What's your name?'

'Tariq.'

'And the rest…'

Tariq shook his head. 'You'll phone the base and the ARWO will come for me.'

Dylan frowned in confusion.

'The recovery officer,' Tariq said.

'Right. That's exactly what I'm going to do. You can't stay here and I can't let you go terrorising the rest of the village.'

'I wasn't trying to terrorise anyone. I just wanted ten minutes to warm up and I would have been gone… I wasn't to know there was a young woman in the house on her own, and I'm sorry for that. Let me go and I'll be on my way.'

'To where?'

He shrugged.

'Don't you have family you can call?' Millie asked.

'They'd be ashamed of me,' Tariq said. 'And they'd be right to, because what I'm doing is cowardly and shameful, but I can't help the way I feel.'

'Have you spoken to any of your friends about this? A commanding officer perhaps? If there's some emotional issue, there must be help available?' Millie glanced at Dylan who nodded agreement.

'There's nobody I can talk to,' Tariq said. 'I'm not like the others – I'm an outsider. They don't trust me. I can see it in their eyes.'

'Why would you say that?'

He studied his hands as he knotted them together. 'You only have to look at me to see why.'

'I don't see anything except a man who needs help,' Millie said gently.

Tariq looked up and held her gaze. 'I'm also a Pakistani Muslim,' he said. 'I'm not ashamed of my religion or my background but the other soldiers… They don't treat me the same as their friends. They laugh and I'm not included in the joke. They share secrets with each other but they don't share them with me. I see them watching me when they think I'm not looking and all I see in their eyes is distrust. I joined the British Army because I wanted to serve my country, the place I've grown up, but it seems that same army thinks I can't have allegiance to more than one home.'

'I can't imagine everyone views you that way. Have you tried talking to someone about it? Maybe even the people you think are doing this to you?' Millie asked.

'And running away isn't going to solve anything,' Dylan added.

'Have you ever served in the forces?' Tariq asked him.

'No.'

'Then you can't understand.'

'You're right. But I do know that burying your head in the sand is not the answer. You will get taken back, whether it's here and now or a few days down the line. I would imagine that going back sooner of your own accord and telling your superiors what you've told us will go a long way to them understanding your concerns and being more lenient in their dealings with you.'

'I don't want to go back.'

'Then why don't you leave for good? Tell them you're quitting the army?' Darcie asked.

'I can't do that either. It would bring shame on me and my family.'

Dylan let out a breath and pulled a chair from a table to sit in front of Tariq. 'Well, if you don't want to be there and you don't want to leave, you're on a pretty sticky wicket.'

'How long have you been missing?' Millie asked.

'A few hours,' Tariq said.

'So they might not have realised anything's wrong yet?' she pressed.

'Someone will have noticed by now.'

She paused. 'Would you like a hot drink? It might make you feel better? And I expect you're hungry too.'

Tariq gave a tiny nod, but Dylan looked sharply at Millie.

'It's just a cup of tea,' she said. 'Maybe a leftover cake. It's not like we don't have any of those.'

She made her way to the kitchens and Dylan leapt up to follow her. 'Don't move!' he ordered Tariq as he went.

'Don't be afraid,' Tariq said to Darcie. 'I'm not moving, because he's right… There is nowhere for me to go. Even if I wanted to go home they're hundreds of miles away from here and I have hardly any money with me.'

'Where are they?'

'Yorkshire.'

Darcie was thoughtful for a moment. 'Why *did* you run away? Millie is right – you could have gone and talked to someone. They must have counsellors and stuff for soldiers. You must have at least one friend there you could confide in?'

'Nobody. I don't know why, I just haven't ever seemed to fit in. And approaching a counsellor… Well, they just think you're a wimp then, that you can't hack it. Then today I just felt as if I would explode if I stayed there any longer, and before I knew what I was doing I was running.'

'And then you ended up here.'

'Yes. What are you going to do?'

'Dylan and Millie are good people. Dylan is just protecting his family but I think he's listening and I think he has sympathy for you. The problem is that it puts us in an awkward position. We have to do something.'

'You could pretend you've never seen me.'

'We could, but I don't think that would sit well with any of us, and not because of stupid laws or anything, but because we would worry about you – where you were, what you were doing, if you were safe or in danger.'

Tariq nodded. 'I understand.'

'If you go back...' Darcie paused. She didn't want to ask the next question, but she couldn't get it from her mind and she knew it wouldn't leave her alone until she did. 'You wouldn't do anything silly, would you?'

'I wouldn't kill myself if that's what you mean.'

'Only... Well, you seem...'

'Crazy?' he finished for her.

'I wasn't going to say that. I'm not sure what I was going to say but I don't think you're crazy.'

'Maybe I am. I must be for doing something as stupid as running.' He sighed. 'Maybe your Dylan is right... I should go back and face the music.'

Darcie looked out of the window. It was snowing again, fat flakes backlit by the street lamps. 'I don't know if it's a good idea tonight, though.'

Millie and Dylan returned. Dylan threw a black look in the direction of Tariq as Millie placed a small teapot, milk and sugar on the table next to him. It was clear they'd been arguing and it didn't take a genius to guess that they had very different opinions on what to do with their unexpected guest.

'Thank you,' Tariq said as he poured some tea into the cup.

'Do you want something to eat?' Millie asked.

He shook his head.

'You must be hungry,' Millie insisted.

He smiled thinly. 'It must be the stress, but I'm not hungry at all.'

'Sit with us for a while,' Millie said. 'We won't make you go anywhere just now. When you've warmed up and had a hot drink, you might feel more able to make a decision.'

'There's no decision to make,' Dylan cut in. 'You have to go back so I don't see the point in delaying the inevitable.'

'He doesn't have to go back until he's ready,' Millie said, shooting a defiant look at Dylan. 'There's no reason he can't pull himself together first, and I thought we had just agreed on that.'

'I never agreed to anything,' Dylan began, but Tariq got to his feet.

'I don't want to cause an argument. You've been more than kind to me and I'll leave now.'

'No,' Dylan said, but Millie interrupted.

'Please, what my boyfriend means is that you are free to go if you want to, but we want to help you. So if you'd like to stay and finish your tea, maybe talk about things for a while, you might decide to return to the barracks of your own free will and you might walk back in there with your soul a little lighter.'

Darcie gave Tariq an encouraging smile. Millie always did have a way with words and a gift for making people feel at ease. Darcie often thought that if Millie ran the world, it would be a pretty nice place. Tariq seemed to think so too, sitting down again and offering a nervous smile of gratitude.

'I don't know about returning, but my soul is already a little lighter with the kindness you've shown me tonight,' he said.

'I'm glad to hear it,' Millie replied. Dylan simply grunted and sat on a nearby chair, broom handle slung across his knees as he watched Tariq closely.

'Maybe you would feel better if you slept on it?' Darcie asked. 'I know I always do.'

'Here?' Dylan asked, stiffening in his seat.

Darcie realised her mistake immediately. This wasn't her home and it wasn't her place to make offers like that, even though it was probably what she would have done.

'I'm sorry,' she said quickly. 'Maybe there's room at the Dog and Hare?'

Dylan shook his head. 'Best not to involve anyone else if we can help it.'

'Would we get in trouble for having you here?' Darcie asked Tariq.

He gave his head an uncertain nod. 'I'm not sure. Possibly. But if I were to go now nobody need know I was ever here.'

Dylan's tone softened as he looked at him thoughtfully. 'You know it's better for you in the long run if you go back tonight? Let me drive you – it's not that far.'

'You'd do that for me?' Tariq asked.

'Why not?'

Millie glanced at the window. 'I don't think it's a very good idea in this snow. Can't we call your barracks to send a vehicle out?'

'But then they would know you were involved,' Tariq replied.

'Yes, but we'd also be returning you,' Millie reminded him.

He shook his head. 'I'll return the way I came.'

'Walking? In this?' Darcie asked, following Millie's gaze back to the window.

He smiled faintly. 'I'm a soldier – I'm trained to survive.'

'But you're not Captain America,' Dylan replied. 'It's a bit late to be noble now you're here. You may as well let us help, and if it means you going back then I'm all for helping… Not because I want to get rid of you,' he added turning to Millie with a look to thwart any argument, 'but because we all know it's the right thing to do.'

Tariq inclined his head slowly as he let out a long breath. 'Ok,' he said. 'I'm ready when you are.'

Millie looked at the window again and then at Dylan. 'Can I have a word… in the kitchen?'

Dylan nodded and glanced at Darcie.

'We'll be fine,' she said, understanding his silent question. 'I'll call if I need you.'

Millie went out and Dylan followed.

'He still doesn't trust me,' Tariq said. 'That's the same look I get from the other soldiers.'

'It's not you he doesn't trust, he's just protecting his home. See it from his point of view – you were snooping around in the middle of the night and he has two women living here with a baby sleeping upstairs. I think you'd react the same if it was the other way around. I think most people would.'

Tariq's gaze went to his feet. 'I'm sorry for scaring you.'

'It's alright. I know you didn't mean to, and being on my own makes me jumpier than I would usually be.'

'I suppose anyone would be jumpy if a strange man was hanging around the place. No wonder Dylan is angry with me.'

'He's not angry, and you're not *that* strange.'

'Thank you,' Tariq said, and for the first time he returned her smile with one of his own, and the warmth and goodness of his soul shone from the depths of his dark eyes.

Something switched on inside Darcie, and as she looked at him her heart seemed to beat that little bit faster. She felt a strange pull towards him, but not in the way she felt pulled towards Nathan; it was a deep, inexplicable wrench that came from a place she had no control over.

'I suppose you'll be in big trouble,' she said.

'I don't honestly know. Maybe they'll be lenient because I've gone straight back. I suppose I'll have to try and explain the best I can and hope they understand.'

'Will you be punished?'

'I expect so.'

'They'll ban you from having days off maybe? Official ones, I mean.'

'I'm not sure. It wouldn't be much of a punishment anyway – when I do have days off I don't do a lot with them, not unless I go home and I can't do that at the moment.'

'Oh, I didn't mean that,' Darcie said. 'I meant...'

'If I did get a day off, maybe I could come and see you?' he asked, seeming to read her thoughts.

She blushed. 'If you didn't have anything else to do. Although I'd understand if you didn't want to or you didn't have time—'

'I'd really like to,' he said. 'In better circumstances than this too, I hope.'

'Me too,' she said. 'I'd love that.' Her mind went back to the decision she'd made to go home after Christmas. Maybe there was a reason to stay for a while after all.

The moment was broken by the bleeping of her phone from the table. She didn't have to check it to know who it was, and then she remembered that she had already made arrangements to see Nathan again. How could she forget him? And what kind of person was she to forget him as soon as Tariq appeared? But where she had felt Nathan was someone perhaps worth taking a chance on, she felt more certain of Tariq, and she was sure that giving her heart to him would be a safer place for it. She could be terribly wrong, of course, but the conviction was there all the same.

Dylan and Millie returned to the room. Dylan looked at Tariq. 'Ready to go?'

Darcie watched as Millie folded her arms and pursed her lips. It was clear she wasn't happy about the arrangement and that she was allowing Dylan to take Tariq back under duress, so whatever argument they'd had in the kitchen, she'd lost.

Tariq rose from his chair.

'Wait!' Darcie said suddenly. She ran to the counter, pulling a notepad and pen from a drawer. A few seconds later she ran to Tariq and handed him a sheet of paper. 'You don't have to feel alone. If you ever want to talk, well…' She blushed again. 'That's my phone number.'

He took the page with a smile. Darcie glanced across at Millie to see her exchange a half-amused look with Dylan, who didn't seem nearly so entertained. If he had disapproved of Nathan, he was probably going to have major issues with Tariq but, for the first time ever, she didn't really care what Dylan thought.

'Thank you, again,' Tariq said, looking from Darcie to Millie.

Dylan went over and touched his arm to lead him out. He turned to Millie. 'Lock up when we've gone and don't let anyone in. I have my keys.'

'How long will you be?' Millie asked.

Dylan glanced at the snowy window. 'I'll be as quick as I can be. I don't want to stay out in this any longer than I have to. And I *still* have that bloody Christmas wrapping to do.'

'That's what comes of leaving things to the last-minute,' Millie said with a faint smile.

'You know me – it's the only way I know how to do things. See you later.'

'Be careful,' Millie said.

He nodded. And then they were gone.

'Tori! Let them go if they want to…' Spencer reached for her arm as she stood to follow her parents to the cab waiting outside the restaurant. She spun around to face him.

'I'm leaving with them because you need to talk to your parents about acceptable boundaries,' she hissed. 'My folks are trying their best but yours aren't doing a damn thing to get along!'

'But—'

'No, Spencer! I've had enough!'

Spencer's arm dropped to his side. 'So *we're* in the wrong again? Figures…'

'What does that mean?'

'Your parents are narrow-minded snobs. If they can't even enter into an intelligent discussion where opinions different than theirs are aired without getting upset, then they must be. Why do your parents get to have the only opinion that matters?'

'My parents don't insult people when they express their opinions!'

'Neither do mine!'

'Lewis called my dad a misguided fool! How is that not an insult?'

Spencer raised his hands in a gesture of surrender. 'Ok. Maybe he got a bit emotional at that point, but your dad drove him to that, being so pig-headed about everything. He might as well have stuck his fingers in his ears and started singing!'

'Spencer,' Tori said, lowering her voice and glancing around at the packed restaurant. It was decorated with sumptuous red and gold and strung with paper lanterns, a tiny Christmas tree perched on the bar the only concession to the season, 'people are starting to stare at us. I don't want a scene, I just want to go back to the Dog and Hare with my mom and dad.'

'And not come back to my house?' Spencer asked.

Tori paused. 'I have a lot of thinking to do.'

'About us?'

She sighed. 'Maybe this is just more difficult than we thought – you and me. There's so much against us and right now it feels like too much.'

'We never thought it was going to be easy.'

'But it shouldn't have to feel like a war.'

'I love you! You love me, right?'

'You know I do.'

'Then shouldn't that be enough?'

'No, Spencer, it isn't. Love is never enough because sooner or later the love takes a back seat and you have to think about rent and your job and how you raise your kids. Love will take you so far but it's not enough.'

'You're saying there's no future with me?'

'I'm saying I need to think.' A car horn sounded from outside. 'I have to go.'

'You can't just leave without talking this through!'

'I can and I am. Right now.'

'Tori!'

'Spencer, stop. This is not the time or place.'

'It bloody well is! We need to talk and I won't let you go until we do!'

She held him in a stony gaze. 'You want to talk? Why don't you go and find Jasmine?'

'What? Now you're being ridiculous!'

'No more than you.'

'I thought we'd cleared up the Jasmine thing.'

'Me too. But maybe it's just a symptom of a dying relationship we ought to be taking more notice of.'

'Tori, please... I don't want you to go – not like this!'

She was silent for a moment, and he wondered if she might relent. But then she reached up and placed a brief kiss on his cheek. 'Good-bye, Spencer.'

He watched as she pushed open the glass doors of the restaurant and disappeared into the night. Something had broken, and this time it felt unfixable. If he had stopped her from leaving the restaurant, maybe he could have saved what they had. But his stupid pride had got in the way and now all felt lost, as if letting her leave had fired her so far from his orbit that they would never be right again. She would go back to the Dog and Hare and she would talk to her parents, and she would decide not to come back to his house that night. It was only a small step from that to never coming back at all. She would fly back to Colorado with her parents instead of him and then she would be gone.

He turned and made his way back to the table, where his parents silently watched him. Perhaps Tori was right – perhaps they were too different to ever make it work and had been foolish to think otherwise.

'We're sorry,' Jenny said as he sat down.

'It's not your fault,' Spencer said wearily.

Jenny exchanged a shamefaced look with her husband. 'We could go and talk to them,' she said. 'Clear the air.'

Spencer shook his head. 'I don't think that's such a good idea tonight. I'm not sure it's a good idea any night... Mum, I sometimes wonder if Tori and I... well, if I've been just a bit too optimistic about our chances together. I mean, straight off the bat there are more barriers than most couples have to get over and that's without all the small stuff that can destroy a marriage.'

'Is that really how you feel?' Lewis asked.

Spencer shrugged. He didn't know what to say, because the only thing he felt right now was numb and defeated, and he couldn't see a way out of the mess he was creating.

'If it is then you need to think carefully about what you're doing. You've already proposed, but going through with it... that's not a decision you can take lightly and if you have doubts now—'

'Not about whether I love her, Dad,' Spencer cut in.

'*Any* kind of doubts,' Lewis continued.

'It hasn't helped that you don't get on with her parents,' Spencer muttered.

'We get on with them just fine.'

'You could make an effort to—'

'Agree with their stupid opinions even though we don't share them? Smile and nod at the ridiculous things they say?'

'Other people do it all the time. It's called keeping the peace.'

'It's how dictatorships begin,' Jenny said. Spencer faced her.

'Seriously, Mum? You're actually saying that with a straight face? Can you stop being a politics-obsessed academic and be my mum just for one minute of your life? They're my prospective in-laws, not Joseph Stalin!'

'I don't see them making an effort.' Lewis prodded his leftovers with a fork.

'Then you be the bigger man and make the effort,' Spencer said. 'Would it kill you?'

'How has a conversation about your doubts become one about our culpability?' Jenny asked.

'Because you're not exactly making things easier for us! I didn't have these doubts before this week!'

Jenny raised her eyebrows. 'Really? Because I hear something much deeper than just parental differences. Maybe it's the differences between you and Tori that are really bothering you, and the differences between us just serve to remind you of that.'

'This is ridiculous.' Spencer scanned the restaurant, looking for a waiter to bring their bill. He needed to get back to Honeybourne and talk to Tori. He hadn't wanted to blame his mum and dad for any of this, but they were making it very tempting right now. They were entitled to express their opinions and he would defend that right until the last, but he couldn't help feeling that they were going out of their way to wind up the Dempseys when they could just as easily retreat for his sake. It was as if they wanted him and Tori to split up. He could understand it coming from the Dempseys, who had always dreamed of some successful, handsome, white-toothed, hotshot lawyer for their daughter instead of a slightly weedy teacher from England – but from his own parents, who professed to like Tori and ought to be going out of their way to ensure their only son's happiness? He just wanted to escape to the quiet of his own home and lock himself away for an hour to sort his head out and decide what he was going to do next. And perhaps it would be good to talk it through with someone impartial, someone who always said the right thing and whose solutions made perfect sense. Millie. It was always Millie who made things right, and he just hoped he could rely on her this time because he was running out of ideas.

Darcie watched as Millie paced the floor. She looked at the phone clasped in her hand yet again and then turned her gaze to the window, where the snow cascaded from the sky in heavy flakes.

'Of all the times for his phone to be off, it has to be tonight,' she muttered. 'Why the hell would he have his phone off?'

'He'll be back soon,' Darcie replied, not at all certain of her prediction but feeling the need to say something soothing. Oscar snuffled in her arms. She'd just got him back to sleep, but it was an uneasy slumber and she didn't expect it to last long. Millie certainly didn't have the patience to deal with one of his screaming fits right now so Darcie had kept hold of him, thinking that he was likely to be at least a little calmer with her if he did wake.

'I told him not to go,' Millie said. 'He's always so stupid and stubborn about these things.'

'He was just trying to be kind. He's a good person and he wanted to help Tariq.'

'What if he's stuck in the snow? What if he freezes to death out there?'

'I don't think it's bad enough for that,' Darcie replied, not feeling the conviction of this argument either.

'What did he think was going to happen when they got there? Did he think he could sneak Tariq under the fence and nobody would know he'd been gone? What if Dylan's being questioned by army officers? What if he's in trouble for taking him back?'

'I don't see how he could be in trouble for that – he did a good thing.'

'But they might get him for aiding and abetting.'

'Millie…' Darcie swept a soothing finger along Oscar's cheek as he stirred. 'Nobody's been murdered. I don't think Dylan will be in trouble for driving him back. Maybe we would have been if we'd let him stay and he'd been found here—'

'I don't like not being able to get hold of him, it's driving me mad.'

'I know. How about we call someone else to see if they can get through to his phone? Maybe it's just your network?'

'Good idea.' Millie pulled out her phone and scrolled down the list of contacts. She held the handset to her ear and waited. 'Jasmine,' she said after a pause, 'you haven't heard from Dylan, have you?'

Darcie listened to Millie's half of the conversation as she tried as concisely as possible to explain the night's events. She didn't keep any of it back – there was no need with Jasmine, who was as sensible with secrets as she needed to be. Millie nodded tensely during each pause in her flow of conversation, and after a couple of minutes she ended the call. She turned to reply to Darcie's silent question.

'Rich can't go out, he's been drinking, but Jasmine hasn't had anything yet so she's going to take the car and pick me up. We'll have a drive along the road to Larkhill and see if we can spot Dylan's car.'

'Isn't that a bit dangerous in this weather?' Darcie asked, a new sense of alarm building inside her at the thought of being alone in the house again with Oscar while Millie battled the elements and possibly ended up just as stuck as Dylan apparently was.

'We don't have a lot of choice.'

'What can I do?' Darcie asked.

'You're already doing it. Please just keep Oscar calm and we'll be back as soon as we can.'

Darcie chewed her lip as she pondered her responses to this. She could see the logic in the plan, but she didn't like it one bit, and she couldn't help feeling that it might make a bad situation twenty times worse. Instead of two people lost in the snow, there would be four, and two of them would be mothers who were very much needed.

'Why don't I go with Jasmine? You should be home with Oscar – he's much happier with his mum than he is with me.'

'I wouldn't expect you to go out in this.'

'I know but if you're positive that someone needs to then I think it should be me.'

Millie was thoughtful for a moment. 'If you're worried about being on your own here I could get someone to come over and stay with you? Or you could stay at Jasmine's place with Rich?'

'But then what if Dylan got back and there was nobody here?'

Millie was about to reply when her phone rang. 'Hey, Spencer... Now's not really a great time unless you can tell me where my boyfriend is.'

Darcie listened again to a second tense exchange as Millie explained Dylan's mission and the lack of phone contact. When she eventually locked her phone, she turned to Darcie with a faint smile. 'Good old Spencer. Luckily for us he hasn't had much to drink tonight so he's coming right over.'

'I though he was out having a meal in Winchester?'

'So did I, but I don't think it went to plan. I expect we'll find out later. First we need to get Dylan back.'

'Do you think it was a good idea to tell him about Tariq?'

'I would trust Spencer with my life – he won't tell anyone about it. And it's only fair if we're asking for his help that he knows everything. If Tariq is still with Dylan, he would have found out for himself anyway.'

'What about Jasmine?'

'The same goes for Jasmine – she can be trusted. And there's no way she won't come over now, even if I tell her Spencer is, so we might as well let her. But at least someone will be able to stay here with you until the other two get back.'

'I'd have been alright,' Darcie said feeling a little shamefaced at her lack of courage.

'I know.' Millie gave her a tight smile. 'But I'd feel better knowing you weren't alone with Oscar. It's alright for an hour while we sing carols but for anything longer we know he can be a handful.'

'Jasmine seems to cope alright.'

'Jasmine has a lot more experience, don't forget. And I think she might have some secret mum superhero power or something – she must have to keep those triplets in line the way she does.' Millie started towards the kitchens. 'I'm going to make a flask of hot coffee with sugar. If anyone is stuck out there they'll be freezing and I might need to warm them up.'

Darcie stared after her. It sounded like Millie was almost fearing the worst, and surely things couldn't be that bad? She hurried after her with Oscar still dozing in her arms. 'Maybe they're just having to drive really slowly in the snow?' she ventured.

Millie turned to her. 'Of course they are,' she said with forced brightness. 'But I want to be prepared.'

It took ten minutes for Jasmine to arrive, but after another five there was still no Spencer. Millie had put Oscar to bed, and she and Jasmine agreed that they would go on without Spencer and he could stay with Darcie. While Darcie was relieved to have some company, she had been hoping it would be someone she knew a little better. Things were tense enough without having to make small talk with a man she'd only met a couple of brief times. But then she was saved by a light tap on the front door.

'Sorry, had to make sure the parents were ok before I came across. They wanted to come and help but I didn't think there was any point and if we have to pick up Dylan for any reason in our car it's sort of defeating the object if the car is full already. You've no idea how difficult Mum can make an argument when she wants to, though.' Spencer kicked snow from his shoes at the threshold before stepping in. 'It's awful out there now too. Seriously treacherous to drive in.'

'That's ok, you can stay with Darcie,' Jasmine said.

Spencer blinked. 'Surely it's better that Millie stays? After all, what will I do if Oscar wakes up? You might as well hand me a live grenade as a baby. I thought that was the idea.'

'I want to go,' Millie said. 'It'll drive me mad if I have to wait around much longer.'

'I know but it makes sense that you stay here,' Spencer insisted.

Millie opened her mouth to reply but Jasmine spoke first.

'Maybe Spencer does have a point. I can look after Oscar but it makes sense for you to be here if you can.'

'I think so,' Darcie agreed. 'I can look after Oscar too but when he gets really awkward he only wants his mum.'

Millie let out a sigh. Clearly she knew that the argument was valid, even if she didn't like it. 'Fine,' she agreed. 'But please be careful out there.'

Spencer nodded and turned to Jasmine. 'The sooner we get going the sooner we can be back.'

There was a faint whimper from the baby monitor. Millie gave an apologetic shrug. 'Sounds like I'm needed elsewhere.'

'Don't worry,' Jasmine said. 'Knowing my idiot brother he's probably driven into a snow bank or something and doesn't have a shovel in the car to dig himself out. We'll be back in no time.'

Millie smiled tightly. 'Of course... You're probably right.'

It was frustratingly slow going on the roads. Nobody had been prepared for this amount of snow to fall and no precautions had been taken by the local authorities. That, coupled with the almost total darkness on the smaller roads, deeper drifts deceptively hidden in hollows, made Spencer feel that they would have made better progress walking.

'At this rate we'll be home for Boxing Day lunch.' Spencer was hunched over the steering wheel, peering through the windscreen as he tried to get a fix on the road ahead, only the occasional flash of a flimsy steel wire fence keeping him from going off course completely. 'What was Dylan thinking, driving out in this?'

'He does have his moments of supreme stupidity,' Jasmine agreed. 'Although he's better than ever with Millie we can't expect her to perform miracles with him.'

'Not yet, anyway. I imagine us men take a lifetime to train.'

'And then some,' Jasmine replied with a wry smile.

There was a pause filled with the revving of the engine and the whirring of tyres trying to get purchase on the ice and snow.

'Is everything ok with you?' Spencer asked carefully. Perhaps it wasn't his place to ask about Jasmine and Rich's relationship, particularly given his history with the two of them and his apparent feelings for her, but he felt compelled to show that he knew something wasn't quite right, and that if she wanted to talk, then he was willing to listen.

'Depends on what you think is ok,' Jasmine said. She let out a sigh. 'You know better than anyone what it's like with Rich and me. It's a spat – it's nothing really.'

'You don't sound certain of that.'

'I'm never certain of anything with him these days. We were ok after the... you know, the thing last summer when you told me how you felt about me.'

Spencer winced at the memory as it dragged old and conflicted feelings to the surface yet again. In a moment of supreme stupidity, during a tense thunderstorm that had almost ended in tragedy, he had not only admitted to Jasmine that he had loved her for years, but he'd told Rich about his feelings for her too. Spencer's revelation had saved their marriage in a strange way, but so many times since then he had recalled the incident and wished he had kept his feelings to himself. He said nothing about it now, though, and she continued.

'But things did change. It was inevitable that they would. I never assume to know what he's thinking and feeling anymore and I'm always wondering whether he might be tempted to hurt himself again, but with more meaning. I know it's daft, and this is Rich we're talking about, but look what happened to Millie's ex-boyfriend and she wasn't expecting that. In moments of desperation, people do terrible things... even some who don't really mean to.'

'So you feel you have to compromise to keep him happy even when you're not?'

'No, I feel that it's more difficult to push an argument I would have once loved having. Our relationship was healthy before, it could stand up to a tempestuous episode or two. But now... I'm never quite as sure.'

Spencer was thoughtful, his eyes trained on the road ahead. 'Want to tell me about it? Maybe you'd feel better if you could get it off your chest, and you know I wouldn't breathe a word.'

'Millie already knows about it...' She shot a sly sideways glance at him. 'Don't tell me she hasn't already spilled to you... I know how close you two are.'

Spencer smiled awkwardly. 'If you're talking about what I think you're talking about then I do know a little.'

'Then you'll know it's an argument that could go around in circles for a long time and probably will if one of us doesn't back down. The problem is, I can understand his stance, and I wish I didn't have to be so bloody reasonable about that – it makes it tough to stand my ground.'

'Can he see your point of view as clearly though?'

'It's Rich we're talking about. Probably not.'

'You shouldn't always feel you have to compromise. It will only breed resentment,' Spencer said, and his mind went back to his own situation with Tori. Did he really believe his own wisdom? Because it didn't feel like it right now.

Suddenly, there was a cascade of snow from a tree just ahead, and then a large dark shape crashed to the road. Spencer squeezed on the brakes and after a breath-sapping skid, the car finally came to a halt. Spencer threw a worried glance at Jasmine. 'Looks like a branch.' He killed the engine and clambered from the car, Jasmine following. 'Must have been the weight of the snow,' he commented as he touched it with the toe of his boot. 'Broke it clean away from the tree.'

'Can we move it?' Jasmine asked. 'It looks massive.'

'We'll have to try. If Dylan is somewhere ahead on this same road, and even if we don't get to him, he's going to need to come back this way. He won't be doing that if there's a huge branch blocking the way.'

Jasmine took hold of one end and Spencer the other and they tried to lift the branch. It inched across the snow but didn't move nearly as much as one would expect an object travelling across a slippery surface to travel.

'This is going to be tougher than it looks,' Jasmine said.

'A bit like your fall out with Rich then,' Spencer said shooting her a wry smile. 'Again?'

Jasmine nodded and they gave the branch another shove, but the distance it travelled was tiny once again. 'I think it's stuck on something,' Jasmine said. She looked up and grinned. 'A bit like me and Rich.'

Spencer laughed as he straightened up to inspect the problem more thoroughly. 'Maybe if we can tear off some of those twigs at the top that are snagged on the fence we might loosen it a bit so we can slide it to the side of the road.'

'Typical,' Jasmine said. 'The road is like an ice rink when we're driving but the minute we want it to be slippery it's rubbish.' She moved along and started to tug at a smaller branch. 'This isn't easy either.'

'You need a bit of weight behind it,' Spencer grinned as he stamped on one. 'Take your frustration out on it.'

'I can do that,' Jasmine said, leaping on the nearest clump of twigs, which collapsed with a satisfying crack. 'I hope Rich can't read my thoughts right now.'

'Well, as long as it's a bit of tree and not his head you're beating up he can't complain.'

'He's lucky this tree decided to cross our path or I might have been driving him to hospital tomorrow instead of cooking turkey for him.'

Spencer stopped and held her in a frank gaze. 'It's that bad?'

'No,' she replied after a pause. 'I'm just frustrated.' She brushed the snow from the log and sat for a moment. Sensing that she was ready to share, Spencer sat alongside her. She looked at him. 'It's just a baby. It's not like I'm asking for the world and he knows how much I love kids. I mean, he loves them too so I don't see the problem. I bet you'd give me a baby, wouldn't you?'

Spencer gave her a half smile. 'You've always known I'd give you anything you asked for.'

And then it happened. Jasmine leaned over and kissed him. It took a moment for his brain to catch up, and he couldn't help but melt into it. But then he wrenched away and stared at her.

'I'm sorry,' Jasmine mumbled, leaping from her seat and shuffling backwards. 'I don't know why I did that.'

'It's ok,' Spencer said. It was strange, but as he processed the event he was calm. For years he had dreamed of kissing Jasmine, but it wasn't at all how he'd imagined it would be. He hadn't wanted to grab her and wrestle her to the floor, driven wild with desire, nor had he been intoxicated by the very taste of her. Far from being the moment he'd always dreamed of, and despite the tingle of electricity he had always felt when she was near, the kiss, when it finally came, had just felt very awkward, and it was clear that Jasmine was feeling the same. He got up from his seat and turned to the branch. 'We should get this out of the way before we become a part of the snow banks ourselves.'

Jasmine nodded, and if the light had been better, Spencer would have seen that she was blushing furiously.

They worked in charged silence, only speaking to give the occasional instruction or suggestion as they tried to move the branch, until, eventually, it groaned far enough out of the way to let them pass.

'Why don't you try Dylan again?' Spencer asked as they got back in the car and he restarted the engine.

Jasmine nodded and dialled the number, cutting the call off as it went straight to voicemail once again. 'For some reason it's still off. He probably let his battery run right down,' she said.

'Right. Helpful…'

There were things that needed to be said and Spencer wondered who would be brave enough to say them first. The tyres slipped and squealed as the car tried to get going on the road again, and for a moment Spencer was absorbed in the task of moving it along, so that when Jasmine did bring it up, the breaking of the silence was almost a surprise.

'I suppose that was a bit weird,' she said. 'Not that I think you're weird…' she added quickly, 'but it's weird that I did it. I mean, I love Rich… You know that. And we had the moment… Last summer, I mean, before you went to Colorado, and I didn't know how I felt about you, but then we cleared it and I thought—' she stopped, breathless, as she looked at him for answers.

'I'll admit,' he began slowly, 'when I came back to Honeybourne for Millie's bakery opening I thought I was over you. And it *was* fine back then. But this time when I came home again, the old feelings returned. I don't know why. Maybe I was just uncertain about this huge, terrifying future I was carving out with Tori, and everything seemed to be running away from us when the families arrived... They still are,' he added quietly. 'How do you feel about it now?'

'I love Rich. That much I know, and I'm so sorry for leading you on. Of all the times to do something that stupid...' She shook her head with a flurry of pink curls. 'You're ok with that? I mean, we're ok? Because I could never forgive myself if I'd hurt you. But I can't leave Rich, and it's not that the kiss didn't matter because it was nice... I mean, not nice, but not horrible... If we'd been in love it would have been nice... not that I couldn't love you... But I love Rich... you see?'

Spencer smiled. 'It's ok. You didn't hurt me, and I feel like, in a weird way, it's finally put the ghost to rest.'

'You're not just saying that to make me feel better? Because you're the best, kindest friend I could ever have and that's exactly the sort of thing you would do, which is why you're the best and kindest friend.'

'I'm not just saying it. Jas, you know how I felt about you, but I'm with Tori now. I was confused, but in a strange way, now I can see things clearly for the first time. I love Tori. I just hope I haven't screwed things up with her for good.'

'I would never tell her – not anyone – about tonight. You can trust me.'

Spencer shot her a sideways look. 'There's nothing to tell, is there?' he asked, raising his eyebrows.

'No,' Jasmine smiled. 'Nothing to tell. So we're ok? We can be friends and it won't be weird?'

'Yes. We're ok.'

But, of course, it would be weird for a while – how could it be anything else? Even if Spencer himself was ok with it, Jasmine would feel awkward and guilty, but Spencer was confident that, in time, they would get past it, especially considering how strangely enlightened he felt right now. As long as Jasmine was still certain of her marriage and that the kiss was an impetuous mistake, they could forget all about this, and their relationship could be what it was always meant to be – just a brilliant, reliable friendship and nothing more.

'We're ok,' he repeated, almost to reassure himself as much as her. Then he trained his eyes on the road ahead and the car became silent.

Half an hour later Spencer spotted Dylan's car. It was at an odd angle at the side of the road, as if it hadn't so much parked up but slid into position, hazard lights blinking through the gloom and Dylan desperately pulling with his gloved hands at a pile of snow around the back wheels. Spencer gently squeezed his brakes to stop alongside and killed the engine.

Dylan straightened up as Spencer leapt out of the car.

'Am I glad to see you!'

Spencer glanced at the interior of the car, but Dylan appeared to be alone. 'He's gone back then?'

Dylan's reply was mute, uncertain surprise, and Spencer laughed. 'Don't worry. Millie told us all about it. I don't think you need to be concerned about us dobbing you in.'

Dylan gave him a sheepish smile. 'I know. I'm just jittery – it's been a hell of a night.'

'Sounds like it.' Jasmine stood next to Spencer now, surveying Dylan's car. 'What's going on here?'

'Slid into a bloody ditch, didn't I?' Dylan said. 'Got one of the front wheels stuck and now all I'm doing is kicking snow all over the place trying to reverse it out. I think I'm getting more dug in than anything else.'

'And I bet your phone is out of battery too?' Jasmine said, arching an eyebrow at him.

Dylan scratched a hand through his hair with an apologetic smile.

'Nothing ever changes,' Jasmine said to her brother. 'You always were the opposite of a boy scout – ready for absolutely nothing ever.'

'I never said I was perfect,' Dylan replied in a slightly offended tone. 'I bet Millie sent you out, didn't she?'

'She'd have had half of Honeybourne out if we hadn't stopped her. I'd better phone and let her know we've found you.'

Jasmine stood to one side and as she spoke to Millie, Spencer folded his arms against the cold and surveyed the puzzle of how to get Dylan's car out of the ditch with him.

'If it wasn't snowing I bet we could tow it out,' he said.

Dylan nodded. 'Probably. But it would take more than your puny car.'

Spencer shot him a sideways glance. 'You know I came out to rescue you, but if my car isn't macho enough I can just as easily leave you here to fend for yourself.'

'You'd never do that – you're too nice.'

Spencer was silent for a moment. 'You could try telling that to my girlfriend and her parents,' he muttered. 'I can guarantee that *nice* is one word not being used about me right now.' The mood shifted in an instant from banter to rueful reflection.

'They don't know you yet,' Dylan said, clapping Spencer on the back. 'Give it time.'

'I don't think I have time, that's the problem. After tonight I wouldn't be surprised if she's flown straight back to Colorado with them. And the worst of it is, a bit of me wouldn't even care.'

'What happened?'

Spencer shook his head. 'My luck, that's what happened. It doesn't matter now.'

Jasmine returned, stowing her phone in her coat pocket. She looked at the car. 'There's no way we're pulling that out. You'd better come back with us.'

'I can't leave it there. It's all skew-whiff and half blocking the road – someone might smash into it.'

'It's not that bad,' Jasmine said. 'And there's hardly anyone about. I doubt there would be much traffic on these roads on Christmas Eve if it wasn't snowy, let alone with this blizzard.' She looked at her brother. 'You have breakdown cover?'

Dylan shook his head. Jasmine let out a sigh. 'See? Backwards boy scout.'

'All this responsibility is still new to me. Cut me a bit of slack for not thinking of everything that grown-ups think about.'

'Well, you'll have to think about leaving this here now. We certainly can't move it and I, for one, don't really want to try. It's Christmas Eve, I'm freezing, Rich will be three sheets to the wind by now and the kids will be up way past their bedtime because he won't have the wit to make sure they're in bed.' Jasmine plunged her hands into her pockets and stamped her feet in the snow. 'So I vote we get home and sort this mess out tomorrow.'

'You want to come out on Christmas Day?' Dylan asked. 'Won't that be worse?'

She shrugged. 'I'll be up early anyway with the kids and at least it will be light. We'll be able to get some help too – someone with a bigger, stronger car.'

'Again with the car insults!' Spencer said in a theatrical tone of deepest offence. 'Unlike some, I don't feel the need to demonstrate my manhood through the medium of my wheels.'

'Alright,' Jasmine smiled. 'Your car is great, it's just not big enough. We all know that size doesn't matter… But sometimes it does.'

Dylan laughed. Spencer laughed too, but he couldn't help wondering if Dylan would be laughing quite so hard if he knew about the kissing incident earlier that night. Worse than Rich or Tori finding out would be Dylan discovering the secret. It had taken him a long time to trust Spencer again, and Spencer quite liked having him as friend rather than foe.

The atmosphere was completely different on the drive back to Honeybourne, the tension between Spencer and Jasmine diluted by Dylan's presence as he teased, cajoled and apologised in equal measure, his banter directed at both Jasmine and Spencer. Spencer had a feeling that there were many reasons for this: not only was it his default setting anyway, but Dylan was probably feeling more than a little bit silly that he had needed rescuing, and, in his own ham-fisted way, was also trying to cheer him up – he appreciated the gesture.

It was a welcome distraction for Spencer, who had now started to worry just how he and Jasmine were going to be after tonight. The more he thought about the kiss, the more it posed a new question… Jasmine's actions had been completely out of character, even for someone as free-spirited as her. Had her feelings for him suddenly become something more? Or had she simply been so angry and frustrated at Rich that she'd reacted impulsively, sought refuge in a man she had always known to have feelings for her and who would have given her anything?

Would have, Spencer thought, because the kiss for him had been an unexpected epiphany. Just like the fairy stories, the spell had been broken by a kiss and Spencer was free. The only thing that wouldn't follow was true love – at least not with Jasmine. He could move on, he hoped they both could, and they could be real friends at last without the emotional baggage of unrequited love. Now he just needed to fix things with Tori and he could get the future back on track. But he was afraid that was going to be a rather taller order.

Once again, Tori found herself sitting in her parents' suite at the Dog and Hare while Spencer was somewhere else. How did they keep getting to this place? With a nod of thanks, she took the coffee offered by her mother from the pot just brought up by Colleen.

'Those people...' Adrienne Dempsey folded her arms and pursed her lips so tightly it was quite possible they might never open again.

'Please stop complaining about it, Mom. I don't want to think about what happened tonight.'

'But they're so opinionated!'

Tori glanced up at her. It would have been easy to point out that she and Todd weren't so different from Lewis and Jenny Johns, but she was too heartsick and just too tired to care anymore.

'Honey,' Mrs Dempsey said, her tone softening, 'your father and I love you very much, and we just want what's best for you.'

'What does that have to do with upsetting Lewis and Jenny?'

'They're upsetting us!'

'Mom, there's no point in going over it again. I'll see Spencer in the morning and we'll talk. I can't do it now; I don't have the strength.'

'You want to see him? All the times he's proved he's not worthy of you and you still want to give him another chance?'

'He hasn't done anything wrong, Mom. We've had a disagreement.'

'What about all the other women?'

'Other women?' Tori forced out a short laugh. 'Don't be ridiculous. Have you been listening to Ruth's gossip?'

'There's no smoke without fire,' Mrs Dempsey replied primly.

Tori looked over the rim of her coffee cup as she took a sip. 'There was only one, and we got to the bottom of that. Spencer promised me there was nothing to worry about now.'

'And you believe that?'

'He has no reason to lie.'

'He has a million reasons.'

'I can't help feeling this is about his parents, not Spencer and I…'

'Nonsense!' Mrs Dempsey scoffed. 'I could give those two oddballs a run for their money any day when it comes to an intelligent debate.'

'Just because you could, it doesn't mean you should,' Tori said, 'and that's the problem.'

'The problem is that you're throwing your life away on a man who isn't good enough for you and it's breaking my heart to see.'

'You mean he's not earning enough?'

Adrienne clutched at her breast in a rather dramatic fashion. 'You don't know how your words cut me. Sometimes you can be so cruel and I don't know where you get it from. I care about you and that's why I feel so strongly.'

'You also want me to have a husband you can present to the other country club members without having to apologise for the lack of zeros on his salary.'

'Tori! You take that back this instant!'

She let out a sigh. 'I'm sorry, Mom. I know you mean well… I'm just tired and my head hurts. I want to go to sleep and make this go away. I want Christmas morning to arrive and be the happy day I've been looking forward to. Right now, everything is a mess.'

'It doesn't have to be, honey. We've always looked out for you and we can continue to do that if you'll let us.'

Tori opened her mouth to reply, but they were interrupted by her dad, who had just returned from the pub downstairs. 'Colleen and Doug are going to bed now,' he said. 'I told them not to worry if we needed anything else, and that we'd go and get it ourselves.'

'So we're paying for accommodation and now we have to do our own chores?' Adrienne asked, planting her hands on her hips.

'Doug looked whacked. They've had a busy night, he's still in a wheelchair and it's Christmas Eve. Let's give them a break, huh?'

Adrienne offered no reply, and he turned to Tori. 'How's your head? Are you feeling better?'

'Yes, thanks, Daddy. A little.'

Adrienne looked down at her daughter. 'I still say we ought to get on the next plane and go home. There's time.'

'I don't want to go home,' Tori said. 'I'm going to call him—'

'Are you crazy?' Adrienne exclaimed. 'That's the last thing you should be doing!'

'He's already sent me a message to say he's sorry.'

'One measly text message – it means nothing. And he keeps saying he's sorry! Which means he keeps stuffing up and that he keeps on needing to apologise for hurting you.'

'But—'

'You can't seriously want all this heartbreak?' Adrienne insisted. 'Come home with us and at least think things over. If you still feel the same way once there's some distance between you and Spencer, then you can try again with our blessing.'

'I don't want to go home,' Tori repeated. 'And I wouldn't get your blessing because I know that once I'm home you'll work on me.'

'Work on you? I can't make you do something you don't want to, even if I know it's the right thing. I think we've seen plenty of evidence of that over the last few days.'

'I doubt we'd get a flight on Christmas Day anyway,' Todd said.

'That's not helpful,' Adrienne shot back.

'But true.'

'London then? There must be plenty of hotels in London? Let's go and see the sights, have Christmas dinner somewhere with a bit of class and leave this terrible village. We can still make our original flight back after a mini vacation in London.'

'Mom! I don't want to go to London and I don't want to go home! I just want to work things out with Spencer and you're not helping!'

'If he's worth it, then where is he now? We've been back for an hour and he hasn't called.'

'But he sent me a message—' Tori began.

Adrienne cut her off. 'That's easy – it's just words. He hasn't come here begging for forgiveness. What does that tell you? Maybe he doesn't care about the relationship quite as much as you think. Maybe he's already found comfort in the arms of that… Petal, or whatever her name is.'

'Jasmine,' Tori corrected. 'And he would never do that.'

'Where is he then? He may not be with her but that doesn't change the fact that he isn't with you either.'

Tori chewed on her lip. She didn't know why Spencer hadn't come. It wasn't like him. Perhaps he'd been driven to the point where he felt as stubborn about making the first move as she did, but she missed him like hell and if he'd suddenly found a set of balls she wished he'd lose them again and go back to being the kind and understanding guy she fell in love with. She'd never backed down in the rare arguments they'd had because she'd never had to. What if this one was the last, the one they couldn't come back from? What if he'd decided to give up on them? What if he had sought solace in the arms of Jasmine…? She pushed the last thought away. He had told her that his feelings for Jasmine were in the past and she wanted to believe him. She wanted him to come over now and take her in his arms and tell her everything was ok, that he loved her and not Jasmine, but he hadn't, and she didn't know what to do. Maybe everything really wasn't ok after all. Maybe it would never be ok again.

Adrienne sat down next to Tori, her tone softer now. 'You don't belong here. I know that you don't want to have anything to do with Hunter, and if this is some sort of rebellion against that, then it can stop. Come back home with us and forget about this village and Spencer. We won't push anymore suitors on you and we'll wait for you to find the right man by yourself… But trust me, honey, this one is not it.'

'Spencer is the right man!' Tori squeaked, tears strangling the words as they came out. She had said it, so why didn't she feel it?

Why did it feel as if her world was about to implode? Adrienne pulled her into an embrace. It felt good – safe and right. Hadn't her parents always looked out for her? Weren't they the people above all others who had her best interests at heart? What if they were right about Spencer and she just couldn't see it?

Chapter Ten

Spencer could hear his mum laughing downstairs, and the deep tones of his dad as he teased her. It was a strange thing to wake up to after all these years of living without them, and it catapulted him back to the Christmas mornings of his childhood. They used to keep him up as long as possible on Christmas Eve just to make sure he slept in a few hours the following morning. The plan worked so well that they would usually be up before him no matter how excited he had been the night before and how hard he tried to get up early for his presents. He smiled for a moment, until the crushing realisation came back that Tori had spent the night with her parents again. As if that wasn't bad enough, this time he hadn't been able to talk to her, what with all the drama over Dylan the previous night. He leaned over to the bedside table and picked up his phone. Tori had sent one message in reply to the one he had sent apologising, right before the call he then made to Millie.

'We need to talk. Call me.'

He hadn't seen it until the early hours and she probably would have been asleep by then, so he had left it, too afraid to call her at such a late hour and too tired to worry any longer. What would she have made of his non-response? Had she been awake all night dwelling on what had happened between them? He cursed himself for being so stupid. Why hadn't he called her straight away or gone over to the pub? He should have climbed the guttering, broken in, done whatever it took to see her, no matter the hour. She mattered more than anything else, and in the cold light of day he could see that more clearly than ever. Without a second thought he dialled her number and waited. Her phone went straight to voicemail, which meant it was probably switched off. That didn't sound good. They had a Christmas dinner date with Millie – did Tori plan to turn up for that? Was she ever planning to see him again or would she and her parents be on the first plane back to Colorado?

Pulling his jeans and sweatshirt on, he thundered downstairs to tell his parents he was going to the pub to sort things out. As soon as he entered the living room their laughter stopped.

'Happy Christmas,' Jenny greeted him, though her tone was subdued.

Lewis was less subtle, and expressed what must have been on both their minds as they watched their son walk into the room. 'How are you feeling?'

'You mean about last night?' Spencer said. 'Hollow… That's the only word I can find to describe it. I feel as if someone has scooped me out.'

'I meant are you tired?' Lewis said. 'Going out to pick up Dylan so late.'

Spencer frowned. 'That wasn't the most pressing problem of the night, as I recall.'

Lewis looked to his wife, who simply threw him an exasperated look and then turned to Spencer. 'You're going to talk to Tori?'

'When I've pulled myself together and decided what to say. I don't know that I've done myself any favours and she probably doesn't want to listen, but I have to try.'

'Spencer,' Lewis began, 'for what it's worth your mum and I are sorry. You're right – we were out of order and we should have tried harder. We've never had to curb our natural tendencies to be opinionated before and we've always dealt with people who were open to debate, but Tori's parents... well, you tried to explain it to us and we feel really bad that we didn't get it. We were selfish and thoughtless for what it would do to you, and if we can make it up in any way we will.'

'I appreciate that, Dad. I'm not sure what I'm going to do but if Tori and I can put this behind us one more time, I'd like to think that at least for the very rare occasions you might have to deal with the Dempseys you'll be able to keep it civil.'

'We'll do our best,' Lewis said.

'I know.' Spencer took the few steps across the room to hug him before hugging his mum too. 'But first I've got to talk to her.'

'Want us to come?' Jenny asked.

Spencer shook his head. Taking them with him was quite probably the very worst thing he could do right now. 'It has to be me. You might as well enjoy your Christmas morning and get ready for dinner at Millie's later.'

'Will that still go ahead?' Jenny frowned. 'In light of last night's events?'

Spencer gave a half smile. 'If I know Millie it will take a lot more than a late night and family feuding to stop her filling the bakery with guests. I'll call her but I don't imagine for a minute she'll be cancelling.'

'She's lovely,' Jenny said.

'She is,' Spencer agreed, wondering if she wished he was dating Millie instead of an awkward American girl with the parents from hell.

'Why don't I make you a coffee before you leave?' Lewis said. 'You might as well call ahead first to make sure they're up before you go dashing off.'

Spencer nodded shortly and his dad went off to the kitchen. Jenny followed him, presumably to talk about the situation some more in private, but whatever they were saying, Spencer couldn't worry about it right now. He dialled the number of the Dog and Hare. After enough rings to almost have him hanging up, Colleen answered. She sounded flustered.

'Dog and Hare.'

'Colleen, it's Spencer. Can I just check, are Tori and her parents up and about?'

'They are,' Colleen replied sounding very unhappy about it. 'But they won't be here for much longer.'

'What do you mean?'

'They woke me up at the crack of dawn demanding breakfast in the room. They're checking out as soon as they've packed.'

'Where are they going?' Spencer asked in a strangled voice. 'I mean,' he added, trying to calm himself, 'it's Christmas Day. Where can they go on Christmas Day?'

'I don't know.' Spencer got the distinct impression that she wanted to add *and I don't care.* 'They seem to know what they're doing so who am I to argue?'

He took a deep breath. 'So it's Mr and Mrs Dempsey leaving Honeybourne? Not Tori?'

'I'm not sure,' Colleen replied uncertainly.

Spencer keenly felt the awkward position she was being put in but he had to know.

'I got the impression they were all going. I heard them say they would get the taxi to come and fetch her things from your house before they went on.'

Spencer ended the call and shoved the phone in his pocket. He ran into the hallway and ripped a jacket from the coat rail. 'I've got to go!' he shouted.

The sound of footsteps followed him, and he heard his father call him back, but Spencer had already slammed the front door shut. Whatever his dad had to say, it couldn't be as important as stopping Tori from leaving. He knew now that he needed her, whatever that took – whether he had to kiss her parents' feet or move to the moon. Whatever she wanted, he would do it, just to have her love him again. He knew now that he was walking away from the one, the love of his life, and he had been stupid to let all his doubts and fears turn into mistakes that would drive her away from him. He had one last chance to make it right, and he couldn't screw up this time.

As he put the car into gear and took off the handbrake, the wheels spun on the now compacted snow, but the vehicle didn't move. He applied pressure to the accelerator again, with more violence this time, and the car shot forwards, sliding sideways on the ice and slamming into his gatepost.

Spencer threw his foot on the accelerator again, trying to stay calm and keep his mind on the driving, but all he could think about was reaching Tori before she left, and if that meant totalling his car he didn't really care. He was even less concerned about totalling himself; being alive at the end of the journey would mean nothing without Tori.

As the car left the drive, he spotted his mum and dad through the rear-view mirror, out on the doorstep, watching him tear off. He owed them a Christmas Day too, but it would have to wait.

The snow had stopped and the sky was a fresh blue, but the roads were worse than they had been the night before, the snowfall hardened to ice in temperatures that had dipped well below freezing in the early hours. Spencer groaned and swore as the car refused to behave, swerving all over the road, sticking in places, sliding in others, and hindering his progress as if it too wanted to stop Spencer and Tori from being together. It was lucky that traffic around the tiny roads of Honeybourne was non-existent that morning. As it was, most of the other residents of his home village would be doing what normal people did on Christmas morning – spending time with their families in their warm homes, maybe opening presents or kissing under mistletoe, or at the very least nursing comfortable and well-earned hangovers from fun-filled Christmas Eve revelling. Certainly not driving erratically towards their destiny, any chance of happiness in Spencer's future seemingly about to be thwarted.

Then the sheep appeared in the middle of the lane. There were about twelve of them, standing around looking dazed and not a bit concerned for the blue tin box that was sliding towards them. Spencer slammed the breaks on and the car pirouetted with the grace of a Russian ballerina before coming to a halt ten yards away but facing the wrong direction.

'Tree branches, snow and now bloody stupid sheep,' Spencer muttered under his breath as he put the car back in gear and tried to manoeuvre it into the right direction again. 'You think you can beat me, world, but you can't – not yet.' With frustrating slowness, he moved the car back and forth, trying to turn it around, wheels spinning and black smoke pouring from the bonnet as it squealed with the effort, but even the noise and smell didn't seem to deter the sheep, and when he finally got the car facing something like the right way, they still blocked his exit, staring at him.

'Dopey sods!' He punched his fist on the horn. Nothing moved. He leaned out of the window. 'Shift, you stupid bloody animals!' he yelled, but not a single sheep showed any sign of concern at his aggression. Leaving the engine running he leapt out of the car and ran towards them. 'Shoo!' he cried, flapping his arms at them. 'Go home! Get off the road!'

The sheep stared at him but continued to huddle together, looking for all the world as if they intended to set up a permanent roadblock. Spencer had never felt so close to tears, the frustration building inside him like a bomb ready to explode. He'd lived in the country nearly his whole life, and yet he'd never encountered a flock of maverick road-hog sheep before. Why now, of all the times? He tipped his face to the sky. 'If this is your idea of a joke, or you're getting your own back because I dissed you the other day, then I get the message. I'll come to church every Sunday, even if my parents laugh at me, but please tell your sheep to move!' His gaze went back to the road. The sheep stared him down but there was no movement. Spencer let out a sigh.

Going back to the car, he pulled it in to the side of the road, as close as he could to the edge and stopped the engine. Leaving cars on the sides of roads seemed to be a new habit developed over the last couple of days. At this rate half the cars of Honeybourne would be parked on the sides of country lanes. But there was nothing else for it. There was no time to wait for the road to clear, and if Spencer was going to reach the Dog and Hare in time, he would just have to run the rest of the way.

The air of the bakery was already sweet with the smells of French toast, made for Darcie and Millie by Dylan as an apology for worrying them the night before, and as a Christmas morning treat. Millie pushed her empty plate away with a contented smile. 'I do believe I did an excellent job of teaching you to cook.'

'Why, thank you,' said Dylan, grinning. 'No allowances for natural talent, though?'

'I saw what you were eating when you lived alone. If you had natural talent you certainly weren't showing it.'

Darcie dropped her knife and fork and held her stomach. 'I don't think I could eat Christmas dinner until at least New Year now.'

'I suppose I'd better think about preparing that,' Millie said, making to leave the table, but Dylan stopped her.

'Not yet. I'm sure nobody will mind if it's a little late, considering the night we had last night.'

'We have guests, though... Very fussy guests by the sounds of things.'

'That's if they bother to turn up. If what Spencer told us is anything to go by, we might be eating turkey for a lot longer than we bargained for.'

Millie was thoughtful for a moment. 'Do you think Spencer and Tori will have worked things out?'

'If I know him I'm sure he'll have gone all girly on us and poured out his heart to her. That usually works, doesn't it?'

Millie smiled. 'It has been known to, on occasion. It certainly beats the caveman approach, so don't think of going all nineteenth century on me next time we have a misunderstanding or I'll be forced to take a pan to your head.'

Dylan's grin spread. 'Noted! But don't worry about Spencer and Tori. They're probably snogging each other's faces off right now.'

'Not if her parents are anywhere around.'

'Hmm... they are hard work, aren't they?' Dylan agreed. 'But the weird thing is, I kind of get where they're coming from.'

Millie raised her eyebrows in a silent question.

'Well,' Dylan continued, 'now that we have Oscar, I want everything in his life to be perfect for him, and I want him to be happy in everything he does – it comes with the territory as a parent, right? So if they feel that Tori is having to compromise in some area of her life – like moving to Honeybourne when she might not really want to – or if they feel strongly that Spencer isn't the right bloke for her, or any other reason that might be odd to us but makes sense to them... All I'm saying is that if it was me, then maybe I'd be making things awkward too, just because I want my son or daughter to make the right choices in life.'

'They could have a lot worse than Spencer for a son-in-law,' Millie commented.

'We know that, but they don't really know him from Adam.'

Darcie watched and listened as the conversation went back and forth, and her heart went out to Spencer. She didn't know him well, but she recognised something in him, a kindred spirit, someone who saw the world a little like she did. And she also saw kindness and humility in him, in the way he gave everything of himself to those around him, the way he always put others first. She knew what it was like to have life deny you the things you wanted, and then to think that you might get them after all only to have them whipped from under your nose again at the whim of fate. She had never fought for what she wanted, and had regretted that every time. But then she also understood, as she looked across at Dylan, that there were some things you had to let go of. And as Millie had paced the floor the previous night, almost out of her mind with worry for a missing Dylan, she had finally understood that. It was time to kill her stupid feelings for him once and for all.

As Millie got up to clear the table, Darcie's mind went back to Spencer. She wondered if his fight was one worth seeing through to the bitter end, or whether it was a battle he needed to walk away from if he was going to fight another day. Whatever it was, she hoped he would get his happy ending.

Darcie helped Millie stack the dishwasher, and as Millie closed the door and went to the fridge to start pulling out the mountains of vegetables she would need for dinner, Dylan popped his head around the kitchen door.

'My God! What are you doing?' he asked with mock horror.

Millie spun to face him. 'What?'

'Presents first!'

He disappeared from the doorway again and Millie smiled at Darcie. 'It'll take hours for Dylan to open all of Oscar's, which is really what he means when he says presents. He's been dying to open them all week!'

'He'll probably spend the rest of the day playing with them,' Darcie agreed, and Millie giggled.

'You know him so well already, big man-child that he is. A few years ago I would have thought a man like that an absolute nightmare, but it's weirdly cute in Dylan.'

Darcie smiled. 'You really love him, don't you?'

'More than life itself. And I never expected it really, at the beginning. That's the funny thing about love, I suppose, sometimes it creeps up on you, sometimes it leaps out and scares you half to death, but more often than not you're totally unprepared for it. I came to Honeybourne for a quiet life, and look what I got…'

'It's a good life, isn't it?' Darcie asked. 'In Honeybourne, I mean. It's a good place to live.'

Millie regarded her frankly. 'What do you think? You've never actually told me whether you like it here or not.'

'It's nice,' Darcie replied carefully.

'But sometimes you're lonely because everyone seems to know everyone else and you're left on the sidelines?'

Darcie nodded.

'I get that,' Millie said. 'If you're still thinking of going home after Christmas then I completely understand. But maybe you should give it one more chance, and I'm not just saying that because I like having your help… although I do.'

'I think I might,' Darcie said, her mind going back to Tariq. Her thoughts had gone that way a lot over the last twelve hours, which had provoked feelings of extreme guilt when she remembered Nathan and the arrangements she had made to see him again. She liked Nathan, and she didn't want to hurt him, but she desperately wanted to see Tariq again. Millie had mentioned her being lonely, and Darcie now wondered whether it might be easier to be lonely than to be faced with this awful choice. And that was assuming that Tariq felt the same way about her as she did about him. He had seemed to give all the signals, but she had never been very good at reading those, so there was no guarantee that what she thought she had seen in him was even there at all. But maybe it was worth sticking around a little longer to see what life in Honeybourne might bring next.

Millie pulled her into a hug. 'I'm so glad. I love having you around, and you're welcome to stay in the annexe as long as you want. We've got big plans for the summer, and if you were happy to stick with us that long, I wanted to put you in charge of some of them. How would that sound?'

Darcie blinked. 'In charge?'

'Yes,' Millie nodded. 'A proper job with a salary, and you'd get to make decisions with me about the business. You're up for the challenge?'

'You'd trust me?'

'Of course I would!' Millie laughed. 'We both love you to bits and we both think that you have a lot more business acumen than you let on. You're going to be fantastic – wait and see!'

Darcie couldn't help the broad grin that stretched across her face. 'I'll do my best!' she cried, flinging her arms around Millie. It was a complete surprise to her that Millie trusted her so much, but it was a lovely one and it meant a lot. With the appearance of Tariq and the promise of what might be, it felt like the start of something good. It felt like the best of reasons to stay in Honeybourne after all.

Dylan's voice came from the living room. 'Ladies! Come on, these presents won't open themselves, and Oscar's awake now so it's a race against time!'

Millie linked her arm in Darcie's. 'We'd better go and put him out of his misery.'

Despite Millie's constant reminders that she needed to start dinner if they were going to have everything ready on time, Dylan managed to cajole her into sitting through the unwrapping of the entirety of Oscar's pile of gifts. Then came Darcie's turn to open the few she had amassed, which amounted to the ones from Millie and Dylan, some sent from home by her parents and, surprisingly, some very nice chocolates from Colleen and Doug to thank her for her help in the Dog and Hare since Doug's fall. She then handed Millie and Dylan the gifts she had bought them. Millie was thrilled with the aromatherapy kit, and Dylan just as happy with his aftershave, although Darcie wished she could have been just a little bit more original, even though she'd struggled to choose as it was. Dylan then opened various gifts from Millie, Jasmine and Rich, and Spencer. There was also one from Colleen and Doug and one from Ruth Evans, a slightly concerning pair of boxer shorts in a leopard-print design.

'She's still got it bad for you,' Millie said with a giggle.

'I wish she'd get rid of it,' Dylan replied with a grimace as he held them up for inspection.

Before Millie's pile was handed to her, she got up from the floor where they'd been sitting next to the tree and handed Oscar over to Dylan. 'I really need to get on. Mine can wait until after dinner.'

Dylan's face fell. 'You're not going to open them now?'

Millie laughed and kissed him. 'They'll wait. I'll be able to appreciate them better if I'm not fretting about being behind schedule.'

'But I wanted to see you open mine.'

'And you will – later. Now I need to start prepping veg and I can't very well serve turkey if it's still gobbling.'

Dylan took Oscar from her. He looked like a balloon with all the air let out.

'Don't sulk,' Millie said. 'It's Christmas Day.'

'That's why I wanted you to open your presents.'

Millie smiled. 'It's Christmas Day for quite a while yet. I won't forget about the presents.'

'Maybe I could start the dinner for you?' Darcie cut in. 'Then you could open your gifts.'

Millie shook her head. 'This is supposed to be a day off for you.'

'I want to help. I am going to be eating the dinner, after all.'

Millie pretended to look shocked. 'Were we supposed to be feeding you too? I had an appointment at the soup kitchen set up for you.'

Darcie giggled, but Dylan didn't laugh, he just sat looking crestfallen and sulky in equal measures.

'Why don't you play with Oscar's Lego for a while,' Millie said, not a bit fazed. 'We all know you've really bought it for yourself anyway and not for your two-month-old son. He might be a child prodigy in the making but even he can't build a Death Star just yet. By the time you've built something I'll have the turkey in and then I'll come and open my presents. How does that sound?'

Dylan nodded sullenly, and Millie's laughter could be heard above the strains of 'Merry Christmas Everybody' as she went into the kitchen and turned the radio on. Darcie followed her in, determined to help no matter what Millie said.

Spencer clutched at his side. He'd never run a marathon, but right now he had a pretty good idea of how it might feel. His lungs felt as though they couldn't contain the oxygen he was pulling in to keep going, and the air he was breathing was so cold his head felt like it might freeze and shatter. When Tori had nagged him back in Boulder to go jogging with her, and he had laughed and patted his flat stomach saying he didn't need to, perhaps he should have gone after all. In different circumstances, had she been here, she'd have laughed and reminded him of his cockiness, and how it had come back to bite him on the bum. But she wasn't, and that was why he had to keep running no matter how sick he felt, or how many times he lost his footing on the ice, or how much sweat poured from his brow. He had to get there before she left – it might be his last chance to tell her how much he loved her, how much he needed her in his life.

Finally, the Dog and Hare was in sight. A minibus was parked outside, with Tori and her parents directing the driver who was hauling their many suitcases into the boot, cigarette hanging from his mouth and looking as though he'd been called out of bed before he'd had a chance to shave or wash. He probably had, Spencer reflected, if the Dempseys had had anything to do with it. He wondered how they had persuaded the nearest cabbie to come out for them on Christmas morning, and just how much it might be costing them, but it was a vague notion that he didn't have time to ponder now.

Tori's head whipped around at the sound of her name being called. She saw Spencer running towards her, and at the same time, so did her dad.

'I hope you haven't come to cause trouble,' he said, advancing on Spencer.

'I… just… want to talk… to Tori…' Spencer panted.

'What are you doing?' Tori asked coldly.

'Came to stop you…'

'Stop me doing what?'

'Going.'

She paused. 'Who told you I was going?'

Spencer shook his head. 'Doesn't matter. You are, aren't you?'

'I don't know yet.'

He wiped a hand across his brow, conscious now that he was a sweaty mess. 'So we can talk it through?'

'I'm going to London.'

'Now?'

She nodded.

'But you just said you weren't going!'

'I'm helping my parents find somewhere to stay.'

Spencer glanced at Mr Dempsey and then back to Tori. He lowered his voice. 'Can't they do that without you?'

'I want to go with them. I need time to clear my head.'

'So you're coming back? You're not coming to my house to get your clothes?'

Tori chewed on her lip. 'I was going to. Just in case...'

'So Colleen was right! You were going to leave! Why did you tell me you weren't?'

'Because I didn't want to have this conversation out on the street in front of my parents!' Tori fired back. 'Because I knew this would happen if I told you the truth and I can't deal with it right now!'

Spencer stared miserably at her. 'I don't want you to go.'

'I know.'

'I love you.'

'I know that too. But it's too late. If you loved me like you say you do, you would have come to me last night, but you didn't.'

'I couldn't, there was a thing and Dylan—'

'I don't want to hear it,' Tori interrupted. 'You didn't even reply to my message. I don't care what excuse you have cooked up. You should have come to me and you didn't.'

The back door of the minibus slammed shut, and Mr Dempsey touched Tori on the arm. 'Time to go.'

'No!' Spencer cried. 'You can't go! Just give me five minutes… Our relationship is worth at least that, isn't it?'

'I'm sorry.'

'But…' Spencer thought quickly, 'you've got to come and get your stuff from my house, right? So I can ride with you in the taxi back there and we can talk?'

'I don't think that's a good idea. Are your parents home?'

'Yes, but—'

'If they'll let me in I'll pick up my stuff.'

'But I love you!'

Tori turned to the waiting cab. Mrs Dempsey watched through the window as Spencer followed.

'Tori, please!'

'I'll call you. It's better that we talk when we've both had time to calm down.'

'I *am* calm!' Spencer insisted, his voice rising in contradiction of his words. Tori climbed into the cab and shut the door. Spencer hammered on the window. 'Why are you doing this?'

She looked straight ahead, her eyes wide as if she was trying to stop herself from crying, but she didn't reply and she didn't look at him.

'Why are you doing this?' he repeated in a small voice as the cab pulled away. 'I love you…'

As Tori became a speck in the distance, Spencer collapsed onto the front step of the Dog and Hare and held his head in his hands. He'd lost her now for sure. *Merry Christmas, Spencer. Welcome to the rest of your life.*

He looked around at a gentle hand on his shoulder.

'I'm sorry,' Colleen said. She gave him a sympathetic smile.

'I was an idiot,' he said in a dull voice. 'I let stupid things get in the way when I should have been fighting for her.'

'You let your compassion get in the way. You always did try to juggle the happiness of everyone at once, but sometimes you have to let one or two of the balls go, and that's something I've never seen you do in all the years I've known you. It doesn't make you a bad person that you wanted to make everyone happy; she just can't see that right now. If you ask me, she doesn't know what she's throwing away but I think she will realise it, and when she does she'll be back.'

'Thanks for trying to make me feel better, but you're wasting your breath on me. It's Christmas morning, Colleen. You should be inside enjoying it with Doug now that the Dempseys are out of your hair, not wasting it on a loser like me.' He pushed himself up from the step and dusted the snow from his backside. 'I might as well go home.'

'Come in for five minutes. You look exhausted and I bet you would feel better with a brandy inside you.'

'I'm fine…' Spencer began to wave away the offer, but Colleen stopped him.

'Just one. Doug would be happy to see you.'

Spencer was pretty sure that Doug wouldn't care either way, but it seemed to matter to Colleen, so he nodded shortly. It wasn't as if he could get back to his house before Tori anyway, and even if he did she wasn't budging on her decision to go to London with her parents.

'I don't know where on earth they think they're going to stay,' Colleen added as Spencer followed her into the bar. 'It's not like you can just walk into a hotel on Christmas morning and demand a room.'

'I bet they can,' Spencer replied, the bitterness in his tone unmistakable. He didn't care right now whether he sounded like a petulant child or not, but he realised that he probably did. 'Would you say no to those two scowling faces?'

'And I bet that cab is costing an arm and a leg,' Colleen continued. 'What happened to get them so angry?'

'I don't really want to talk about it,' Spencer said. 'I'm sorry, but I'm still trying to make sense of it all myself.'

'I understand. For now, let me fix you that brandy and just you sit for five minutes before you go back – pull yourself together.'

Doug was in the bar in his wheelchair. He looked as if he was nursing his first alcoholic drink of the day. Spencer supposed that Christmas morning tipples went with the territory when you were a publican – they certainly wouldn't get much chance to sit and relax with a drink once they opened at lunchtime.

'He's here,' Doug said, nodding at Spencer. 'Poor bugger. If you ask me it's good riddance.'

'Doug!' Colleen chided. 'He's heartbroken!'

'Oh, I don't mean the girlie – she's grand. But her folks… I thought Yanks were supposed to be friendly.'

'And Englishmen are supposed to be sensible but I don't see you showing much of that,' Colleen replied as she handed Spencer a glass.

'It's alright,' Spencer replied, taking a seat at the table with Doug. 'I feel sorry for you two having to look after them. I would never have suggested they stay here if I'd known what they were like.'

'Not your fault. A paying customer is a paying customer and you have to take the business where you can,' Doug said sagely. 'We'd have put them up regardless. But I can't say I'll miss them now they're gone.'

Spencer knocked back his brandy in one go. He wasn't one for drinking neat spirits and felt it go straight to his head. But it had a pleasant warming effect too; he hadn't realised just how cold he'd become as he sat outside on the step, the sweat freezing on his skin.

'Fancy another one?' Doug asked, raising an eyebrow.

Spencer shook his head, but Colleen took his glass and filled it anyway, placing a new drink in front of him. Spencer took that and knocked it back too. He pulled his phone from his pocket and unlocked it. There was a missed call from his dad, and one from Dylan, but no call or text from Tori. A small part of him had hoped she would change her mind, that she might message him to say she was turning the cab around and coming back, but he knew deep down that it was a silly, forlorn hope. Even if she'd considered it, her parents would see to it that she didn't. God, how he hated them – almost as much as he loved their daughter. It seemed like a ludicrous position to be in and so very unfair. They had been alright before, and then her stupid parents had come and messed everything up. They hadn't liked him from the start, and they had set out to destroy him and Tori. It looked as though they'd got what they came for.

'I've just got to check on the turkey,' Colleen said, offering Spencer a conciliatory pat on the shoulder. Spencer nodded and fiddled with his glass as she left him with Doug.

'I'd get you another one, but I'm a bit indisposed,' Doug said. Spencer looked up and couldn't help a wan smile.

'I'm sorry. Here's me feeling sorry for myself and you've got far bigger problems. I should be thankful that I have all my limbs working.'

'And youth on your side,' Doug grinned.

'I know I haven't lost a limb or anything, but it feels like I've lost something… something I can't put a name on, like there's this huge gaping hole inside me.' Spencer shook his head. 'Listen to me – I sound like an idiot. Why do you need to know all this?'

'I might be a bit long in the tooth and stuck in a wheelchair but it doesn't mean I can't have a bit of sympathy for you.' He nodded up at the bar. 'Fetch yourself another, and get me one while you're at it.' He tapped the side of his nose. 'On the house – we won't mention it to Colleen.'

Spencer couldn't be bothered to argue. Comfortably numb might just be a nice state of being right now. He strode over to the bar and squeezed a couple of shots from the optics, taking them both back to the table where Doug waited.

'Last year Colleen and I nearly split up,' Doug said. He held his drink up to the light with a satisfied look before downing it.

'You did? What happened?'

'Well, we worked it out, didn't we?'

Spencer blinked. He waited for more, some elaboration on the story, but none came. Instead he knocked back his own measure with a grimace.

'It'll work out for you too,' Doug said, holding him in a steady gaze.

'I wish I could be so sure. What do you think I should do about it?'

Doug shifted in his seat. 'Beats me.'

Spencer stared at him. *Brilliant advice, Doug.* But he had to admire the stoicism with which the landlord of the Dog and Hare viewed life's problems. For him, almost splitting from Colleen was just like being stuck in a wheelchair with two broken legs – things would come right if they were meant to and it was pointless worrying about it. Spencer wished a little of it would rub off on him.

Colleen returned from the kitchen wiping her hands on her apron. 'I bet you could do with a top up,' she said to Spencer, glancing at the empty in front of Doug with a slight frown as she took Spencer's glass. 'Then if you need a friendly ear, you can tell me all about it.' She was about to return to the bar when there was a knock on the front doors of the pub. Spencer's head flicked around as Colleen scurried off to answer it. But he was to be disappointed, because it was not Tori at the door, but his mum and dad. Colleen let them in and they came bowling over to the table.

'What the hell happened?' Jenny demanded. 'Your car was abandoned at the side of the road, there was no sign of you and you weren't answering your phone! We were worried sick and now we find you here drinking with not a thought for letting anyone know you're alright! We thought…'

Spencer could see she'd been crying and his heart almost broke all over again. 'God, Mum, please don't be upset.'

Jenny dropped to a chair. 'I thought you'd done something stupid… I thought…'

Spencer grabbed her hand. 'I'm sorry. You're right, it was selfish of me. I just wanted to get to Tori before she left and then when I got here she wouldn't let me explain.'

Jenny gave a jerky nod. 'Ignore me. I'm being silly. I should be apologising to you, not the other way around.'

'It's not your fault everything went wrong.'

'But I feel responsible.'

Spencer hesitated. He didn't want to ask the next question, because to say it out loud might mean an answer he didn't want to hear. But he had to. 'She's been to collect her things then?'

Lewis nodded. 'And she wouldn't listen to a bit of reason. Or rather her stubborn old cow of a mother wouldn't.'

'We tried to apologise, to tell them that it wasn't your fault and to make them see what a mistake it was driving you and Tori apart but…' Jenny didn't need to finish her sentence for Spencer to know exactly how that conversation had gone.

'Your mum's taking it hard,' Lewis said. 'We both feel responsible.'

'So you bloody well should!' Everyone looked around to see Ruth Evans standing in the doorway. 'The door was unlocked,' she added, by way of an apology for her outburst. 'I thought you might have opened early.'

'Trust you to be skulking around where you're not needed,' Jenny said under her breath.

'I take it your lady friend has gone home and left you high and dry?' Ruth said, looking at Spencer.

'You know she has,' Jenny replied for him. 'You know everything that happens in this village so I can't even imagine why you're asking. I wouldn't be surprised to hear that you've bugged everyone's living rooms and have CCTV in their bedrooms.'

'I keep my wits about me and I learn enough,' Ruth said haughtily. 'I've also been around the block a few times myself, and I think I know enough about life to be able to give some friendly advice.'

'Come on then,' Jenny said, arms folded tightly across her chest. 'Let's hear the wisdom of Ruth Evans. This should be good.'

'Mum,' Spencer said, 'don't.'

'He's right,' Ruth said. 'The way I see it, you didn't make things any easier for poor Spencer here than Tori's parents did.'

'We know that.'

'So why didn't you stop? You must have known at the time you were making trouble.'

'Do you really think we'd have caused all this deliberately?' Lewis asked.

'You tell me,' Ruth said. 'Seems to me you wanted them apart as much as her folks did.'

'That's ridiculous,' Jenny said.

'Not from where I'm standing.'

'Ruth,' Doug cut in, 'if you've come in just to insult people then you can go. In fact, we're not open yet so you can go anyway.'

'The money I've given you over the years!' Ruth squeaked. 'And I helped behind the bar when Doug threw himself off the roof!'

'Doug didn't throw himself off the roof! And we're grateful for your help,' Colleen began, before both Lewis and Jenny cut into the argument with their own opinions, until everyone was talking at once.

Spencer looked around at them all. This was too much. They barely noticed him get up from his seat, and without another word he left them all shouting in the pub and began the walk to the bakery.

Chapter Eleven

The cabbie had thrown Tori's suitcases into the back of the van, and they pulled away from Spencer's house with his parents watching from the doorstep. They had looked a good deal more distraught and repentant than they had in the Chinese restaurant the night before. Tori understood that they were probably sorry, and at any other time she might have said something to make them feel better, even listened to their requests to give Spencer another chance. But she had made her decision and she had to stay strong, even though it was killing her. She had held onto the tears and her dignity as best she could, but as the taxi left the borders of Honeybourne, they flooded out.

'It hurts now, honey, but you've made the right decision,' Mrs Dempsey said, pulling her close and stroking her hair away from her face. 'Here…' She handed her a newly washed handkerchief. 'Dry your eyes. By the time we get to London things will seem better.'

'Will they, Mom? Because it doesn't feel like it. It feels like things will never be better.'

'Time is a great healer and one day you'll see that the tough decision was the right one.'

'I don't think I want to be healed and I don't think I'll ever see things your way.'

'Nonsense. You have a wonderful future ahead of you once you get this out of your system. The eligible bachelors will be lining up for you.'

'Your mom's right,' Mr Dempsey said, leaning across to pat Tori's hand.

Out of her system? She wasn't some lovesick teen with a crush on her teacher or her father's best friend. This was a huge decision… This was the rest of her life. Why couldn't they see that? But she was too confused, too heartsick, to argue it now.

'Mom, what if I'm wrong? What if I'm throwing away something special, something I'll never find again?'

'You're not backing down now,' Mrs Dempsey replied, rubbing Tori's arm vigorously as if to massage some resolve back into her. 'You've done the hard part and it would be ridiculous to come this far only to go back again.'

Tori gazed out of the window. The landscape flashed by: layers of white and grey against a blue sky, patches of deep green here and there, roads almost ghostly in their desertion as the rest of the country celebrated Christmas Day in their homes. Tinny music echoed around the cab from the driver's radio.

'Couldn't you turn that down?' Mrs Dempsey snapped at the driver. 'We're trying to have a conversation in here and you're drowning it out! And in case you hadn't noticed, my daughter is very upset and she needs calm!'

'He's just trying to be happy,' Tori said in a dull voice. 'Leave him alone.'

Mrs Dempsey looked as though she might argue, but instead straightened her skirt and said nothing. The volume of the music reduced, but Tori could see the driver grinding his teeth in the rear-view mirror. Further along the road, the first large signpost for the motorway, and for London, loomed into view.

Tori dried her eyes and took a deep breath. This was it: there was no going back now.

Darcie couldn't remember the last time she had felt so happy and relaxed. Millie was in high spirits, dancing around the kitchen as she cooked. Considering the late hour they had all ended up climbing into bed the night before, it was a miracle she was up and about at all, let alone so cheerful about it. But it seemed the Christmas spirit had got to everyone, and even Oscar gurgled happily in his bouncing seat as everyone scurried to and fro getting the bakery ready for their guests. It all made Darcie feel contented, and more secure in her decision to stick around for a while than she had felt so far. The bakery was beginning to smell like Christmas too, the air filled with the aromas of cooking turkey and glasses of spiced mulled wine for the chefs as they worked. Dylan was still quiet, and Darcie wondered whether he was angry about Millie refusing to open her presents, but when she snuck into the living room to check, she found him crooning to Oscar as he demonstrated the wonders of Lego and figured that he seemed happy enough.

'So,' Millie asked as they peeled sprouts together, 'which one will you choose?'

Darcie shot her a sideways glance. 'Which what?'

'Boy…' Millie said with a smile.

Darcie stared at her.

'Don't think I haven't noticed!' Millie laughed. 'You've already told us that you've been thinking about Nathan, and I saw the way you and Tariq looked at each other. I wasn't born yesterday.'

'I don't know that Tariq likes me at all,' Darcie said.

'Ah! So it's him you're interested in!'

'I didn't say that,' Darcie mumbled, blushing.

'You didn't need to. What about Nathan? How does he fit in?'

Darcie sighed. 'I don't know. I like him, and I feel bad that I'm even thinking about someone else.'

'But he did mess you around, and you don't know for sure that all the business with his ex is over.'

'I think it is.'

'But you think that Tariq might be more reliable?'

'I can hardly say that. I've met him for half an hour when he was running away from the army. I'm not sure that's the behaviour of someone who is reliable.'

'True.' Millie smiled at her. 'Maybe emotional reliability is what I mean.'

'I'm not sure he could offer that either. I don't know. I just felt…'

'A connection?'

'Sounds silly, doesn't it?'

'Not one bit,' Millie replied. 'That's exactly how I felt about Dylan. I mean, on the face of it he couldn't have been more unsuitable, but there was something about him I couldn't put my finger on, and I was drawn to him even though I didn't know why. I can only describe it as a connection.'

'So maybe it's not that mad after all?'

'I think you might need to keep a clear head about it, but if that's what you feel you shouldn't dismiss it out of hand. You got his number last night?'

Darcie shook her head. 'No. But I gave him mine. I suppose that means I have to wait and see if he calls. At least it saves me making the decision.'

'There is that. Though it might be a bit of a nail-biting wait.'

The conversation was interrupted by Dylan hurrying into the kitchen, looking worried. Millie read the expression immediately and turned the radio off.

'What's the matter?'

'Spencer's here. I'd say he needs a stiff drink but judging by his breath he's already taken care of that. Tori's left him.'

Millie and Darcie exchanged a look of alarm. Reaching for a cloth to wipe her hands, Millie rushed through to the living room.

'Sorry…' Spencer sat in the armchair, looking so deflated that he was in danger of being swallowed up by the cushions.

'What are you sorry for?'

'Ruining your Christmas Day, being a complete loser, for ever thinking it was a good idea to come home… Take your pick.'

Millie looked at Dylan. 'Be a love and get some coffee, would you.'

Dylan fastened Oscar back into his bouncy seat and went off to the kitchen while Millie and Darcie both sat on the sofa across from Spencer.

'Want to talk about it?' Millie asked.

'There's nothing to talk about. I'm an idiot and she's gone.'

'I think that's a bit harsh,' Millie said. 'You're far from an idiot. The Spencer Johns I know is a smart, caring man who also happens to be a bit of a secret hero. So if she's gone, then I suspect there's more to it than that.'

He shook his head. 'I wish all those things were true, but you're being too kind.' He stood up. 'I don't know why I've come. You've got things to do, and I'm ruining your morning with my miserable face.'

Millie leapt up and caught him by the arm. She smiled. 'Don't be silly. Your face is a very nice face and I want to help. If you like, we can cook dinner together and you can tell me about it that way. It might help to take your mind off things and make you feel a bit brighter about it all.'

'How is it that you always know exactly the right thing to say?' Spencer asked.

'I don't know about that. I think Dylan would tell it differently.'

'Dylan wouldn't,' Dylan said, returning with a coffee for Spencer. 'Dylan thinks Millie is practically perfect in every way – just like Mary Poppins.'

'I wish,' said Millie. 'I could do with some of that finger clicking to tidy up after you from time to time.' She looked at Spencer. 'Come on, let's get dinner on.'

'Would you mind if I try to call Tori again first?'

Millie nodded. 'Do whatever it takes.'

Spencer placed his coffee on a small table and stepped into the vast kitchens. He dialled the number, and as he had suspected, the call went straight to voicemail.

'Tori,' he began, 'please talk to me. I want to apologise, and I can't talk to a machine. So if you'd just call me we can talk and I'll explain…' Spencer ended the call and, with a sigh, went back through to the living room.

'Well?' Millie asked.

Spencer shrugged. 'I don't suppose someone wants to come with me to fetch my car? I kind of left it with some sheep at the side of the road. And as I've already downed a couple of brandies, it'll have to be someone who can drive.'

Dylan looked at Millie, who nodded.

'Darcie and I can cope here for an hour while you go,' she said. 'But don't even think about calling at the Dog and Hare on the way back.'

Spencer and Dylan stepped out into the crisp white landscape, azure skies stretching above. 'Nice day for a brisk walk,' Dylan said.

'How about a sweaty run?' Spencer shot him a sideways glance.

'Shameful,' Dylan said. Spencer looked at him, but although Dylan wore the ghost of a smile, it wasn't the usual mocking one he reserved just for his oldest friend. 'You had it bad for her, didn't you?'

'I think she was the one.'

'It's too bad, my friend.'

'Yeah.'

'She'll come back. She's not going to throw away what you had over some stupid stink her parents kicked up.'

'I don't think it's just about that.'

'What are you going to do?'

Spencer shrugged.

'We could hit the Dog and Hare tonight? A pint or two of Doug's finest guest ale might cheer you up.'

'Tori and I were going to help out on the bar at the Dog and Hare tonight,' Spencer said. 'I suppose I might as well still do it. And if a drink slips down at the same time, well, I don't suppose that will hurt. I could do with blotting out the misery, just for today. Some Christmas Day this is turning out to be.'

'Tell me about it.'

Spencer turned to him. 'I thought you and Millie were blissfully happy?'

'Oh, we are. It's just, well, you know what she's like. Always busy fussing over everyone and sometimes she forgets the things closer to home.'

'Like what?'

Dylan shook his head. 'It doesn't matter.'

'Yes, it does. What's she forgotten?'

'Everyone has opened their presents, but she hasn't opened hers from me.'

Spencer broke into a puzzled smile. 'That's it? The big issue?'

'Now I feel like a tit – thanks for that.'

'To be honest, mate, you sound like a tit. You're the luckiest guy on the planet getting that woman to put up with you.'

'Yeah, I know. And she is amazing. It's just that I needed her to open her presents because... Forget it.'

They trudged on in silence, the ground heavy going beneath them and their breath curling into the blue skies. Honeybourne was at its most peaceful, the streets bathed in a strange, ethereal calm, the only sounds other than the crunching of their boots on the snow were the faint strains of laughter or music as they passed a dwelling. Then, in the distance, the church bells began to ring out the first service of the day.

As they passed the Dog and Hare, Jenny and Lewis rushed out to them.

'Where have you been?' Jenny cried.

'To the bakery,' Spencer said, angling his head at Dylan as if it was the most obvious reply in the world. Which, really, it was.

'We're not due there for a couple of hours yet,' she said, ignoring Dylan. 'Come home and talk to us.'

'There's nothing to say, Mum. I don't blame you and I don't want you to blame yourself either. I need to sort this mess out and I will, in my own time and in my own way.'

'Where are you going now then?' Lewis asked.

'To get the car I abandoned… remember?'

'Right. Well, how about we go and get it?'

'What for?'

'To help.'

'Dad, what will that achieve?' Spencer asked. He wasn't angry, but he was tired of his parents' pointless platitudes and gestures. 'It won't help me get Tori back and as I have nothing better to do right now, I might as well go and get it. And before you say anything, Dylan is going to drive it back to the bakery.'

'So you're not coming home to open your presents?'

'I'm not really in the mood.'

Jenny looked at Lewis and her lip trembled.

'Please, don't be upset, Mum. I will, but I just can't face it right now. Surely you can understand that and forgive me this once?'

'What shall we do?' she asked in a small voice.

Spencer looked at Dylan. He did feel sorry for his parents, who seemed to realise now the part they had played in the events leading up to today; their guilt was easy to see. He didn't want to hurt them but he just couldn't help it.

'Why don't you head off to the bakery?' Dylan suggested. 'Millie could do with a hand and we'll be back as soon as we can.'

Lewis nodded and took Jenny's hand as they headed off in the direction Spencer and Dylan had just come from.

'Thanks, mate,' Spencer said.

Dylan gave him a tight smile. 'It's what friends are for, isn't it?'

Darcie listened to the message again with a huge smile.

Hi, Darcie, it's Tariq. I just wanted to let you know that there is good news and bad news. The bad news is I got some pretty severe punishments for going AWOL. But the good news is that I haven't been sent to the firing squad so I'm still alive. Seriously, though, it wasn't as bad as I thought it would be and that's because I came back sharpish. I can't thank you enough for listening to me last night, it means so much to have a friendly ear. I'm really glad you talked some sense into me and persuaded me to come back, and please thank Dylan for driving me here.

So, you might have guessed that this is my number. I hope you'll keep it in your phone now and maybe use it to tell me when you're free for a drink. I promise I won't hide behind your bins and scare the life out of you next time we meet... and I hope we do.

I'm not really into Christmas, but I know you are, so Merry Christmas.

Tariq.

He wanted to meet her for a drink. She wanted to send him a text, but she didn't have a clue what to say. She began one, but then deleted it. Then she began another before deleting that too. Nothing sounded right. Maybe she needed to wait until she'd thought about it. But she couldn't wait because he might take that as a sign she wasn't interested. But then if she replied straight away, wouldn't that make her seem desperate and needy? Maybe she'd go and ask Millie. But that was ridiculous – she was twenty-two, after all, and if she couldn't reply to a simple text by now it was time to give up. Not only that, but she had texts on her phone from Nathan, who still seemed very keen, though she tried not to think about those as the little worm of guilt worked into her thoughts. She would need to make some decisions, but maybe today wasn't the day to do that.

She looked up as Millie came into the kitchen with Oscar in her arms.

'He would wake up now, just when we don't have Dylan around…' Millie gave a vague smile as she glanced at the phone still clutched in Darcie's hand. 'What are you looking so pleased about? You look like someone's just given you an extra big bit of Christmas pudding.'

'I wouldn't look like this,' Darcie grinned. 'I don't like Christmas pudding.'

Millie frowned. 'Yes, you do – you've always eaten it.'

'Only at Christmas, because you're supposed to, and only when you cooked Christmas dinner for me because I felt guilty that you'd made it and I was so happy that you'd cooked for me when my parents were being useless and I wanted to get out of the house. I hate it really.'

'So all those times you had dinner with me…'

Darcie shrugged and offered an apologetic smile. 'Sorry.'

Millie shook her head. 'That's mental. So what's the thing that has you so chipper?'

'I can be happy for no reason, can't I?'

'Ok, don't tell me then.'

'Tariq left me a message!' Darcie blurted out, beaming.

'I knew he would.'

'Really?'

'It was pretty obvious that he liked you,' Millie laughed.

'Not to me.'

'That's the frustrating thing about these situations – the person who is the object of the other person's affections is usually the last to work it out, and it's hard to give encouragement when you're clueless.'

'What do you think?' Darcie asked.

'About what?'

'Do you think he's worth a shot? Do you think he seems ok?'

'I'm not sure I'm qualified to comment. What's your gut feeling?'

'I like him.' Darcie was thoughtful for a moment. She did like him – a lot. And now that she had said it out loud she realised just how much, and how right he seemed already. She also realised another strange thing – she hadn't thought about Dylan in that way since Tariq had appeared the night before. Maybe he was more right for her than she had even realised.

'Then go for it. You get one life, so go out, take chances, make mistakes, fall in love, get your heart broken and then fall in love all over again. There's no point in half measures, and I can say that with a great deal of authority.'

Darcie grinned. 'Do you think I should call him?'

'Right now? Maybe better to text. He might be doing press-ups in the training ground with some big grumpy general's boot on his back. Probably best to arrange a time to phone, or let him know that he can call you when it's a good time.'

'Of course,' Darcie said. 'I never thought of all that. It must be stifling sometimes to be in the army, with all those rules and restrictions. No wonder he felt like running away.'

'It's certainly not a life I'd fancy,' Millie agreed. 'But he signed up so rules and restrictions are what he's got. I would hope there's some support there for him so there are no repeats of last night.'

They were interrupted by a knock at the front door booming through the house. Millie looked at the clock.

'If that's guests they're a bit early. Or maybe Dylan's left his key behind again.'

'I'll get it,' Darcie said, racing for the door and feeling giddier than she had done in a very long time.

Today felt like the Christmases of old, when she was a kid and the world was still a wondrous and shiny place. It was nice to have that feeling back.

But then she opened the door to a very sober looking Jenny and Lewis, and she was reminded that not everyone was having the Christmas Day they'd been hoping for.

Millie and Dylan had utilised the bakery café, pulling together the tables to create one huge place to eat. With Darcie's help they had decorated it with gold place settings, tiny stars sprinkled over the pure white cloth and a centrepiece arrangement of holly and deep red roses. The whole effect was simple but stunning, and Darcie had almost been sorry to ruin it with the cheap crackers she had bought in Salisbury, which she deposited next to each set of cutlery. Seated around the table were Jasmine, Rich, the triplets, Jenny, Lewis, Spencer, Ruth Evans and Darcie herself. Millie and Dylan were up and down from their chairs as they remembered things to bring in, or as the various courses became ready, or simply to fetch more wine, while baby Oscar slept in his cot close by. Nobody spoke of the three empty places. Spencer had taken Millie to one side and asked her to leave them set, just in case (although it seemed a forlorn hope) and Millie had quietly agreed.

Despite the obvious strain on certain members of the party, the atmosphere was jovial and good-natured, and people seemed to be doing their best to put differences and heartbreak aside so as not to ruin the day for Millie, who had gone to so much trouble to arrange it. Ruth was already on her way to being cheerfully drunk and was telling the table in a rather loud voice about a particularly vicious water infection she'd just got rid of, while Jenny and Lewis, although doing their best, were notable in that they barely drank at all, especially compared to their usual amount at such a gathering. Spencer was quiet, which was to be expected, but he smiled in all the right places, even if Darcie could see it was a smile of someone who was dying inside, and he nodded and answered questions when they were asked. Darcie couldn't help noticing that he ate very little, even though he made a fuss of each course and told Millie that it was wonderful, and his wine glass seemed to be emptying as fast as it was filled. Darcie wished she could take him to one side and hug him. Though she barely knew him, Millie had told her so many things about the sort of man he was and Darcie couldn't bear to see him hurting so obviously.

Jasmine and Rich seemed to be getting along. Although the triplets took a great deal of their attention, the frosty atmosphere that had been palpable between them was gone, and they laughed together, even snatching the odd kiss between courses.

Darcie herself kept her phone close. She was not one for using it at the dinner table usually, but she had finally sent Tariq a message and had been hoping for an instant reply, only to get a Christmas message from Nathan instead. It had been quite sweet, but it filled her with guilt. She had sent a brief message back to wish him a Merry Christmas too, and realised she would have to deal with the break-up as soon as she could. It wasn't fair to string him along like this, but it seemed even less fair to dump him today of all days. In many ways she was annoyed at herself for letting this happen – she should have known from the start that Nathan wasn't right for her and had the courage to hold out until the right man came into her life. But as she looked across at Dylan, whose sulk over Millie not opening his Christmas presents had obviously been forgotten, she understood why she had done that. It was strange how that longing for him had turned into a gentle, platonic fondness so quickly, but she was more relieved than she could say to have the pain finally lifted from her.

The last thing Spencer wanted to do was eat, drink and be merry. But although his heart was in a million pieces, he forced himself to look as happy as he could manage. He was sure he wasn't fooling anyone, but his parents felt guilty enough about the way things had turned out with Tori, and Spencer looking like a man who was just waiting for the next bridge to jump off was not going to make them feel any better. His Christmas had been a disaster, but that didn't mean he couldn't salvage theirs.

'What time is Colleen opening for the annual Christmas knees-up?' Dylan asked, breaking into his thoughts.

'Hmm?'

'I asked what time Colleen was opening.' He lowered his voice. 'You're still thinking about Tori, aren't you?'

Spencer shrugged. 'What else am I meant to do?' he replied quietly. 'I'm trying my best not to. Is it that obvious?'

'Only to me, mate. Listen, if you're not up to helping in the pub today, let me go. I'm sure Millie won't mind and Darcie has already said she's happy to babysit.'

'It's good of you to offer, but I'm fine. It'll stop me from moping around at home and at least it will make Mum and Dad think I'm alright.'

'I don't think they're that easy to fool,' Dylan replied with a wry smile.

'Yeah, I know. Ok, so what I mean is they can't interrogate me about my feelings and give me a ton of well-meaning but pointless advice if I'm stuck behind the bar of the pub, and I can't lose my temper again and ruin their Christmas completely. How's that for an excuse?'

'Better,' Dylan said. 'I get that. Well, we'll be over as soon as we've cleared up here, so if you need a hand or a bit of moral support then you can count on me.'

Spencer gave him a sideways look. 'You really have changed, haven't you? There was a time you'd have told me to snap out of it and be a man.'

'There was,' Dylan laughed. 'I needed to change, and Millie could see that. She's done a pretty good job, hasn't she?'

Spencer smiled slightly. He glanced across the table to where Jasmine laughed with Rich. How different was this new Dylan? If he'd known about their kiss last night, would he still be the same Dylan who had given him a pasting last time he'd revealed his feelings for Jasmine, all those years before? The kiss was one secret that could never come out, even amongst the best of friends, and Spencer decided quickly that he needed to erase it from his own memory too. It seemed safer that way, for him and for Jasmine. 'She's done a great job. You were ok before, but I like this new and improved version a lot more.'

'Thanks!' Dylan said with a broad grin. 'At least, I think that's a compliment!' His grin faded. 'But seriously, there's one thing I know for sure – I was half a man without Millie. I can't believe how she's opened the world up to me and turned my life around, and she hasn't even had to try. Just being with her makes me want to be better and more than I ever thought I could be…' he paused. 'That sounds mushy, right?'

'From you, yes. But it makes sense. It means things are good and right. You're lucky.'

'I know. I'm sorry about Tori, I really am. But you know what?'

'What?'

'I think she'll come back when she's had time to think it through.'

'I've called her about twenty times today and her phone is always off. I've sent her about another twenty text messages. You're right about a lot of things, my friend, but I don't think you're right this time.'

Dylan clapped him on the back. 'You're right about a lot of things too, but I hope this time you're very wrong.'

Spencer nodded. 'Thanks, mate.'

Millie stood from the table and made her way over. 'Can you help take some of these dishes away?' she asked Dylan.

'I'll help,' Spencer began, getting up from his chair, but Millie stopped him.

'It's ok, Dylan can do it.'

Dylan stood up and kissed her. 'Is this just an elaborate ruse to get me alone in the kitchen?' he teased.

'It's a not-so-elaborate ruse to get you doing some actual work,' said Millie, cocking an eyebrow at him.

'No fair,' Dylan pouted. 'I've peeled potatoes and everything to-day!'

'And I've never seen more finely peeled potatoes. Now I need you to do an equally masterful job of clearing dishes and maybe I'll be really impressed.'

'Enough for an extra Christmas present later?' Dylan asked with an impish look.

Millie's laughter was like music as she glided away from the table with the glasses she had just collected. Spencer looked up to see Dylan watch her go with the expression of a lovesick teenager. It was the same look Spencer imagined he wore when he watched Tori – one that said he was well aware how much she was out of his league, and that he thanked his lucky stars for every day she allowed him to stay in her life. He was glad things had worked out so well for Dylan, who had been subjected to more than his fair share of tragedy, and who had needed an anchor to stop him drifting so far off course that he would never find his way back. He was wrong about one thing, though. Millie had not made him a better man – she had helped him find the man who was in there all along. He had drunk too much, dabbled in substances far more illegal, had gambled, womanised, and not cared a jot for the consequences... But to see him now, anyone who hadn't known him before Millie would scarcely believe the man who did all those things had ever existed.

He looked down at Spencer. 'I suppose I'd better be a good boy and do as I'm told.'

Spencer stood up too. 'I think I might get some air.'

'Go out into the backyard if you like,' Dylan replied, understanding immediately Spencer's need for a moment or two of quiet. 'It's nice and private out there and there's a little seat. The door is already unlocked.'

Spencer stood against the wall of the bakery, watching the first stars appear in a sky washed in lilac and blues. They'd only just finished a long and lazy lunch, but already the night of deepest winter closed in. It was cold, but he didn't notice it. Somewhere, under the sky he looked up at now, Tori existed. What was she doing? What was she thinking about? Was she thinking of him? Did she feel regret for the things they'd said and done, or relief that it was all over? He tried not to think it might be the latter. He had hoped to be looking up at this sky with her tonight, but for a very different reason, and he had rehearsed the moment over and over again in his mind, certain that she would have been thrilled. It would never happen, not now.

Spencer had never smoked, but there were times when it seemed quite appealing, if only for the excuse for solitary moments outside like this one. Everyone meant well, but the bakery was too crowded, too noisy and just too happy right now. He didn't want cheering up, he only wanted to reflect on how everything had gone so wrong and work out what to do next. The other thing he wanted was to hide that melancholy from his parents. They'd cheered up considerably during lunch and he was glad of it. They blamed themselves for what had happened, but Spencer didn't. The way he saw it, if he had been stronger and more committed, if his relationship with Tori had been as rock solid as he had thought, then nothing would have torn them apart, not even warring parents. The blame fell squarely on his shoulders and it was up to him to carry it.

As the evening air lulled him into a strange sort of calm reflection, the back door opened, letting a slice of yellow light out onto the step and a snatch of merriment into the air, which both disappeared again as it closed. Jasmine stood before him with a faint smile.

'Mind if I join you? It's far too hot in there now and I could do with a bit of air myself.'

Spencer nodded. He didn't believe for one moment that Jasmine had come out because she was too hot, but he appreciated the tact on her part. She had come to explain, to clear the air, maybe even to ask him not to mention their moment of intimacy to Rich, though she must have known that she didn't need to worry, and it needled Spencer slightly to think that she didn't trust him after all these years. 'There's room for two,' he said.

'And not much more than that,' Jasmine replied, pulling her cardigan tighter and taking a seat.

Spencer continued to lean against the wall, and looked down at her expectantly, waiting for her to say what she needed to get off her chest.

'It's been a nice dinner – Millie knows how to put on a spread.'

'Yes,' he replied, still waiting for the real conversation to start.

They lapsed into silence. There was a muffled cheer from inside, followed by laughter.

'So… are you ok?' Jasmine asked.

'Honestly? I don't know. I'm still processing stuff.'

'But *we're* ok?' she asked tentatively. 'You and me, after…'

'I told you not to worry about it,' Spencer said, immediately regretting the brusqueness of his tone. 'I'm sorry. I'm just not myself today.'

'I understand. But I still feel that I haven't helped to make things any easier. It was a stupid thing I did last night, and I don't know what made me do it, but I owe you an explanation.'

'You gave me one.'

'A proper one,' she said.

Spencer sensed that she needed to offload this more than he needed to hear it, and so he nodded and waited.

'You know me and Rich,' she began. 'We're happy but we've always been what you might call… volatile. Others might see it as a sign of things breaking down, but it's just us, it's the way we function as a couple. So I've been angry with him, and I've been frustrated and resentful, and—'

'You wanted to get back at him?'

'No,' Jasmine replied quickly, 'not like that. I suppose I just needed to vent it, and you've always been there for me. I just felt that pull towards you at the same time you just happened to pull towards me and, well, you know…'

'It's as much my fault as yours, Jas. How I've always felt about you is no secret – even to most of the village, it seems – and I shouldn't have put myself in a position where I could be tempted. If it makes you feel better, though, you don't need to feel guilty, or that you've led me on, because in a strange way, it was a good thing. After it happened I suddenly saw everything clearly, and I saw that it was Tori I wanted. I love you as a friend, but I'm in love with Tori, and I want to spend my life with her. I came back to Honeybourne and saw a future with her that was somehow closer and more real than ever before, and I was suddenly scared that I wouldn't be good enough. I was scared that I would disappoint her so much she would leave me. I freaked out and I looked for excuses to fail. I didn't mean to, but my doubts were like a self-fulfilling prophecy and everything I was scared would happen happened. I wasn't good enough, and she ended up leaving me. But that was my fault. The thing last night… that was just the final nail in my self-made coffin. But you know you can trust me not to breathe a word to anyone, ever, about it. If you ask me never to speak of it again, I won't.'

'That's exactly what I'm asking. More for your sake than anyone else's. Rich has only just started to trust you again and…'

Spencer couldn't help a small smile. 'Won't he be wondering what we're doing out here then?'

'I doubt it. He has his face in a bowl of Millie's excellent Christmas pudding right now.'

'That's alright then. Millie's Christmas pudding is a far less complicated situation than our relationships. I wish having my face in a bowl of that was the only thing I had to worry about right now.'

'You really think she's gone for good?'

'Yes, and I wouldn't blame her.'

'Have you tried to speak to her?'

'About a dozen times today. She won't answer the phone. What's your suggestion? How can I get her to listen?'

'I don't know. It's hard if she won't give you a chance. Do you know where she is?'

'London, I think. At least that's what they were planning this morning. I need to do something – some grand gesture to somehow get her to notice, but I don't know what. I can't drive down there in this state – I'd be done for drink driving. Maybe I should borrow one of Frank's horses and gallop down there like Dick Turpin or something.'

'I don't think Frank or his horse would thank you for that. Besides, everyone knows Dick Turpin was a twat.'

Spencer laughed. Jasmine always made him feel better. 'So what should I do?'

'Try one more time. If she doesn't pick up, leave her a message, and tell her everything you've told me tonight about how you feel, how scared you were and how you want to make things right. Be straight and honest with her and that's all you can do. If she still doesn't want to know, that makes her a fool in my book, but I think she will listen.

She must know that you're a good man who made a mistake, and you will make more mistakes in the future, as she will. Forgiving those mistakes and getting past them is what marriage is about.'

'Like you and Rich?'

'Yeah, like me and Rich.' She stood up. 'Speaking of which, I'd better go in and stop him from eating too much pudding, or he'll spend the evening rolling around in agony clutching his stomach. That's one of the other things that marriage is about.' She gave Spencer a quick hug. 'I'm so glad we had this chat.'

'Me too,' he smiled.

'You're going to call her now?'

'Yes. One more try.'

Jasmine nodded and then headed back inside. Spencer pulled his mobile from his pocket and took a deep breath, thinking about everything he needed to say. But his mind was blank. He dialled the number anyway. If he didn't do it now, he would lose all the courage Jasmine had given him. He just hoped that once he got through, the right words would come. But the phone went straight through to voicemail again. At the tone he began to speak:

'Tori... you're probably going to delete this message as soon as you hear my voice, but I'm going to leave it anyway. I need to say this...

'I love you. I've loved you since the first moment we met over bitter coffee in the school staffroom. I've behaved like an idiot these past few days and there's no excuse. I should have put your love above everything else. I should have told you that I will do anything to spend the rest of my life with you – change my name, shave my hair off, disown my parents, move to Boulder, move to Mars... as long as I'm with you. But I was scared. I'd asked you to marry me and I was suddenly terrified that I wasn't good enough for you, that I'd disappoint you and you'd wish you'd never met me. And it made me do things I shouldn't have done. I'm still scared about that, but I'm even more scared of a future without you in it. So I want you to know that I will do anything for you, if you just give me a chance to show you that I love you enough to face that fear, and I'll do anything to be the best husband, to give you the life you deserve—'

There was a beep to signal that he'd run out of message space. Spencer stared at the phone. He could call back and begin again, but what was the point? He's spoken from his heart, and he'd laid bare everything in it, and if she didn't come to him now then she never would and he would have to learn to live with that.

Jasmine looked up as he returned to the table. They exchanged a look of special understanding. It was strange, but though he hadn't been able to talk to Tori, he felt lighter for leaving the message, the burden of the words he had needed to say somehow lifted now that they were out. All he could do now was wait and hope.

Christmas evening in the Dog and Hare was something of a Honeybourne tradition and almost everyone always went, even the teetotallers. Like the carol service, it was an excuse for the village to come together, to exchange stories of the past, problems of the present and hopes for the future, to remember old friends who had gone before and appreciate those who still remained, and most importantly, it was a party where everyone was invited, no matter who they were or what their neighbours thought of them the rest of the year. It was a night of peace and goodwill to all men (and women) and everyone was welcome. Doug may have been in his wheelchair and Colleen frazzled from looking after him and the pub, but that didn't seem to be a reason for them to cancel what was the most eagerly anticipated night of the year. In fact, Colleen had insisted that everyone's first drink was on the house, as a thank you for the support they had shown since Doug's accident.

Spencer looked on from the bar as everyone began to arrive, Colleen at the other end wiping it down. Millie's dinner guests were already in, having walked together as a party, with the exception of Darcie who had been adamant that she was happy to stay at home and babysit Oscar so Millie could go. Dylan had given her a grateful nod and Spencer couldn't help but wonder if there was some big secret between them, but perhaps it was better not to ask. Everyone had their secrets, after all.

'Need a hand?' Lewis asked as Spencer set a gin and tonic in front of Amy Parsons, who had just arrived.

'I'm good, Dad. If things get too busy behind here I'll give you a shout. I think being busy will be good for me anyway – help to take my mind off things.'

'I think you're coping with this in a very mature way,' Lewis replied. 'I just wanted you to know that.'

The comment wasn't exactly helpful, and it wasn't going to bring Tori back, but Spencer gave his dad a tight smile. 'Thanks, Dad. There's no point in moping, though, is there. I don't have a lot of choice but to get on with things.'

'Not everyone would say that.'

Spencer gave a short nod, and then turned his attention to Ruth as she waddled over to the bar. 'What can I get you?'

'Apart from a young stud of a man to keep me warm tonight?' Ruth said with a worryingly tipsy grin.

'We're fresh out of those,' Spencer replied with a patient smile.

'Well, you're free now, aren't you?' she asked.

Spencer heard the sharp breath of his dad, but he turned to him with an expression that said he was ok with it. Ruth was just being Ruth, and she had a habit of blurting out the first thing that came into her head, no matter how ill-advised, and especially when she was a bit drunk. As she'd been knocking the spirits back all day, it was hardly a surprise that tactless comments were falling out of her mouth with more regularity than her rickety old false teeth as she chewed on a bag of Doug's pork scratchings. She didn't mean any harm, though, and everyone who knew her well knew that.

The arrival of the vicar and his wife saved Spencer from having to reply, as Ruth immediately set her sights on worming as many intimate details as she could from the couple. Before he had even got halfway to the bar, Ruth had tottered over with surprising speed and was standing in his way.

'He'll need God and all those angels on his side tonight if Ruth is interrogating him,' Lewis said as they watched her in action.

'I thought you didn't believe in God,' Spencer said.

'I don't, but I could be persuaded if I thought it would save me from a grilling by Ruth Evans.'

'Oh, so you're a fair-weather supporter?'

'Something like that,' Lewis grinned.

Jenny left Millie and Dylan getting settled at a table and joined them.

'Can I get you a drink, Mum?' Spencer asked.

'I think I might just have a cola for now – give my liver a break.'

Spencer raised his eyebrows. 'You're having a Coke?'

'It's not that much of a shock.'

'It's Christmas Day, the one day of the year it's practically obligatory to be blind drunk,' Spencer said.

'I know, and I'll probably have one later, but for now a soft drink will do.'

Spencer reached for a glass and scooped some ice into it. He suspected that his mum was still feeling guilty for drunken comments that had been hurled around over the previous few days, and that was why she was taking it easy tonight. But there didn't seem much point when the damage was already done. Maybe it just made her feel better, and Spencer couldn't really argue with that. He placed her drink on the bar and took her exact change to the till. When he turned around again, Jenny was buried in Lewis's arms. Another time he might have turned away, feeling keenly the awkwardness of a child watching his parents in an intimate moment, but not this time. This was a hug of consolation, not of passion. It twisted the knife in Spencer's heart. Despite his best efforts, they still blamed themselves, and he knew that no matter what he said, they would continue to do so. There was nothing he could say, and so he left them to it and moved down the bar to serve someone else.

The bar got steadily busier and louder, but Spencer was glad of the distraction. He hadn't even had a chance to check his phone, but as all the previous opportunities of the day had only resulted in disappointment, maybe that wasn't a bad thing either. He could hardly say he was happy or cheered by the high spirits and lively atmosphere of the Dog and Hare, but he was content to soak it up and there was something quite comforting about the feeling of belonging he had to be there amongst friends and family, part of a tradition that had been going on in Honeybourne for as long as he could remember.

An hour or so passed before Dylan strode up to the bar. It wasn't his first visit, but this one was different. Spencer watched him closely.

The jovial mood of earlier had gone, and if Spencer hadn't known better, he would have said that he looked tense and nervous – scared even.

'Mate, I need a whisky,' he said.

'What's the matter with you?' Spencer asked, turning for the optic and squeezing a measure out.

'I need a bit of Dutch courage.'

'Ice?' Spencer placed the tumbler on the bar in front of him.

'No, I need it as neat as you can possibly get.' He knocked it straight back and handed the glass to Spencer. 'Another one.'

Spencer frowned. 'Seriously, what's happened?'

'It's not what's happened,' Dylan said grimly as he took the refill. 'It's what's about to happen.'

'What?' Spencer asked, starting to feel somewhat alarmed. 'Is it something you want to talk about? Can I help? Do you think maybe you should give me a heads up if it's going to kick off in here in a minute?'

Dylan slammed the glass down a second time and shook his head. 'That ought to do it,' he said before walking back to the table where Millie waited for him with a broad smile.

Spencer shook his head slightly. He was tempted to go and sit with them, just so he could be on hand if or when the thing that had got Dylan so worked up happened. They may have had their differences in the past, and their daily lives may now be separated by thousands of miles, but Dylan was still his best friend and he would stick by him, fair weather or foul.

He was about to call to Colleen that he needed to leave the bar for a moment when he glanced across again and realised that he needn't have worried. The table Dylan and Millie occupied was close, and

Spencer strained to hear what was being said, because he had a feeling it wasn't going to be so bad after all.

Dylan pulled a small parcel from his pocket. It was wrapped in gold paper and secured with a red metallic bow. 'As you didn't have time to open your presents this morning, I brought one of them with me for you to open now.'

'It could have waited,' Millie said. 'It would have been something to look forward to later when all the other excitement of Christmas is over.'

'Not this one,' he said. 'This one couldn't wait another minute, because the suspense is killing me.'

Millie frowned slightly as she took it from him. Unravelling the knot on the bow, she slid the paper off to reveal a small red-velvet box. She looked up at him with a silent question, before turning her attention back to the box and opening it. A hush fell over the pub, every eye now on the mini drama unfolding at their table. Millie caught her breath as the glint of a diamond peeked from within and she opened it fully to reveal the ring. Dylan slid from his chair onto one knee.

'Millicent Hopkin… Would you do me the honour of being my wife?'

Millie's eyes filled with tears and she bent to kiss him forcefully on the lips. 'Of course I bloody will!' she cried. 'I thought you'd never ask!'

A cheer went up around the pub, and everyone surged forwards to congratulate the couple as Millie clung onto Dylan's neck and held on for dear life. Dylan wore a grin so huge it looked as if it would burst from his face. Tears poured down Millie's cheeks, and she laughed and cried and didn't seem to know quite what her emotions were doing.

Spencer smiled as he watched them. He was happy for his friends, but somewhere that unwanted little voice got to him. It should have been like that for him and Tori – they were supposed to be looking forward to a long and blissful future together. Instead, he was manning a bar alone while he watched someone else get their happy ending. It seemed to be the way his life would always go, and perhaps things would be easier to bear if he stopped hoping for anything different.

But then his attention was drawn away from the happy couple. He couldn't say what had made him look, but one person in the bar that night looked far from pleased for Dylan and Millie's announcement: Amy Parsons. Sweet, pretty, unassuming Amy. Married Amy, whose expression of deepest jealousy was very out of place. Spencer had long suspected history between her and Dylan, and village gossip had confirmed the same, but if Amy's reaction was anything to go by, it wasn't history for her. Spencer couldn't help a wry smile. If only he could get himself some of whatever Dylan had, maybe he could keep at least one girlfriend, even if half of the western world wasn't in love with him. But he hoped that Amy would at least keep her unfinished business to herself and let sleeping dogs lie. The Dylan she had known was in the past now and that was the best place for him.

Dylan climbed onto his table. 'It looks like I'm getting married!' he shouted, and was met by another cheer that echoed around the room. 'So this round of drinks is on me!'

There was an immediate tidal wave of bodies towards the bar, and many people ended up there whether they actually wanted to be or not. It looked as though it was going to be a busy half hour, and Spencer shot a helpless glance at Colleen, who simply smiled. But in the next moment, he found his mum and dad beside him.

'We weren't going to leave you floundering,' Jenny said as she pulled a pint of Guinness for Saul. Lewis nodded agreement and grabbed Spencer in a manly hug.

'What she says,' he laughed.

Then someone turned up the music and The Pogues started to sing 'Fairytale of New York', and pretty soon afterwards half the pub was shouting along, with Lewis and Jenny louder than anyone. It was hard for Spencer not to grin, and even harder for him not to soak up some of the love in the room, despite his own private sadness. It felt more like Christmas than it had done for days, and it looked as though the next year was going to be an amazing one for his friends. It was hard to be unhappy about any of that.

He looked over to see that Millie and Dylan were dancing together in a space cleared from the floor for them, a sort of mixed-up, crazy foxtrot-waltz that seemed to defy all rules and that only they knew, kissing, crying and laughing alternately. They looked delirious with happiness, like they couldn't fall deep enough into each other's eyes, and Spencer, though he was happy, felt that pang too. He looked away and swallowed it back, turning to Ruth who had appeared at the bar again for what had to be her eighth or ninth refill of the night. He didn't want to feel this jealousy; he wanted only to be happy for them.

'What can I get you, Ruth?' he asked with all the brightness he could muster.

She hooked a thumb over her shoulder with a drunken grin. 'You should see what your young lady wants first.'

Spencer looked up. At the door of the pub stood Tori.

Chapter Twelve

She was smiling, and from her hand swung a sprig of mistletoe. Spencer looked from her to Ruth and back again. He couldn't quite trust his own senses. Had Tori really come back?

'What are you waiting for?' Ruth asked, rolling her eyes.

He didn't need a second invitation. With one fluid movement, he leapt up onto the bar top and then down to the other side. He didn't know where the energy or strength had come from, but it didn't matter. All he could think about was getting to Tori as he jostled his way through the heaving mass of bodies now occupying the bar of the Dog and Hare. And as people began to work it out, they moved out of his way, so that he ran the last few yards and flung his arms around a laughing Tori, lifting her from the ground and kissing her hard on the lips.

'I missed you so much,' he murmured in her ear before kissing her again. 'I was so miserable without you.'

'I missed you too,' she smiled. 'I just didn't know how much I would until we were apart.'

He held her tight, like he could make the two of them one whole if he pulled her close enough. He never wanted to let go.

After a moment, she gently prised herself away to look up at him. 'I guess I didn't need the mistletoe after all.'

'Seems a shame to let it go to waste, though.'

'Hmm… Yes, it does.' She held it up over their heads, and their lips locked again, this time with less urgency and more passion. 'What time does your shift end?' she asked with a wicked smile. 'I want you and I don't know how much longer I can hold out. While kisses are fantastic, they just aren't cutting it.'

Spencer glanced back at the bar. Jenny was still on duty, next to Lewis, who looked across with a nod that told him everything he needed to know. 'I think they'll manage without me for a while,' he said. 'The only problem is I've had too much to drink so we'll have to walk back to my place.'

Tori slid her hand down his arm and wove her fingers into his. 'I can do that. It'll give us time to talk.'

Tori couldn't remember the last time making love to Spencer had been so natural and comfortable. It was like they were laying their souls completely bare to each other for the first time ever, giving the whole of themselves with nothing held back. When it was over, she lay in his arms, head on his chest, and she knew that this time, something had changed. They really were one, and nothing was going to break them.

'I love you,' she said. It was a simple sentence, three little words that didn't feel anywhere near huge enough to express what was in her heart. *I love you*. It was said so easily and so often by so many people. How could it be enough? And yet, it was; pure and uncomplicated, it was the most perfect sentence in the history of language. She loved him, and there was nothing more to say.

'I love you too,' he said.

She nuzzled in closer, trailing a lazy finger down his torso towards his groin, and though they had only just finished, he twitched to life again.

She smiled as he rolled her over and kissed her. They would need to talk, and there were things they would have to put right before they could move on, but it would wait. This moment was perfect, and she wasn't about to ruin it for anything.

Much later still, Tori was wearing Spencer's dressing gown, curled up by the fire. He handed her a mug of coffee and settled next to her with one of his own. 'Nearly chucking out time at the pub, which means Mum and Dad will be back soon. And knowing them, they'll bring half the pub back with them, especially as Dylan and Millie will still be celebrating,' he added, glancing up at the clock. 'Maybe we should think about making ourselves decent.'

'I feel like a teenager sneaking around,' she said.

'I know...' Spencer rubbed a hand through his hair with a lop-sided smile. 'Sorry about that.'

'It's funny. I don't mind. We have all the time in the world to think about becoming grown-ups.'

'It makes me so happy to hear you say that. Listen... If you want, I can ask my parents to take the room at the Dog and Hare that your parents have vacated. It might make it easier on us for the rest of the holidays.'

'No, I wouldn't do that, it doesn't seem fair. Besides, I like your parents just fine. It's my mom and dad who had a problem with them, and as they've decided to stay in London until their flight home...'

'Are you ok with that?' he asked. It wasn't the first time that night he'd asked the same question, and she had reassured him that she was, but it still bothered him. He hated to think that she was compromising for his sake, because if anyone had to make compromises, he would happily let that person be him.

'They made their choice and I made mine. I'll go and see them when I get home and smooth things over. For now, if they're not prepared to accept my future husband with all his baggage, then I'm not interested in what they think.'

'Baggage?' Spencer cocked an eyebrow at her.

'You know what I mean,' she laughed. 'God, I missed you so much today. It hurt like hell, the thought that we were over. I know I went off to London with my parents, but I didn't really want to.'

'You don't need to explain it to me,' he said, kissing her. 'I don't care what happened before; I only care what happens now. And as long as that involves you and me together, I can face anything.'

'Even dragging all the suitcases I left at the pub back here tomorrow?'

'Even your unfeasibly large amount of luggage.'

'And the fact that you won't be able to open any of the Christmas gifts I got you until tomorrow because they're still in that luggage?'

Spencer shot up. 'Christmas presents! I haven't given you any either!'

'Sit down,' she smiled. 'I don't care about that. The best gift is being back here with you.'

Spencer was thoughtful for a moment. 'There is one I want to give you right now.'

Tori grinned. 'I think you already gave me that one… Twice.'

'Not that,' he laughed. 'Get your coat and shoes on.' He leapt from the sofa and went rummaging under the Christmas tree. A moment later he returned holding a parcel wrapped in gold paper. He frowned. 'I thought you were getting your coat on?'

Tori looked up at him from the sofa. 'You hardly gave me a chance!' Handing him her mug, she shuffled through to the coat peg in the hall and returned a couple of seconds later shrugging her jacket on. 'Where are we going? Don't you think I ought to get dressed?'

'It's only the back garden,' he said, taking her hand. 'But it's freezing out there tonight.'

'The back garden?' she asked, stamping her feet into her boots as he tugged her towards the kitchen. 'What for?'

'You'll see,' he said, unlocking the back door and leading her outside.

The moon was full and high, bathing the garden in pearly light. There was a deep hush over it and the fields beyond, still peppered with glistening peaks of hardened snow. Spencer turned his face to a clear sky full of stars.

'It's no good,' he said after a moment. 'Wait here.' He rushed inside, killed all the lights in the house and then returned to her. Looking up again, he gave a little cry of triumph. 'There you are, you little minx!' Pulling Tori close, he pointed up into the sky. She followed the direction of his finger. 'See that bunch of stars?' he asked. 'That's Cygnus, the constellation of the swan. It's a kind of crucifix shape.'

'I think so,' she said, peering up. 'I still don't get it, though. Why am I looking at that?'

'Because...' He lit the torch on his phone and handed her the Christmas gift. 'Open it up and you'll understand better. Besides, I can't figure out where the ruddy thing is without the map.'

'Oh,' she said, reading the scroll inside her parcel and then looking up at him, her face alight with joy. 'You did this for me?'

He nodded. 'Let me see...' he said, bending to look at the map with her. 'Right.' He pointed at the sky again. 'Round about there... See? That's your star!'

'I love it!' she beamed. 'It's the most beautiful thing anyone's ever done for me!' She kissed him. 'And you called it "This Much"?' she asked, bending to the scroll again. 'That's an interesting name…'

'It makes more sense than you think. You want to know why I called it that?'

She nodded. 'Kinda.'

'Because when you ask me how much I love you, I'll point up to the star and say: *this much.*'

Tori flung her arms around him. 'Oh my God, I love you so much it hurts!'

'I love you too. I could tell you every minute of every day and it still wouldn't be enough.'

'Try me anyway,' she laughed. 'I want to hear it.'

'I love you.'

'I love you too, you Limey fool.'

'Promise you'll never leave me again,' Spencer whispered.

'I promise. Never again.'

He pulled her close and buried his face in her hair. He was home at last. And no matter where in the world they ended up, no matter what life threw at them, he would always be home, because home was with Tori.

A Letter From Tilly

I really hope you've enjoyed reading *Christmas at the Little Village Bakery* as much as I enjoyed writing it. And I hope you've grown to love the new characters as much as old friends from *The Little Village Bakery*, just as I have. If you liked *Christmas at the Little Village Bakery*, the best and most amazing thing you can do to show your appreciation is to tell your friends. Or tell the world with a few words on a social media site, or a review online. That would make me smile for at least a week. In fact, hearing that someone loved my story is the main reason I write at all.

If you ever want to catch up with me on social media, you can find me on Twitter @TillyTenWriter or Facebook, but if you don't fancy that, you can sign up to my mailing list and will get all the latest news that way. I promise never to hassle you about anything but my books. The link is below:

http://www.bookouture.com/tilly-tennant

So, thank you for reading my little book, and I hope to see you for the next instalment!

Love Tilly x

@TillyTenWriter

TillyTennant

Acknowledgements

The list of people who have offered help and encouragement on my writing journey so far must be truly endless, and it would take a novel in itself to mention them all. However, my thanks go out to each and every one of you, whose involvement, whether small or large, has been invaluable and appreciated more than I can say.

There are a few people that I absolutely must mention. Obviously, my family, who bear the brunt of every plot-fail tantrum and yet still allow me to live with them. The staff at the Royal Stoke University Hospital, who have let me lead a double life for far longer than is acceptable. The lecturers at Staffordshire University English and Creative Writing Department, who saw a talent worth nurturing in me and continue to support me still, long after they finished getting paid for it. They are not only tutors but friends as well. I have to thank the team at Bookouture for the way they have welcomed me on board and have supported me through every step of my journey with them, particularly Kim Nash, Lydia Vassar-Smith and Natasha Hodgson. Their belief and encouragement means the world to me. My friend Louise Coquio merits a special mention, never too busy to read a first draft no matter how awful it is, always ready with an endless supply of tea, sympathy and plot suggestions. Also Kath Hickton, who's always there and has been for over thirty years. I have to thank Mel Sherratt and Holly Martin, fellow writers and amazing friends who have both been incredibly supportive over the years and have been my shoulders to cry on in the darker moments. Victoria Stone, my litmus test and my cheerleader, who will cheerfully tell me exactly what she thinks! Thanks to Liz Tipping, Emma Davies, Jack Croxall, Dan Thompson and Jaimie Admans: not only brilliant authors in their own right but hugely supportive of others. I have to thank all the brilliant and dedicated book bloggers and reviewers out there, readers, and anyone else who has championed my work, reviewed it, shared it, or simply told me that they liked it. Every one of those actions is priceless and you are all very special people.

Last but never, ever least, is my agent, Peta Nightingale. Where do I begin? She is more than an agent, she is a friend, and she has never lost faith in me, even when I lost faith in myself. She is incredibly hard-working, endlessly patient, warm and fuzzy, and great fun to share a glass of Prosecco with! I wouldn't be writing this now if it wasn't for her and the team at LAW literary agency, and I feel sure that my future with this incredible bunch of people is going to be a very interesting one!

Lightning Source UK Ltd.
Milton Keynes UK
UKOW05f0916231116
288348UK00016B/389/P